ELECTRONIC
TEXTUAL
EDITING

ELECTRONIC
TEXTUAL
EDITING

EDITED BY
Lou Burnard,
Katherine O'Brien O'Keeffe,
AND
John Unsworth

THE MODERN LANGUAGE
ASSOCIATION OF AMERICA
NEW YORK
2006

For information about obtaining permission to reprint material from MLA book publications, send your request by mail (see address below), e-mail (permissions@mla.org), or fax (646 458-0030).

Guidelines for Electronic Text Encoding and Interchange (P4 ed.), edited by C. M. Sperberg-McQueen and Lou Burnard, is reprinted by permission of the Text Encoding Initiative Consortium. © 2002 Text Encoding Initiative Consortium.

Library of Congress Cataloging-in-Publication Data
Electronic textual editing / edited by Lou Burnard, Katherine O'Brien O'Keeffe, and John Unsworth.

    p. cm.

  Includes bibliographical references and index.

  ISBN-13: 978-0-87352-970-9 (hardcover : alk. paper)

  ISBN-10: 0-87352-970-7

  ISBN-13: 978-0-87352-971-6 (pbk. : alk. paper)

  ISBN-10: 0-87352-971-5

  1. Editing.   2. Editing—Data processing.   3. Scholarly publishing.   4. Electronic publishing.   I. Burnard, Lou.   II. O'Keeffe, Katherine O'Brien, 1948–   III. Unsworth, John, 1958–

  PN162.E55 2006

    808'.027—dc22   2005030710

Published by The Modern Language Association of America
26 Broadway, New York, New York 10004-1789
www.mla.org

CONTENTS

PART II
PRACTICES AND PROCEDURES

FOREWORD

G. THOMAS TANSELLE

In his essay "The Electronic Book," D. T. Max describes his conversation with a six-year-old who was excited over her developing ability to read. She had gone through *Charlotte's Web* both in a conventional printed book (with illustrations) and in an e-book, and Max asked her which she preferred. Her answer was, "Any book." Max was at first surprised but then realized that she had implied a crucial point about the new technology: "Bits, atoms, paper, plastic are going to change Citizen X's life, but what's going to matter most is what she reads" (28). This interpretation of the girl's reply—that substance is more important than form—is indeed the way to begin thinking about her comment. The question itself reflected a generation gap: to anyone whose earliest reading matter was in both forms—which therefore seem routine and interchangeable—the question appeared almost foolish, or at least of no more significance than asking, "Do you prefer paperbacks or hardcover books?" Of course, whether e-books are as convenient to handle and use as the codices that preceded them is not an irrelevant matter, but convenience is not entirely a function of developing technology, for what one becomes accustomed to is a fundamental factor. As more people grow up using e-books, they will not find the technology a distraction, and the six-year-old's attitude will become a common one.

Despite the turn-of-the-century fascination with predicting the future role of electronic texts, this point is probably all that needs to be said about whether e-books will triumph over printed books. But it is not the only point that the little girl's comment should lead us to. Although she was more comfortable with e-books than many adults would be at present, her comment was similar to what most adults say about conventional books, in that it did not take into account the role that physical presentation plays in the reading experience. An increasingly populated field of literary study has made scholars acutely aware of what psychologists, in their different way, have long understood: people may think that "any book" will do for reading a given work, but all the details of graphic design, which are likely to vary from printing to printing (and from e-book to e-book), do affect readers' responses. Whether those details, or some of them, were intended by the author to be part of the work is a separate question—and one not necessarily of interest to the few readers who think of it—but the details do nevertheless have their effect. (And if one wishes to try to recapture the reading experience of a prior time, one must turn, not to a scholarly edition, whether printed or electronic, but to the original physical objects that carried the text at that time.) Another way that one book claiming to contain a particular work is not the equivalent of the others claiming to contain it—a possibly more obvious way, if no more often recognized by most readers—is that the texts may vary. Textual scholars have documented, in their essays and editions, how important it is for readers to understand the textual history of the works they read and thus the relation of one text to another; but the bulk of readers remain unaware of the value of questioning the makeup of the texts they encounter, in whatever form.

Since these points are applicable to all appearances of texts in all forms, the little girl was in one sense right to answer as she did. In saying essentially that the distinction between electronic and printed texts was not one that she considered significant, she was quite correctly implying that the question had been misconceived. With more sophistication, she might have said, "I know that letterforms, layouts, and other physical aspects of textual presentation affect reading, and I know that the text of a work may not be the same in all the physical objects that claim to display it, but whether a text is electronic or printed has nothing to do with these matters. Electronic appearances of texts are appearances after all, and it would be pointless for me to say that in general I prefer them to printed appearances, or vice versa. The appearance I prefer for each work depends on the particular text and design features it offers." This expanded reply suggests the lesson we should extrapolate from her terse answer. It is a lesson, one might think, too obvious to need teaching, but many people have a hard time keeping it in mind in the midst of all the hyperbolic writing and speaking about the computer age, as if the computer age were basically discontinuous with what went before.

Even those engaged in textual criticism and scholarly editing have sometimes been swept along by the general euphoria and lost their sense of perspective. Their concerns, after all, are at the heart of the new developments, because what the computer offers, as far as verbal communication is concerned, is a new way of producing and displaying visible texts. It can be of such great assistance to editors and other readers that they would be foolish not to make use of it and be excited about it. But when the excitement leads to the idea that the computer alters the ontology of texts and makes possible new kinds of reading and analysis, it has gone too far. The computer is a tool, and tools are facilitators; they may create strong breaks with the past in the methods for doing things, but they are at the service of an overriding continuity, for they do not change the issues that we have to cope with.

The common claim that the arrival of electronic texts is comparable to the dawn of the age of Gutenberg five and a half centuries ago should in fact be understood as reinforcing this point (though the comparison is often used to suggest discontinuity). The invention of printing from movable type greatly facilitated the production of tangible verbal texts, but it did not change the questions that readers need to ask about the nature of a verbal work. The development of computers is another such invention, assisting us with our old inquiries but not rendering them irrelevant or outmoded. When we create and use an electronic text, we still have to ponder the mode of existence of the linguistic medium; we still have to think about the relations among mental, audible, and visible texts; we still have to consider whether it is meaningful to pursue authorially intended texts or whether the documentary texts that survive from the past (perhaps purged of their obvious errors) are the only ones we should study; we still have to decide how to present the results of our textual research to other readers. Editors have always dealt with these questions, and different answers to them have produced the great variety of editions that exist today. The use of the computer in editing does not change the questions, and the varying temperaments of editors will continue to result in editions of differing character.

When people say that the computer makes possible certain kinds of textual research, such as locating all the appearances of particular words in a given text or group of texts, they are using the word *possible* inexactly to mean "feasible." But what is feasible is a relative matter, as much related to individual attitudes as to technology. We may now find it sad that some scholars of the past spent large portions of their lives compiling and proofreading concordances, but our sympathy is misplaced: there is nothing sad about scholars' performing heroic tasks by the only means available to them. Word searching has been greatly facilitated, of course, by the existence of searchable electronic texts, but it has always been possible; and whether something takes more time than one is willing to spend is a question relevant to all tasks, one that in each instance may be answered differently by different people. The misuse of *possible* is not a trivial matter, for it is symptomatic of the exaggerated claims one often hears about computers, and these claims do not provide a useful foundation for thinking productively about what computers can in fact do for us.

The idea that electronic texts encourage a new kind of reading has also been overstated. Because the press of a key or the click of a mouse can (if such links exist) take one instantly from a given point in one transcribed text to a given point in another and can make it easy to locate the same points in images of the relevant documents or to go to reproductions of relevant visual art and music, there has been a feeling that new reading habits will emerge: the reader will constantly move around and backtrack rather than take a straightforward linear path. No doubt many (perhaps even most) people will find it easier to read this way in electronic editions than in printed ones; but the codex is not in fact an inefficient instrument for radial reading (as non-linear reading is now often called), and most readers—of all kinds of books, not just scholarly editions—have always done a great deal of it. What makes such reading easier is less a matter of technology than of how thoughtfully a text or set of texts is cross-referenced—with tables of contents, running heads, footnote numbers, indexes, and lists of variants and other textual data, in codices; or with a network of searching capabilities as well as linked apparatuses and other editorial material, in electronic texts. Such aids to radial reading can be well or poorly constructed whether the means of presentation is printed or electronic.

The matter of readability involves other issues as well. Electronic editions raise in clear form a question that has always been present: Are scholarly editions meant for prolonged reading or only for reference? Some people have felt that, even in codex form, they are not designed for reading and that on the screens of monitors they are even less conducive to it. But future improvements in e-books will eliminate the problems of screen reading, and the idea that reading and reference cannot be simultaneously accommodated, whatever the form, is at odds with the concept of radial reading (which combines both). Surely the richest kind of reading depends on having at hand, for constant reference, the information that textual scholars have amassed. The real issue is how best to provide guidance for readers. In a codex edition, where there is usually enough space for only one long text to be offered in full (the other relevant texts being present in apparatus form), the reader is in effect instructed to use the full text (which may be a documentary text or an editorially emended one) as the base from which to engage in radial reading that embraces variants in other texts. In an electronic edition, where there is unlimited space, all the relevant texts are likely to be presented in full, and readers may feel disoriented without some direction from the editor. (A few multivolume archives of reproductions of documentary texts do exist in codex form, and they pose the same problem for readers, along with a greater logistical challenge.)

It is a distinct advantage, of course, for readers to be able to choose the points of entry they wish to use; but to engage in radial reading effectively, they need the editor's assistance in the form of comments on the textual history of the work, organized records of variants in the relevant documentary texts, and the like. They also need editorially emended texts in order to see how the mass of evidence has been used in reading by scholars who have made themselves expert in the textual history of the work. Unlike codex editions, electronic ones can easily include many such emended texts, attempting to reconstruct authorial intentions at different stages, publishers' intentions, and any other sets of intentions that seem relevant; they can also offer texts as emended by earlier editors, for each previous edition is a document attesting to the history of the work. Up to now, scholarly projects for publishing electronic texts have tended to take the form of archives, and it is understandable that editors would revel in their newfound freedom to offer images and transcriptions of all relevant primary documents. But their goal of giving readers the freedom, in turn, of conveniently studying different textual manifestations of a work cannot be fully realized without their offering a variety of editorial helps and emended texts. This point shows, once again, that the advantages of the electronic form are maximized when one recognizes that the technology contributes to the process of building on past accomplishments.

The difficulty people have in defining just what changes the computer has brought about in the reading and study of verbal texts can be illustrated by a passage in David Scott Kastan's *Shakespeare and the Book*. His discussion (in his final chapter) of the shift from codex to computer is a particularly thoughtful one, yet even a person as perceptive as Kastan is can falter in locating the line between the old and the new. He observes initially that people's feelings about electronic texts seem to be aroused more strongly by the form in which those texts appear than by the technology that underlies them. But then he notes that, whereas ink remains on a piece of paper, a saved electronic file is reconstituted every time it is called up on the screen.

Therefore, he says, "It seems to me that it is actually this ontological distinction between the electronic text and the printed text that unsettles, which if true means that the mode of production is, in fact, every bit as much the issue as the mode of display. Texts in this form are fluid and transient, clearly separate from the physical instantiations that enable them to be read" (115). Whether or not we wish to claim an ontological distinction between ink and pixels, the concept of text has obviously shifted its meaning between the two sentences. In the first, a text is a physical thing, an arrangement of words and punctuation in a particular visible form. In the second, it is the sequence of words and punctuation itself, an abstraction that can be given any number of concrete renderings (in the same medium or different media). Printed and electronic renderings are thus not ontologically different; they may be made of different physical materials, but the conceptual status of the texts in each case is identical. The philosophical conundrum as to where a text resides is exactly the same as it always was.

We should be enthusiastic about the electronic future, for it will be a great boon to all who are interested in texts; but we do not lay the best groundwork for it, or welcome it in the most constructive way, if we fail to think clearly about just what it will and will not change. Procedures and routines will be different; concepts and issues will not. For editors and other readers, the computer dramatically increases the efficiency of manipulating information, and the storage capacity of electronic editions can result in improved accessibility to variant texts. But these desirable changes do not alter the questions we must ask about texts or guarantee a greater amount of intelligent reading and textual study. We will be spared some drudgery and inconvenience, but we still must confront the same issues that editors have struggled with for twenty-five hundred years.

ACKNOWLEDGMENTS

The editors should like to acknowledge the generosity of the Andrew W. Mellon Foundation in supporting the planning, writing, and editing of this volume. The MLA has housed the project as it developed, and we are grateful for the expert technical assistance of Judith Altreuter, Elizabeth Holland, Michael Kandel, and David G. Nicholls during the production of the volume. We should also like to thank the members of the MLA's Committee on Scholarly Editions, whose advice over the years of the project has helped and cheered us. It is a pleasure to acknowledge the Text Encoding Initiative Consortium for contributing the TEI guidelines, included at the back of this volume on CD. Sebastian Rahtz was exceedingly generous with his time and expertise in preparing the manuscript for review. Technical editorial assistance at the University of Notre Dame was provided by Scott Thompson Smith and supported by funds from the Notre Dame Chair in English.

NOTE ON THE CD

T he CD that accompanies this volume provides background support for the essays in *Electronic Textual Editing*. It contains the complete text of the current TEI guidelines (P4 edition), in both HTML and PDF formats. The HTML format can be read with any Web browser, the PDF format with the *Adobe Acrobat* free browser (not included).

The Text Encoding Initiative's *Guidelines for Electronic Text Encoding and Interchange* was first published in April 1994 as two substantial green volumes known as TEI P3 (P for "public"). In 2001, the Text Encoding Initiative was reestablished as a membership consortium, jointly hosted by two United States and two European universities. Its first act was to sponsor a revision of the TEI guidelines. This edition, known as TEI P4, was a maintenance release, bringing the guidelines up-to-date with changes in the technical infrastructure—most notably in the use of the W3C's extensible markup language (XML) as its means of expression rather than the ISO standard, SGML, used by earlier editions. TEI P4 was published in 2002 under the imprint of the University of Virginia Press and forms the current reference standard.

But nothing written in digital form is ever really finished. Work has been proceeding on the next major revision, to be known as TEI P5, which will include far more substantive changes than were needed for P4. A first release of TEI P5 appeared in January 2005: see www.tei-c.org/P5/ for its current status.

The TEI guidelines comprise detailed definitions and documentation for hundreds of textual features and a formal representation of those definitions. The system is highly modular: the guidelines are intended to provide not a single monolithic markup scheme but rather an environment for creating customized DTDs or schemata.

TEI P4 comes in two big blue books and is also expressed as a modular, extensible, document type definition (DTD) covering most kinds of electronic texts. At the TEI Web site, you can find the whole of the TEI DTD as a single archive: to use it, you need to unpack this archive into an appropriate folder, then configure your XML software to use the required modules from it, as further described in the text of the guidelines. You can configure these files for use either as an SGML or an XML DTD.

The revisions needed to make TEI P4 were deliberately restricted to error correction only, with a view to ensuring that documents conforming to TEI P3 would not become illegal when processed with TEI P4. During this process, however, many possibilities for other, more fundamental, changes were identified, and a program of work was begun to enhance and modify the guidelines more fundamentally.

In January 2005, the preparation of TEI P5 moved to a new level with the decision to make the source text of the new edition of the guidelines available under an open-source license. For this new edition, it was decided to replace the SGML/XML DTD version of the TEI scheme with a version that could be expressed in any of the three schema languages now in wide use: DTD, W3C Schema, and RelaxNG. The current state of this work is now accessible to all from the TEI's repository at http://tei.sf.net.

INTRODUCTION

E ver since the invention of the codex, the long and distinguished history
of textual editing has been intimately involved in the physique of the
book. The format of that remarkable invention, less fragile by far than
the scroll and amenable to a more rapid retrieval of information, has determined, until the present, the ways in which writers brought texts into the
world and readers encountered them. In obvious but also subtle ways, the
physique of the book and its economics have both enabled scholarly textual
recovery and set limits on it. Certainly, the carefully elaborated sets of rubrics
for the recovery of textual artifacts (whether addressing problems of Greek
tragedy, Jewish or Christian scriptures, medieval vernacular literatures, early
modern drama, or the novel) were substantially governed by the realities of
book format. Notably, these rubrics required considering how the material
to be edited could be represented within the confines of the page and recognizing practical limits on the plethora of information that might be brought
to bear on a textual problem. Such limits were not merely matters of structural
design (e.g., replacement of the manuscript's marginal gloss by foot- or endnotes or appendixes, introduction of split levels for an apparatus criticus, space
limitations on synoptic presentations). Such a book had to be bindable; lift-
able; and, perhaps most important, affordable. The scholarly debates over
what sort of editions to produce—whether favoring the textual object, the
author of the text, or the text's reception history—were driven as much by
economics as by ideology. Quite simply, one could not have it all.

The rapid spread of computing facilities and developments in digital
technology in the 1980s and 1990s offered the possibility of circumventing a

number of practical (both physical and economic) limitations posed by the modern printed codex. Over the last two decades, it has become increasingly evident that the written word, in all its manifestations, has taken on a digital form. The implications of this adoption appear to be as radical as those of the codex itself. This metamorphosis, if it is one, has naturally been most keenly debated in the home of the written word: the world of scholarly editing and textual theory. The debate has involved practitioners at either end of a spectrum that runs from metaphysical speculation on the nature of textuality at one extreme; through questions of editing theory; to pragmatic concerns about machinery, software, markup, and best practice at the other. The present volume offers, we hope, an emerging consensus about the fundamental issues in electronic textual editing, together with guidance on accepted current wisdom.

Coincident with the spread of computing facilities, and with their adoption as the basic means of communication among academics at all levels, has been an extraordinary democratization in the production of textual editions. Professional academics, researchers, students, and enthusiasts at all levels and from many different fields frequently put texts online for teaching or research purposes. The democratization of publishing through access to the Internet has not brought with it, however, a concomitant broadening in the reliability of such editions. And the index of a text's reliability is unfortunately inversely proportional to its innocence of the canons of editing. In the light of these realities, the world of possibility presented by individual electronic publication raises questions and a challenge. What is the point of contact between the canons of textual editing, formulated as they have been for the technology of the printed word in the codex, and the emerging possibilities of the digital text? Through what structures can we imagine a new form of editing whose limits, theoretical, practical, and economic, are other than those of the printed book? The challenge is to make available to prospective editors—either to those approaching the task for the first time or to seasoned veterans of print—the kinds of information they must have to engage with electronic textual editing at the level of needed knowledge, conceptual and practical. Currently, such information is thin on the ground. While there is a rich literature on virtually any kind of scholarly editing designed for the printed book, the fruit of multiple experiments in electronic scholarly editing remains, substantially, at the level of individual experience, and when that experience is shared in published form, it tends to be shared in the form of theoretical speculation rather than as practical guidance.

THE COMMITTEE ON SCHOLARLY EDITIONS

The publicly distributed version of the guidelines of the Modern Language Association's Committee on Scholarly Editions (CSE) that was in use up until the inception of this volume was last revised in 1992, and it took the form of an essay setting out a mixture of principles, best practices, and a checklist of very specific guiding questions for the vetter of a print edition (and, by implication, for its editor). The essay consisted of seven pages of outline distributed under four large headings: "Conception and Plan of Volume/ Edition," "Editorial Methods and Procedures," "Parts of the Edition," and "Preparation for Publication." Interestingly, the largest part of the guidelines was "Parts of the Edition" (not methods and procedures), which detailed considerations for the production of text, the components of the textual essay, the critical-textual apparatus, and extratextual materials. The guidelines themselves were meant to be, and indeed were, useful within this understanding of the task of scholarly editing. Although they clearly attempted to be catholic in recognition of variation, they showed their pedigree, descending from the copy-text theory that drove the Center for Editions of American Authors (1963–76; CEAA)—though in that process of descent the CEAA broadened its purview to include other kinds of editions and reinvented itself as a committee (the CSE) designed to offer advice to editors with work in progress as well as to commission the evaluation of ready-to-be-published editions.

The four major divisions of the 1992 checklist occupied some six printed pages, a mere twenty lines of which were devoted to electronic media, which were imagined only as a kind of handmaiden to the traditional editorial procedures of making a book. The primary consideration under "Use of Electronic Files" was the three issues on which the editor and the publisher had to come to agreement: which software would be used (with attention to linkage of notes and to nonstandard characters); whether the "electronic files" were to supply simply data for the galleys or also page makeup; who would be responsible for final changes or corrections—editor, publisher, or typesetter. Other considerations were more in the line of reminders or helpful hints: electronic files to drive the typesetter still required proofing; hard copy was required as well as disks; electronic files required considered archiving. The last item (number 5) under "Use of Electronic Files" should be quoted in full: "Consideration should be given to publication of the edition on floppy disks, CD-ROM, or other electronic text formats" (CSE, "Guidelines" 8). It commands our interest not simply because it points to how far we have come (who today could imagine publishing on floppy disks?) but also because it identifies precisely the presupposition behind the 1992 guidelines—that an edition was a print-bound object and that medium defined and dictated the procedures for producing a scholarly edition.

In December 1993, Peter Shillingsburg produced a document for the CSE called "General Principles of Electronic Scholarly Editions," and in 1997, Charles Faulhaber advanced that effort by bringing the 1993 document forward as "Guidelines for Electronic Scholarly Editions," more or less in parallel with the "Guidelines for (Print) Scholarly Editions." The difficulty with this solution to the short shrift of the 1992 guidelines was that, although admittedly more detailed and helpful, it reified the split that the 1992 guidelines took for granted: there were "scholarly editions" and "electronic scholarly editions." Further, because many of the same principles applied in both media, parallel guidelines raised the problem of coordinating additions and revisions across two documents. An outside review of the draft "Guidelines for Electronic Scholarly Editions," conducted by a group of editors working on electronic scholarly editions, produced the suggestion that there should be only one set of guidelines and that they should be structured to facilitate maintenance—in particular, new examples should be added and frequent revisions made to reflect changes in technical best practices. More specifically, that review committee recommended that the CSE develop a three-tiered document to address both print and electronic scholarly editing. The first tier would state, briefly and at the general level, the necessary characteristics of a scholarly edition. The second tier would address best practices within specific traditions of editing and with respect to particular kinds of source material. The third tier would offer a technical best-practices manual in two parts, one for producing print editions and one for producing electronic editions. The guidelines included in this volume have been thoroughly revised and restructured in accordance with their advice and so represent an important recognition on the part of the CSE, the MLA, and the community of scholarly editors represented by them that scholarly editing as an intellectual activity is independent of the medium of publication, even if the methods used to achieve reliability in an edition may vary somewhat by medium.

THE TEXT ENCODING INITIATIVE

An international and interdisciplinary standards project, the Text Encoding Initiative (TEI) was established in 1987 to develop, maintain, and promulgate hardware- and software-independent methods for encoding humanities data in electronic form. Even in 1987, it was clear that without such an effort the academic community would soon find itself overwhelmed by a confusion of competing formats and encoding systems. Part of the problem was simply a lack of opportunity for sustained communication and coordination, but there were more-systemic forces at work as well. Longevity and reusability were clearly not high on the priority list of software vendors and electronic publishers, and proprietary formats were often part of a business strategy that might benefit a particular company but at the expense of the broader scholarly and cultural community. At the end of the 1980s there was a real concern that the entrepreneurial forces that (then as now) drove information technology forward would impede such integration by the proliferation of mutually incompatible technical standards.

The TEI guidelines, like the CSE guidelines, outline a set of best practices, but they also embody them in a formal and computable expression, originally constructed using standard generalized markup language (SGML) and since the fourth revision of the guidelines (published in 2002) expressible in extensible markup language (XML) as well (Sperberg-McQueen and Burnard, *Guidelines for Electronic Text Encoding*). The TEI guidelines are an extraordinary example of international interdisciplinarity, having been produced by hundreds of scholars from many different humanities disciplines, working in dozens of groups over more than fifteen years to specify a formal representation for what were considered the most important features of literary and linguistic texts.

The TEI guidelines today take the form of a 1,300-page reference manual, documenting and defining some six hundred elements that can be combined and modified in a variety of ways for particular purposes. Each such combination can be expressed formally as a kind of document grammar, technically known as a document type definition (DTD). The size of the guidelines would be daunting, were the TEI encoding scheme not highly modular. The designer of a TEI DTD reviews the available tag sets (modules, each containing semantically related element definitions) and decides how they are to be combined. Individual elements may be renamed, omitted, or modified, subject only to some simple architectural constraints. The TEI maintains Web-accessible software (for example, the TEI *Pizza Chef*) that helps users in carrying out this task. The size of TEI guidelines in book form is also somewhat daunting, particularly as they have gone through four editions since 1990.[1] The digital form of the guidelines has always been widely available without constraint on the Internet and should be consulted for up-to-date authoritative information (see www.tei-c.org/).

The work of the TEI has been supported by many organizations, including the United States' National Endowment for the Humanities, the United Kingdom's Arts and Humanities Research Board, the Modern Language Association, the European Union's Expert Advisory Group for Language Engineering Standards, and many agencies around the world that fund or promote digital library and electronic text projects. The impact of the TEI on digital scholarship has been enormous. Today, the TEI is internationally recognized as a critically important tool, both for the long-term preservation of electronic data and as a means of supporting effective usage of such data in many subject areas. It is the encoding scheme of choice for the production of critical and scholarly editions of literary texts, for electronic text collections in digital libraries, for scholarly reference works and large linguistic corpora, and for the management and production of item-level metadata associated with electronic text and cultural heritage collections of many types.

ELECTRONIC TEXTUAL EDITING

There is work for a generation or more of textual editors in the transmission of our cultural heritage from print to electronic media, but if that work is to be done, then a rising generation of scholars must receive professional credit for doing it. For that credit to be given, tenure and promotion committees will need to evaluate work of this kind. Our aim is to facilitate that evaluation, at both scholarly and technical levels. In this volume, the updated version of the CSE guidelines and the most recent release of the TEI guidelines frame a wide-ranging collection of essays that covers both practical and theoretical issues in electronic textual editing. The need for such a volume is immediate: there are currently few manuals, summer courses, or self-guided tutorials that would help even trained textual editors transfer their skills from print to electronic works.[2] Put another way, the evidence of need is to be found in the tens of thousands of poorly selected, unedited, and (most often) unidentified editions of literary texts one can find instantly on the Web. In response to that situation, our main goal has been to encourage careful work in the production of new digital editions by providing scholarly editors with pragmatic advice from expert practitioners (who are also internationally respected authorities in this expanding and interdisciplinary field) as well as by reproducing and uniting the best standards so far developed for such work. This volume may also serve another useful purpose: recording how, in the present moment, the community of textual editing is changing and evolving in response to the emergence of new technologies.

We ask the casual reader—who may at first see only a cacophony of unrelated specialist voices here—to look a little deeper for the common concerns that link all the contributors. First in the volume, we provide a complete revision of the MLA's CSE Guidelines for Editors of Scholarly Editions, which updates the checklist for vetters of print editions and adds a glossary to explain the terminology of the checklist (revised and explicated by Robert Hirst); it also includes new checklist items and glossary entries specifically aimed at vetters of electronic editions, compiled by Morris Eaves and John Unsworth, and a detailed annotated bibliography covering the whole field of editorial methods, compiled by Dirk Van Hulle. Then the volume editors briefly discuss the most basic principles of scholarly editing. The twenty-six essays that follow are grouped under two headings: material and theoretical approaches ("Sources and Orientations") and actual practices and procedures.

"Sources and Orientations" is appropriately opened by a joint contribution from two leading theorists of textual editing from complementary fields of expertise, Dino Buzzetti (medieval philosophy) and Jerome McGann (nineteenth-century English literature). Their reflections on the disciplinary transformations brought on by the development of powerful digital tools demonstrate in compelling ways the new opportunities and the new problems arising from "born-digital artifacts." There follow eleven case studies exploring specific problems and solutions for electronic editing in different genres, disciplines, and media. Editing from manuscript materials and fragments constitutes in itself a set of particular problems. Peter Robinson draws on his experience editing Chaucer for CD-ROM to offer a series of "lessons" for anyone contemplating the edition of a medieval text with multiple witnesses. Quite another set of challenges for electronic editing is posed by historical documents: Bob Rosenberg uses the papers of Thomas Edison (comprising some 1.5 million documents) to explore the problems and decision processes involved in the documentary editing of the papers and drawings of so prolific an inventor. In both cases, the computer's ability to handle, integrate, and manipulate vast amounts of disparate materials opens up new possibilities of access.

Next, electronic editing strategies for print-based texts are addressed by genre. Neil Fraistat and Steven Jones, coeditors of the collaborative *Romantic Circles* Web site, define the particular challenge of electronic editing: "to produce an electronic edition that doesn't simply translate the features of a print edition onto the screen but instead takes advantage of the truly exciting possibilities offered by the digital medium for the scholarly editing of poetry."

By framing the questions before scholarly editors of letterpress editions in the terms of an electronic medium, they address the fundamental questions that electronic editors of poetry must answer before beginning their task. Drama is a genre with problems both overlapping those of poetry and distinct from them. David Gants illustrates these problems from the early modern theater, discussing *The Cambridge Edition of the Works of Ben Jonson*. It is a distinctly hybrid edition, envisioned as two separate projects: six volumes in print form and a networked electronic edition that is expected to grow over time. Gants pays special attention to the problems of encoding peculiar to drama as a genre.

Julia Flanders draws on her experience migrating an editing project, the Women Writers Project, from print to electronic form. This large, multi-author collection "has been described variously as an archive, an edition, and an anthology and serves, in a sense, the purposes of all three." She shows how the digital anthology in its variety may serve as the "scale model" of the digital world.

Authorial translations are a separate case for editing, and Dirk Van Hulle discusses the twenty versions of Samuel Beckett's *Stirrings Still / Soubresauts*, which cross two languages. We see here the development of a genetic electronic edition that aims to capture the work in all its states. Van Hulle shows how the genesis of the work might be approached through different traditional editorial methods and gives a comprehensive presentation of how this edition represents Beckett's complex text. Edward Vanhoutte defines an electronic edition and its aims and offers as a case study in fiction his electronic edition of the classic Flemish novel *De teleurgang van den Waterhoek* by Stijn Streuvels.

Two essays consider the possibilities of electronic editing for nonfiction texts. Claus Huitfeldt sets out the thinking behind the design of a documentary edition, containing a facsimile, diplomatic transcription, and normalized transcription, for Wittgenstein's manuscript *Nachlass*. In establishing the procedures for ensuring consistency across the three parts of the edition, Huitfeldt also shows how such a project recapitulates the classical philosophical problems of representation and interpretation. Some pressing considerations for the electronic editing of religious texts are offered by D. C. Parker. In surveying how to define a religious text and how to treat scriptures considered sacred, his essay ranges widely across the peculiar difficulties of editing scripture, no matter what the medium. It might be considered a cautionary tale of editing in a sea of variants.

The final two essays in this section are composites of different kinds.

Morris Eaves draws on his experience with the *Blake Archive* as he explores the problems peculiar to a multimedia electronic edition of a single author, with particular attention to the technical and intellectual problems posed by the need to achieve a balance between art and text in an electronic scholarly edition. The field of epigraphy presents a range of problems and solutions, applicable also to all forms of surviving writing, whether complete or fragmentary. Anne Mahoney addresses digitization projects in Greek and Latin inscriptions and discusses the extent to which it is possible to preserve both information and its interpretation in such a context.

In "Practices and Procedures," the main focus of the essays is a practical issue of general importance to those undertaking digital textual editing. Some readers may find portions of what is discussed here overwhelmingly technical, but we have tried to retain accessibility without rendering discussion vacuous. This part opens with a very accessible essay on how to produce machine-readable text from manuscript and print sources, contrasting the practical experiences of two major digital editing projects: the *Piers Plowman* Project and the *JSTOR* service. Eileen Fenton and Hoyt Duggan demonstrate both unexpected similarities and differences in the not so mechanical processes of transforming medieval manuscript and modern print materials into digital form. M. J. Driscoll discusses how TEI may be used in the transcription of letterforms, abbreviations, structure, layout, emendations, and other features of a manuscript text. Kevin Kiernan also addresses working with manuscripts but focuses on issues raised by the use of digital facsimiles in editing. Presenting the possibilities of the digital, image-based edition of early medieval manuscripts, he shows how high-resolution facsimiles and digital restoration allow editors to represent the historical state of primary texts far better than would be possible with print technology. His considerations of the promise of such editions point to the need to bring the humanities and computing science together to develop more-flexible tools for image search and textual encoding.

A group of editors at the Australian Scholarly Editions Centre (Phill Berrie, Paul Eggert, Chris Tiffin, and Graham Barwell) explore the difficult question of how textual reliability can be maintained in the electronic environment. Next, Greg Crane explains the inner workings of the *Perseus Digital Library*, one of the oldest and largest collections of electronic editions. *Perseus*—originally focused on, and still best known for, editions of classical-era texts—has for nearly two decades grappled with changes in language technology. Christian Wittern explains in lucid detail where those technologies stand today, shows how text encoding is built on character encoding, and demonstrates the importance to editors of understanding how character encoding actually works. Patrick Durusau explains why it is important for electronic textual encoding projects, no matter how small, to record and explain the choices they make as they work their way through applying the TEI or any other markup scheme to the editorial problems that their texts present. Sebastian Rahtz convincingly shows what can be achieved using current standards-based Web technologies to store, analyze, and display digital texts.

There is some nontechnical discussion as well. We include, for example, a short account by John Lavagnino of circumstances in which the TEI might not be an appropriate solution, because we recognize that all representational schemes, including the TEI, must be informed by an ontology that in some cases will be inadequate, inefficient, or inappropriate. Hans Walter Gabler presents a detailed meditation on the experience of moving a print-based editorial project into electronic form, which should be useful to the growing number of editors who find themselves in analogous positions. The final two essays deal with important issues raised by the new modes of publication and distribution. No scholarly editor can afford to proceed far with a project without some basic understanding of copyright and contracts. In their detailed and indispensable essay, Mary Case and David Green review the relevant law on rights and permissions and its implications for scholarly editions—both for authors and editors. Marilyn Deegan addresses questions of what editors can do to facilitate library collection and preservation of their electronic editions.

No printed book that deals with information technology can avoid obsolescence: we fully expect that certain parts of this volume will be outdated, if not by the time that the book is published, certainly before it has been in print for even a year or two. For that matter, even if we start the history of electronic scholarly editions with Father Busa's punch-card Aquinas in 1949, we are not many decades into developing an understanding of how to make and use electronic documents in general, let alone electronic scholarly editions in particular. It took five hundred years to naturalize the book and a hundred and fifty years to develop the conventions of the scholarly edition in print. Those schedules reflect the time required for social, not technological, change, and while the acceleration of technological change in this case may rush the social evolution of rhetoric for digital editions of print and manuscript sources, it will still be generations before the target of this volume stops moving. Even before that happens, as Matthew Kirschenbaum has pointed out, we will soon be grappling with the problem of editing primary sources that are themselves digital—a problem with entirely new practical and theoretical dimensions ("Editing"). Precisely because, in these circumstances, no book can be definitive and no rules or guidelines can be the last word on their subject, we need organizational mechanisms for the continued maintenance, development, and dissemination of standards and best practices. The MLA's CSE and the TEI are two such mechanisms. The volume editors would therefore like to point out, in closing, that both organizations depend on the work of individuals and the support of institutions to persist in and to carry on their mission, and we invite your membership and participation.

NOTES

1. At the time of writing, a fifth major revision known as TEI P5 is in preparation.
2. The recently published Blackwell's *Companion to Digital Humanities* includes a chapter by Martha Nell Smith describing electronic scholarly editing; however, since the *Companion*'s intent is to serve as a textbook or reference work covering the entire field of humanities computing, it does not offer in-depth coverage of any particular practice in that field.

GUIDELINES FOR EDITORS OF SCHOLARLY EDITIONS

COMMITTEE ON SCHOLARLY EDITIONS, MLA

1. GUIDELINES FOR EDITORS OF SCHOLARLY EDITIONS

1.1. Principles

The scholarly edition's basic task is to present a reliable text: scholarly editions make clear what they promise and keep their promises. Reliability is established by

    accuracy
    adequacy
    appropriateness
    consistency
    explicitness

—accuracy with respect to texts, adequacy and appropriateness with respect to documenting editorial principles and practice, consistency and explicitness with respect to methods. The means by which these qualities are established will depend, to a considerable extent, on the materials being edited and the methodological orientation of the editor, but certain generalizations can be made.

Many, indeed most, scholarly editions achieve reliability by including a general introduction—either historical or interpretive—as well as explanatory annotations to various words, passages, events, and historical figures.

Scholarly editions generally include a statement, or series of statements, setting forth the history of the text and its physical forms, explaining how the edition has been constructed or represented, giving the rationale for decisions concerning construction and representation. This statement also typically describes or reports the authoritative or significant texts and discusses the verbal composition of the text—its punctuation, capitalization, and spelling—as well as, where appropriate, the layout, graphic elements, and physical appearance of the source material. Statements concerning the history and composition of the text often take the form of a single textual essay, but it is also possible to present this information in a more distributed manner.

A scholarly edition commonly includes appropriate textual apparatus or notes documenting alterations and variant readings of the text, including alterations by the author, intervening editors, or the editor of this edition.

And finally, editors of scholarly editions establish and follow a proofreading plan that serves to ensure the accuracy of the materials presented.

1.2. Sources and Orientations

1.2.1. Considerations with Respect to Source Material

Is the date of the material known? For example, in William Blake's *The Marriage of Heaven and Hell*, because the work itself bears no date, the date and its place in the author's oeuvre have to be inferred, and on such inferences other editorial decisions (decisions based, for example, on authorial intentions, which may vary over time) may depend. More generally, the location of a text in time and place may influence the editorial representation of a text.

Is there an author? La chanson de Roland, for example, took a specific written form after a long life as a heroic poem or poems delivered orally from memory. Folktales, which may or may not originate with individual authors, are usually known to editors only in forms that have been shaped by transmission through communities of performers and listeners. W. B. Yeats and Georgiana Yeats claimed to have taken dictation from the spiritual world. Sacred texts are often attributed to divine authors or divinely inspired human authors.

Is the author known? Authorship has been one of the most powerful and influential categories of textual criticism, where the "authority" of a text has often been determined by its convenient proximity to a known author writing in a specifiable time and space (traditionally, texts that come from an author's hand, such as an autographic manuscript, tend to have more authority in an edition than texts published after the author's death). When a text (for example, *Lazarillo de Tormes*) has no known author in the modern sense, or when authorship has been collaborative or communal, or when texts have taken shape over an extended period of time, editorial decisions must be based on other grounds.

Is there more than one author? For example, Francis Beaumont and John Fletcher collaborated in writing over a dozen dramatic works between 1606 and 1616, such as *The Knight of the Burning Pestle*; in addition to working together, these two writers also corrected and collaborated on texts with numerous other playwrights, including William Rowley, Philip Massinger, Thomas Middleton, and Ben Jonson, making it difficult, if not impossible, to assign authorship in some of these works to any one specific individual. Harriet Mill's role in the authorship of J. S. Mill's *Autobiography* might be labeled coauthorship; Theodore Dreiser sometimes revised his novels on the advice of a circle of family, friends, and associates. Max Perkins might be considered the coauthor of the novelists he edited as an employee of Scribner's—most notably Thomas Wolfe, whose published novels bear little resemblance to the manuscripts that Wolfe turned over to Perkins.

If there is an author (or authors), how far back in the process of authorship is source material available? For example, there are no surviving manuscripts or working drafts for the majority of Daniel Defoe's more than 250 works, including his novels, such as *Moll Flanders* and *Robinson Crusoe*. The editor must rely instead on printed texts produced during Defoe's lifetime as the earliest sources.

Does the author play any other roles in producing the object being edited? For example, Vladimir Nabokov translated his own early works from Russian into English at a later point in his career; Blake printed and watercolored his illuminated books with the assistance of his wife, Catherine; Charles Dickens became his own publisher, first as an editor of *Bentley's Miscellany*, then as founder and editor of *Household Words* and *All the Year Round*.

How many other people are involved in producing the object being edited, and what are their roles? For example, John Wilmot, the earl of Rochester, never published any of his works during his lifetime. Some of his poems were printed without his authority in songbooks and miscellanies, and they were widely circulated and preserved in manuscript copies. The subsequent posthumous editions gathered together many of these scattered pieces, but a modern editor must untangle the numerous variations found in the verses collected from these various manuscript and unauthorized printed versions. Another example would be the famously vexed case of James Joyce's *Ulysses*, drafted in longhand, typed by a typist, typeset by printers who spoke no English, and reset as many as five times, after Joyce's editing of page proofs.

Is it important, and is it feasible, to reproduce the material sources in facsimile as part of the edition? A facsimile reproduction of an author's manuscript (or diary, or letters, or draft of an unpublished poem or novel) may make it easier to follow the process of composition than any translation of the manuscript into typographic form. For example, recent editors of Emily Dickinson have argued that something important is lost when Dickinson's "jottings" on scraps of paper are translated to the more familiar form of printed poems. In principle, it would seem always desirable to reproduce the source material for a scholarly edition in facsimile, but in print editions it is often impractical, and even in electronic editions it may be too expensive, or it may be impossible for lack of permission.

1.2.2. The Editor's Theory of Text

Editorial perspectives range broadly across a spectrum from an interest in authorial intention, to an interest in the process of production, to an interest in reception, and editors may select a given methodology for a variety of reasons. In very general terms, one could see copy-text, recensionist, and best-text editing as being driven by an interest in authorship—but best-text editing might also be driven by an interest in the process of production, along with "optimist," diplomatic, scribal, documentary, and social-text editing. Social-text editing might also be driven by an interest in reception—as "versioning" and variorum editing might be. And, of course, an editing practice that is primarily interested in authorship might very well be interested in production or reception or both—any good editor will be aware of the importance of all these things. However, when an editor has to choose what to attend to, what to represent, and how to represent it, there should be a consistent principle that helps in making those decisions. See the CSE's "Annotated Bibliography: Key Works in the Theory of Textual Editing," below, for further information on editorial methods and perspectives.

1.2.3. Medium (or Media) in Which the Edition Will Be Published

The decision to publish in print, electronically, or both will have an impact on a number of aspects of the edition, on its fortunes, and on the fortunes of its editor. Some questions an editor should consider in choosing the medium of publication:

> Is the source material itself manuscript, printed, electronic, or a combination of formats?

> What is the desired or potential audience for the work? Is there more than one audience? Will one medium reach the desired audience more effectively than another?

What rights and permissions are required for publication, and do the terms differ by medium?

What kind of apparatus can the edition have, and what kind should it have?

Are there standard symbols or methods in a given medium for representing the typography, punctuation, or other textual features of the material being edited (Peirce's symbols, Shelley's punctuation, size-of-letter problems, spacing problems)?

What is the importance of facsimile material, color reproductions, multiple versions, multiple states, interactive tools in this edition?

Working with and from originals is of utmost importance; but some photographic, digitized reproductions make visible certain marks that have deteriorated and are no longer visible to the naked eye, even in the best light. If legibility has been enabled by the photographic or digitizing process, has that fact been explicitly noted to readers?

How important is permanence or fixity? How can these qualities be attained?

Alternatively, is there a possible benefit to openness and fluidity (for example, the certainty that new material will come to light)?

Is there a publisher willing to publish in the medium you choose?

How important is peer review (and if it is important, how will it be provided)?

2. GUIDING QUESTIONS FOR VETTERS OF SCHOLARLY EDITIONS

(This section is available as a checklist at the MLA Web site [www.mla.org/cse_guidelines#d0e354].)

Title vetted: _____

Edited by: _____

Date vetted: _____

Vetter: _____

For each question listed below, the vetter should enter *Yes*, *No*, or *Not applicable* as appropriate. Vetter should also indicate whether additional comment on this point is made in the attached report.

I. Basic Materials, Procedures, and Conditions

1.0   Has the editor missed any essential primary or secondary materials?

2.0   Has the editor constructed a valid genealogy, or stemma, of all relevant texts?

2.1   Have you tested the validity of this stemma against the collation data and included your findings in the report?

3.0   Have all transcriptions been fully compared by the editor with the original documents, as distinct from a photocopy of those documents?

3.1   If any transcriptions have not been fully compared with the originals, is there a statement in the edition alerting the user to that fact?

3.2   Has someone other than the original transcriber carried out a thorough and complete check of each transcription, whether against the original or a photocopy of the original?

3.3   Have you sampled the transcriptions for accuracy and included the results of that sampling in your report?

4.0   Have all potentially significant texts been collated?

4.1   How many times have the collations been repeated by different people?

4.2   Have you sampled the collations for accuracy and included the results of your sampling in your report?

II. Textual Essay

5.0   If the edition under review is one in a series, have you examined textual essays and vetters' reports (if any) from earlier volumes?

5.1   Does the textual essay provide a clear, convincing, and thorough statement of the editorial principles and practical methods used to produce this volume?

5.2   Does it adequately survey all pertinent forms of the text, including an account of their provenance?

5.3   Does it give an adequate history of composition and revision?

5.4   Does it give an adequate history of publication?

5.5   Does it give a physical description of the manuscripts or other pertinent materials (including electronic source materials, if any)?

5.6   Are ways in which photographic or digital reproductions manipulate the text (sometimes leading to greater legibility) plainly described?

5.7   Does it give a physical description of the specific copies used for collation?

6.0   Does the textual essay provide a convincing rationale for the choice of copy-text or base text or for the decision not to rely on either?

6.1   Does it adequately acknowledge and describe alternative but rejected choices for the copy-text or base text?

6.2   If there are forms of the text that precede the copy-text or base text, can they be recovered from the edited text and its apparatus?

6.3   If not, is it practical, desirable, or necessary to make them recoverable?

7.0   Does the editor give an adequate account of changes to the text made by authors, scribes, compositors, et cetera?

7.1   Are such changes to the text reported in detail as part of the textual apparatus?

7.2   If such changes are recorded but the record will not be published, has the decision not to publish it been justified in the textual essay?

8.0   Is the rationale for emendation of the copy-text or base text clear and convincing?

8.1   Are all emendations of the copy-text or base text reported in detail or described by category when not reported in detail?

8.2   Are the emendations of the copy-text or base text consistent with the stated rationale for emendation?

8.3   Do the data from collation support the editor's assertion of authority for emendations drawn from the collated texts?

8.4   If the author's customary usage (spelling, punctuation) is used as the basis for certain emendations, has an actual record of that usage been compiled from this text and collateral texts written by the author?

8.5   Have you sampled the edited text and record of emendations for accuracy, and have you included the results in your report?

8.6   Are emendations recorded clearly, avoiding idiosyncratic or ill-defined symbols?

9.0   Does the essay somewhere include an adequate rationale for reproducing, or not, the significant visual or graphic aspects of the copy-text or base text?

9.1   Are all illustrations in the manuscript or the printed copy-text or base text reproduced in the edited text?

9.2   If not, are they adequately described or represented by examples in the textual essay?

9.3   Are the visual aspects of typography or handwriting either represented in the edited text or adequately described in the textual essay?

9.4   If objects (such as bindings) or graphic elements (such as illustrations) are reproduced in the edition, are the standards for reproduction—sizing, color, and resolution—explicitly set forth in the textual essay?

III. Apparatus and Extratextual Materials

10.0   Has a full historical collation been compiled, whether or not that collation is to be published?

10.1   Is the rationale clear and convincing for publishing a selective historical collation (e.g., one that excludes variant accidentals)?

10.2   Does the selective collation omit any category of variants you think should be included or include any you think should be excluded?

10.3   Is the historical collation to be published accurate and consistent?

11.0   Are the textual notes clear, adequate, and confined to textual matters?

12.0   Have ambiguous hyphenated compounds (e.g., "water-wheel") in the copy-text or base text been emended to follow the author's known habits or some other declared standard?

12.1   Have ambiguous stanza or section breaks in the copy-text or base text been consistently resolved by emendation?

12.2   Are both kinds of emendation recorded in the textual apparatus to be published?

12.3   For words divided at the end of a line in the edited text and stanzas or section breaks that fall at the end of a page in the edited text, can the reader tell how these ambiguous forms should be rendered when the text is quoted?

13.0   Does the apparatus omit significant information?

13.1   Can the history of composition and/or revision and/or the history of printing be studied by relying on the textual apparatus?

13.2   Is the purpose of the different parts (or lists) in the apparatus clearly explained or made manifest?

13.3   Is cross-referencing between the parts (or lists) clear?

13.4   Is information anywhere needlessly repeated?

13.5   Is the format of the apparatus adapted to the audience?

13.6   Are the materials well organized?

14.0   Does the historical introduction dovetail smoothly with the textual essay?

14.1   Has the editor quoted accurately from the edited text in the introduction and the textual essay?

14.2   Has the editor verified references and quotations in the introduction and the textual essay?

14.3   Has the editor checked the author's quotations and resolved the textual problems they present?

14.4   Have you spot-checked to test the accuracy of quotation and reference in the introduction, textual essay, and text, and have you included the results of that spot check in your report?

15.0   Are the explanatory notes appropriate for this kind of edition— for example, in purpose, level of detail, and number?

15.1   Is there a sound rationale for the explanatory notes, whether or not the rationale is to be made explicit anywhere in the published work?

IV. Matters of Production

16.0   Did you see a final or near-final version of the edition or a substantial sample of it?

16.1   If you did not see final or near-final copy, were you satisfied with the state of completion of the materials you did see?

17.0   Has the editor obtained all necessary permissions—for example, to republish any materials protected by copyright?

18.0   If there is a publisher involved in producing the edition, has the publisher approved the content and format of the edition?

18.1   Has the publisher approved the amount of time needed for proofreading?

18.2   Has the publisher approved the requirements of the edition's design?

18.3   Has the publisher approved cuing the back matter (textual apparatus and notes) to the text of the edition by page and line number (if this is a print edition) or by other unambiguous means (if this is an electronic edition)?

18.4   Has the publisher approved the printer's or other production facility's copy requirements?

19.0   Has ultimate responsibility for maintaining accuracy throughout the production process been clearly assigned to one person?

19.1   Are the proofreading methods sufficient to ensure a high level of accuracy in the published edition?

19.2   How many proofreadings are scheduled?

19.3   How many stages of proof are there?

19.4   When a new stage of proof is read to verify changes or corrections, is adequate provision made for ensuring that all other parts of the text have not been corrupted?

19.5   Is there a provision in place for collation or comparison of the first correct stage of proof against the production facility's final prepublication output (e.g., bluelines from a printer or text as rendered for final delivery in an electronic edition)?

20.0   If the edition—whether print or electronic—is prepared in electronic files, are those files encoded in an open, nonproprietary format (e.g., TEI XML rather than *Microsoft Word* or *WordPerfect*)?

20.1   Will anyone other than the editor create or edit these files?

20.2   Is the editor directly involved in encoding (e.g., in doing XML markup or in coding for typesetting)?

20.3   If automated processes are applied to the text, is the editor checking the result for unintended consequences?

20.4   If an index or search engine is to be used as part of the edition, will it be checked or tested in detail by the editor?

21.0   Can the edited text be easily republished, excerpted, or repurposed?

21.1   If the edition is printed, is it suitable for photographic reproduction? If it is electronic, does it provide PDF or other pretty-printing output?

21.2   Will all electronic files used in producing the edition be archived?

21.3   Will a correction file be set up and maintained for correcting the text after its initial publication?

21.4   Is the current state of the correction file available to readers of the edition (on the Web, for example, or on request in printed form)?

V. Electronic Editions (see glossary for expansion of abbreviations)

22.1   Does the edition include help documentation that explains the features of the user interface and how to use them?

22.2   Does the edition carry a clear statement of the appropriate reuse of its constituent elements, especially those protected by copyright or used by permission?

23.0   Is the text of the edition encoded in an ISO standard grammar, such as XML or SGML?

23.1   Is the XML or SGML applied using relevant community guidelines (e.g., the Text Encoding Initiative guidelines)?

23.2   If the answer to the previous question is no, does the essay on technical methods provide a rationale for departing from community practice?

23.3   Is the edition designed to make its underlying markup (rather than markup that results from a rendering process) available to the reader for examination?

24.0   Is character encoding in the edition done according to an ISO standard (e.g., Unicode)?

24.1   Are rendering or transformation instructions (e.g., stylesheets) encoded in an ISO standard grammar, such as XSL?

24.2   Does the edition use ISO standard formats (e.g., JPEG, PNG) for the distribution copies of its digital images?

24.3   If there are time-dependent media elements in the edition (e.g., audio or video), are these encoded using ISO standard formats (e.g., MPEG/MP3)?

25.0   Are the distribution copies of multimedia elements (image, sound, video) sufficiently high-resolution to allow close study?

25.1   Are ways in which photographic or digital reproductions manipulate the text (sometimes leading to greater legibility) plainly described?

25.2   Are the distribution copies of multimedia elements stored at reasonable file size, given the intended method of distribution?

25.3   Are the sources for those distribution copies archived?

25.4   Are those sources captured at a sufficiently high resolution to allow for the future derivation of higher-resolution distribution copies?

26.0   Does the edition have, and does it validate against, a DTD or schema?

26.1   Is the DTD or schema used in marking up the edition adequately documented (e.g., with a tag library)?

26.2   If the edition includes one or more databases, is referential integrity enforced within the database(s)?

26.3   Are the database schemata documented?

26.4   Are the stylesheets (or other rendering instructions) documented as to their intended effect?

27.0   Is there a definitive and documented method for determining what constitutes the electronic edition?

27.1   Is there a definitive and documented method for determining whether all the constituent elements of the edition actually exist?

27.2   Is technical, descriptive, and administrative metadata provided for all the components of the edition, using a library-approved schema (such as METS)?

27.3   If any software has been uniquely developed for this edition, is source code for that software available and documented?

27.4   Has a copy of the edition and its images, software, stylesheets, and documentation been deposited with a library or other long-term digital object repository?

3. GLOSSARY OF TERMS USED IN THE GUIDING QUESTIONS

The glossary was drafted by Robert Hirst and subsequently revised and expanded by the committee.

accidentals   A collective term invented by W. W. Greg and now widely used to mean the punctuation, spelling, word division, paragraphing, and indications of emphasis in a given text—things "affecting mainly its formal presentation," as he put it (21). Greg distinguished between the accidentals of a text and its words, or substantives (q.v.). Accidentals and substantives are conceptually important for Greg's rationale of copy-text, which assumes that authors are more proprietary about their words than about their accidentals, while typesetters and other agents of textual transmission (copyists, typists, proofreaders, copyeditors) are the reverse. For this reason, at least for an edition aimed at preserving the author's accidentals as well as substantives, the rationale for choosing a copy-text is first and foremost that, of the available texts, it is the most faithful to the author's accidentals and contains the fewest changes to them by other hands. It is therefore often the first or earliest text in a line of descent, but any author who carefully revised the accidentals (say, in the second edition) might oblige an editor to choose that text rather than an earlier one.

authority   A property attributed to texts, or variants between texts, in order to indicate that they embody an author's active intention, at a given point in time, to choose a particular arrangement of words and punctuation. Authority therefore always derives from the author, even when *author* is defined and understood as coauthor, collaborator, or a collective (like the vorticists). Where the author is unknown or uncertain, authority will need to be argued. It is even possible to invert the usual pattern and assign authority to agents who produce variants commonly regarded as unauthoritative, such as typesetters, proofreaders, or reprint publishers—though one hesitates to call such agents "author." However defined, the author produces texts or variants that have authority. Some reprints may be said to have "no authority" because the author had no role in producing them. On the other hand, texts that were set from copy revised by the author are said to contain "new authority," meaning that some of their variants arose from the author's revision. The authority of a holograph manuscript is usually greater than any typesetting of it, but the manuscript's authority at any given point may be superseded if the typesetting incorporates authorial changes—a case of "divided authority."

base text   The text chosen by an editor to compare with other texts of the same work in order to record textual variation among them. Its selection can be to some extent arbitrary, or it can be selected because it is (among the available texts) simply the most complete. Unlike a copy-text (q.v.), it is not assigned any presumptive authority and may not even be used to construct a critical text, serving instead only as an anchor or base to record textual variants.

collation   Comparison. A collation is either the record of the substantive and accidental differences between two or more texts or the act of comparing two or more texts for the purpose of documenting their differences.

copy-text   The specific arrangement of words and punctuation that an editor designates as the basis for the edited text and from which the editor departs only where deeming emendation necessary. Under W. W. Greg's rationale the copy-text also has a presumptive authority in its accidentals (that is, the editor will default to them wherever variant accidentals are "indifferent"—meaning not persuasively authorial or nonauthorial). But *copy-text* may also designate texts for which no later variants are possible or anticipated. It is now commonplace to designate a manuscript letter that was actually sent as a copy-text for a personal letter. In such cases, emendations of the copy-text would normally consist not of the author's subsequent revisions but solely of elements in the original manuscript that the editor could not, or elected not to, represent in the transcription. Contrary to certain common misconceptions, *copy-text* does not mean the copy an editor or author sends to the printer, and it need not represent the "author's final intention." Indeed it is more likely to be the author's first draft than the author's final printed revision of a text. Its selection is based on the editor's judgment that the authority of its accidentals is on the whole superior to other possible texts that could be chosen for copy-text.

digital object repository   A means of storing, retrieving, and administering complex collections of digital objects. If the repository is to meet the needs of scholarly editions, it should have a secure institutional basis (like a university research library), and it should have a commitment to long-term preservation, migration, and access. For an example, see www.fedora.info.

DTD (document type definition)   The set of rules that specifies how the SGML or XML grammar will be applied in a particular document instance.

emendations   Editorial changes in the copy-text or base text. These changes may be made to correct errors, to resolve ambiguous readings, or to incorporate an author's later revisions as found in printed editions or other sources, such as lists of errata, assuming for the moment that the editorial goal is to recover the author's textual intentions. Different editorial goals might well call for emendations of some other kind, but they would all still be editorial changes to the copy-text or base text and would under normal circumstances be reported as part of the editor's accounting of the handling of available evidence.

end–of–line hyphens   Hyphens in a word that fall at the end of a line in a manuscript or in typeset material. End-of-line hyphens may sometimes be ambiguous. They may be either (a) signs of syllabic division used to split a word in two for easier justification of a line of type (or to fit it on the end of one and beginning of the next manuscript line) or (b) signs that a compound word is to be spelled with a hyphen. A word like *water-wheel* or *jack-o'-lantern* if broken after a hyphen at the end of a line might be ambiguous—that is, it is unclear whether the word is intended to be spelled with or without the hyphen. For any source text these ambiguous hyphens require judgment as to how the word was intended to be spelled, and such ambiguities would ordinarily be resolved in the way other ambiguous readings in a copy-text are resolved—by editorial choice, recorded as an emendation (change) in the copy-text. In the text as finally edited and printed, if hyphenation of certain words falls at the end of a line and is therefore ambiguous, the editor should likewise resolve this ambiguity for the reader.

explanatory notes   Notes devoted to explaining what something means or why it is present, rather than textual notes, which are devoted to explaining why the text at a certain point reads in the way it does and not in some other way.

historical collation   A record of variants for a given text over some defined number of editions (e.g., from the first through the seventh editions) or some period of time (e.g., from different impressions of the same edition made between 1884 and 1891). The purpose of historical collations is to put before the reader as complete a record as possible of all variants among a group of texts from which the editor has had to choose. In the past, but only to save space, historical collations have tended to omit variant accidentals and confine themselves to a record of variant substantives.

ISO   The short name for the International Organization for Standardization, a worldwide federation of national standards bodies from more than 140 countries, one from each country. ISO is a nongovernmental organization established in 1947. The mission of ISO is to promote the development of standardization and related activities in the world with a view to facilitating the international exchange of goods and services and to developing cooperation in the spheres of intellectual, scientific, technological, and economic activity. See www.iso.org.

JPEG (Joint Photographic Experts Group), or JPG   An open, nonproprietary ISO standard (official name ITU-T T.81 | ISO/IEC 10918–1) for the storage of raster images. For more information, see www.jpeg.org.

machine collation   Collation by means of a Hinman collator or other mechanical or optical device, allowing very slight differences between states of the same typesetting to be located visually, without the need for a traditional point-by-point comparison of one text against the other. Machine collation is only possible between different states of the same typesetting.

modernizing   Changing the spelling or punctuation of a text to bring these into conformity with modern standards, as distinct from the standards at the time of first composition or publication.

METS (Metadata Encoding and Transmission Standard)   A standard for encoding descriptive, administrative, and structural metadata regarding objects within a digital library, expressed using the XML schema language of the World Wide Web Consortium. The standard is maintained in the Network Development and MARC (machine-readable cataloging) Standards Office of the Library of Congress and is being developed as an initiative of the Digital Library Federation. For more information, see www.loc.gov/standards/mets.

MPEG (Moving Picture Experts Group)   The nickname given to a family of international standards used for coding audiovisual information in a digital compressed format. The MPEG family of standards includes MPEG-1, MPEG-2, and MPEG-4, formally known as ISO/IEC-11172, ISO/IEC-13818, and ISO/IEC-14496. Established in 1988, the MPEG working group (formally known as ISO/IEC JTC 1/SC 29/WG 11) is part of JTC1, the Joint ISO/IEC Technical Committee on Information Technology. For more information, see www.mpeg.org.

PNG (portable network graphics)   An extensible file format for the lossless, portable, well-compressed storage of raster images. The PNG specification is on a standards track under the purview of ISO/IEC JTC 1 SC 24 and is expected to be released eventually as ISO/IEC international standard 15948. See www .libpng.org.

raster image   An image stored and shown in terms of points, each one based on a set number of bytes that define its color. Arranged in a grid of pixels on a monitor, the points represent the tones, colors, and lines of the image. Common raster formats include TIFF and JPEG. Sometimes called bitmapped images, raster graphics are often contrasted to vector graphics, which represent images by such geometrical elements as curved lines and polygons rather than points in a grid. Vector graphics are typically used in programs for drawing and computer-aided design (CAD).

rendering process   The application of rules to transform content from storage format (e.g., TEI XML) to delivery format (e.g., XHTML), for the purpose of display in a Web browser. A vetter usually encounters these rules embodied in XSL stylesheets, but they could take other forms as well (PHP, CSS, etc.).

schema   A means for defining the structure, content, and semantics of XML documents. For more information, see www.w3.org/XML/Schema.

SGML (standard generalized markup language)   A grammar for text encoding, defined in ISO 8879. For more information, see http://xml.coverpages.org/sgml.html.

silent emendations   Editorial changes to the copy-text that are not recorded, item by item, as they occur but are only described somewhere in the textual essay as a general category of change and are thus made "silently," without explicit notice of each and every change.

stemma   A schematic diagram representing the genealogical relation of known texts (including lost exemplars) of a given work, showing which text or texts any given later text was copied from, usually with the overall purpose of reconstructing an early, lost exemplar by choosing readings from later extant texts, based in part on their relative distance from the lost source. A stemma may also be used simply to show graphically how any given text was copied or reprinted over time, even if the goal is not to recover an early, lost exemplar.

substantives   W. W. Greg's collective term for the words of a given text—"the significant . . . readings of the text, those namely that affect the author's meaning or the essence of his expression," as distinct from its accidentals (21). Under Greg's rationale for copy-text, the authority for substantives could be separate and distinct from the authority for the accidentals, thus permitting an editor to adopt changes in wording from later texts, even though maintaining the accidentals of an earlier one virtually unchanged.

tag library   A document that lists all the tags, or elements, available in a DTD, with a brief description of the intended use of each, a list of its attributes, and statements identifying elements within which this element can occur and which elements it can contain. See www.loc.gov/ead/tglib/index.html for an example.

textual notes Notes devoted specifically to discussing cruxes or particular difficulties in establishing how the text should read at any given point. Compare "explanatory notes."

user interface In an electronic edition, the on-screen presentation of content, including navigational methods, menus of options, and any other feature of the edition that invites user interaction or responds to it.

variants Textual differences between two or more texts. These would include differences in wording, spelling, word division, paragraphing, emphasis, and other minor but still meaning-bearing elements, such as some kinds of indention and spacing.

XML (extensible markup language) A simplified subset of SGML (q.v.), developed by the World Wide Web Consortium. For a gentle introduction to XML, see www.tei-c.org/P4X/SG.html.

XSL (extensible stylesheet language) A language for expressing stylesheets. An XSL stylesheet specifies the presentation of a class of XML documents (e.g., TEI documents) by describing how an instance of the class is transformed into an XML document that uses the specified formatting vocabulary (e.g., HTML). For more information, see www.w3.org/Style/XSL.

4. ANNOTATED BIBLIOGRAPHY: KEY WORKS IN THE THEORY OF TEXTUAL EDITING

The bibliography was drafted by Dirk Van Hulle and subsequently revised and expanded by the committee. For a more extensive compilation of works on the topic, see William Baker and Kenneth Womack, *Twentieth-Century Bibliography and Textual Criticism: An Annotated Bibliography* (Westport: Greenwood, 2000).

Bédier, Joseph. "La tradition manuscrite du *Lai de l'ombre*: Réflexions sur l'art d'éditer les anciens textes." *Romania* 54 (1928): 161–96, 321–56.

Bédier advocates best-text conservatism and rejects the subjectivity of Karl Lachmann's method (see Maas), with its emphasis on the lost authorial text, resulting remarkably often in two-branch stemmata. Instead, Bédier focuses on manuscripts and scribes, reducing the role of editorial judgment.

Biasi, Pierre-Marc de. "What Is a Literary Draft? Toward a Functional Typology of Genetic Documentation." *Drafts*. Spec. issue of *Yale French Studies* 89 (1996): 26–58.

> In a continuous effort to present manuscript analysis and *critique génétique* as a scientific approach to literature, Biasi designs a typology of genetic documentation, starting from the *bon à tirer* ("all set for printing") moment as the dividing line between the *texte* and what precedes it, the so-called *avant-texte*.

Blecua, Alberto. "Defending Neolachmannianism: On the *Palacio* Manuscript of *La Celestina*." *Variants*. Ed. Peter Robinson and H. T. M. Van Vliet. Turnhout: Brepols, 2002. 113–33.

> A clear position statement by the author of the noteworthy Spanish *Manual de crítica textual* (1983) in defense of the neo-Lachmannian method. Blecua argues that stemmatic analysis is superior to the methods based on material bibliography and that only the construction of a stemma can detect the presence of contaminated texts.

Bornstein, George, and Ralph G. Williams, eds. *Palimpsest: Editorial Theory in the Humanities*. Ann Arbor: U of Michigan P, 1993.

> On the assumption that texts are not as stable or fixed as we tend to think they are, these essays examine the palimpsestic quality of texts, emphasizing the contingencies both of their historical circumstances of production and of their reconstruction in the present. They mark a theoretical period of transition, shifting the focus from product to process in editorial theory and practice.

Bowers, Fredson. "Some Principles for Scholarly Editions of Nineteenth-Century American Authors." *Studies in Bibliography* 17 (1964): 223–28.

> Concise and systematic elaboration of W. W. Greg's theories, arguing that "when an author's manuscript is preserved," this document rather than the first edition has paramount authority and should serve as copy-text. Bowers's principles for the application of analytic bibliography in an eclectic method of editing have been most influential in Anglo-American scholarly editing.

Bryant, John. *The Fluid Text: A Theory of Revision and Editing for Book and Screen*. Ann Arbor: U of Michigan P, 2002.

> Bryant draws attention to textual fluidity, which results from processes of revision. In terms of scholarly editing, this implies a method of representation that does not obviate but rather emphasizes moments of textual instability. Although the examples are mostly taken from Melville's works, the ideas are generally applicable to other writings.

Cohen, Philip, ed. *Devils and Angels: Textual Editing and Literary Theory*. Charlottesville: UP of Virginia, 1991.

> The "increasingly theoretical self-consciousness" characterizing textual criticism and scholarly editing marks an impasse, indicative of a paradigm shift. Assumptions that have been self-evident for several decades are rethought in eight stimulating essays and three responses.

Deppman, Jed, Daniel Ferrer, and Michael Groden, eds. *Genetic Criticism: Texts and Avant-Textes*. Philadelphia: U of Pennsylvania P, 2004.

This representative collection of eleven essays by French critics (such as Louis Hay, Pierre-Marc de Biasi, Almuth Grésillon, and Jean Bellemin-Noël) introduces genetic criticism (*critique génétique*) to an Anglo-American audience, distinguishing this critical mode from textual criticism. Apart from the elucidating general introduction, each of the essays is preceded by an informative introduction and bibliography.

Eggert, Paul. "Textual Product or Textual Process: Procedures and Assumptions of Critical Editing." *Editing in Australia*. Ed. Eggert. Canberra: U Coll. ADFA, 1990. 19–40.

Starting from a comparison with new techniques of x-raying paintings, Eggert proposes a valuable ideal for a critical edition that allows the reader to study both the writing process and the finished product.

Ferrer, Daniel. "Production, Invention, and Reproduction: Genetic vs. Textual Criticism." *Reimagining Textuality: Textual Studies in the Late Age of Print*. Ed. Elizabeth Bergmann Loizeaux and Neil Fraistat. Madison: U of Wisconsin P, 2002. 48–59.

Ferrer defines the difference between genetic and textual criticism on the basis of their respective foci on invention and repetition. He pleads for a hypertextual presentation as the best way to do justice to the diverse aspects of the writing process.

Finneran, Richard J., ed. *The Literary Text in the Digital Age*. Editorial Theory and Lit. Criticism. Ann Arbor: U of Michigan P, 1996.

The availability of digital technology coincides with a fundamental paradigm shift in textual theory, away from the idea of a "definitive edition." Fifteen contributions reflect on the shift toward an enhanced attention to nonverbal elements and the integrity of discrete versions.

Fiormonte, Domenico. *Scrittura e filologia nell'era digitale*. Turin: Bollati Boringhieri, 2003.

Taking Italian *filologia* as his frame of reference, Fiormonte includes advances in various fields of research and different national contexts to expound his view on the theoretical implications of electronic editing and digital philology or "postphilology." In the appendixes, Fiormonte discusses a number of existing electronic editions and useful tools for textual criticism and digital philology.

Gabler, Hans Walter. "The Synchrony and Diachrony of Texts: Practice and Theory of the Critical Edition of James Joyce's *Ulysses*." *Text* 1 (1981): 305–26.

The work's "total text," comprising all its authorial textual states, is conceived as a diachronous structure that correlates different synchronous structures. A published text is only one such synchronous structure and not necessarily a privileged one.

Gabler, Hans Walter, George Bornstein, and Gillian Borland Pierce, eds. *Contemporary German Editorial Theory*. Ann Arbor: U of Michigan P, 1995.

With its representative choice of position statements, this thorough introduction to major trends in German editorial theory in the second half of the twentieth century marks the relatively recent efforts to establish contact between German and Anglo-American editorial traditions.

Gaskell, Philip. *From Writer to Reader: Studies in Editorial Method*. Oxford: Clarendon, 1978.

In 1972, as *A New Introduction to Bibliography* was replacing R. B. McKerrow's manual, Gaskell had already criticized W. W. Greg's copy-text theory, arguing that authors often expect their publishers to correct accidentals. *From Writer to Reader*
zooms in on the act of publication and the supposed acceptance of the textual
modifications this may involve.

Greetham, David C., ed. *Scholarly Editing: A Guide to Research*. New York: MLA, 1995.
The most comprehensive survey of current scholarly editing of various kinds of
literatures, both historically and geographically, with elucidating contributions by
textual scholars from different traditions.

———. *Textual Scholarship: An Introduction*. New York: Garland, 1992.
An impressive survey of various textual approaches: finding, making, describing,
evaluating, reading, criticizing, and finally editing the text—namely, biblio-, paleo-,
and typography; textual criticism; and scholarly editing. The book contains an extensive bibliography, organized by discipline.

Greg, W. W. "The Rationale of Copy-Text." *Studies in Bibliography* 3 (1950–51): 19–36.
This pivotal essay has had an unparalleled influence on Anglo-American scholarly
editing in the twentieth century. Greg proposes a distinction between substantive
readings (which change the meaning of the text) and accidentals (spelling, punctuation, etc.). He pleads for more editorial judgment and eclectic editing, against
"the fallacy of the 'best text'" and "the tyranny of the copy-text," contending that
the copy-text should be followed only so far as accidentals are concerned and that
it does not govern in the matter of substantive readings.

Grésillon, Almuth. *Eléments de critique génétique: Lire les manuscrits modernes*. Paris: PUF,
1994.
An introduction to textual genetics or *critique génétique*, which was developed in the
1970s and became a major field of research in France. In spite of correspondences
with textual criticism, it sees itself as a form of literary criticism, giving primacy to
interpretation over editing.

Groden, Michael. "Contemporary Textual and Literary Theory." *Representing Modernist
Texts: Editing as Interpretation*. Ed. George Bornstein. Ann Arbor: U of Michigan P, 1991.
259–86.
An important plea for more contact between textual and literary theorists, by the
general editor of the *James Joyce Archive* facsimile edition of Joyce's works.

Hay, Louis. "Passé et avenir de l'édition génétique: Quelques réflexions d'un usager."
Cahier de textologie 2 (1988): 5–22. Trans. as "Genetic Editing, Past and Future: A Few
Reflections of a User." Trans. J. M. Luccioni and Hans Walter Gabler. *Text* 3 (1987):
117–33.
Genetic editing, presenting the reader with a "work in progress," is a new trend,
but it revives an old tradition. The founder of the Institute for Modern Texts and
Manuscripts (ITEM-CNRS), in Paris, points out that editing has always reflected
the main ideological and cultural concerns of its day.

Maas, Paul. *Textkritik*. Leipzig: Teubner, 1927. Vol. 2 of *Einleitung in die Altertumswissenschaft*. Trans. as *Textual Criticism*. Trans. Barbara Flower. Oxford: Clarendon, 1958.

> One of Karl Lachmann's main disciples, Maas systematizes Lachmannian stemmatics, requiring thorough scrutiny of witnesses (*recensio*) before the emendation of errors and corruptions (*emendatio*, often involving a third step of divination or *divinatio*).

Martens, Gunter, and Hans Zeller, eds. *Texte und Varianten: Probleme ihrer Edition und Interpretation*. Munich: Beck, 1971.

> An epoch-making collection of German essays with important contributions by, among others, Zeller (pairing "record" and "interpretation," allowing readers to verify the editor's decisions), Siegfried Scheibe (on fundamental principles for historical-critical editing), and Martens (on textual dynamics and editing). The collection's central statement is that the apparatus, not the reading text, constitutes the core of scholarly editions.

McGann, Jerome J. *Critique of Modern Textual Criticism*. Chicago: U of Chicago P, 1983. Charlottesville: UP of Virginia, 1992.

> Textual criticism does not have to be restricted to authorial changes but may also include the study of posthumous changes by publishers or other agents. McGann sees the text as a social construct and draws attention to the cooperation involved in the production of literary works.

———. "The Rationale of HyperText." *Text* 9 (1996): 11–32. Rpt. in *Electronic Text: Investigations in Method and Theory*. Ed. Kathryn Sutherland. Oxford: Clarendon, 1997. 19–46. Rpt. in *Radiant Textuality: Literature after the World Wide Web*. New York. Palgrave, 2001. 53–74.

> Conceived in an expressly revisionist relation to W. W. Greg's rationale, McGann's ambitious essay presents the book as a machine of knowledge and evaluates the advantages of hyperediting and hypermedia over editions in codex form. As the earliest hypertextual structure, the library organization illustrates the theoretical design of a "decentered text."

———. *The Textual Condition*. Princeton: Princeton UP, 1991.

> McGann makes several valuable and innovative suggestions, from the idea of a "continuous production text" to a clear distinction between a text's bibliographic and linguistic codes (in the important essay "What Is Critical Editing?").

McKenzie, D. F. *Bibliography and the Sociology of Texts: The Panizzi Lectures, 1985*. London: British Lib., 1986.

> McKenzie extends the scope of traditional bibliography to a broader sociology of the text, including video games, movies, and even landscapes. This perspective has been a major stimulus to the advancement of the sociological orientation in scholarly editing.

McKerrow, R. B. *An Introduction to Bibliography for Literary Students*. Oxford: Oxford UP, 1927.

McKerrow's manual of "new bibliography" reflects the early-twentieth-century editorial method that made extensive use of analytic bibliography. The author of *Prolegomena for the Oxford Shakespeare* was rather averse to the idea of emending the copy-text from other sources.

Nutt-Kofoth, Rüdiger, Bodo Plachta, H. T. M. Van Vliet, and Hermann Zwerschina, eds. *Text und Edition: Positionen und Perspektiven*. Berlin: Schmidt, 2000.

As a younger generation's counterpart of *Texte und Varianten* (see Martens and Zeller), this state of the art of current scholarly editing in Germany also includes interesting survey articles on Anglo-American scholarly editing (e.g., Peter Shillingsburg) and "genetic criticism and philology" (Geert Lernout; trans. in *Text* 14 [2002]: 53–75).

Parker, Hershel. *Flawed Texts and Verbal Icons: Literary Authority in American Fiction*. Evanston: Northwestern UP, 1984.

Starting from analyses of revisions by Herman Melville, Mark Twain, Stephen Crane, and Norman Mailer, Parker pleads for more attention to textual composition and the development of (sometimes self-contradictory) authorial intentions, which an institutionalized editorial method is often unable to represent.

Pasquali, Giorgio. *Storia della tradizione e critica del testo*. Florence: Le Monnier, 1934.

Pasquali criticizes some of the basic Lachmannian principles and proposes to take the history of the witnesses and the scribes into account. The current emphasis on textual tradition in Italian philology is to a large extent his legacy.

Pizer, Donald. "Self-Censorship and Textual Editing." *Textual Criticism and Literary Interpretation*. Ed. Jerome J. McGann. Chicago: U of Chicago P, 1985. 144–61.

Pizer emphasizes the social aspects of texts, arguing that even when authors personally change their texts under external pressure, it may be more important to present the reader with the censored versions because of their social resonance.

Reiman, Donald H. "'Versioning': The Presentation of Multiple Texts." *Romantic Texts and Contexts*. Columbia: U of Missouri P, 1987. 167–80.

Reiman suggests "versioning" (or multiversional representation) as an alternative to "editing." The main purpose of this textual approach is to offer readers and critics the opportunity to figure out for themselves how the work evolved.

Robinson, Peter M. W. "The One Text and the Many Texts." *Making Texts for the Next Century*. Spec. issue of *Literary and Linguistic Computing* 15.1 (2000): 5–14.

In answer to the question "Is there a text in these variants?," which Robinson asked in a previous essay, he argues that a scholarly edition is more than merely presenting an archive of variants. The aim of the editor should be to offer a useful tool so as to allow readers to make the connection between variation and meaning. A critically edited text (presented along with "the many texts") is the best means to that end.

Schreibman, Susan, Ray Siemens, and John Unsworth, eds. *A Companion to Digital Humanities*. Oxford: Blackwell, 2004.

This collection of thirty-seven essays consolidates its broad, authoritative coverage of the emerging field of humanities computing in four sections: history; principles; applications; and production, dissemination, and archiving. Topics range from computer basics and digital textual editing to speculative computing, project design, and preservation.

Shillingsburg, Peter. *Resisting Texts: Authority and Submission in Constructions of Meaning.* Ann Arbor: U of Michigan P, 1997.

The editor's main task, Shillingsburg argues, is to relate the work to the documents and to take responsibility for the integrity of the agency of texts, which is a responsibility to both the author and the social contract. Shillingsburg designs a map with four major forms of textual concern, placing the physical documents at the center of textual and literary theory.

————. *Scholarly Editing in the Computer Age: Theory and Practice.* 3rd ed. Ann Arbor: U of Michigan P, 1996.

An indispensable introduction to practical procedures and controversial issues in editorial theory, offering clear definitions in matters of textual ontology and a survey of different orientations in scholarly editing.

Stillinger, Jack. *Multiple Authorship and the Myth of the Author in Criticism and Textual Theory.* New York: Oxford UP, 1991.

Stillinger pleads for a broader conception of authorship to include collaboration as an inherent aspect of creation. Case studies include John Stuart Mill and his wife, John Keats and his helpers, and William Wordsworth revising earlier versions of his texts.

Tanselle, G. Thomas. "The Editorial Problem of Final Authorial Intention." *Studies in Bibliography* 29 (1976): 167–211.

Authors' revisions do not automatically reflect their final intentions. In the case of *Typee*, Herman Melville was responsible for the changes in the second edition, but they represent his "acquiescence" rather than his intention, according to Tanselle, who is well aware that a reader does not have access to an author's mind and who advises editors to always take the context into account.

————. *A Rationale of Textual Criticism.* Philadelphia: U of Pennsylvania P, 1989.

In his profound analysis of the ontology of texts, Tanselle makes a clear distinction between *work* and *text*. A work is an entity that exists in no single historical document. Scholarly editing entails, just like any act of reading, the effort to discover the work that "lies behind" the text(s) one is presented with.

Thorpe, James. *Principles of Textual Criticism.* San Marino: Huntington Lib., 1972.

As an early critic of the principles advocated by W. W. Greg and Fredson Bowers, Thorpe argues that specific compositional peculiarities and contingencies tend to be left out of consideration.

Timpanaro, Sebastiano. *La genesi del metodo del Lachmann.* Florence: Le Monnier, 1963. Rev. ed. Padua: Liviana, 1985.

The genealogical study of manuscript transmission originated in New Testament criticism toward the end of the eighteenth century. By reexamining Joseph Bédier's criticism regarding two-branch stemmata, Timpanaro does not so much aim to correct them as to understand how they came into being.

Van Hulle, Dirk. *Textual Awareness: A Genetic Study of Late Manuscripts by Joyce, Proust, and Mann*. Ann Arbor: U of Michigan P, 2004.

The first part of the book gives a concise but thorough overview of the three editorial traditions (*Editionswissenschaft*, *édition critique* and *critique génétique*, and textual criticism and scholarly editing). The second part of the book is a genetic analysis of three major works of world literature: James Joyce's *Finnegans Wake*, Marcel Proust's *À la recherche du temps perdu*, and Thomas Mann's *Doktor Faustus*.

Zeller, Hans. "A New Approach to the Critical Constitution of Literary Texts." *Studies in Bibliography* 28 (1975): 231–63.

In his evaluation of Anglo-American copy-text theory from a structuralist point of view, Zeller contrasts the practice of editing an "eclectic (contaminated) text" with German editorial methods, showing crucial differences with respect to the notions of "authority," "authorial intention," and "version."

NOTE

These guidelines were last revised 7 April 2006.

A SUMMARY OF PRINCIPLES

Scholarly editing as a discipline encompasses interlocking sets of procedures that must be responsive in various ways to the nature of the material to be edited, to developments in the theory of editing, and to the technical possibilities and limitations of the medium in which a text is to be published. If the horizon of texts to be edited has changed little in the last quarter century,[1] the same cannot be said for the theory of editing such texts or for the publication possibilities opened up for them by electronic editing. While in these two areas the practice of scholarly editing has seen prodigious change in the last few decades, the principles and goals of this form of editing (as opposed to its particular procedures or techniques) have, nonetheless, remained essentially the same. The challenge posed in articulating these principles, given the possible range of editorial theory and the burgeoning developments in electronic editing, is both simple and daunting: In the face of significant differences in textual materials (by date, medium, genre, mode of dissemination), textual theories (author-centered, social-text, reception-oriented, etc.), and manner of publication (print-based or electronic), how can we express what is common to them all?

The Modern Language Association's first corporate involvement with scholarly editing was the Center for Editions of American Authors (CEAA), established in 1963 to coordinate, evaluate, and fund editorial work in the United States on texts by American authors. The MLA reorganized that body in 1976 and created the Committee on Scholarly Editions (CSE). This committee's change in name and charge reflected a broader interest in textual editing of material from any period or language covered under the general umbrella of the MLA. Since 1976 the CSE has itself developed in order to respond to developments in editing theory and, most recently, to embrace the challenges posed by the growth of electronic editing. A broader scope requires a more general (and indeed, more abstract) statement of the principles that guide good practices in scholarly editing, across periods, languages, and methodological commitments. In the light of that broader scope, the CSE most recently revised its guidelines to present, in their most applicable form, the principles that must underlie any formal scholarly edition.

The first of these principles is, in effect, a summary of the discipline: "The scholarly edition's basic task is to present a reliable text: scholarly editions make clear what they promise and keep their promises" (CSE, *Guidelines*).

The clause before the colon is the simplest statement of the principle that guides scholarly editing, and it is only slightly embellished by the explanation that follows. The CSE neither can nor wishes to prescribe the exact manner in which reliability will be achieved; rather, it stipulates that a text must be reliable with respect to a clearly stated set of editorial commitments. An edition is to be judged by the scholarly promises it makes and the degree to which it keeps those promises.

"Reliability" would be merely a shibboleth without a set of criteria establishing the bases on which the editing may be trusted. The guidelines specify five criteria on which to build the trustworthiness of any scholarly edition:

accuracy   Accuracy is the goal of any scholarly edition. For an edition to be reliable, the text "made" in the process of editing must be a faithful representation, whether the goal is a best text, a documentary text, or a social text, to name some common editorial approaches. Whatever theory of editing is applied, a comprehensive proofreading plan is required to ensure that the scholarly text, so carefully established through numerous iterations of the editing and production process, has been purged of errors and typos.

adequacy and appropriateness   Adequacy and appropriateness are the goals at two distinct points in the process of editing. In the preliminary stages of designing an edition, they are measures of the fit between editorial principles and practice and the textual materials to be edited. At the stage of writing the introduction to the edited text, adequacy and appropriateness are goals for documenting editorial principles and practice.

consistency and explicitness   Consistency and explicitness are required of a scholarly edition with respect to the methods used in establishing its text. Editions must make explicit the principles on which their texts are founded, and those principles must be clearly followed in the text that is subsequently produced. Consistency is the measure of agreement between editing principles and edited text.

The first section of the CSE guidelines, "Principles," is the briefest and least frequently revised section in that document. It deliberately offers no medium-specific advice and no advice that applies only to editions of certain kinds of material or editions in certain editorial traditions. By design, it speaks only to general and enduring principles, acting as an introductory overview for readers new to editing and as a general reminder for those with some experience. And throughout, it prompts editors to consider and make explicit their methodology. Thomas Tanselle offers a convenient statement of these ideas ("Statement"). In keeping these principles severely spare, the CSE has hoped to provide a starting point and a frame of reference for the widest possible range of scholarly editing projects. From these few principles held in common, editors embark on the many-forked paths of decision making in producing a text.

Note

1. See, for example, Kirschenbaum's discussion of the challenges that will be raised when we come to do scholarly editions of born-digital, multimedia texts ("Editing").

PART I

SOURCES AND ORIENTATIONS

CRITICAL EDITING IN
A DIGITAL HORIZON

DINO BUZZETTI AND JEROME McGANN

Just as the machinery of the codex opened radically new ways to store, organize, study, transform, and disseminate knowledge and information, digital technology represents an epochal watershed for anyone involved with semiotic materials. For scholars of books and texts, and in particular for editorial scholars, digital tools have already begun their disciplinary transformations, and we can see as well the promise of further, perhaps even more remarkable, changes on the near horizon of our work.

In this essay, we describe and reflect on these changes, but first we briefly review the forms and procedures of scholarly editing that are licensed by codex technology. This survey is important because present work and future developments in digital scholarship evolve from critical models that we have inherited. The basic procedures and goals of scholarly editing will not change because of digital technology. True, the scale, range, and diversity of materials that can be subjected to scholarly formalization and analysis are all vastly augmented by these new tools. Besides, the emergence of born-digital artifacts creates entirely new critical opportunities, as well as problems, for librarians, archivists, and anyone interested in the study and interpretation of works of culture. Nonetheless, the goals of the scholar remain unaltered—preservation, access, dissemination, and analysis-interpretation—as does the basic critical method, formalization.

If our traditional goals remain, however, these new technologies are forcing us to revisit and rethink some of the most basic problems of textuality and theory of text. We address these matters in the two central sections of this essay, and in the final section we reflect on certain practical methodological implications of these reflections. First, however, we must step back and make a brief review of the current state of text-editing theory and method.

CODEX-BASED SCHOLARSHIP AND CRITICISM

Scholarly editing is the source and end and test of every type of investigative and interpretational activity that critical minds may choose to undertake.[1] Well understood by scholars until fairly recently, the foundational status of editorial work is now much less surely perceived. Hermeneuts of every kind regularly regard such work, in René Wellek's notoriously misguided description, as "preliminary operations" in literary studies (Wellek and Warren 57). Odd though it may seem, that view is widely shared even by bibliographers and editors, who often embrace a positivist conception of their work.

Scholarly editing is grounded in two procedural models: facsimile editing of individual documents and critical editing of a set of related documentary witnesses. In the first case, the scholar's object is to provide as accurate a simulation of some particular document as the means of reproduction allow. Various kinds of documentary simulation are possible, from digital images and photoduplications on one end to printed diplomatic transcriptions on the other. Facsimile editing is sometimes imagined as a relatively straightforward and even simple scholarly project, but in fact the facsimile editor's task is every bit as complex and demanding as the critical editor's. In certain respects it can be more difficult, precisely because of the illusions that come with the presence of a single documentary witness, which can appear as a simple, self-transparent, and self-identical object.[2]

Securing a clear and thorough facsimile brings with it more problems than the manifest and immediate technical ones, though they are real enough. In addition, the facsimile editor can never forget that the edition being made comes at a certain place and time. At best, therefore, the edition is an effort to simulate the document at that chosen moment. The document bears within itself the evidence of its life and provenance, but that evidence, because of the document's historical passage, will always be more or less obscure, ambiguous in meaning, or even unrecoverable.

Every document exhibits this kind of dynamic quality, and a good scholarly edition will seek to expose that volatility as fully as possible. Being clear about the dynamic character of a document is the beginning of scholarly wisdom, whatever type of work one may undertake (hermeneutical or editorial) and—in editorial work—whatever type of edition one has chosen to do.

The other foundational pole (or pillar) of scholarly editing is critical editing. This work centers in the comparative analysis of a set of documentary witnesses each of which instantiates some form or state of the work in question. We name, for example, Dante Gabriel Rossetti's "The Blessed Damozel" with that one name, as if it were a single, self-identical thing (which, in that special perspective, it in fact is—that is to say, is taken to be). But the work so named descends to us in multiple documentary forms. Critical editing involves the careful study of that documentary corpus. Its main purpose is to make various kinds of clarifying distinctions among the enormous number of textual witnesses that instantiate a certain named work.

The critical editor's working premise is that textual transmission involves a series of translations. Works get passed on by being reproduced in fresh documentary forms. This process of reproduction necessarily involves textual changes of various kinds, including changes that obscure and corrupt earlier textual forms. Some of these changes are made deliberately, many others not. A classical model of critical editing, therefore, has involved the effort to distinguish the corruptions that have entered the body of the work as a result of its transmission history. That model often postulates a single, authoritative, original state of the work. The scholar's analytic procedures are bent on the effort to recover the text of that presumably pristine original.

A key device for pursuing such a goal is stemmatic analysis. This is a procedure by which the evolutionary descent of the many textual witnesses is arranged in specific lines. A stemma of documents exposes, simply, which texts were copied from which texts. Understanding the lines of textual transmission supplies a scholar with information that guides and controls the editorial work when decisions have to be made between variant forms of the text.

The problematic character of every documentary witness remains a key issue for the critical editor. That difficulty emerges at the initial stage of editorial work—that is to say, at the point when a decision is made about which documents will come into the textual analysis. In no case can all the witnesses be included. On one hand, the number of actually available documents will be far too numerous; on the other, many documents that formed part of the transmission history will be inaccessible.

In some cases—they are a distinct minority—a relatively small and manageable set of documents offers itself for scholarly analysis. Print technology brought about a massive proliferation of textual works. These are passed on to us edition by edition, and of course each edition differs from every other, nor are the differences between editions always easy to see or understand.

But the play of these kinds of textual differences is still more extreme. An unschooled view, for example, will assume that every copy of a print edition of some work is identical to every other copy. Editorial scholars themselves often make this assumption, and sometimes deliberately (in order to simplify, for analytic purposes, the ordering of the editorial materials). But the textual scholar usually knows better, and in producing a critical edition from an analysis of printed documents, editors regularly understand that multiple copies of a single edition must be examined. (As we see below, even multiple copies that appear to be textually identical always incorporate material differences that can be, from the scholar's point of view, crucial for anyone trying to understand the work in question.)

In recent years a special type of critical editing gained wide currency: the so-called eclectic editing procedure, promoted especially by Fredson Bowers. This method chooses a copy-text as the editor's point of departure. The editor then corrects (or, more strictly, changes) this text on the basis of a comparative study of the available readings in the witnesses that are judged to be authoritative by the editor. When variant readings appear equally authoritative, the editor uses judgment to choose between them.

In considering these matters, the scholar must never lose sight of the fundamentally volatile character of the textual condition. The pursuit of a correct or authoritative text is what a poet might call "a hopeless flight" (Byron 3.70.5). Editors can only work to the best of their judgment, for the texts remain, in the last analysis, ambiguous. One sees how and why by reflecting on, for example, the editorial commitment to achieve an authoritative text—which is to say, a text that represents the author's intention. That pervasive editorial concept is fraught with difficulties. Authors regularly change their works, so that one often must wrestle with multiple intentions. Which intentions are the most authoritative? first intentions? intermediate? final? Are we certain that we know each line of intentionality, or that we can clearly distinguish one from another? For that matter, how do we deal with those textual features and formations that come about through nonauthorial agencies like publishers? In respect to the idea of textual authority, more authorities sit at the textual table than the author.

Scholars have responded to that textual condition with a number of interesting, specialized procedures. Three important variations on the two basic approaches to scholarly editing are especially common: best-text editions, genetic editions, and editions with multiple versions. The best-text edition aims to generate a reproduction of the particular text of a certain work—let's say, the Hengwrt manuscript of Chaucer's *Canterbury Tales*—that will be cleared of its errors. Collation is used to locate and correct what are judged to be corrupt passages. Unlike the eclectic edition, a best-text edition does not seek to generate a heteroglot text but one that accurately represents the readings of the target document. If a facsimile or diplomatic approach to the editorial task is taken, editors will even preserve readings that they judge to be corrupted. If the approach is critical, editors will try to correct such errors and restore the text to what they judge to have been its (most) authoritative state.

Genetic editing procedures were developed in order to deal with the dynamic character of an author's manuscript texts. These editions examine and collate all the documents that form part of the process that brought a certain work into a certain state. Usually these editions aim to expose and trace the authorial process of composition to some point of its completion (for example, to the point where the text has been made ready for publication).[3]

Multiple version editions may take a best-text, an eclectic, or a genetic approach to their work. They aim, in any of these cases, to present multiple-reading versions of some particular work. (Paull Baum edited Rossetti's "The Blessed Damozel" in this way, and Wordsworth's *The Prelude* as well as Coleridge's "The Rime of the Ancient Mariner" have regularly been treated in a versioning editorial approach.)[4]

Finally, we should mention the proposal for social text editing that was especially promoted in recent years by D. F. McKenzie. In McKenzie's view, the scholar's attention should be directed not only at the text—the linguistic features of a document—but at the entirety of the material character of the relevant witnesses. McKenzie regarded documents as complex semiotic fields that bear within themselves the evidence of their social emergence. The critical editor, in his view, should focus on that field of relations and not simply on the linguistic text. Unfortunately, McKenzie died before he could complete the project he had in mind to illustrate his editorial approach—his edition of William Congreve.

TEXTUAL AND EDITORIAL SCHOLARSHIP WITH DIGITAL TOOLS

The advent of information technology in the last half of the twentieth century has transformed in major ways the terms in which editorial and textual studies are able to be conceived and conducted. This transformation has come about because the critical instrument for studying graphic and bibliographic works, including textual works, is no longer the codex (see McGann, "Rationale"). Because the digital computer can simulate any material object or condition in a uniform electronic coding procedure, vast amounts of information that are contained in objects like books can be digitally transformed and stored for many different uses. In addition, information stored in different kinds of media—musical and pictorial information as well as textual and bibliographic information—can be gathered and translated into a uniform (digital) medium and of course can be broadcast electronically. We go online and access the card catalogs, and often the very holdings, of major research archives, museums, and libraries all over the world.

The implications of this situation for scholarly editing are especially remarkable. For example, one can now design and build scholarly editions that integrate the functions of the two great editorial models, the facsimile and the critical edition. In a codex framework these functions are integrated only at the level of the library or archive, so that comparative analysis—which is the basis of all scholarship—involves laborious transactions among many individuals separated in different ways and at various scales. A complete critical edition of the multimedia materials produced by figures like Rossetti, William Blake, or Robert Burns can be designed and built, and Shakespeare's work need no longer be critically treated in purely textual and linguistic terms but can be approached for what it was and still is: a set of theater documents. Digitization also overcomes the codex-enforced spatial limitations on the amount of material that can be uniformly gathered and re-presented. In short, digital tools permit one to conceive of an editorial environment incorporating materials of many different kinds that might be physically located anywhere.

The accessibility of these resources and the relative ease with which one can learn to make and use them have produced a volatile Internet environment. The Web is a petri dish for humanities sites devoted to every conceivable topic or figure or movement or event. Noncopyrighted texts are available everywhere as well as masses of commentary and associated information. And of course therein lies the problem, for scholarship and education demand disciplined work. Scholars commit themselves to developing and maintaining rigorous standards for critical procedures and critical outcomes. The truth about humanities on the Internet, however, is that tares are rampant among the wheat. Nor do we have in place as yet the institutions we need to organize and evaluate these materials. Those resources are slowly being developed, but in the meantime we have metastasis.

Here is an example of the kind of problem that now must be dealt with.

We have in mind not one of the thousands of slapdash, if also sometimes lively, Web sites that can be found with a simple *Google* search. We rather choose the widely used (and in fact very useful if also very expensive) *English Poetry Full-Text Database* (600–1900) developed and sold by Chadwyck-Healey. From a scholar's point of view, this work is primarily an electronic concordance for the authors and works in question. While its texts have been for the most part carefully proofed, they are nearly all noncopyrighted. The status of the source text therefore must be a primary concern for any but those whose use is of the most casual kind. Thomas Lovell Beddoes, for example, comes in the 1851 Pickering edition—an edition no scholar now would use except in the context of inquiries about Beddoes's reception history. In addition, although the database calls itself full-text, it is not. Prose materials in the books that served the database as copy-text are not part of the database. The prefaces, introductions, notes, appendixes, and so forth that accompany the poetry in the original books, and that are so often clearly an integral part of the poetry, have been removed.

Economic criteria largely determined the database's choice of texts (and, presumably, the removal of the prose materials). The decision brings certain advantages, however. The 1851 edition of Beddoes, for example, while not a rare book, is not common (the University of Virginia, which has strong nineteenth-century holdings, does not own a copy). The database is of course far from a complete collection of all books of poetry written, printed, or published between 600 and 1900, but it does contain the (poetical) texts of many books that are rare or difficult to find.

Two further important scholarly facts about the database. First, it is a proprietary work. This means that it does not lie open to Internet access, which would allow its materials to be integrated with other related materials. The database is thus an isolated work in a medium where interoperability—the capacity to create and manipulate relations among scattered and diverse types of materials—is the key function. Second (and along the same fault line), its texts can only be string-searched: they have not been editorially organized or marked up for structured search and analysis operations or for analytic integration with other materials in something like what has been imagined as a semantic web (see below).

Scholars whose work functions within the great protocols of the codex—one of the most amazing inventions of human ingenuity—appear to think that the construction of a Web site fairly defines digital scholarship in the humanities. This view responds to the power of Internet technology to make materials available to people who might not otherwise, for any number of reasons, be able to access them. It registers as well the power of digitization to supply the user with multimedia materials. These increased accessibilities are indeed a great boon to everyone, not least of all to students of the humanities. But in a scholarly perspective, these digital functions continue to obscure the scholarly and educational opportunities that have been opened to us by the new technology.

Access to those opportunities requires one to become familiar with digital text representation procedures and in particular with how such materials can be marked and organized for formal analysis. That subject cannot be usefully engaged, however, without a comprehensive and adequate theory of textuality in general.

MARKING AND STRUCTURING DIGITAL TEXT REPRESENTATIONS

Traditional text—printed, scripted, oral—is regularly taken, in its material instantiations, as self-identical and transparent. It is taken for what it appears to be: nonvolatile. In this view, volatility is seen as the outcome of an interpretive action on an otherwise fixed text. The inadequacy of this view, or theory, of text must be clearly grasped by scholars, and especially by scholars who wish to undertake that foundational act of criticism and interpretation, the making of a scholarly edition.

We may usefully begin to deconstruct this pervasive illusion about text by reflecting on the view of text held by a computer scientist, for whom text is "information coded as characters or sequences of characters" (Day 1). Coded information is data, and data is a processable material object. By processing data, we process the information it represents. But digital text, unlike the information it conveys, is not volatile. It is a physical thing residing in the memory cells of a computer in a completely disambiguated condition. That precise physical structure matters for digital text, just as precise physical structure, very different, matters for paper-based text. The digital form of the text defines it as an object on which computers can operate algorithmically to convey sense and information. A digital text is coded information, and a code has a syntax that governs the ordering of the physical signs it is made of. In principle, therefore, digital text is marked by the syntax of its code, by the arrangement of the physical tokens that stand for binary digits.

Any explicit feature of a text can be conceived as a mark. We may thus say that digital text is marked by the linear ordering of the string of coded characters that constitutes it as a data type, for the string shows explicitly its own linear structure. The primary semiotic code of digital text is cast by the structural properties of a string of characters. The linearity of digital text as a data type puts an immediate constraint on its semiotics. It is a stream of coded characters, and each character has a position in an ordered linear succession.

But in common technical parlance, a string of coded characters is regarded as unmarked text. Markup is a special kind of coding, one laid on a textual object that has already been coded in another textual order entirely—that is to say, in the textual order marked by bibliographic codes. When we mark up a text with TEI or XML code, we are actually marking the preexistent bibliographic markup and not the content, which has already been marked in the bibliographic object. This situation is the source of great confusion and must be clearly grasped if one is to understand what markup can and cannot do for bibliographically coded texts.

Markup is described, correctly, as "the denotation of specific positions in a text with some assigned tokens" (Raymond, Tompa, and Wood, *Markup*). In this sense, it adds to the linear string of digital characters its "embedded codes, known as tags." A marked-up text is then commonly and properly understood as a tagged string of characters. But what function do tags perform with respect to bibliographic text, which is most definitely not a linear character string (though it can appear to be that to a superficial view)?

Let us continue to approach the problem from a computational point of view. In first-generation procedural markup systems, tags were used to add formatting instructions to a string of characters. With the introduction of declarative markup languages, such as SGML and its humanities derivative TEI, tags came to be used as "structure markers" (Joloboff 87). By adding structure to the string, semiotic properties of the digital text emerge as dependent functions of the markup with respect to the linear string of characters. It has been observed that adding structure to text in this way—that is, to text seen as flat or unstructured character data—enables "a new approach to document management, one that treats documents as databases" (Raymond, Tompa, and Wood, "From Data Representation" 3). But what does that understanding mean in semiotic terms?

The answer depends on the status of markup in relation to the bibliographically coded text. Markup makes explicit certain features of an originally paper-based text; it exhibits them by bringing them forth visibly into the expression of the text. It is therefore essentially notational. It affects the text's expression, both digital and bibliographic, adding a certain type of structure to both.

But then we want to ask, How is that structure related to the content of the bibliographic object it is meant to (re)mark?

To show the crucial status of that question, let us make a thought experiment. Suppose we choose SGML as the markup language. Its syntax, a context-free grammar expressed by a document's DTD (document type definition), assigns a given hierarchical structure—chapters, sections, paragraphs, and so on—to the linear string of characters, the computer scientist's text. Text can thus be conceived as an "ordered hierarchy of content objects" (DeRose, Durand, Mylonas, and Renear 6; this is the OHCO textual thesis). But can textual content be altogether modeled as a mere set of hierarchically ordered objects? Are all textual relations between content elements hierarchical and linear? The answer is, clearly, no. Traditional texts are riven with overlapping and recursive structures of various kinds, just as they always engage, simultaneously, hierarchical and nonhierarchical formations. Hierarchical ordering is simply one type of formal arrangement that a text may be asked to operate with, and often it is not by any means the chief formal operative. Poetical texts in particular regularly deploy various complex kinds of nonlinear and recursive formalities.

Whatever the complexity of a bibliographic text's structure, however, that structure may be defined as "the set of latent relations" among the defined parts of the text (Segre and Kememy 34). Only through markup does that formal structure show explicitly at the level of textual expression. In principle, markup must therefore be able to make evident all implicit and virtual structural features of the text. Much depends on the properties of the markup system and on the relation between the markup tags and the string of character data. The position of the tags in the data may or may not be information-bearing. Forms of in-line markup, like those based in an SGML model, can exhibit only internal structure, that is, a structure dependent on "a subset of character positions" in textual data (Raymond, Tompa, and Wood, *Markup* 4). But textual structures, and in particular the content features of the text's structure, are "not always reducible to a functional description of subcomponents" of a string of characters (7). Textual structure is not bound, in general, to structural features of the expression of the text.

From a purely computational point of view, in-line "markup belongs not to the world of formalisms, but to the world of representations" (4). A formalism is a calculus operating on abstract objects of a certain kind, whereas a representation is a format or a coding convention to record and to store information. Unlike a calculus, a format does not compute anything, it simply provides a coding mechanism to organize physical tokens into data sets representing information. We can say, then, that markup is essentially a format, or again, in a semiotic idiom, that markup is primarily notational. Inasmuch as it assigns structure to character strings or to the expression of textual information, it can refer only indirectly to textual content. In computational terms, it describes data structures but does not provide a data model or a semantics for data structures and an algebra that can operate on their values.

Attempts to use the DTDs in SGML systems as a constraint language, or formalism, to operate on textual data face a major difficulty in dealing with the multiple and overlapping hierarchical structures that are essential features of all textualities. Some circuitous ways out have been proposed, but in the end the solutions afforded provide "no method of specifying constraints on the interrelationship of separate DTDs" (Sperberg-McQueen and Huitfeldt, "Concurrent Document Hierarchies" 41). The use of embedded descriptive markup for managing documents as databases that can operate on their content is thus severely hampered by the dependence of SGML systems on internal structure. Content relations are best dealt with by forms of out-of-line markup, which "is more properly considered a specific type of external structure" (Raymond, Tompa, and Wood, *Markup* 4).

In general, we may therefore say that adding structure to textual data does not necessarily imply providing a model for processing the content of a text. A model applicable to document or internal structures can be appropriate only for directly corresponding content relations. To adequately process textual content, an external data model that can implement a database or operate some suitable knowledge representation scheme is required. The crucial problem for digital text representation and processing lies therefore in the ability to find consistent ways of relating a markup scheme to a knowledge-representation scheme and to its data model.

The Semantic Web project proceeds in that direction with its attempt to "bring structure to the meaningful content of Web pages" (Berners-Lee, Hendler, and Lassila). It is an effort to assign a formal model to the textual data available on the Web. The introduction of XML, a markup language profile that defines a generalized format for documents and data accessible on the Web, provides a common language for the schematic reduction of both the structure of documents—that is, their expression or expressive form—and the structure of their content. In this approach, the problem to solve consists precisely in relating the scheme that describes the format of the documents to the scheme that describes their content. The first would be an XML schema, "a document that describes the valid format of an XML dataset" (Stuart), and the second would be a metadata schema such as the resource description framework (RDF) being developed for the Semantic Web.[5]

An RDF schema can be described as an "assertion model" that "allows an entity-relationship-like model to be made for the data." This assertion model gives the data the semantics of standard predicate calculus (Berners-Lee). Both an XML schema and an RDF schema can assign a data model to a document, but in the first case the model depends on internal relations among different portions of the document, whereas in the second case it consists in an external structure independent of the structure of the document. In this context, XML documents act "as a transfer mechanism for structured data" (*Cambridge Communiqué*). XML works as a transfer syntax to map document-dependent or internal data structures into semantic or external data structures and vice versa. It is through markup that textual structures show up explicitly and become processable.

MARKUP AND THE GENERAL
THEORY OF TEXTUALITY

In this context, an important question rises to clear view. Since text is dynamic and mobile and textual structures are essentially indeterminate, how can markup properly deal with the phenomena of structural instability? Neither the expression nor the content of a text are given once and for all. Text is not self-identical.[6] The structure of its content very much depends on some act of interpretation by an interpreter, nor is its expression absolutely stable. Textual variants are not simply the result of faulty textual transmission. Text is unsteady, and both its content and expression keep constantly quivering. As Valentin Voloshinov has it, "what is important about a linguistic form is not that it is a stable and always self-equivalent signal, but that it is an always changeable and adaptable sign" (68).

Textual mobility originates in what has been described as "the dynamic[s] of structures and metastructures [that lie] in the heart of any semiotic activity" (Y. Neuman 67), and it shows up specifically in the semantic properties of those kinds of expression that set forth what linguists call reflexive metalinguistic features of natural language.[7] Diacritical signs are self-describing expressions of this kind, and markup can be viewed as a sort of diacritical mark. A common feature of self-reflexive expressions is that they are semantically ambiguous. They are part of the text and they also describe it; they are at once textual representations and representations of a textual representation. Markup, therefore, can be seen either as a metalinguistic description of a textual feature or as a new kind of construction that extends the expressive power of the object language and provides a visible sign of some implicit textual content.

A diacritical device such as punctuation, for instance, can be regarded as a kind of markup (Coombs, Renear, and DeRose 935), and by adding punctuation to a medieval text, a modern editor actually marks it up. Editorial punctuation, therefore, can be considered either as part of the text or as an external description related to it. In the first case, it produces a textual variant; in the second, a variant interpretation. Accordingly, any punctuation mark is ambivalent: it can be seen as the mark of an operation or as the mark of an operational result. If it is regarded as part of the text, it brings in a variant reading and has to be seen as a value for an operation of rephrasing; at the same time, by introducing an alternative reading, it casts a new interpretation on the text and must be seen as a rule to an action of construing. Yet the very same punctuation mark can be regarded as an external description of the text. In that case, it assigns a meaning to the text and must be seen as a value for an operation of construal. By providing a new interpretation, how-ever, it adds structure to the wording of the text and must be seen as a rule to an action of "deformance" (for a definition of this term, see McGann, *Radiant Textuality*). Marks of this kind, viewable either way, behave just as Ludwig Wittgenstein's famous duck-rabbit picture (*Philosophical Investigations* 2.11).

This sort of semantic ambivalence enables any diacritical mark, or for that matter any kind of markup, to act as a conversion device between textual and interpretational variants. Far from stabilizing the text, the markup actually mobilizes it. Through markup, an interpretational variant assumes a specific textual form; conversely, that explicit form immediately opens itself to in-terpretive indeterminacy. Markup has to do with structure or logical form. It describes the form or exposes it in the text. But the logical form of a textual expression is only apt to show or to express itself in language, and, as Wittgenstein puts it, "that which mirrors itself in language, language cannot represent."[8] The only way to represent a logical form is to describe it by means of a metalanguage. The markup, on its part, may either exhibit or describe a logical form, but it can perform both functions only by changing its logical status: it has to commute between object language and meta-language, so as to frame either an external metalinguistic description or an object-language, self-reflexive expression. Markup, therefore, is essentially ambivalent and sets forth self-reflexive ambiguous aspects of the text, which can produce structural shifts and make it unstable and mobile.

Text is thus open to indeterminacy, but textual indetermination is not totally unconstrained. Because of textual mobility, we may say that text is not self-identical. But putting things the other way around, we may also say that text is, virtually, identical with itself, because the whole of all its possible variant readings and interpretations makes up a virtual unity identical with itself. Text in this view is not an arbitrary unity, for if it were seen as such, no text would differ from any other. The entirety of all latent capacities of the text is virtually one and the same, and this self-identity imposes limiting conditions on mobility and indetermination. The latent unity of the text brings about phenomena of mutual compensation between the stability of the expression and the variety of its possible interpretations or, conversely, between the instability of the expression and the steadiness of its conceptual import. With any given expression comes an indefinite number of possible interpretations, just as for any given conceptual content we may imagine an indefinite number of possible concrete formulations. But for a given text, the variation of either component is dependent on the invariance of its related counterpart, and such variation can come about only under this condition.

Semantic ambiguity may be thought of as an obstacle to an automatic processing of textual information, but actually it can serve that very purpose. Markup can provide a formal representation of textual dynamics precisely on account of its diacritical ambivalence and its capacity to induce structural indeterminacy and compensation. The OHCO thesis about the nature of the text is radically insufficient, because it does not recognize structural mobility as an essential property of the textual condition. The OHCO view builds on the assumption of a syntactically well-determined expression, not acknowledging that a fixed syntactic structure leaves the corresponding semantic structure open to indetermination. A nonsemantically identifiable string of characters is thus regarded as the vehicle of a specific content. A digital text representation need not assume that meaning can be fully represented in a syntactic logical form.[9] The automatic processing of the text does not depend on a condition of this kind and need not fall victim to the snares of classical artificial intelligence. A formal representation of textual information does not require an absolute coincidence between syntactic and semantic logical form. In this respect, the role of markup can be of paramount importance in bringing their interconnections to the fore. Markup, turning to account its operational dimension, can act as a transfer mechanism between one structure and the other. It can behave as a performative injunction and switch to a different logical function.

Viewing markup as an operator in this sense, we may say, as has been proposed, that "to describe the meaning of the markup in a document, it suffices to generate the set of inferences about the document which are licensed by the markup," or even more assertively, that "in some ways, we can regard the meaning of the markup as being constituted, not only described, by that set of inferences" (Sperberg-McQueen, Huitfeldt, and Renear 231). Actually, to describe markup in this way amounts to seeing it as a kind of "inference-ticket," to use Gilbert Ryle's locution—as an assertion, belonging to a "different level of discourse" from that to which belong the expressions it applies to (121). So described, markup functions as a higher-order object-language statement—as a rule that licenses the reader, or for that matter the machine, to interpret the text in a certain way and to assign dynamically a structure to its content. Markup can therefore be conceived as a transfer mechanism from a document's structure to its semantic structure or, the other way around, from a semantic structure to a document's structure (as in the implementations being imagined in the Semantic Web project).

Diacritical ambiguity, then, enables markup to provide a suitable type of formal representation for the phenomena of textual instability. By seeing markup in this way, we can regard it as a means of interpretation and de-formance (see Samuels and McGann), as a functional device both to interpret and to modify the text. But in the OHCO view, the structure assigned to the expression of a text (by marking it up) and the structure assigned to its content coincide, with the result that the capacity of the markup to account for textual dynamics is prevented. Markup should not be thought of as in-troducing—as being able to introduce—a fixed and stable layer to the text. To approach textuality in this way is to approach it in illusion. Markup should be conceived, instead, as the expression of a highly reflexive act, a mapping of text back onto itself: as soon as a (marked) text is (re)marked, the meta-markings open themselves to indeterminacy. This reflexive operation leads one to the following formulation of the logical structure of the textual condition:

$$(A = A <=> A \neq A) <=> A \xrightarrow{m} A$$

(Buzzetti, "Digital Representation" 84)

In this view markup (m) is conceived as the expression of an operation, not of its value, for the nature of text is basically injunctive. Text can actually be seen as the physical mark of a sense-enacting operation (an act of *Besinnung*). But in its turn, the result of this operation, the expression of the text, must be seen not as a value but as an operation mark, otherwise its interpretation is prevented. Such an expression of the text is then regarded as a rule for an act of interpretation, an operation that is essentially undertermined. Inter-pretation, as an act of deformance, flags explicitly its result as a self-reflexive textual mark, which imposes a new structuring on the expression of the text.

Again, the newly added structural mark, the value of the interpreting operation, converts back into an injunction for another, indeterminate act of
interpretation.

Textual dynamics is thus the continual unfolding of the latent structural
articulations of the text. Any structural determination of one of its two primary subunits, expression and content, leaves the other underdetermined and
calls for a definition of its correlative subunit, in a constant process of im-
permanent codetermination. In more detail, and referring to the interweav-
ing of textual content and expression, we may say that an act of composition
is a sense-constituting operation that brings about the formulation of a text.
The resulting expression can be considered as the self-identical value of a
sense-enacting operation. By fixing it, we allow for the indetermination of
its content. To define the content, we assume the expression as a rule for an
interpreting operation. An act of interpretation brings about a content, and
we can assume it as its self-identical value. A defined content provides a model
for the expression of the text and can be viewed as a rule for its restructuring.
A newly added structure mark can in turn be seen as a reformulation of the
expression, and so on, in a permanent cycle of compensating actions between
determination and indetermination of the expression and the content of the
text.

This continual oscillation and interplay between indetermination and
determination of the physical and the informational parts of the text renders
its dynamic instability very similar to the functional behavior of self-
organizing systems. Text can thus be thought of as a simulation machine for
sense-organizing operations of an autopoietic kind. Text works as a self-
organizing system inasmuch as its expression, taken as a value, enacts a sense-
defining operation, just as its sense or content, taken as a value, enacts an
expression-defining operation. Text provides an interpreter with a sort of
prosthetic device to perform autopoietic operations of sense communication
and exchange.

Textual indeterminacy and textual instability can thus be formally described, like most self-organization processes, through the calculus of indications introduced by George Spencer-Brown (see Buzzetti, "Diacritical
Ambiguity"). His "nondualistic attempt" to set proper foundations for mathematics and descriptions in general "amounts to a subversion of the traditional
understanding on the basis of descriptions," inasmuch as "it views descriptions as based on a primitive *act* (rather than a logical value or form)." In
Spencer-Brown's calculus "subject and object are interlocked" (Varela 110),
just as expression and content are interlocked in a self-organizing textual

system. Only an open and reversible deforming or interpreting act can keep them connected as in a continually oscillating dynamic process. Louis Kauffman's and Francisco Varela's extension of Spencer-Brown's calculus of indications (Kauffman and Varela; Varela, ch. 12) accounts more specifically for the "dynamic unfoldment" (Varela 113) of self-organizing systems and may therefore be consistently applied to an adequate description of textual mobility.

FROM TEXT TO WORK:
A NEW HORIZON FOR SCHOLARSHIP

Exposing the autopoietic logic of the textual condition is, in a full Peircean sense, a pragmatic necessity. As Varela, Humberto Maturana, and others have shown, this logic governs the operation of all self-organizing systems (Maturana and Varela; Varela et al.). Such systems develop and sustain themselves by marking their operations self-reflexively. The axiom that all text is marked text defines an autopoietic function. Writing systems, print technology, and now digital encoding license a set of markup conventions and procedures (algorithms) that facilitate the self-reflexive operations of human communicative action.

Scholarly editions are a special, highly sophisticated type of self-reflexive communication, and the fact is that we now must build such devices in digital space. This necessity is what Charles Sanders Peirce would call a "pragmatistic" fact: it defines a kind of existential (as opposed to a categorical) imperative that scholars who wish to make these tools must recognize and implement. We may better explain the significance of this imperative by shifting the discussion to a concrete example. Around 1970, various kinds of social text theories began to gain prominence, pushing literary studies toward a more broadly cultural orientation. Interpreters began shifting their focus from the text toward any kind of social formation in a broadly conceived discourse field of semiotic works and activities. Because editors and bibliographers oriented their work to physical phenomena—the materials, means, and modes of production—rather than to the readerly text and hermeneutics, this textonic shift in the larger community of scholars barely registered on bibliographers' instruments.

A notable exception among bibliographic scholars was McKenzie, whose 1985 Panizzi lectures climaxed almost twenty years of work on a social text approach to bibliography and editing. When they were published in 1986, the lectures brought into focus a central contradiction in literary and cultural studies (*Bibliography*). Like their interpreter counterparts, textual and bibliographic scholars maintained an essential distinction between empirical-analytic disciplines on one hand and readerly-interpretive procedures on the other. In his Panizzi lectures McKenzie rejected this distinction and showed by discursive example why it could not be intellectually maintained.

His critics—most notably Thomas Tanselle and T. Howard-Hill—remarked that while McKenzie's ideas had a certain theoretical appeal, they could not be practically implemented (Howard-Hill; Tanselle, "Textual Criticism and Literary Sociology"). The ideas implicitly called for the critical editing of books and other socially constructed material objects. But critical editing, as opposed to facsimile and diplomatic editing, was designed to investigate texts—linguistic forms—not books or (what seemed even more preposterous) social events.

In fact one can transform the social and documentary aspects of a book into computable code. Working from the understanding that facsimile editing and critical editing need not be distinct and incommensurate critical functions, the *Rossetti Archive* proves the correctness of a social text approach to editing: it pushes traditional scholarly models of editing and textuality beyond the Masoretic wall of the linguistic object we call the text. The proof of concept would be the making of the archive. If our breach of the wall was minimal, as it was, its practical demonstration was significant. We were able to build a machine that organizes for complex study and analysis, for collation and critical comparison, the entire corpus of Rossetti's documentary materials, textual as well as pictorial. Critical, which is to say computational, attention was kept simultaneously on the physical features and conditions of actual objects (specific documents and pictorial works) as well as on their formal and conceptual characteristics (genre, metrics, iconography).[10] The archive's approach to Rossetti's so-called double works is in this respect exemplary. Large and diverse bodies of material that comprise works like "The Blessed Damozel" get synthetically organized: scores of printed texts, some with extensive manuscript additions; two manuscripts; dozens of pictorial works. These physical objects orbit around the conceptual thing we name for convenience "The Blessed Damozel." All the objects relate to that gravity field in different ways, and their differential relations metastasize when subsets of relations among them are revealed. At the same time, all the objects function in an indefinite number of other kinds of relations: to other textual and pictorial works, to institutions of various kinds, to different persons, to varying occasions. With the archive one can draw these materials into computable synthetic relations at macro- as well as microlevels. In the process the archive discloses the hypothetical character of its materials and their component parts as well as the relations one discerns among these things. Though completely physical and measurable (in different ways and scales), neither the objects nor their parts are self-identical; all can be reshaped and transformed in the environment of the archive.

The autopoietic functions of the social text can also be computationally accessed through user logs. This set of materials—the use records, or hits, automatically stored by the computer—has received little attention by scholars who develop digital tools in the humanities. Formalizing its dynamic structure in digital terms will allow us to produce an even more complex simulation of social textualities. Our neglect of this body of information reflects, I believe, an ingrained commitment to the idea of the positive text or material document. The depth of this commitment can be measured by reading McKenzie, whose social text editing proposals yet remain faithful to the idea of the "primacy of the physical object" as a self-identical thing ("What's Past" 274).

Reflecting on digital technology in his lecture "What's Past Is Prologue," McKenzie admitted that its simulation capacities were forcing him to rethink that primary article of bibliographic faith (272–73). He did not live to undertake an editorial project in digital form. Had he done so, we believe he would have seen his social text approach strengthened by the new technical devices. All editors engage with a work in process. Even if only one textual witness were to survive—say, that tomorrow a manuscript of a completely unrecorded play by Shakespeare were unearthed—that document would be a record of the process of its making and its transmission. Minimal as they might seem, its user logs would not have been completely erased, and those logs are essential evidence for anyone interested in reading (or editing) such a work. We are interested in documentary evidence precisely because it encodes, however cryptically at times, the evidence of the agents who were involved in making and transmitting the document. Scholars do not edit self-identical texts. They reconstruct a complex documentary record of textual makings and remakings, in which their own scholarly work directly participates.

No text, no book, no social event is one thing. Each is many things, fashioned and refashioned in repetitions that often occur (as it were) simultaneously. The works evolve and mutate in their use. And because all such uses are always invested in real circumstances, these multiplying forms are socially and physically coded in and by the works themselves. They bear the evidence of the meanings they have helped to make.

One advantage digitization has over paper-based instruments comes not from the computer's modeling powers but from its greater capacity for simulating phenomena—in this case, bibliographic and sociotextual. Books are simulation machines as well, of course. Indeed, the hardware and software of book technology have evolved into a state of sophistication that dwarfs computerization as it currently stands. In time this situation will change through the existential imperative—digitization—that now defines our semiotic horizon. That imperative is already leading us to design critical tools that organize our textual condition as an autopoietic set of social objects—that is to say, objects that are themselves the emergent functions of the measurements that their users and makers implement for certain purposes. Our aim is not to build a model of one made thing, it is to design a system that can simulate the system's realizable possibilities—those that are known and recorded as well as those that have yet to be (re)constructed.

McKenzie's central idea, that bibliographic objects are social objects, begs to be realized in digital terms and tools, begs to be realized by those tools and by the people who make them.

NOTES

1. The best introduction in English to this broad subject is Greetham, *Textual Scholarship*; see also his important *Theories of the Text*. A brief introduction can be found in Williams and Abbott.
2. On the nonself-identity of material objects, see McGann, *Radiant Textuality*, chapters 5 and 6.
3. This genetic work was initiated with Friedrich Beissner's project (begun in 1943) to edit the work of Hölderlin. It was continued in the edition of D. E. Sattler, begun in 1975. The best known English-language genetic edition is Hans Walter Gabler's Ulysses: *A Critical and Synoptic Edition* (1984; Gabler, Steppe, and Melchior).
4. A good example of versioning is provided by Wordsworth's The Prelude: *1799, 1805, 1850.*
5. For good bibliographic sources on RDF, see www.w3.org/RDF/.
6. For a more thorough discussion of this assertion, see McGann, *Radiant Textuality*, especially chapter 5 and the appendix to chapter 6.
7. Cf. Hjelmslev 132: "Owing to the universalism of everyday language, an everyday language can be used as metalanguage to describe itself as object language."
8. *Tractatus* 4.121: see also 4.1212: "What can be shown cannot be said."
9. "If you take care of the syntax, the semantics will take care of itself" (Haugeland 23).

10. Since its initial conception, the *Rossetti Archive* has been subjected to further digital transformations—most notably a translation into XML format—that extend the archive's translinguistic critical functions. The digital logic of the archive's structure leaves it open to more comprehensive scales of interoperability, such as those being developed through the Semantic Web and the Open Knowledge Initiative (OKI). For an introduction to OKI see www.okiproject.org.

THE CANTERBURY TALES AND OTHER MEDIEVAL TEXTS

PETER ROBINSON

O ver the last decade (and longer), editorial activity in older English literature has been marked by fascination with the possibilities of the digital medium. There have been several large-scale editorial projects and a host of smaller initiatives, built from the beginning on computer methods. Some of these have now had more than ten years' experience of the possibilities, problems, and actual achievements of the medium—long enough for us to begin to suggest some general propositions about the nature of editorial work in it. In this essay, I use my experience with the *Canterbury Tales* Project, with which I have been involved since its beginnings in 1989, to explore five such propositions.

These propositions are:

1. The use of computer technology in the making of a particular edition takes place in a particular research context.
2. A digital edition should be based on full-text transcription of original texts into electronic form, and this transcription should be based on explicit principles.
3. The use of computer-assisted analytic methods may restore historical criticism of large textual traditions as a central aim for scholarly editors.
4. The new technology has the power to alter both how editors edit and how readers read.
5. Editorial projects generating substantial quantities of transcribed text in electronic form should adopt, from the beginning, an open transcription policy.

While I concentrate on the *Canterbury Tales* Project, it should be emphasized that it is far from being the only editorial project in older English (and medieval vernacular) literature. Indeed, all the major editorial projects undertaken in this domain over the last decade seem to have a significant computer component: thus the cluster of projects undertaken by Kevin Kiernan, beginning with the Electronic *Beowulf*; the *Piers Plowman* Project and other SEENET (Society for Early English and Norse Electronic Texts) initiatives associated with Hoyt Duggan; the *Middle English Compendium* (itself growing from the digitization of the *Middle English Dictionary*); individual enterprises by Murray McGillivray, Larry Benson, Peter Baker, Graham Caie; the Bestiary Project at Aberdeen; and the *Roman de la rose* project at Johns Hopkins.[1]

One could speculate at some length about the reasons for the speed with which scholars working in older areas of English literature have taken up the new technologies. One severely practical reason has been the reluctance of traditional publishers to commit to publishing the results of large editorial projects. Also, editors of medieval texts rely heavily on manuscript sources, some of which are famous and fascinating objects in their own right (if not beautiful, indeed), and these lend themselves very well to digitization: thus, for instance, the manuscripts published under the Turning the Pages initiative by the British Library. It is a material help too that all these texts are comprehensively out of copyright (though rights in manuscript images do need to be negotiated with the individual owners). Medieval authors are safely dead, and so too are any relatives who might have any copyright interest. It is also something of a fortunate chance that at least three of the leading editors of older English texts in the 1970s and 1980s were fascinated by computers and were among the early adopters of the technology: Kiernan, Benson, and Duggan.

Proposition 1: The use of computer technology in the making of a particular edition takes place in a particular research context.

Beside these practical considerations (which are hardly unique to medieval English literature), a key reason for the particular receptivity of scholars working in early English studies in the last decades of the twentieth century to the promise of computer methods was the state of thinking about editing in this area. There are two aspects to this receptivity. First, many editions in this domain—notably those produced for the Early English Text Society since the late nineteenth century—have been closely based on single manuscripts. Such editors of early English texts were best-text editors before Joseph Bédier, and such editions lend themselves easily to computer representation. One can see Kiernan's Electronic *Beowulf* as in a direct line of descent from Julius Zupitza's facsimile, which over a hundred years ago presented a full-image record alongside a transcription of the whole text. Second, for editors in Middle English particularly, there has been the influence of the Athlone edition of *Piers Plowman* and George Kane's writings about textual editing (Piers Plowman: *The A Version*). This edition is famously uncompromising and controversial in its insistence on the failure of stemmatic and indeed any other methodology apart from the application of editorial judgment at every point of the text (see, e.g., on this controversy, Adams; Brewer; E. Donaldson; Patterson). For many editors, the sheer confidence (not to say extremism) of Kane's assertions about textual scholarship has provoked a reaction: Is this really what editing is? The advent of computer methods has offered a new domain, in which editors might explore approaches that run counter to the vision offered by Kane. I return later to the influence of his edition on my own work.

In this context, the conception of the *Canterbury Tales* Project in the early 1990s sprang from the same impulse that variously moved Kiernan and Duggan (among others): to apply the new methodology not just to convert existing printed editions into digital form but also to try to solve long-standing textual difficulties. This effort can be seen at a literally microscopic level, in Kiernan's use of fiber optics to recover readings lost at the charred edges of the *Beowulf* manuscript. For the *Canterbury Tales* Project, the textual difficulty is indeed the whole text, the whole tradition. There are (by the latest count) eighty-four manuscripts and four incunable editions of the *Tales* dating from before 1500. Further, not only did Chaucer notoriously leave the text unfinished, but he seems to have taken no care (as some other medieval authors did) to prepare something like an authorized text or to control the form in which his text was distributed. As a result, editors of the *Tales* are left with the documents—all the manuscripts and incunables—and no authorial declaration of any kind to help make sense of them all. The very earliest manuscripts bear eloquent witness to the struggles by scribes and their supervisors to put Chaucer's original materials (in whatever form they were) into shape. Later editors have inherited the struggle and with it the record of earlier scribes and editors. One can see too the history of textual scholarship in the West through the lens of *The Canterbury Tales*: through the medieval scribes trying to impose a coherent *ordinatio* and *compilatio* on incomplete and complex texts; through the first incunable printers printing a text from a single source, either a manuscript or earlier printing, then progressively modifying the text by reference to other sources; then in the eighteenth century through the *ad fontes* movement, reflected in Thomas Tyrwhitt's determination to return to the manuscripts and attempt to establish a new text from study of the originals; then, in the nineteenth and early twentieth centuries, through attempts to set the manuscripts in some kind of order that might in turn justify the choice of one or more manuscripts as base for the edition (Ruggiers). This enterprise culminated in the massive effort of John Manly and Edith Rickert to collate all the known manuscripts of the *Tales* to establish a historical recension of the entire textual tradition, on something like Lachmannian principles (Manly and Rickert).

Manly and Rickert's work appears as a late expression of a nineteenth-century confidence (they began their work in the early 1920s) in the ability of editors to establish definitive texts. It is exactly this confidence that editorial thinking through the latter part of the twentieth century has undermined. Editors of older English texts have found themselves engaged in the same problems, of versioning, of variance, of copy-text theory, as their counterparts in other editorial domains.[2] In this context of increasing editorial anxiety, the clarity of Kane's view of editing has found many followers. Over this period, apart from asserting the eminence of the Hengwrt manuscript of the *Tales*, Manly and Rickert's work has had little influence and was heavily attacked by Kane in an article in *Editing Chaucer: The Great Tradition*. Indeed, Manly and Rickert's failure (as Kane sees it) to create any kind of valid historical account of the tradition is a cornerstone of Kane's wider argument that editorial judgment alone must be used to fix the text ("John M. Manly").

The failure of Manly and Rickert's attempt to create a historical account of the textual tradition, and the vehemence of Kane's assertion that no such account could possibly be created for the *Tales*, set out a clear challenge. It seemed arguable that the failure did not occur, as Kane suggested, because of a fundamental theoretical flaw in method. Possibly Manly and Rickert failed because the sheer volume of data generated by their collation (some three million pieces of information on sixty thousand collation cards) quite overwhelmed the tools of analysis available to them: basically, pencil, paper, and Rickert's memory. Until the late 1980s, a few experiments and articles appeared to suggest that a combination of the computer, with its ability to absorb and reorder vast amounts of information, and new methods of analysis being developed in computer science (in the form of sophisticated relational databases) and in mathematics and in other sciences might be able to make sense of the many millions of pieces of information in a complex collation and provide a historical reconstruction of the development of tradition.[3]

From this account, we can see that any decision to use computer technology in the making of a particular edition takes place in a particular research context. What has been done before, the controversies reigning at any one moment, determines our sense of what is to be done. It may seem a rather obvious point, that electronic editions are made in a context of editorial theory, just as print editions always have been. But it happens that over the last decade many electronic texts have been made that present the text alone—often with images yet with only a minimum of the additional material (variant apparatus, descriptive and analytic commentaries) that has in the past characterized scholarly editions. There is a place for such plain-text enterprises, but their inability to engage with the wider issues surrounding the texts they offer limits their utility.

Proposition 2: A digital edition should be based on full-text transcription of original texts into electronic form, and this transcription should be based on explicit principles.

The perceived failure of Manly and Rickert to create a historical account of the relations among the manuscripts of *The Canterbury Tales* sets a clear challenge: to apply the emerging methods of computer analysis to create such an account, based on analysis of the agreements and disagreements among the texts they contain. This challenge was the starting point of the *Canterbury Tales* Project.

The immediate problem was to gather the record of agreement and disagreements on which this analysis would be based. We decided first to make a full-text transcription of the whole text of the manuscripts, then to use computer tools to compare the transcripts, to create the record of agreements and disagreements among the manuscripts. Accordingly, in 1989, with the help of Susan Hockey, I wrote an application to the Leverhulme Trust for a grant to carry out a series of experiments in the use of computers in textual editing. We proposed to develop a computer collation system for comparing different versions of texts word by word and to experiment with different methods of analyzing the results. Given the intractable nature of the editorial problems posed by *The Canterbury Tales*, we chose Chaucer's Wife of Bath's Prologue (830 lines in fifty-four manuscripts and four incunables) as one of the exemplary texts for this experiment.

We were successful with this application, and work began September 1989. We were fortunate indeed in the time and place. In time: the three-year project began just after the inception of the Text Encoding Initiative (TEI), and in those three years the first steps were being made toward electronic publishing, first on CD-ROM and later over the Internet as the Web began to take shape. In place: Oxford, where the project began, was intensely involved in the TEI through Hockey and Lou Burnard. Hockey was the project leader, and the project was based in the same building (Oxford University Computing Services) as Burnard, who was the European editor. This close link with the TEI became crucial because of something to which I had not given much thought before: the need for a stable and rich encoding scheme both to record the transcripts of the original texts we were to make and to hold the record of variation created by the collation program. One could say that the *Canterbury Tales* Project, the TEI, and the Web were born and have grown side by side, and that the TEI has been the crucial enabling factor in the project.

A first, critical impact of the TEI on this project was in the shaping of the transcription guidelines. We needed to make transcripts of the manuscripts in electronic form, ready to submit to the collation program we would develop. Because there were many different people working on the transcriptions, we had to work out a scheme of transcription that could be applied uniformly. There were two aspects to this task.

The first aspect concerned the structure of the text: its division into tales, links, lines, blocks of prose, with marginalia, rubrics, glosses, and more. Clearly, we needed some means of indicating these elements, even if only (at the most basic level) to be able to locate all the different forms of any one line in the manuscripts so they could be collated. From the very first meetings of the TEI, the rich repertoire of structural encodings it offered was apparent. Accordingly, I designed a set of markup protocols for the *Collate* program to replicate the TEI structural encodings, with the aim of being able to translate these encodings into the TEI implementation of SGML (later XML) as needed. Over the years, this approach has proved very successful, and we have experienced no difficulty in moving our files into SGML/XML for publication. We have been able to use readily available commercial SGML/XML software (first *DynaText*, later *Anastasia*) to achieve excellent results. However, we decided at the very beginning of the project that we would not encode the working transcripts themselves in SGML. There was a simple, practical reason for this: the SGML editors then available (basically, emacs!) were rather formidable, well beyond the slender computer abilities of the transcribers we then had. Many years on, the gap between the programs and the transcribers has narrowed but persists (emacs is still the tool of choice for many).

There is no doubting the value of SGML/XML for interchange systems, and the TEI work of creating a set of guidelines for interchange of an enormous range of humanities texts is one of the great scholarly achievements of our time. But what is good for interchange is not necessarily good for capture, where an efficient and focused system is required for the transcribers. Nor may it be good for programming, as attempted by the XSLT (extensible style-sheet language transformation) and similar initiatives—but that is another subject. I have no time for the shibboleth that one must use SGML or XML everywhere one has a text. One should use it where it is efficient (for interchange and archiving, for example); one should not use it where it is not.

The second aspect of transcription concerned the words and letters themselves, the marks on the parchment themselves. Encoding the words and letters in a printed text can be quite simple: just establish the characters used by the printer and allocate a computer sign to each. All the transcriber has to do is recognize the character in the text and press the appropriate button. But in a manuscript, where the range of marks that can be made by a scribe is limitless, matters are not so simple. The transcriber must decide which of these marks is meaningful and then which of the range of signs available on a given computer system best represents that meaning. One can see a world of problems emerging just from this bare outline. What do we mean by meaning? Meaning for whom? by whom? to whom? Are we speaking of the meanings intended by author or by scribe, or the meanings that might be mediated by ourselves and received by our readers? How can the limited range of signs available in any computer system (let alone the fewer than two hundred available in most text-computing environments, pre-Unicode) represent all the possible meanings?

In our first experiments in the early 1990s, we were influenced by the capacity (only just recently developed) to add characters to fonts. So we thought we had an excellent solution. Where we saw a meaningful sign that could not be represented in the characters available in our computer font, we would just add to the font a character for that sign. In theory, this solution is very attractive. Scribes use many different graphic (or graphetic) forms for one letter. It seemed possible that the choice of forms by any scribe (*r* rotunda, or *z*-shaped, or long, or ragged; sigma *s*, kidney-shaped *s*, long *s*, *s* ligatured with a following letter; and so on) might be distinctive of that scribe. It might be possible to use this information to find one of the philosopher's stones of manuscript studies: a means of distinguishing and identifying both individual scribes and scribal schools, as suggested by Angus McIntosh ("Scribal Profiles" and "Towards an Inventory"). This delusion lasted about one month— actually, until the moment we started transcribing manuscripts written later than around 1410. We had naturally begun the transcription with the manuscripts generally regarded as oldest and most important: essentially, those commonly dated before 1410. It happens that these manuscripts (or at least four of them) do form something of a coherent group. Their scribes worked closely together, and the scripts share many common characteristics. So it did appear possible to map the marks in these manuscripts to a finite set of signs and represent each sign by a single computer character. So long as we dealt only with these manuscripts, this system seemed to work. But when we came to a much later manuscript, we found a character we had not dealt with (a distinctive *s* in final word position). Fine, we thought: add the character to the font. Then we noticed something very alarming: when we looked back at the first manuscripts we had transcribed, we found that the character was indeed present in these—just not in final position. Worse still: as we looked at more manuscripts, more and more such signs appeared (to the point where it became prohibitively time-consuming to add them to the font). Worse still: we kept discovering that whenever we identified such a sign in a new manuscript, we would find that it was indeed present in manuscripts we had already seen—we had simply not noticed it.

At this point we discovered ourselves asking, How new is new? Take the long *s*: there are long *s* forms that tower proudly over the other letters and wave a luxuriant tail into the line below; there are others that skulk among the other characters, ducking their head and tucking in their tail so they barely show. Should we distinguish each and all of these? Where do we stop? Worst of all: one of the letters we observed at this late stage was a distinctive form of *s*, used in some manuscripts—almost universally—in final position. We could see an argument developing, that certain letterforms were reserved for final word position and that their function (in a time of uncertain word division) was to mark the ends of words. But we realized that interesting and valid as that argument might be, we could not confidently assert it on the basis of our transcripts. Such an argument would have force only if we were sure that the occurrence of this particular letterform in this particular position was really distinctive. Not only would we have to recognize and transcribe this letter securely in each place where it appeared, we would also have to distinguish competing forms of the letter and recognize and transcribe them securely. Increasingly, we found ourselves lacking that confidence. It became clear to us that the more signs we distinguished, the greater the possibility of error. Because there were so many, it would be easy for our transcribers to overlook individual signs. Further, the more distinctions we made, the narrower the differences would be among them and the easier it would be for a transcriber to misallocate characters. But if we could not support such an argument with these distinctions in our transcribing, what use was it to make them? At the same time, we noticed another phenomenon that gave us pause: in a pair of manuscripts written probably by a single scribe, in one he commonly used a long-stemmed *r*, in the other the more normal *r*. This rather clear distinction might have appeared to justify our experiment, but it did not. What did it tell us? Really, not very much: just that the scribe adjusted his practice from manuscript to manuscript. Further, one hardly need go to the trouble of transcribing the whole of both manuscripts, spending hours on meticulous discrimination of the various *r* characters, to make this one rather facile observation.

In the last paragraphs I spoke of "us": by this time (early 1992) Elizabeth Solopova, then a graduate student at Oxford, had come to work as a transcriber on the project, just as I was wrestling with these problems. She brought with her an understanding of semiotics and an awareness of the range of signs on a manuscript page. We decided to discard the whole elaborate effort to separate signs according to fine graphic criteria. Instead we asked, What are our transcriptions for? Why are we making them? How will we use them and for what purposes? Who else might use them? In essence, we determined to concentrate on our work as mediators: interpreting the manuscripts for our use and for others'. This approach had one signal advantage. Questions such as, What did this scribe mean by this mark?, can never be answered, but the question, What do we want to do with these transcripts?, can be answered. We wanted to compare them by computer program and then use the results of the analysis to determine, if possible, the relations among the manuscripts in terms of genetic descent. Rather clearly, all this additional information concerning variant letterforms was irrelevant to this purpose (or so rarely relevant that we could not justify the effort of gathering the information). By definition, our transcription then could focus on lexical variation, on the kinds of differences that might survive copying from one manuscript to another. Even such transcription is problematic: purely lexical variation involves removal of differences at the level of spelling as well as letterform. But if transcribers regularized all spelling as they transcribed, to what would they regularize it? The collation tool we had developed by then had the ability to regularize as we collated, thereby shifting the responsibility for deciding exactly what a variant was to the editor from the transcriber. We decided therefore to adopt a graphemic system: as transcribers, we would represent individual spellings but not (normally) the individual letter shapes. We also included in our transcriptions sets of markers to represent nonlinguistic features, such as varying heights of initial capitals, different kinds of scribal emphasis, and the like: what Jerome McGann calls bibliographic codes (*Textual Condition* 52). By the strict interpretation of our goal—to analyze only lexical variation—we should not have recorded these features. We felt a need to record them, nonetheless, for various reasons. First, these features were undeniably there, were indeed the most striking phenomena about the manuscripts, and so should have been somehow noted. Second, while we could not see how we might use this information, its prominence in the manuscripts, an increasing interest in manuscript layout (not least in Solopova's own graduate work), and the likelihood that we might publish the transcripts all persuaded us that we should retain this information on the chance that it would be useful to others.[4]

Through 1992 and 1993 therefore, Solopova and I prepared a set of transcription guidelines that has since become the foundation of the project (Robinson and Solopova). These guidelines amount to a hypothesis of significant difference. One can hardly overestimate the importance of a defined set of transcription guidelines for any project built (as ours is) on full-text transcripts. Perhaps more to the point: the new medium had forced us to define exactly what variation was, for our purposes, and to build a transcription-and-collation system to capture that variation. Thus the second proposition offered here.

The route of full-text transcription we chose was not so obvious as it appears now. Traditionally, editors of texts would prepare collations by selecting a base text, comparing each version one at a time against that text, and recording the differences. One could—in theory—just input this record of difference into the computer and analyze that and thereby save vast amounts of time. This method would have the apparent advantage of circumventing all the difficult questions about transcription discussed above. But it was exactly this shortcut that raised the most serious doubts. In traditional collation the three parts of the editorial process—observing the actual spellings in the manuscript, noting those seen as different, and recording the differences—are so compressed into a single act as to make it very difficult to determine just what the editor sees in the manuscripts. But if a collation is not based on an explicit declaration of what the editor sees, what is it based on? The advantage of full-text transcription is that it forces us to state exactly what we see, and it makes it possible for readers to check what we say we see against what the reader can see.

Proposition 3: The use of computer-assisted analytic methods may restore historical criticism of large textual traditions as a central aim for scholarly editors.

By mid-1992, we had begun to consider what to do with all the information we were gathering. Rather obviously we should publish it. But what, exactly, would we publish? And how? We had a body of transcripts in electronic form, we had electronic tools to compare and analyze them, and we had various additional materials (discussions, descriptions of the manuscripts) in electronic form. We were also becoming aware of the possibility of digital imaging, and CD-ROM publication, as a means of distributing large volumes of text and perhaps images, had been established through the pioneering ventures of Chadwyck-Healey and the Oxford University Press. We seemed to have an obvious answer: we should publish electronically. From the work of Chadwyck-Healey, we knew that the *DynaText* program (then a product of Electronic Book Technologies) was able to publish, on CD-ROM, large volumes of SGML-encoded text such as we were then developing. By fortunate chance, it happened that Cambridge University Press was investigating electronic publication and saw our project as an opportunity to explore the possibilities. So we formed an alliance: Cambridge would purchase *DynaText*, and we would work out how to use it both to publish our own CD-ROMs with Cambridge and help Cambridge publish other CD-ROMs.

Accordingly, in 1996 the first of our CD-ROMs was published: the Wife of Bath's Prologue on CD-ROM (*Wife*). It included all transcripts of the fifty-eight witnesses, images of all pages of the text in these manuscripts, the spelling databases we had developed as a by-product of the collation, collation in both regularized spelling and original spelling forms, and various descriptive and discursive materials. It presents a mass of materials such as an editor might use in the course of preparing an edition. This mass quite overwhelms the rather slender explanatory and discursive materials included on the CD-ROM. As a result, the CD-ROM on its own may give the impression that the aim of the project is to gather the sources of the text, to transcribe and collate them, and then publish all this as an "electronic archive" (as Matthew Kirschenbaum has suggested [Kirschenbaum and Kraus]).

But transcription for us was always a means, never an end in itself. We sought to compare the transcripts to discover what the texts had in common and what they did not. The comparison itself was only a means: what we really wanted to know was why the texts differed. A reasonable guess was that the process of copying had caused the difference; that scribes introduced new readings into copies; and that these copies were themselves copies, introducing yet more new readings. This process, of course, is the basis of the traditional, Lachmannian, stemmatics, and it was precisely the denial by Kane of the grounds for this method that sparked our project (Piers Plowman: *The A Version*). There is an obvious analogy between the processes of copying and descent we might hypothesize for manuscript copying and those of replication and evolution underlying biological sciences: both appear instances of "descent with modification," to use Darwin's phrase. Therefore, it seemed possible that the techniques developed for tracing descent in evolutionary biology, especially through comparison of DNA sequences, might be applicable to manuscript traditions. With the aid of Robert O'Hara, then at the University of Wisconsin, Madison, and later with Chris Howe, Adrian Barbrook, and Matthew Spenser at the University of Cambridge, we were able to show that phylogenetic software developed for biological sciences gave useful results when applied to manuscript traditions. That is, we can turn our lists of agreements and disagreements among the manuscripts into a form that can be input into a program used by biologists to hypothesize a tree of descent among species; we can then use the program to hypothesize a tree of descent among manuscripts. But what exactly does such a hypothetical tree of descent represent? Is it useful for editors or just a curiosity?

As to the first question, our experiments suggest that such programs may indeed produce representations of relations among manuscripts that correspond with historical sequences of copying. That is, if a group of manuscripts is shown by the software as descended from a single point in the tradition, there is a good chance that they have in fact descended from just one exemplar in the tradition. To convert chance to probability, one would need to analyze further: to look at the history of the manuscripts, so far as we can recover it from external evidence, and to look at the readings that cause the software to hypothesize this descent. In at least one instance, for the manuscript tradition of the Old Norse *Svipdagsmøl*, we were able to compare external evidence of manuscript relations with the representation offered by phylogenetic software, and the software did succeed in showing close links between manuscripts known to be near relatives by copying (Robinson and O'Hara, "Cladistic Analysis").

As to the second question (Are such reconstructions useful for editors?), where these techniques show a group of manuscripts as apparently descended from a single exemplar in the tradition, one should be able to deduce just what readings were introduced by the exemplar. One could go further: scrutiny of these readings might give answers to a question such as, Did the variants come from authorial revision or from scribal interference? In a long article on the Wife of Bath's Prologue, I suggested that one could discriminate some six fundamental groupings among witnesses for this text, and one could use these groupings to identify contamination and shifts of exemplar ("Stemmatic Analysis"). One could also isolate through this means the variants characteristic of each group and therefore apparently descended into each group from a single ancestor in the tradition. These variants could then be examined and a judgment made on whether they were scribal or authorial in character. From this, I arrived at a reasonably firm set of conclusions: that there was no evidence of word-by-word revision by Chaucer in the groupings; that the so-called added passages were present very early in the tradition, reinforcing the argument that Chaucer himself wrote them; and that their scattered attestation across the manuscripts might have resulted from these passages' having been marked for deletion in very early manuscripts.

After decades of doubt and uncertainty, historical criticism of large textual traditions may return as a central tool of scholarly editors. The denial by Kane and his followers that any kind of genetic reconstruction is possible or useful left the text and the editor in a historical vacuum: an editor must use only judgment, based on a sense of the author's intention and an intuition for how this intention might be corrupted, to create a pristine text. Against this, our work suggests that historical analysis of textual traditions, in terms of "descent with modification" by the flow of readings from manuscript to manuscript, is possible. It does appear useful to explore the development over time of the tradition: to attempt to trace it both forward, from the first surviving manuscripts to the latest incunables, and back, from the extant witnesses to the hypothetical ancestors underlying the texts we now have. If so, here is a remarkable instance of the effect advances in one field (evolutionary biology) can have on a second, quite distinct field (textual scholarship).

Proposition 4: The new technology has the power to alter both how editors edit and how readers read.
The Wife of Bath's Prologue on CD-ROM was published before these analyses were complete. By the time we came to publish our next CD-ROM, Solopova's edition, *The General Prologue on CD-ROM*, we had considerably more experience with these phylogenetic methods. For the Wife of Bath's Prologue, materials and analysis were separated between the CD-ROM and the printed article. This time, we were determined to unite them. So I wrote an "Analysis Workshop" section for the new CD-ROM along the same lines as the Wife of Bath article ("Stemmatic Analysis"). Because of the electronic publication mode, we were also able to include the actual software and all the data we used for the analysis, with exercises that allowed readers to run the software themselves, so that they might confirm, extend, or deny the hypotheses suggested in the article. My "Stemmatic Commentary" took some 120 individual places in the General Prologue and attempted to use the results of the stemmatic analysis to clarify the range of readings at each place.

The movement from the first to the second CD-ROM marked a significant shift in our thinking. In the general editors' introduction to the General Prologue CD-ROM, this change was expressed: "One might summarize the shift in our thinking in the last two years, underlying the differences between the two CD-ROMs, as follows: the aim of *The Wife of Bath's Prologue on CD-ROM* was to help editors edit; our aim now is also to help readers read." Elsewhere on the CD-ROM, I give this approach the name "new stemmatics" and explain it: "Like the stemmatics of the last century, its aim is to illuminate the history of the text. Unlike the stemmatics of the old century, its aim is not a well-made edition, but a well-informed reader" ("Stemmatic Commentary"). This shift coincided with (and was indeed largely caused by) an increasing sense of the expressive power of the computing medium. As standard browsers grew in stability and capacity, it became possible to build attractive and responsive interfaces for the vast range of material at our disposal. Not in *DynaText*, however: this system, now venerable (ten years old!), lacked many of the features we could see appearing on the Web and elsewhere. We wanted to do much more than have text and image appear in a window when you clicked (about all you could do in the early days of hypertext). We wanted to be able to have images resize and scroll as you moved over them, to have boxes with text appear or the text itself change when you clicked or as the mouse moved, and more. With JavaScript and other technical advances, all this became possible. We developed a new software tool, *Anastasia*, specifically to offer a bridge between the XML, into which we now decanted all our files, and the new JavaScript-and-HTML interfaces now appearing. Our first publication to make use of this combination was our third CD-ROM, the *Hengwrt Chaucer Digital Facsimile* (Stubbs). For this we had a new aspiration: it should be beautiful. We sought out a clean and efficient interface that would allow the manuscript to speak for itself as clearly as possible. The editor, Estelle Stubbs, wished to present the manuscript as much more than a container of text, as a physical object, with distinctive orderings of page, quire, tale, and ink, and we devised a set of tables to show this. Our motivation was to make the manuscript as accessible to as many people as possible, at least down to undergraduates beginning their first work on Chaucer and manuscripts. For us, this was an opportunity to give practical expression to what was becoming a core belief of the project, that we could use the new tools and our materials to change the way people experience a text.

In our most recent publications, beginning with *The Miller's Tale on CD-ROM* (Robinson and Stevenson), we are applying the technology used for

The Hengwrt Chaucer Digital Facsimile to our single-tale editions, where (as earlier with the Wife of Bath's Prologue and the General Prologue) we bring together all the transcripts and images of the many versions of any one tale with collations and analyses based on them. These offer readers the opportunity to check efficiently the stability of the text at critical points and offer too an agreeable means of discovery of how the text came to be how it is. By inviting exploration rather than baffling it, such editions might help us all be better readers.

Proposition 5: Editorial projects generating substantial quantities of transcribed text in electronic form should adopt, from the beginning, an open transcription policy.

This compressed account rather elides the many difficulties we faced in our (now) sixteen years' progress. One difficulty, however, looms so large that it must be mentioned. We are necessarily a collaborative project: over forty people, and some six institutions, have contributed significantly to our work. Typically, transcripts are started by one person at one institution, then checked and rechecked by other people elsewhere. This collaboration is of course a great strength: no one person or institution could have done all this. But it can be a source of trouble. If only one of these people or one of these institutions decides to insist on control of his, her, or its part of the project and attempts to use this control to determine how the work should be published (or to deny its publication altogether), then we have a problem. If materials central to the project are affected, then the existence of the whole project is threatened. Of course, insisting on control might be done for the best of motives, but the effect is the same. The reason for this difficulty lies in copyright law and in the legal status of projects such as ours. The *Canterbury Tales* Project is not a legal entity and so cannot own anything, including copyright. Copyright in the transcripts varies, belonging either to the individuals who did them or to the institutions in which those individuals were based. Therefore we typically need permission from at least two or three institutions before we can publish a transcript. As time passes and more institutions become involved (if the project continues), every one of these institutions must be contacted for each and every act of publication. This necessity alone threatens the future viability of the transcripts on which we have spent so much energy. We would like others to take them, reuse them, elaborate on them (e.g., they could include the graphetic information we rejected), and republish them: exactly the means of scholarship promoted by the fluid electronic medium. But if future scholars must go through a process of increasingly lengthy, multisided negotiation, then the transcripts will become unusable, walled from the world by legal argument.

The answer to this problem, we can now see, is an open transcription policy, modeled on the copyright licensing arrangements developed by the Open Software Foundation (now part of the Open Group). It is important to note that this policy does not mean that institutions and individuals give up all copyright control. The originators of the transcripts still retain this and so can still (where possible) make commercial arrangements for their publication and prevent inappropriate use. What it does mean is that the copyright holders assert that the transcripts may be freely downloaded, used, altered, and republished subject to certain conditions (basically, republication must be under the same conditions, all files must retain a notice with them to this effect, and permission must still be obtained for any paid-for publication). It seems to me appropriate that copyright holders retain a measure of control in a collaborative environment. But they should not have exclusive control, to the point where it might, unilaterally and without consultation, determine the conditions under which transcripts can or cannot be published, to the possible detriment of others who have worked on the transcripts. The open transcription policy balances nicely the rights and needs of all those involved in a collaborative scholarly project of this kind. The policy, accepted by the project steering group in 2002, became the official policy of the project. I regret greatly that we did not adopt this course at the very beginning.[5]

One should not finish this article with the impression that the *Canterbury Tales* Project is all there is to the electronic editing of medieval texts. We have had perhaps a longer continuous history than any comparable born-digital project in the medieval realm, but we are certainly not alone. The roll of names given at the beginning of this essay shows the vigorous activity in the field in just England and America. There is also a wide range of similar editorial projects in Europe: one could mention Michael Stoltz's work on the *Parzival* tradition; the initiatives of Andrea Bozzi at the Consorzio Pisa Ricerche and associates in the BAMBI (Better Access to Manuscripts and Browsing of Images) and other projects; the electronic publications of SISMEL (Società Internazionale per lo Studio del Medioevo Latino); the "virtual reunification" of the Arnamagnæan Collection under way in Copenhagen and Reykjavik (Driscoll, "Virtual Reunification"), and several other projects in Old Norse; the Forum Computerphilologie in Germany; and many more.[6] This massive burst of activity across all the traditional domains of medieval philology puts one in mind of the grand editorial projects of the nineteenth century. The comparison is humbling: it remains to be seen whether the work we are now doing will last so well.

NOTES

1. Kiernan's *Beowulf* edition is introduced at www.uky.edu/~kiernan/eBeowulf/ guide.htm. The lessons of this project have been subsumed into the ambitious ARCHway Project, which aims to create a whole architecture for research, teaching, and learning in the digital medium, and particularly in the Edition Production Technology (EPT) Project, which seeks to create an edition for multimedia contents in digital libraries (Kiernan, "EPT"). SEENET is at www .iath.virginia.edu/seenet/, with links to the *Piers Plowman* Project. For the *Middle English Compendium*, see www.hti.umich.edu/mec/. Perhaps the most fully realized of the other enterprises I refer to is McGillivray's *Book of the Duchess*; versions of it have also appeared online (see www.ucalgary.ca/ucpress/online/pubs/ duchess/Websample/mainmenu.htm). Benson's work underlies the Harvard Chaucer pages at www.courses.fas.harvard.edu/~chaucer/index.html. Baker's work on early English texts can be viewed through www.engl.virginia.edu/OE/; Caie's teaching edition of The Miller's Tale is at www2.arts.gla.ac.uk/SESLL/ EngLang/ugrad/Miller/cover.htm; the Aberdeen Bestiary Project is at www .clues.abdn.ac.uk:8080/besttest/firstpag.html; the Johns Hopkins *Roman de la rose* is at http://rose.mse.jhu.edu/pages/terms.htm. There are many Web sites offering access to older English literary resources: for example, the British Academy portal at www.britac.ac.uk/portal/.

2. A pioneering instance of such discussion is Tim Machan's *Textual Criticism*. See both Hoyt N. Duggan's review of this book and Machan's reply ("Response").

3. The first scholar to explore such methods with an actual tradition appears to have been J. G. Griffith. For a bibliography of work in this area up to 1992, see Robinson and O'Hara, "Computer-Assisted Methods." For work done since then, see the publications of the STEMMA Project, listed at www.cta.dmu.ac.uk/ projects/stemma/res.html.

4. There has been lively debate on the meaning and purposes of transcription. One view, argued by Allen Renear, is that text has an objective existence, which a transcription act may witness: thus his contribution to the MII-PESP Philosophy and Electronic Publishing discussion group on 27 November 1995. The discussion group was established as part of a paper organized by Claus Huitfeldt for publication in an interactive issue of the journal *The Monist* (for Renear, the discussion, and the paper, see Biggs and Huitfeldt). An opposite view, asserted by Alois Pichler, Solopova, and me, argues that a transcription is a text constructed for a particular purpose and has no existence outside this construction (see Pichler; Robinson and Solopova). I tried to find a third way between the two views ("What Text").

5. Paolo D'Iorio has come to exactly the same conclusion concerning the transcripts of Nietzsche materials prepared for HyperNietzsche, a large collaborative editorial project organized on lines very similar to those of the *Canterbury Tales* Project.

6. On Andrea Bozzi and the BAMBI workstation, see Calabretto and Bozzi; for SISMEL, see www.sismel.it/, listing six different series of electronic publication; for the Arnamagnæan Collection, see www.hum.ku.dk/ami/; for the other Old Norse projects, see the Medieval Norse Text Archive at SEENET (note 1); for the Forum Computerphilologie, see computerphilologie.uni-muenchen.de/. These enterprises are only a fraction of the activity in the area.

DOCUMENTARY EDITING

BOB ROSENBERG

The most important point to be made about any digital documentary edition is that the editors' fundamental intellectual work is unchanged. Editors must devote the profession's characteristic, meticulous attention to selection, transcription, and annotation if the resulting electronic publication is to deserve the respect given to modern microfilm and print publications. At the same time, it is abundantly clear that a digital edition presents opportunities well beyond the possibilities of film and paper. In the Edison Papers, both the microfilm and print editions were well under way, and the electronic edition was seen as a means to combine and extend the work done without significantly altering the established editorial principles.

There are a number of principal considerations facing anyone who plans to create an electronic edition of historical documents. If the documents are presented as images, the primary concerns will be construction of a database and creation of those images; if the documents are all transcribed, then preparation and presentation of the text will be foremost concerns. The Edison Papers is working to combine images and text, and I hope that a careful examination of some avenues explored and lessons learned in that process will be helpful to anyone fortunate enough and bold enough to undertake such a task.[1]

The Edison Papers is unusual in several respects, the first and most striking being the size of the archive from which it draws. When the project was launched at the end of the 1970s, it was estimated that the collection at the Edison National Historic Site comprised about 1.5 million pages. In a few years the estimate grew to five million, which made the tens of thousands of Edison pages in other archives, libraries, and repositories seem easily manageable. It was clear that the two editions projected at that time—microfilm and print—would be selective, the microfilm including about ten percent of the holdings and the printed volumes including perhaps two or three percent of that ten percent. A second unusual aspect of the Edison corpus is the central importance of drawings and even physical artifacts to an understanding of its subject's work, which is a direct consequence of Edison's being an inventor and fresh territory for documentary editing. Despite these differences and others more subtle, we decided at the outset to hew as closely as possible to the standard practices of documentary editing.

The original plan was to have the microfilm proceed ahead of the print edition, since the microfilm could capture years of Edison's life while the book editors were dissecting it one day at a time. This strategy worked admirably, even if at first it had the book editors champing at the bit, teasing insight out of reams of photocopies. Organizing, comprehending, selecting, and filming the documents was—and remains—a truly Herculean task. When the first part of the collection was published on film in 1985, the book editors had Edison's early work at their fingertips. At the same time, two crucial pieces of the foundation for the electronic edition had been unwittingly put in place: first was the structure of the descriptive data recorded about each document; second was the high quality of the microfilm itself, which would later allow the creation of excellent digital images.

DATABASE

It had been impressed on the project organizers that the only way to control a collection of this size was with an electronic database. Fortunately, the Joseph Henry Papers Project had already started blazing a trail into that mysterious territory. Using that experience and knowledge as a foundation, the Edison Papers created a database that would prove two decades later to be the heart of their electronic edition. At its inception, the database served two functions: it was the raw material from which was created the detailed, item-level printed index that accompanied the microfilm, and it contained information about the organization and contents of the documents that was used for in-house research.

The first incarnation of the database lived on a university mainframe and was written by a hired programmer in Fortran 77. The main table had twenty-four data fields:

Group   A one- or two-character field identifying the record group to which the document belonged ("A" for accounts, " PN" for pocket notebooks, etc.)

Location　A field of up to eight characters specifying the position of the document in its record group ("7204A" would indicate the first document in the fourth folder for 1872)

Type　A field that held a two-digit code indicating which of the many types of documents this document was (there are currently more than fifty in the edition). A separate table held the codes and their full meaning ("01" = Accounts, "33" = Test Reports, "79" = Interviews, etc.).

Date　Three two-character fields: month, day, year. Dating turned out to be very complex. Although it would be nice to use the date function that is built into most databases, it cannot be done in any straightforward way, because documents are frequently partially dated, and the date function will not allow dates such as "May 1875."

Author　Two fields containing three-character codes. As in the Type field, there was a separate table holding the codes and the names they represented. There were two Author fields (and two Recipient fields) to allow for situations such as an individual's writing on behalf of a company.

Recipient　Two fields containing three-character codes

Name Mention　Two fields containing three-character codes. Limiting name mentions to two fields meant that many names appearing in documents could not be included, which was unfortunate. But computational power and storage were much dearer when the project began.

Subjects　Three three-character subject codes

Status Codes　Six single-character fields that flagged information about the documents and their data: What language is it in? Is it a fragment? Is it a photocopy? Is it an attachment or enclosure? Is some part of the date conjectured?

Reel, Frame, Addframe　These three fields recorded the reel and frame numbers of the document on the microfilm.

This database structure is far from what would now be considered optimal, but it did contain almost all the information needed for searching and retrieval. (Were we to create the database today, we would try to encode document information in some form of metadata rather than use a proprietary database. The editors and Rutgers library staff are now discussing the possibility of creating such metadata from the present structure.) Over time, the database migrated to three new programs: first to a different mainframe program, then to a desktop PC, and finally to a newer desktop program.

Once on the desktop, the number of name mentions and subjects was increased to sixteen each, the Group and Location fields were merged into a single Document ID, and a field was added that held a code for the folder or volume containing the document. With the most recent migration (to *Microsoft Access*), the data have been normalized, which means they are broken up into a larger number of interlinked tables, most of which contain only a few fields. This normalization makes the data easier to manipulate; it also means there is no limit to the number of names or subjects recorded for a document.

I do not mean this discussion to be inordinately detailed and technical. Any digital edition that provides images of original documents, with or without transcriptions, can be no better than its database. At the very least the database must have dates and authors' and recipients' names. It should also contain information about the organization of the edition. One of the great strengths of a microfilm edition is that once a user finds the first page of a letter, an account book, or a legal proceeding, the successive pages usually appear on successive frames. Moreover, documents in a given editorial grouping usually appear together on the film. Digital images, however, must be ordered for the user, and beginnings and ends of documents must be flagged somehow. We return to the issue of the database after discussing images.

IMAGES

In the mid-1990s, after the first graphic browsers had awakened everybody to the Web's potential, a foundation program officer was arguing against the work of entering documents' information into the Edison Papers database. "You don't have to do all that indexing," he said. "Just scan the documents and put them on the Internet!" Not only was he wrong about the indexing; he was wrong about the "just scan." At the time of that conversation, the Edison Papers had published 162 reels of microfilm, each reel averaging slightly more than a thousand images. The market for microfilm scanning was largely driven by institutions such as banks and insurance companies, which had huge collections on microfilm and which wanted greater access to those images. Not interested in subtlety, they were content with black-and-white (one-bit) images. Such images can suffice if a typed or printed document is scanned at a sufficiently high spatial resolution (300–600 dpi [dots/pixels per inch]), but most of the documents in the Edison Papers microfilm edition were handwritten, many of them in pencil or light pen and many of them on paper that had darkened in the century since they were written. There was no doubt that the documents would have to be scanned as eight-bit images (256 shades of gray), a capability the scanner manufacturers were just beginning to explore. Increasing the bit depth of the images allowed us to scan them at a relatively modest resolution of 200 dpi.

After some misadventure, we settled on a vendor. We soon found that the scanning produced better images when we used negative film, as the amount of light that came through positive film tended to overload the sensors and wash out fainter lines. Besides straightforward quality-control issues of light or dark images, we found that the scanner occasionally trapped dust particles between the sensors and the film, creating a streak across dozens or even hundreds of images. Those problems aside, we were pleasantly surprised by the quality of the images. Because the documents were recorded on high-contrast microfilm, we expected little in the way of fine distinction, but in fact the images often revealed details that were nearly or actually impossible to see using a microfilm reader.

The original time estimate for the job was six months. As there were some kinks to be worked out in the technology, the job took about two years. When it was done, we had nearly 1,500 CDs holding a terabyte of data. The images, captured as uncompressed TIFF (tagged image file format) files, averaged around 6 MB each, and before we could deliver them over the Internet, we needed to create smaller versions. Even more important, we needed to somehow link the images to the appropriate document information, so that when a user called up a particular document, the correct images would appear.

The creation of derivative images, like much editorial work, is repetitive but not routine and requires a finicky intelligence. We did not have sufficient storage space to put the full-size images online as a viewing option, so the user was going to get one derivative image, and it had to be legible. We aimed at reducing the spatial resolution to 80 dpi, which is about life-size on most computer screens, and using JPEG compression to wind up with an image that was about one percent the size of the original (an average of 60 KB). Because the microfilm edition grouped documents by subject or type, the images could often be batch-processed and then reviewed for quality. We did not hesitate to lighten or darken an image if the alteration made it easier to read. (Some editors initially winced at this, reflecting a general uneasiness about manipulating digital images, but such adjustment is philosophically no different from changing the lighting while microfilming in order to enhance the contrast of a document. An illegible document is of little use.) Although most of the film was shot at a constant 14:1 reduction, some unusually large or small documents were filmed at other ratios. We tried to scan all the images at the equivalent of 200 dpi on the original, but for agate-type newspaper clippings and other documents with fine detail we increased the spatial resolution of the online images to make them legible for the user.

Linking images to their document information was a painstaking process. There is no simple one-to-one correspondence between images and their information. A document might contain one or more attachments or enclosures, for example, in which case a user who retrieves the covering document will want to see the enclosures as part of the document, while at the same time the enclosures might be recorded as separate documents themselves. That is, the same image may be linked to more than one document. With the help of an outside programmer (and a 21-inch screen), we created an interface that displayed successive digitized images on one side and database information on the other. Using the microfilm frame numbers in the database, the program would calculate the number of images in a document. Most of the time the calculation was right, but when it was wrong the operator—working with the digital images, the database, and the microfilm— could easily override it.

The result is an online image edition that allows the user to sample or assemble the documents in a number of ways—name, date, document type, editorial organization—and to view as a group documents scattered across many reels of microfilm. At the same time, there are certain characteristics of microfilm that are useful to preserve in an electronic edition. A user landing on a page in the middle of an experimental notebook, account book, or scrapbook is likely to want to browse forward and backward through the entire item. This problem was solved by the creation of a new data table, but the solution was possible only because the structural information identifying the collection of individual documents as a unit was already present in the database.

TEXT

As might be expected, the other side of the edition—creating live, linked text from the transcribed documents and their editorial apparatus—presented its own set of issues. Again, the electronic text and apparatus, if not identical to those in the published volumes, reflected the same principles of selection, transcription, and annotation. There were both theoretical and practical considerations in the creation of the digital text for the Edison Papers, as is always the case, but the practical issues predominated.

At the start of the project we had chosen "a conservative expanded approach [to transcription] that does not try to 'clean up the text' . . . to strike a balance between the needs of the scholar for details of editorial emendation, the requirements of all users for readability, and the desire of the editors that all readers obtain a feel and flavor for Edison, his associates, and their era" (Jenkins et al. lv–lvi). Because of the nature of the documents, establishment of an authoritative text—in the sense of choosing between alternative readings—was rarely an issue. Only a tiny percentage of the documents (such as contracts, letters to the editor, or patent specifications) had been written or printed more than once.

Traditional text-editing conventions generally proved a comfortable fit. Where they did not, we tried to keep our improvisations as close as we could to the spirit of traditional models. For example, we used traditional abbreviations to describe the documents: A for autograph, meaning that the document was in the hand of the author; L for letter; D for document; S for signed; and so on. But there was no existing symbol for an artifact, nor was there one for technical notes or notebook entries, both of which we had in abundance. So we created new ones: M (model) for physical objects and X for technical materials. Almost immediately, we realized that notebook entries and similar materials presented a significant new entanglement. From quite early in his career, Edison had coworkers beside him at the bench, people who helped him carry out his research plans. Sometimes one of them would work and another would take notes; sometimes the experimenter would make his own notes; sometimes a group of them would work together with one keeping notes; sometimes the researcher was more or less autonomous; sometimes they were pursuing a line of thought that Edison had assigned. What stumped us was the question of authorship raised by such documents. Was the author the person who did the work? recorded the work? had the idea for the work that was carried out? Even if those puzzles had answers, most of the time we couldn't assign those roles with much surety. Finally we cut the Gordian knot and declared that documents of type X had indeterminate authors, even when Edison wrote them. This solution turned out to reflect the way work was pursued as well as the way many of Edison's coworkers felt about the work. They realized that they were active participants, but they also recognized that when Edison was not in the laboratory, work slowed after a couple of days, and that in fact the work would not have existed without him to drive it.

Although the quantity of Edison's drawings and their importance are unusual for documentary editions, with only a few published scientific documents as distant prototypes, there is one documentary category in which the Edison Papers pioneered and that so far remains unique to the project—technological artifacts (Rosenberg). Edison was, after all, an inventor, and the things he created were the core of his work. In the mid-1980s, when we confronted the problem posed by physical objects, we considered several options for presentation, even exploring videodisc (and, in a lighter moment, paper pop-up constructions). Finally we decided to give each artifact an annotated introductory headnote, presenting the object as a photograph if we had one—preferably our own, if we had access to the object, or a historical image if we didn't—or, failing that, as a historical sketch, patent drawing, or other representation. Dating was a challenge—we decided that the date of design was comparable to the date a text was composed—as was the slippery analogy of transcription for both photographs and drawings. We have found the system satisfactory for print, and the edition's users have seemed to agree. The electronic edition will offer similar presentation of photographs and drawings. For those instances where an artifact still exists, though—stock tickers, electric lighting, and motion pictures, for example—the Internet's potential for displaying sound and motion opens fascinating possibilities for annotation, affording the user detail, depth, and understanding simply not possible with static images and text. As Edison's designs stretch the notion of artifact to include his electric central stations and the Ogdensburg ore-milling plant of the 1890s, modes of presentation will doubtless adapt to them.

It was planned from the beginning of the electronic edition that the text of the print volumes would be included, marked up with SGML (later XML) to take full advantage of the capabilities of live digital text. But before we did any markup, the text itself had to be established, letter for letter, as accurate as in print. This accuracy was not a problem for volumes 3 and 4, because all the corrections, alterations, and additions to the documents and editorial material in those volumes made after their submission to the press—through galleys and page proofs—had been entered into the electronic files of the documents. For the first two volumes, however, edited and published before the electronic edition was on the horizon, the electronic files were uncorrected. Neither scanning with optical character recognition (OCR) nor simply retyping the published text was accurate enough to avoid another full proofreading of the text. However, those two processes combined offered an extremely accurate text, since the computer and the typist did not make the same kinds of mistakes. The scanned text was divided into individual documents, and a second copy of the documents was typed in individually from the volumes. The project secretary then used the Compare function of

WordPerfect to find differences between the two versions and create a corrected one, which she stored. Editorial material, such as front matter, headnotes, and back matter, was treated the same way.[2]

What was not clear at the outset was which DTD would be used, and even less clear was which software would be used to deliver the text on screen.[3] The work done by David Chesnutt, Michael Sperberg-McQueen, and Susan Hockey for the Model Editions Partnership (MEP) was immensely helpful, as was the DTD they developed. The MEP tackled a diverse collection of electronic documentary presentations, and the resultant *Markup Guidelines for Documentary Editions* is now the only reasonable starting place for anyone preparing text for an electronic documentary edition.[4]

We found, as does everyone who attempts markup, that tagging the text is a painstaking process.[5] The situation is admirably described in the *Markup Guidelines*:

> Some of the tagging we recommend can be automated in very simple ways, e.g. by simple macros in a word processor, or in some cases even by simple global changes. Other tagging we recommend can be automated successfully only by a skilled programmer. Some things fall between the two extremes, and can be performed by an astute editor or a journeyman programmer. Some kinds of tagging cannot be fully automated, even by expert programmers, but an automatic process can propose tagging for a human editor to accept or reject, in much the same way that a selective global change in a word processor allows the user to decide whether or not to make the change, on a case by case basis. And, finally, some tagging is done most simply by hand.
>
> Automated and semi-automated tagging can substantially reduce the cost of tagging an edition, but failed attempts to automate what cannot be automated can consume alarming amounts of time, patience, and money. The art and challenge of managing the creation of an electronic edition using limited resources [lie], in no small part, in automating what can be automated, doing manually what must be done manually, and deciding (perhaps with a sigh) to leave untagged what cannot be tagged automatically and is not essential to the edition. It will not always be easy to decide where to class a particular kind of tagging: some kinds of information require manual tagging in some collections of documents, but can be tagged automatically or semi-automatically in others. Right judgment will depend on the body of materials being edited, on the time and resources at hand, and on the skills of the available programming assistance. (sec. 2.4)

Those paragraphs constitute guiding principles for editors. We had the advantage of long familiarity with our word processor, which allowed us to write fairly complex macros that greatly simplified much of the tagging. Nevertheless, the actual work required as much intelligence and care as any other in the project.

The structural tagging of the documents tended to be straightforward (which did not always mean easy). Markup targeted the structure and physical presentation of the text—date lines, paragraphs, closings, signatures, damage to the paper—rather than such details as names of people or places. Perhaps the most important structural decision concerned images in the documents— what in the volumes we call "art" (as opposed to "illustrations," which are images we supply). These images are usually integral to the meaning of the documents, especially in notebook entries, patent documents, and other technical material. Occasionally a selected document has no words on the page at all, and we must insert bracketed letters next to drawings as hooks from which to hang annotation. Often enough the placement of text relative to drawings is meaningful, and there are times when no transcription can fully capture that relation. On paper we tackle these issues with careful explication, thoughtful design, and even inclusion of text in reproduced art; still, there is sometimes meaning lost in a patchwork of text and excised drawings. But in the electronic edition, where the original document is instantly available to the user, the transcribed representation no longer carries the full interpretive burden. The representation becomes an aid to reading, and the design of individual documents—still a nightmare of fluidity on-screen—becomes a secondary consideration. With the text transcribed, "figure" elements that contain the ID of their respective page image are inserted where images exist on the page. Those elements will appear on-screen as icons that, when clicked, call up the entire page image.

Embedding editorial material proved challenging. The first big decision concerned the index. A back-of-the-book index, although created for use in a codex, is a sophisticated intellectual tool whose strength is maintained and arguably increased in an electronic text. Full-text searching can help find specific text known to exist, but it is at best a marginally effective way to explore a body of information.[6] A good index not only provides direction to implicit meaning in the text but also reveals to the user what may be found in the work. In print volumes, an index is often used as a browsing aid; online, where the scope and depth of a work are harder to judge, such an aid is that much more valuable. A full index—or an index for any selected group of documents—can be assembled on the fly for browsing and access.[7] Moreover, index entries can appear on the screen with documents or editorial text and so serve as links to related material.

We had final electronic versions of the volumes' indexes, and we used a macro to convert the alphabetically ordered entries:

Ammonium nitrate, 264n.2
Anders, George, 104, 122, 128, 132n.1, 664; agreement with TAE and Welch, 118–19; and Boston instrument, 109; and Financial and Commercial instrument, 133n.1; and magnetograph, 82n.2, 104; and polarized relay, 110n.9
Anderson, Frank, 253

into a tagged, page-ordered list:

```
103<index level1="Stock-quotation service" level2="in
   Philadelphia"/>
103<index level1="Roberts, Dewitt"/>
104<index level1="Atlantic and Pacific Telegraph Co."
   level2="and double transmitter test"/>
104<index level1="Anders, George"/>
104<index level1="Anders, George" level2="and magnetograph"/>
104<index level1="Edmands and Hamblet" level2="Anders in"/>
```

Having the index prepared this way made it relatively straightforward for taggers to place entries in the text as they serially processed the documents. Afterward, a macro inserted an ID attribute in the element for linking:

```
<index id="d855i1" level1="electric sparks"/>
<index id="d864i1" level1="etheric force"
   level2="experiments"/>
```

The other complex editorial decision involved references and is still very much in process. In an edition where only a small percentage of the documents are transcribed, annotations often direct the reader to the images of other documents that are not. In the books, such annotations take the form of lists of documents on the microfilm, identifications accompanied by reel and frame numbers. For correspondence and many other types of documents, references can be translated into direct links. However, references to material in notebooks are rarely coordinate with the way notebooks are divided into documents.[8] Moreover, Edison and his crew recorded their work in whatever notebook lay at hand, so the background information for a technical document that represents a week's work is as often as not collected from more than one source. What in the book are haphazard strings of frame numbers must become a new type of online document, an artifice that allows the user to see the relevant notebook pages as the assemblage we intend. Just as we made notebooks, account books, and scrapbooks browsable by creating a new data table, these compound references will be a creation of the database. Like the tagging, this work will be half automated and half handwork; with the tagging—and the scanning, the data entry, the myriad editorial decisions, and the work that follows on them—such referencing is part of a foundation for an edition we couldn't imagine when the project started twenty-five years ago, one that combines the known strengths of microfilm and books with the remarkable power and access of the digital world.

Notes

1. The aspiring editor might acquire copies of Kline; Stevens and Burg; and join the Association for Documentary Editing (http://etext.lib.virginia.edu/ade/), which makes available the aggregate expertise of the profession (and discounts both books to members). The two volumes lay out in careful detail the strengths and weaknesses of the many methods used by the best practitioners. I must mention that, although I use "we" for convenience throughout this chapter, the Edison Papers was organized in 1978–79 and I did not join until 1983. I left the project in 2002.
2. There are services that will recapture printed text by double-keying and comparing, and the accuracy is at least as high as can be obtained any other way. Because the work is done overseas, we were concerned about the labor practices involved; our situation allowed us to recapture the text this way. However, it seems that the principal firms doing such work are mindful of their employees' well-being, and it would certainly be worth considering their services if an edition consisted of or included a significant quantity of previously published materials (Farrell and Olsen).
3. This question remains unresolved, awaiting completion of a substantial portion of the markup before a commitment is made. Choices are limited; without a programmer, they are nonexistent. The *Anastasia* suite, created by Peter Robinson and Scholarly Digital Editions, requires programming expertise we do not have but offers a promising mix of power and flexibility.
4. The home page of the MEP is http://adh.sc.edu; its *Markup Guidelines* are at http://adh.sc.edu/MepGuide.html.
5. When we started, in 1998, we did preliminary tagging on each document in Corel's *WordPerfect* and then switched to SoftQuad's *Author/Editor* (which no longer is supported) for most of the work. *Author/Editor* was superior at tagging the text, but we were frustrated by its text-handling and proprietary file format.

When later versions of *WordPerfect* proved capable of handling markup with sufficient sophistication and stability, we used it exclusively. The significance of Corel's 2002 acquisition of SoftQuad and its XML editor *XMetaL* remains to be seen.

6. In April 2000, the University of Vermont and the National Historical Records and Publications Commission funded a meeting to discuss ways to improve and standardize intellectual access to electronically published historical documents— that is, through online indexing and searching. The result of those deliberations, known as the Burlington Agenda, can be found at http://cit.uvm.edu:6336/ dynaweb/burlingtonagenda/.

7. For a related group of editions such as the Founding Fathers, a common index would obviously be a remarkable tool. However, merging existing indexes, which are often created with different intellectual perspectives, would require significant groundwork.

8. It is another idiosyncratic treatment of the documentary record that, in order to make the microfilmed notebooks most useful for readers, the database treated the appearance of a different date in a notebook as the beginning of a new document. This practice allowed us to sort the notebook materials by date in the printed index. (The electronic edition uses the same document definitions.)

THE POEM AND THE NETWORK: EDITING POETRY ELECTRONICALLY

NEIL FRAISTAT AND STEVEN JONES

Editing scholarly editions of poetry has never been an enterprise for the faint of heart. The challenges, however, are several orders of magnitude greater when one sets out to edit poetry electronically, as many scholarly editors now beginning their projects must do. The tasks of learning how to encode, how to adopt or create a DTD (document type definition) sufficiently complex to account for all the poems and manuscripts that will be a part of the edition, how to imagine the overall editorial environment the edition will provide, how to ensure the stability and portability of the edition over time, and how to make deliverable over the Web (if desired) the finished edition can be daunting. They take the sort of time, money, and special expertise that is immensely more difficult to acquire without the strong institutional and pro-gramming support offered to those affiliated with technology centers such as the University of Virginia's Institute for Advanced Technology in the Hu-manities or the University of Maryland's Maryland Institute for Technology in the Humanities. Perhaps the largest challenge of all is to produce an elec-tronic edition that doesn't simply translate the features of a print edition onto the screen but instead takes advantage of the truly exciting possibilities offered by the digital medium for the scholarly editing of poetry. In what follows we offer a few practical examples from our experience as coeditors of the col-laborative *Romantic Circles* Web site as a means of exploring the kinds of issues that must be confronted by those planning to produce electronic editions of poetry.

All scholarly editing requires the editor to pay attention to texts in more than one way, to what Jerome McGann has called the "concurrent structures" that divide the editor's attention between, on the one hand, bibliographic codes for design and presentation and, on the other hand, linguistic codes for structural and semantic communication ("Editing" 90). Imaginative texts, and poetry in particular, clarify the need for this kind of divided attention, since so much of the history of poetic expression is a matter of what is sometimes dismissively treated as layout, the "mere" appearance of the words on the page (or screen). Poetry as a form, then, tests and sometimes strains the resources of any textual encoding system. A predominantly structural approach to markup, such as SGML (standard generalized markup language), may unwittingly encourage critical editors to revert to privileging linguistic codes at the expense of bibliographic codes, though XML (extensible markup language) is an exciting recent development precisely because it points to a more capacious view of electronic textuality, one that enables the kind of double attention that we think is necessary for serious critical editing.[1]

Because poetry, with its enhanced self-consciousness of the physique of texts, expresses itself inextricably through particular interfaces, any editor of poetic texts in the digital medium must be centrally concerned with interface, with matters of textual display and appearance. The venerable dichotomy that divides the digital world into opposing demesnes, one focused on the front end (physical display features) and one on the back end (logical search and navigation) of digital texts, must give way in practice to a more complex approach, as experienced electronic editors know. Editors of poetry in the electronic medium need to possess a clear imagination of the front end, the interface or desired physical display of the text, when going into an editing project, in order efficiently to plan the logical, structural markup—and vice versa. The two sides of electronic editing, like the two foci of all serious critical editing, according to McGann (bibliographic and linguistic codes), are always intertwined, dialectically enmeshed. It seems to us as well that any serious editor of electronic texts must pay attention to an even wider field for such questions, looking outward to the "contextural" relation of multiple individual texts and other materials on the Net as a whole and within hyperlinked clusters, paying attention to the poem *and* the network.[2]

Romantic Circles has from the start been dedicated to producing and providing reliable and theoretically significant electronic editions over the existing dominant network, the World Wide Web of 1995 to the present.[3] This means of course that we have been committed to HTML, the limited tag set derived from SGML that became the lingua franca of the Web as Tim

Berners-Lee and others established it. What is at stake in that devil's bargain with HTML is perhaps best illustrated in one of our very early texts, Shelley's broadside ballad of 1812, "The Devil's Walk." This electronic edition was based on the texts and notes produced for volume I of *The Complete Poetry of Percy Bysshe Shelley*, edited by Donald H. Reiman and Neil Fraistat and published by Johns Hopkins University Press. At the time (1996), the text was essentially encoded in HTML 3.0, including a limited use of tables and frames. In fact, we used tables as a fundamental formatting device, as did many HTML texts of this era, before the advent of cascading stylesheets (CSS) and other devices for giving Web designers and editors more control over the layout of the electronic page.[4] HTML was originally derived from SGML in order to facilitate the exchange of simple, mostly scientific, informational documents over the Web; it inherited a deliberate lack of interest in typeface, indentation, and so on—all the graphic features of a text that matter to serious textual critics and editors (and to most poets). Consequently, HTML was bent and stretched over time, so that, for example, the table element became commonly used as a way to control the relative or absolute placement of bits of text and image on the formatted page. In this way we used table cells to hold individual lines of Shelley's ballad, as this example of the source code for "The Devil's Walk" demonstrates:

```
<TABLE BORDER="0" cellspacing=7>
  <TR>
  <TD COLSTART="1" ALIGN=RIGHT VALIGN=TOP WIDTH="25">
  <a href="variantsb.html#B1">01</a></TD>
  <TD COLSTART="2" ALIGN=LEFT WIDTH="550">
  <p>      </p>
  <p>ONCE, early in the morning,</TD></TR>
  <TR>
  <TD COLSTART="1" ALIGN=RIGHT VALIGN=TOP WIDTH="25">
  <a href="variantsb.html#B2">02</a></TD>
  <TD COLSTART="2" ALIGN=LEFT WIDTH="550">
  <p>        </p>
  <a href="brnotes.html#B2">Beelzebub</a> arose,
  </TD></TR>
```

The pragmatic limitations of HTML markup are clear, here, to anyone with an elementary knowledge of encoding, including the then-necessary but inelegant use of the nonbreaking space tag (" ") to create indentation.

But the result was an accurately formatted, clear text that was viewable on the actual browsers that were then available to users:

01   ONCE, early in the morning,
02   **Beelzebub** arose,

Of course the text availed itself of other features of the Web as a hypertext network, such as hyperlinks to a complete apparatus (the "variants" and "notes" HREF [hypertext reference] tags above). Our edition was not born digital; preliminary work on the text had been done for the Hopkins letterpress edition. But its electronic version was born live on the Web, the historically situated hypertext network of the early to mid 1990s.

One's ability in HTML to divide a screen window into separate frames allowed us to think creatively about how to display the textual apparatus of the "The Devil's Walk" edition in relation to the text proper. At the time, before the widespread use of JavaScript pop-up windows or mouseovers, most hypertextual editions that included such things as annotations placed them on separate Web pages to which one jumped by clicking a link in the primary text. This clicking wasted a great deal of time (waiting for the new page to load), caused user disorientation, and necessitated a liberal use of the Back button. Ultimately, we decided on a more user-centered and aesthetically pleasing interface, dividing the screen window for "The Devil's Walk" into three scrollable frames: (1) the largest frame, covering three-quarters of both the width and length of the entire window, contains the text of the poem, with line numbers and links to the apparatus; (2) immediately to the right of the text frame is a narrower frame, one-quarter of the window's width and three-quarters of its length, that contains annotations to the text; (3) below the frames for the text of the poem and the annotation, running the entire width of the window, is a frame containing the collations of variants (fig. 1). Clicking a link in the text proper, whether to the annotations or the collations, brings to the top of the relevant frame the appropriate gloss or variant.

The advantage of this design is that it visually streamlines the architecture of the edition, making each part of the textual apparatus visible to the user at a glance, to be easily read and referenced in relation to every other part. Because all three frames are scrollable, the user can even read all of the text, annotations, or collations independently. We also took advantage of frames for the contextual material provided in the edition, creating a window with two parallel scrollable frames so that users could compare, side by side, two substantively different versions of "The Devil's Thoughts," a poem by Robert Southey and Samuel Taylor Coleridge that was a major influence on Shelley's

"The Devil's Walk." Because frames were not always successfully read by browsers of the day, and because they create a series of design complications in hypertext navigation and with search engines, we also provided nonframe versions of the edited poem and its apparatus. Along with the Web design community, *Romantic Circles* has since moved away from the use of frames wherever possible, but they served a purpose for a time in the wide-area protocols of the Web, and they illustrate the kinds of provisional editorial solutions the larger context and infrastructure of the network sometimes require.

"The Devil's Walk" made a good choice for an experiment in electronic editing, in part because of the form of its material embodiment as a single surviving copy (in the Public Record Office) of a multistanza ballad printed on a large-format broadside sheet. Shelley had it printed—he may even have had a hand in the typesetting—and it was distributed mainly by his servant. The Web made it possible to link the edition to a zoomable photofacsimile of the unique document that users could examine from any point in the edition. Besides comparing the printed words of the original document with

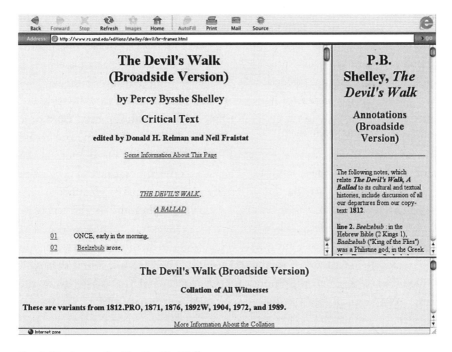

Fig. 1. Start page for *The Devil's Walk*

our edited text, users can get a concrete sense of the dimensions and other physical characteristics of the large sheet (18$\frac{1}{16}$" x 14$\frac{7}{8}$") with its three columns of stanzas, and they can better grasp facts like its mode of distribution: the clandestine posting of the broadside on walls and fences. Evidence for detective work by Reiman and Fraistat, such as establishing that the colophon had not in fact been cut away from the sheet, as it had long been thought, was made immediately available to the user. Hyperlinking allowed for an efficient apparatus, a way of presenting parallel versions and complete variants, along with a wealth of textual and contextual annotation, but the heart of the project is its providing full access to both the facsimile and the carefully edited HTML text at any point in the reading process. The horizontally linked, hypertextual text-and-image architecture of the Web actually helped determine the simple yet powerful shape this edition took.

Hypertext is of course the essence of the World Wide Web, and it extends beyond the poem itself, to allow for apparently encyclopedic possibilities, a potentially infinite expansion of the traditional editorial apparatus.[5] For this reason, the *Romantic Circles* edition of "The Devil's Walk" was eventually used as a source text for a virtual conference in our MOO, the Villa Diodati.[6] Afterward, the transcript of the conference papers and online discussion was linked to and from the text of the ballad, becoming an integral part of the electronic edition. At a later date, a volume of critical essays focused on early Shelley and published in the Praxis series of *Romantic Circles* was also able to cite this edition by hyperlink, in effect incorporating "The Devil's Walk" into that collection.[7]

What has happened to the text of "The Devil's Walk" beyond its initial encoding and publication usefully illustrates the extensibility of an electronic edition on the Web, the interactions that are possible between the poem and the network. In fact, even the text of this single poem is more complicated than we have so far described it. "The Devil's Walk" comes down to us in both the broadside version and a letter version in Shelley's hand; the two versions vary in significant ways. The electronic edition did its best to create parallel versions, something HTML and the hypertext structure of the Web would seem designed for. We aimed to represent the manuscript letter version diplomatically, as a kind of partial typographic facsimile but found that such representation strained the limited formatting capabilities of HTML at the time, even beyond the clumsiness of using table cells to place or paste up the lines of the broadside version.

This is just one example of some of the special complications presented by editing poetic manuscripts electronically, complications operating at both the front end (display encoding) and back end (structural encoding). At present, no single markup scheme is fully adequate to address these editorial complications.[8] The hypertext links that the Web makes so effortless to construct and use, the apparent integration of text and image into a seamless whole in an HTML edition of this sort, really takes place only on the surface, as it were. The digital image of "The Devil's Walk" broadside is not itself marked up or encoded, and we mark up the text to determine its appearance and presentation—for example, where individual lines are to be placed using table cells and how (relatively) far they are to be indented.

If we wish to encode a poetic text at the level of its structure, to describe (not format) its components—stanzas, parts of stanzas, lines, and so on, for search, retrieval, analysis, and recombination by a computer—we must turn to SGML proper and the guidelines developed by the Text Encoding Initiative (TEI). A very simple SGML version of "The Devil's Walk" (encoded using the basic TEI Lite tag set) was in fact produced simultaneously with our HTML version by collaborative agreement with the University of Virginia's Institute for Advanced Technology in the Humanities and Electronic Text Center.[9] This version, translated into HTML by *DynaWeb* middleware, was immediately browsable on the Web, but, under then-current conditions of the network and available browsers—not to mention the limitations of *DynaWeb* itself—it sacrificed the relatively sophisticated visual formatting of the HTML version. It now seems likely that both the HTML 3.0 and SGML (TEI Lite) versions of "The Devil's Walk" will in the near future need to be made available in XML (or the Web-ready standard it has created, XHTML).[10]

This is not the place for a detailed explanation of XML, but the difference between it and HTML can be quickly grasped in this way: whereas HTML tags might indicate a preferred typeface, point size, font color, and even something of the arrangement on the page of a poetic stanza, XML could tag the stanza *as* a stanza (a particular instance of the "line group" element, `<lg>`) and could add to that tag the attribute type with specific content labels of immediate use to literary critics—for example, pointing out that it is a quatrain. Then with every line tagged (surrounded by `<l>` and `</l>`), the encoded stanza would look like this:

```
<lg type="quatrain">
<l>Long banish'd Peace again descends,</l>
<l>Array'd in all her heav'nly charms;</l>
<l>Her dove-like wings to earth she bends,</l>
```

```
<l>Bids Europe drop the deathful arms.</l>
</lg>
```

By nesting multiple sets of tags of this sort, it becomes possible logically to mark the portions of a stanza—octet, sestet, quatrain, couplet—such that software recognizing the document type could parse, search, and manipulate the text in complex ways. To put it in computer terms, we focus on the text's content objects as they can be described in an ordered hierarchy. But the X in XML stands for "extensible," meaning that encoders can develop their own tags (for, say, personification) so long as the tags are incorporated in the overall formal schema (a document type description or DTD is a necessary schema for any valid code) that lists the rules by which the text has been encoded and can be decoded. The point for the would-be editor is that this kind of encoding is a way to think structurally about poetic texts and to allow the computer to think structurally about them as well.

The stanza cited in the example above is taken from *British War Poetry in the Age of Romanticism*, an XML project now in progress at *Romantic Circles*, coedited by Betty T. Bennett and Orianne Smith (with help from Steven Jones). This will be a new electronic edition of a 528-page book originally edited by Bennett and first published in 1976, a collection of poems on war (and peace) published mostly in British newspapers between 1789 and 1815, by a range of authors, including some that remained anonymous. When Garland Press published the book, it was already a reprint edition, a gathering of materials originally published elsewhere; some of the bibliographic and contextural codes with which each poem was first published, while of obvious historical interest to the scholar and critic, have been bracketed off and set aside, at least for the first phase of this project.

Instead of an edition of poems based on first publications, ours will be an entirely new reprint edition of the 1976 Garland volume that anthologized them, making no attempt beyond page numbering to reproduce that volume's original bibliographic codes. The *Romantic Circles* electronic edition of *British War Poetry* will amount to a kind of database of the individual poems extracted and repurposed for the new medium, a thematic anthology with a historical focus, with individual entries retrievable and combinable in various ways, depending on the needs of the reader or scholarly researcher. As such, the project makes a perfect field for editorial experiments with XML.[11]

We are starting with the TEI core tag set but may eventually add other tag sets as necessary (e.g., for verse). Thus creating our own customized DTD,[12] we'll mark the general structural and formal features as well as the basic historical circumstances of the publication of each poem in the collection. XML will allow us to record bibliographic data such as title, author, date, and place of publication, which, for the poem on peace above will include the information that it was titled "From the Belfast News-Letter," was written by William Cunningham, and was published in the *Gentleman's Magazine* for November 1801. In addition, the XML encoding of the poem itself will include structural and formal elements, ranging from the individual lines and, if we wish, their poetic meter, to stanza type and general form (ballad, sonnet, etc.). All this data and metadata will be marked in the text itself, not in a separate file, and will then be carried with the edition in a form that will survive across various platforms and delivery systems.

As we write this, the newest browsers are capable of reading XML, and a number of businesses, publishers, and scientific projects are using it. Humanities scholars and textual editors, it seems likely, will increasingly turn to XML for serious encoding projects. Its advantages for complex editorial projects are many. For example, with the use of XSLT, a special stylesheet language for XML,[13] one large document can, depending on software applications, serve up both scholarly and classroom texts of the same work. In general, XML now promises to overcome the crudest form of the binary opposition between structural and display markup, which is very good news for electronic editions of poetry.

The *British War Poetry* project at *Romantic Circles* is just one example of an XML-based edition that would embody in its plan the complex double attention we have been suggesting is necessary for all editing but especially— and in this inescapable, concrete form, at the level of encoding scheme—for electronic editions of poetry. These two example texts, "The Devil's Walk" and *British War Poetry*, one early and one recent in the history of *Romantic Circles*, demonstrate how fundamental markup schemes are to digital editing—and they also indicate some of the limits of all existing schemes. Those of us who would edit poetry electronically thus find ourselves working at an interesting moment, rife with possibilities but with experiments still to be done and solutions still to be found as new projects attempt new schemes.

As the Web has evolved, *Romantic Circles* has worked with an expanding group of collaborators and contributing editors around the world, deliberately publishing an experimental and diverse list of editions of varying design and editorial approach. Several of these editions have used HTML strategically so as to thicken the interrelations between the poem and the Net. For example, Lisa Vargo and Allison Muri's edition of Anna Barbauld's *Poems* (1773), instead of in effect translating print apparatus into HTML (as "The Devil's

Walk" did), uses a full range of hypertextual links to produce native-to-the-Web representations of context, most especially the "poem web" focused on the lyric "On a Lady's Writing," which includes images from writing manuals of the eighteenth century, extended notes on copybooks and quills, a contextual presentation of the way Mary Wollstonecraft anthologized the poem in *The Female Reader*, and an excerpt from Hugh Blair's influential *Lectures on Rhetoric and Belles Lettres*.

In their edition of Letitia Elizabeth Landon's *"Verses" and* The Keepsake *for 1829*, to cite another example, Terence Hoagwood and Kathryn Ledbetter created an edition that exists mostly as context, emphasizing the interconnectedness of the poet's lyric and the popular annual gift book in which it first appeared, a volume that was itself crafted by its editor, Frederic Mansel Reynolds, to emphasize the contextural relations among its contents, especially between word and image. Hoagwood and Ledbetter's edition thus reproduces several especially important works that appeared in *The Keepsake* for 1829, including an engraving of Edwin Landseer's painting *Georgiana, Duchess of Bedford*, to which Landon's poem refers.

Experiments have also been done at *Romantic Circles* with editions that push the boundaries of HTML, trying to take advantage of the performative and participatory properties of the digital environment. For instance, Fraistat and Melissa Jo Sites's dialogic HTML edition of Shelley's lyric "On the Medusa of Leonardo da Vinci in the Florentine Gallery" presents a critically edited text of the poem with an apparatus that consists entirely of verbal commentary and images provided by users and structured through a forms-based interface that allows the editors to vet all potential contributions to the apparatus.

Of all the electronic editions currently mounted on *Romantic Circles*, one of the most ambitious in terms of design is Bruce Graver and Ronald Tetreault's SGML-encoded edition of Coleridge and Wordsworth's *Lyrical Ballads*, which reproduces in full the texts of both 1798 imprints of the volume, as well as the three subsequent editions of 1800, 1802, and 1805. Photofacsimile images of every page in all five editions are also included, linked hypertextually to the encoded text, which is marked up in TEI Lite. This edition exploits the digital environment to emphasize two important characteristics of *Lyrical Ballads* that have been obscured in print editions: "first, the complex interaction between authors, publishers, and printers that brought it into being, and second, the multiplicity of versions of the collection that readers had available to them in the early nineteenth century." To represent that multiplicity of versions in meaningful ways, Graver and Tetreault replace the standard apparatus criticus with what they call dynamic collation, a script that allows for comparative viewing of textual cruxes in their original contexts (fig. 2). Here's a description from the edition:

> What is seen on the screen is an array of four windows displaying the text of any poem as it varies through the four lifetime editions (1798, 1800, 1802, 1805). This parallel display is accompanied by a fifth window on the left which maps the changes in the poem as descriptive hyperlinks. Clicking on a link in this "variant map" causes the text in each of the four windows to leap to the same line where the revision in question may be observed in context. . . . The variant map acts a guide to revisions that were made at various stages in the poem's development. . . . Scrolling down the variant map, the reader is thus alerted by a sort of palimpsest that an alteration has been made, and by clicking on the "hotspot" or hyperlink can summon up the parallel passages.

This re-imagination of the traditional static foot-of-the-page or back-of-the-book treatment of variants takes advantage of the electronic medium to provide an inviting editorial environment for the meaningful close reading of textual variation.[14]

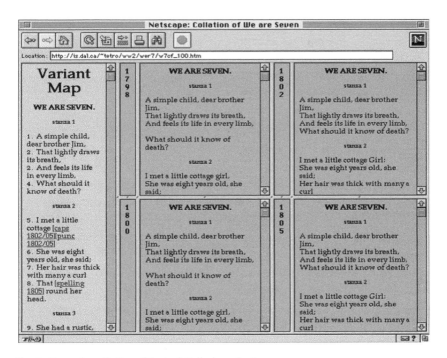

Fig. 2. Dynamic collation of *Lyrical Ballads* variants

More recently, we have moved beyond the Web page and HTML as such in *MOOzymandias*, an ambitious collaborative experiment in editing that situates Shelley's sonnet "Ozymandias" in a text-based multiuser virtual-reality environment, making the edition, its text and apparatus, more like a game or theatrical space than a letterpress artifact.[15] *MOOzymandias* was created to attempt what no existing markup scheme can really do well yet: deal with the multidirectional, spatialized, phenomenological effects of poetic language—and the multilayered complexity with which poems mean, in terms of both their presentational and structural features and in terms of the contextual editorial environments constructed by every edition through its acts of annotation and interpretation. Through *MOOzymandias* we are seeking to learn how the potential of the digital medium might be tapped in pursuit of new kinds of editions that engage editors and scholarly readers and researchers in collaborative editorial environments, foregrounding the making of knowledge as central to the editorial endeavor.

An experiment like *MOOzymandias* serves to highlight some of the limits of editions in traditional markup schemes, whether in HTML or XML.[16] While searchability, retrieval, and textual display are all important to take into account in electronic scholarly editions, there are other dimensions to be explored. Indeed, the digital medium promises to engage makers and users of editions in exciting new ways, to exploit the imaginative energy, ambiguity, and intertextual dynamics of literary works—and of poetry in particular—in ways that may call into question the customary relations between the edited text and its reader-user. Textual editors should be among those attempting such important and innovative experiments in electronic environments. There are, for instance, interesting possibilities for using 3-D editorial environments to interrelate text and apparatus, as suggested by Matthew Kirschenbaum ("Lucid Mapping").[17] We could even imagine future editions or archives structured as databases that could be customized to the needs and interests of individual users: first in response to a user's electronic registration form indicating those interests, then by the distribution of relevant information to users based on their behavior while interacting with the edition or archive, much as Amazon.com tailors itself to the behavior of customers.

In the meantime, we believe that given the current state of markup, institutional expectations, and the Web, editors would be well advised in the near future to use XML for most major electronic editions of poetry. But the challenge for editors of poetry working in such hierarchical markup schemata is to resist letting the computational and analytic powers of the digital environment eclipse an edition's performative and expressive possibilities, its use as an engine of artistic representation. Editors should strive to produce the richest possible editorial environment, to exploit the full range of resources provided by the digital medium. To date, however, as Susan Schreibman has recently noted, editors have largely played the "role of assembler of electronic texts," becoming "on the one hand the literary-librarian, building a library or the more commonly termed *archive* of multimedia objects, and on the other hand, the literary-encoder grappling with a logic more amenable to programmers than literary scholars . . . " (285).

Schreibman's editor as literary encoder has already at some point learned how to grapple with a logic native to computer programmers. As we have discovered over time through our work at *Romantic Circles*, those highly competent textual scholars who do not already possess such knowledge face an extremely steep learning curve, even though there are several helpful XML tutorials online and the TEI guidelines can also be found online or ordered in a two-volume letterpress edition that comes with a CD (see Sperberg-McQueen and Burnard, *Guidelines for Electronic Text Editing*, "Gentle Introduction"). In time, it is likely that tools will be developed that allow editors to produce simple markup by uploading the text and then filling in fields in an online form. (A version of such a form is already in development at the University of Maryland for use by the *Dickinson Electronic Archive*.) But such tools will not do away with the need for careful analysis of the structure of the text, detailed planning for the markup, and editorial judgment. For now, editors planning to use XML markup would do well to purchase a software editor, such as *XMetaL* or *OXygen*, that can facilitate uniform and valid encoding throughout the edition (even though such software, it must be acknowledged, has its own learning curve).

Our general advice to prospective editors of electronic editions of poetry is to consider the same kinds of questions facing scholarly editors of letterpress editions, especially when it comes to ensuring the accuracy and logical relations of the texts in question, but to frame these questions anew in the face of the procedural demands and interactive opportunities of the electronic medium. The relevant set of questions will vary from case to case but might include the following:[18]

1. What is the focus of the edition: form and structure, linguistic intertextuality, contextural relations and publishing history, the larger historical contexts for the material production and reception of the text? What are the relations among the various texts of the poetic work in question? Which variants, versions, or genetic layers will be included in the edition?

2. What markup scheme—HTML or XML, or some other subset of

SGML (using an existing DTD or creating a new one)—will optimize your ability to represent the features of the poetic text for the scholarly user? Is the primary goal an archival edition for computerized search and retrieval or an edition publicly accessible to students and others on the Web? What will be gained and lost in each case?

3. What kind of electronic apparatus or editorial environment will support the poetic text in this edition? Traditional lists of variants, hypertext clusters of other poems or contextual materials (including image, video, or sound files or specialized programs for manipulating the text), or more experimental architectures, such as collaborative editorial environments and forms-based encoding? (The TEI includes helpful standards on the critical apparatus.)

4. What plans are in place for long-term maintenance or updating of the edition, either the text itself or the apparatus? Where will the edition be published—online (and where?) or on CD-ROM or other medium? Will it be portable or translatable from one format or medium to another? Will it be stable? Will the edition's contents survive major changes in platforms, standards, or the protocols of the Internet? (These last questions, it should be clear, are meant to suggest the value of structural, descriptive encoding in SGML/XML.)

5. What electronic editions currently online might serve as helpful models? What can be learned by contacting the editors of such editions to gain the benefit of their experience?[19] These kinds of fundamental questions ought to be asked and answered before the project proper begins, though the initial set of answers is likely to be modified by subsequent experience. The answers, in turn, need to be evaluated by being applied to a test case, a sample poem or group of poems that embody the most challenging issues faced in the edition, so that all these issues are encountered beforehand and addressed at the level of editorial practice.

Finally, we would exhort the editor of an electronic edition to use editorial judgment and creativity (and to consider working collaboratively with others who have experience in technology and encoding) in designing an edition. In uniting a poem and the Net, the larger goal of an electronic scholarly edition should be not only to meet the current needs of the scholarly researcher but also to stimulate and challenge scholars of various kinds, including teachers, students, even poets and specialists in digital media, to use the text in order to make new knowledge—which is to say, to use it in ways none of us has yet fully imagined.

NOTES

1. On the split of "the computerized imagination" into two worldviews and the decision of the *Rossetti Archive* to build along a "double helix" of attention to both structure and appearance, see McGann, "Editing" 89. But note that one of McGann's analogues, "the gulf separating a Unix from a Mac world" (89), no longer applies, given Apple's recent release of OS X, an operating system built on Unix—which serves as a reminder of how quickly the computing landscape can change. The need for such divided attention, given the current state of markup, follows logically from McGann's earlier theoretical distinction between the bibliographic and linguistic codes of any text (e.g., in *Textual Condition* 12–14).

2. For the use of the term *contexture* to denote the contextuality provided for each poem by the larger frame in which it is placed, the intertextuality among poems so placed, and the resultant texture of resonance and meanings, see Fraistat, *Poem.*

3. *Romantic Circles*, coedited by Fraistat and Jones with Carl Stahmer, is found at www.rc.umd.edu. Online since 1996, the site has been published by the University of Maryland since 1998.

4. On the use of cascading stylesheets, see the W3C (World Wide Web Consortium) pages at www.w3.org/Style/.

5. The encyclopedic nature of hypertextuality, however, is often overrated and abused when there is no well-conceived interface to structure the information critically and coherently for users. Resources conceived as electronic archives, with all the expansiveness invited by that master trope, need to be especially aware of this danger.

6. MOO stands for "multi-user domain, object-oriented." The *Romantic Circles* MOO, the Villa Diodati, can be accessed at www.rc.umd.edu:7000.

7. This extension is basically the process that Theodor Nelson, who coined the term *hypertext*, had in mind when he speculated about the explicit intertextuality of virtual copies over the network, or the "transclusion" of one text by another. See his *Generalized Links.*

8. Two sections of the Text Encoding Initiative are especially useful for understanding these issues: on critical apparatus (sec. 19; www.tei-c.org/P4X/TC.html) and on the transcription of primary sources (sec. 18; www.tei-c.org/P4X/PH .html).

9. The TEI Lite–encoded version of "The Devil's Walk" is on the Electronic Text Center Web site: http://etext.lib.virginia.edu/toc/modeng/public/SheDevB .html. See also the larger SGML archive of which it is a part: *British Poetry, 1780–1910: A Hypertext Archive of Scholarly Editions* (http://etext.lib.virginia.edu/ britpo.html).

10. As browsers have conformed to newer and more restrictive standards for HTML, they are losing their ability to read resources encoded in older and more tolerant

HTML versions. XHTML combines the syntax of XML with the standards of HTML 4.01 and is read by browsers as well-formed XML markup. For a useful introduction as well as tutorials for learning XHTML, see www.w3schools.com/xhtml.

11. We have learned a great deal for this project from the Brown University Women Writers Project (www.wwp.brown.edu), which also collects far-flung poems under the rubric of an electronic database or anthology. See the essay by Julia Flanders in this volume.

12. For the use of the TEI *Pizza Chef* to build a customized DTD, see the TEI page www.tei-c.org/pizza.html. We recommend this method for projects in their formative stages; many will find that TEI Lite is sufficient for their purposes; others will quickly discover that they need a wider range of tag sets, for which they can consult TEI documentation.

13. XSLT (XSL transformations) is a subdivision of XSL (extensible stylesheet language), whose purpose is to transform an XML document into another XML document. For XSLT, see www.w3.org/TR/xslt. Samples of two different Java-driven XSLT engines for transforming XML to HTML can be found at *The Melville Electronic Library* (www.iath.virginia.edu/melville).

14. For a more extensive discussion of the rationale and structure of their edition, see Graver and Tetreault.

15. *MOOzymandias* can be browsed on the Web (not in the fully interactive MOO version) by going to www.rc.umd.edu:7000/705/. For a fuller discussion of *MOOzymandias* as a new kind of textual edition, see Fraistat and Jones.

16. Schreibman usefully summarizes the current debate about the limitations inherent in SGML (and its derivatives) to the understanding of a poem as an ordered hierarchy of content objects. To get beyond the limitations of editions or archives that are structured merely as ordered hierarchies, Schreibman suggests that electronic editions might be fundamentally organized to represent multiple versions of the same work and that electronic archives might be developed whose primary purpose is to represent a work's reception history. Those editors interested in textual versioning should know that Schreibman has led a team at the Maryland Institute for Technology in the Humanities in the development of a new and freely available software tool, *The Versioning Machine*, an editorial environment "designed . . . for displaying and comparing multiple versions of texts" (*Versioning*).

17. Elsewhere we discuss, in the light of experiments Robert Coover has been doing in Brown University's Virtual Reality Chamber, the possibility of textual editions in a form that would allow, for example, Shelley or Joyce scholars to make and share discoveries about the text while inside *Prometheus Unbound* or *Ulysses* (see Fraistat and Jones 75).

18. These questions are adapted from the CSE's Guidelines for Scholarly Editions, which appear in the present volume. See also www.mla.org/cse_guidelines.

19. For a list of projects currently using the TEI, see www.tei-c.org/Applications/ index-subj.html.

DRAMA CASE STUDY:
THE CAMBRIDGE EDITION OF
THE WORKS OF BEN JONSON

DAVID GANTS

To engage in textual and editorial scholarship is to enter into a dialogue: with past men and women responsible for the creation and transmission of linguistic works, with current scholars and students negotiating among various theoretical perspectives, and with future readers and teachers who will use and ultimately displace the editions that come down to them from us. Since the emergence of the scholar-editor toward the end of the nineteenth century, the relative emphasis given the voices of the past, present, and future has shifted a number of times, and with those shifts has come a succession of overlapping editorial principles. The current state of affairs is fairly complex,[1] but the essential issues facing an editor embarking on a new project center on the weight given to the role of author or authors in the initial textual creation, to the treatment of historical reception and material production in the overall interpretive presentation of the text, and to the forms in which the planned edition will be issued.

The Cambridge Edition of the Works of Ben Jonson (CEWBJ) project has navigated these critical waters since it emerged from a series of meetings and conferences organized by Ian Donaldson, David Bevington, and Martin Butler in the 1990s, events that sought to generate ideas for a new edition of Ben Jonson's collected works.[2] The current standard edition is the monumental but outdated Oxford *Ben Jonson* of C. H. Herford, Percy Simpson, and Evelyn Simpson. While the eleven-volume work was published between 1925 and 1952, the initial contracts were issued in the 1890s, and the final volume to contain Jonsonian texts (volume 8, *The Poems and Prose Works*) was published in 1947, three years before W. W. Greg's ground-breaking "The

Rationale of Copy-Text." From the perspective of current editorial theory, therefore, the texts of Herford, Simpson, and Simpson present numerous problems. Furthermore, the Oxford edition has no concordance or adequate index; the format of text on page is increasingly arcane and difficult to use; the text lacks serious consideration of the circumstances of staging; and, perhaps most important, materials relating to one work are often distributed among five or six volumes. The goal of the Cambridge general editors is to reedit the Jonson canon for scholars, teachers, and students using current historical, literary, and textual approaches, and to present the results of this initiative in a comprehensive and well-organized fashion that makes full use of all modes of textual reproduction.

To this end, the *CEWBJ* is envisioned as two complementary but materially distinct projects that together attempt to participate in the continuing editorial dialogue: a six-volume traditional edition that will be published in print form, and a networked electronic edition that, while initially released simultaneously with the print edition, will continue to develop dynamically on its own as scholarship and technology advance. The print side will present all Jonson's works in modernized form, with introductions and annotations; essays exploring the historical, social, political, artistic, literary, and theatrical environment in which he worked; and an extensive bibliography of Jonson scholarship. More than two dozen contributing editors have worked on the print edition, proceeding from an editorial rationale based on authorial intention and emerging from fresh examinations of early manuscript and print witnesses, primary documentary evidence, and a reevaluation of four centuries of scholarly commentary.

The initial version of the electronic side will contain all the print edition in digital form as well as the complete old-spelling texts and image facsimiles of all the early print and manuscript witnesses, a full census of those witnesses, life and court-masque primary archives, performance calendars, a reconstruction of Jonson's library, and a diverse collection of other materials that might help us better understand these important works. Once the basic electronic archive is completed, the developmental strategy will shift from traditional to innovative, from compiling and organizing the essential evidence to investigating and analyzing the complex possible interactions among the various elements. As each part of the electronic edition accrues many layers of cross-referencing, the resource will form a dense research matrix in which individual items connect with one another in sophisticated ways. Hypertext theorists refer to this complex and unpredictable texture as *rhyzomatic*, a term that comes from the tangled root structure beneath a field of grass, a non-hierarchical mass of ever-growing links between and among tufts.

The primary research goal of this second and ongoing editorial phase is to explore and exploit the rapidly expanding potential of electronic publishing. In terms of content this goal means fully reconceptualizing the relation between the structural demands placed on information by computer networks and the needs of the scholars, teachers, and students who will use those resources. Many electronic archives and editions rely on relatively simple frameworks that structure material according to rigorous hierarchies branching from a central core. These organizing principles are partly the result of the way computers process information and partly the result of editors' following traditional print-based models. Consequently the digital archives themselves are peculiarly static—they provide for the possibility of addition but not reorganization of material. Unlike such rigid e-text collections, the *CEWBJ* seeks to explore the vision of electronic textuality imagined by Jerome McGann in his influential "The Rationale of HyperText." Rather than simply generate yet one more centralized archive, we will embrace emerging technologies to distribute editorial power among the users, to provide them "the means for establishing an indefinite number of 'centers,' and for expanding their number as well as altering their relationships. One [will be] encouraged not so much to find as to make order—and then to make it again and again, as established orderings expose their limits" (29). The *CEWBJ* will thus create a new paradigm for organizing digital scholarly editions, but at the same time it will seek new ways of delivering and using its complex materials. Current search-and-display strategies serve hierarchically structured collections, but they can only skim the edges of an interwoven information matrix. Concurrent with the shift in editorial design from hierarchical to rhyzomatic, a series of intensive research-and-development initiatives will come into more robust delivery modes designed specifically for this new type of resource.

At the center of any editorial project, of course, resides the text, and the accuracy of the authorial materials must be a continuing concern. The *CEWBJ* derives its core texts from manual and keyboarded transcriptions of the source witnesses, employing either copies of the early quartos and folios owned by editors or the UMI Early English Books series of microfilm facsimiles, along with on-site transcriptions of manuscripts held in research archives.[3] The print edition's contributing editors had the choice of using the keyboarded texts or generating their own transcriptions, which in turn formed the basis for their modernized texts. Proofing of each work and its attendant secondary materials will occur in three stages: the first proofreading sequence is the responsibility of the individual contributing editors, the second will be performed by the general editors, and the third by Cambridge University Press.

The original spelling texts on which the electronic edition is based derive completely from keyboard transcriptions of the printed sources and manual transcriptions of the manuscript sources. The initial texts were keyboarded twice and the resulting copies compared electronically against each other as the first stage of proofing. In addition, because digital facsimiles of early modern books often contain obscured or deleted text, the keyboarding firm was instructed to transcribe only those characters that the persons responsible for the actual data entry could positively identify. Any material not readily identified was tagged with an <unclear> marker. The second stage of proofing consists of concordances generated as a guide for identifying typographic errors, followed by a manual reading of the electronic text against its source facsimile (during which the <unclear> passages are restored).[4] Finally, the general and electronic editors will proof the entire electronic edition.

EDITING DRAMA

Considered structurally, drama consists of spoken language presented in soliloquial or dialogic form. These speeches are usually organized into a sequence of scenes, which in the Western tradition can also be grouped into acts. Typographically the representation of this structure on the printed page has changed very little since the first publication of interludes in the early sixteenth century. Figure 1 shows a few lines of dialogue between Cornelius and a servant named B from *Fulgens and Lucrece*, the earliest extant example of printed drama (Medwall; published by John Rastell c. 1512–16). Despite the use of the now-arcane black-letter face, the exchange looks strikingly

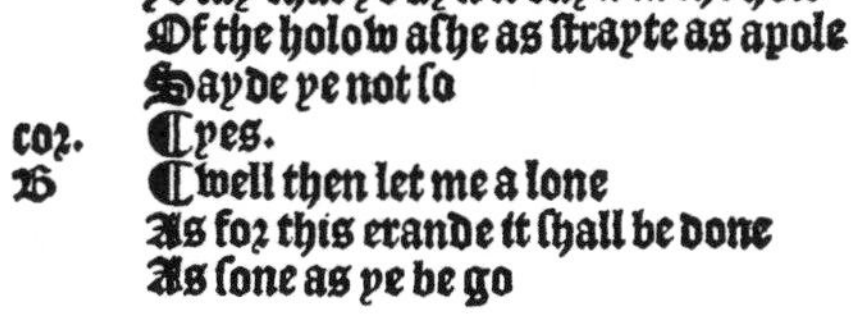

Fig. 1. *Fulgens and Lucrece*, sig. E4r. Reproduced by permission of the British Library, shelfmark C.60.h.19

similar to a contemporary paperback play. The speech prefixes are set left and the initial line of each speech marked with an early version of the paragraph symbol (¶), providing the reader with a simple device for keeping track of who is speaking. During this time, speech prefixes were also centered above the corresponding text and prefixed with a fleuron, as shown in figure 2, in the exchange between Pity and Contemplation from the 1550 quarto edition of *Hycke Scorner*, printed by John Waley.

When printing these early interludes, stationers primarily followed the conventions employed in the production of manuscript collections (the layout of the mystery plays in the N-Town manuscript, for example, closely resembles that of the 1550 *Hycke Scorner*).

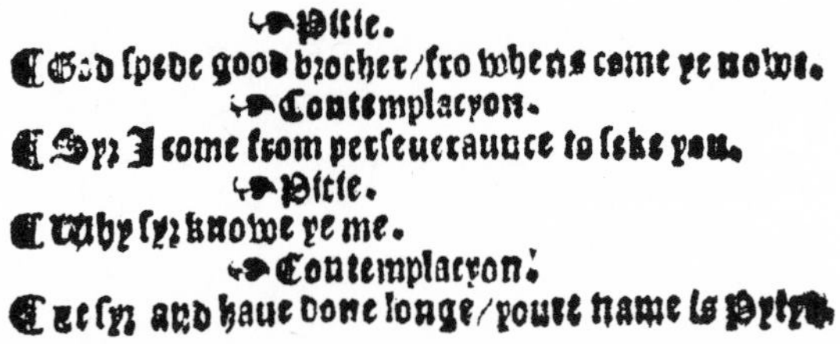
Pitie.
¶ God spede good brother/fro whens come ye nowe.
Contemplacyon.
¶ Syr I come from perseueraunce to seke you.
Pitie.
¶ Why syr knowe ye me.
Contemplacyon.
¶ Ye syr and haue done longe/youre name is Pyte.

Fig. 2. *Hycke Scorner*, sig. A2v. Reproduced by permission of the Bodleian Library, University of Oxford, shelfmark Mal.330

Beyond speech, however, printed drama can also contain a variety of components that interpret the theatrical circumstances of the work for the reader—character lists, stage directions and descriptions, acting notes, and details of real or ideal performance. These details may derive from authorial instructions meant for the stage, ranging from simple sound cues to the complex visual alienation devices employed by Bertolt Brecht. In many cases printed plays will also contain nonauthorial stage directions, added by the editor or publisher to help the reader follow the action in the theater of the mind. Sometimes a play text may include material never meant for the theatrical audience, such as George Bernard Shaw's famous final direction from *Candida*: "They embrace. But they do not know the secret in the poet's heart."

Again, early printed drama provides numerous examples of how printers learned to use format to distinguish among the textual components. Cornelius responds to B's line "As sone as ye be go" (fig. 1) with the lines in figure 3. Here the stage direction "Et exeat corne[lius]" is right-justified to be distinguished from Cornelius's exit line. The early 1520s octavo of John Rastell's *The Nature of the Four Elements* contains a cast of characters, an abstract of the interlude's main points, a musical score for the songs, and even suggestions for cutting the piece:

> whiche interlude yf ye hole matter be playd wyl conteyne the space of an hour and a halfe / but yf ye lyst ye may leue out muche of the sad mater as the messengers pte / and some of naturys parte and some of experyens pte & yet the matter wyl de pend conuenyently / and than it wyll not be paste thre quarters of an hour of length. (sig. A1r)

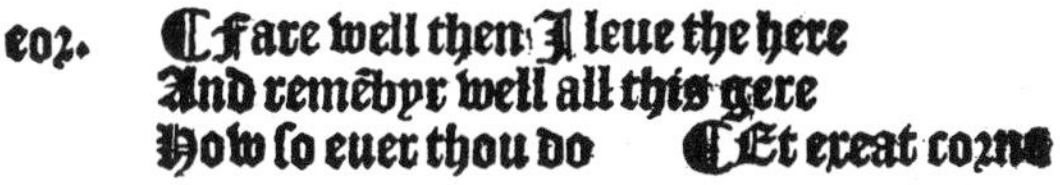

eo². **Cfare well then:I leue the here**
And remēbyr well all this gere
How so euer thou do   CEt ereat corne

Fig. 3. *Fulgens and Lucrece*, sig. E4r. Reproduced by permission of the British Library, shelfmark C.60.h.19

A 1559 octavo translation of Seneca's tragedy *Troas*, printed by Richard Tottle, includes act and scene divisions as well as speech prefixes in-line with the text. Once printers started using roman and italic faces instead of black letter in the 1580s, they could differentiate speech prefix and speech typographically; this differentiation by font became the model for the next four centuries. By the late sixteenth or early seventeenth century, authors began to bring an awareness of format and design elements to their work, sometimes providing in their holograph manuscripts a template for the printed book.[5]

In addition to the text within the covers of a book, theatrical works frequently refer implicitly or explicitly to materials beyond the printed page. The many ballad operas produced and printed following the success of John Gay's *The Beggar's Opera* (1728) assumed a knowledge on the part of the readers of the tunes associated with each song, while Ben Jonson loaded many of his plays and masques with a thick shell of annotation until they resembled not so much popular play texts as religious tomes. In each case the secondary references form part of the work's linguistic and sociohistorical nexus.

Finally, most twentieth-century editorial work rested on the theoretical underpinnings of the new bibliography, proceeded from an assumption of the primacy of the author, and sought "to reconstruct the text of works as intended by their creators" (Tanselle, *Rationale* 92). In the process, less-than-careful editors often treated the physical evidence on which complex editorial decisions were based as sterile accumulations of quantitative data.[6] But recent scholarship on both sides of the Atlantic has underlined the need for editors to recognize anew the expressive nature of physical forms and to investigate "how material texts of all kinds have been conceptualized, produced, marketed, and consumed at specific moments in history" (Marcus 3). Critics such as D. F. McKenzie offered an approach that sought to "show the human presence in any recorded text" (*Bibliography* 20). Exploiting the ability of emerging digital technologies to create and circulate high-quality reproductions of printed books and manuscripts as well as link together disparate classes of evidence, recent projects have attempted to reimagine the scholarly edition in hypertextual terms, freeing the text from the constraints of the physical codex form. The result has been an evolving set of editorial rationales that, as McGann and others have suggested, envision an interactive relation between text and user, one that encourages a creative dialogue in a literary and textual community.

ENCODING DRAMA

From the outset the Text Encoding Initiative recognized the special textual and material requirements of theatrical works, including in its guidelines a set of encoding strategies designed specifically for drama. John Lavagnino and Elli Mylonas have already addressed the issues surrounding the application to performance texts of the earlier TEI guidelines for SGML, and the following XML-based overview is greatly indebted to their insightful and clearheaded analysis.

Speech, the component common to almost every dramatic work throughout history, is encoded with the <sp> element (Sperberg-McQueen and Burnard, *Guidelines for Electronic Text Encoding*, sec. 10.2.2). The two most prevalent materials in this container are the speech prefix, encoded as <speaker>, and the contents of the speech, encoded according to simple generic categories such as <p> or <l> (discussed below). In the printed drama, a speech prefix may vary according to the needs of the work. If the perception of a character by an audience is meant to change over the course of the evening, then an editor may wish to mirror that changing perception on the page by manipulating the speech prefix. For example, in Anthony Shaffer's mystery *Sleuth* the Milo Tindle character adopts the disguise of Inspector

Doppler for the first half of the second act, fooling his antagonist Andrew Wyke and (one hopes) the audience as well. Similarly characters may first appear on stage anonymously and have their characters revealed only later. Plays that deal with English historical subjects will often alter the speech prefix assigned a character as the title and status of that character change— for example, Bolingbroke becomes Henry IV and Gloucester becomes Richard III. In each case the contents encoded in the `<speaker>` tag will change, even though the character remains constant. The device linking these shifting prefixes is the who attribute to the `<sp>` tag. Asper, one of the three characters who act as a sort of chorus in Jonson's *Every Man out of His Humour*, steps from his role as commentor at the beginning of the piece and into that of Macilente, one of the lead roles in the play proper. His opening speech of act 1, scene 1, might be tagged:

```
<sp who="Asper"><speaker>Macilente</speaker>
<l>Viri est, fortunæ cæcitatem facilè ferre.</l>
<l>'Tis true; but, Stoique, where (in the world)</l>
<l>Doth that man breathe, that can so much command</l>
<l>His bloud, and his affection?</l></sp>
```

Application of the constant who attribute allows researchers to interrogate the linguistic aspects of a character across an entire play or, in play cycles,[7] across multiple works.

The contents of a speech (see Sperberg-McQueen and Burnard, *Guidelines for Electronic Text Encoding*, sec. 10.2.4) usually consist of prose or verse text in a variety of arrangements; a prose paragraph is encoded as `<p>`, while a line of verse appears within the `<l>` tag. Furthermore, verse organized in stanzas, verse paragraphs, or other poetic structures can be encoded in linegroup `<lg>` tags. For lines and line groups, the TEI supports a set of attributes to help editors further define the characteristics of the subject text. Multiple characters in a scene, particularly in early modern works, sometimes share complete lines of verse. In such instances it is helpful to use the part attribute to the `<l>` element, assigning the values "I," "M," or "F" according to whether the line segment in question is in the initial, medial, or final position. This sequence from act 1, scene 2, of Jonson's *The Alchemist* consists of verse lines shared between two characters, which the 1612 quarto and 1616 folio editions represent thus (fig. 4). The printer has retained the visual integrity of the individual verse line while using small caps to indicate speech prefixes

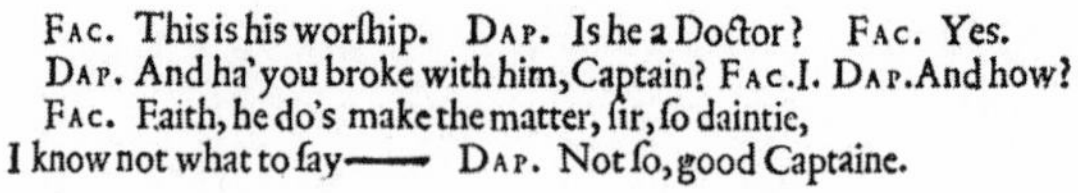

Fᴀᴄ. This is his worſhip. Dᴀᴘ. Is he a Doᴄtor? Fᴀᴄ. Yes.
Dᴀᴘ. And ha' you broke with him, Captain? Fᴀᴄ.I. Dᴀᴘ.And how?
Fᴀᴄ. Faith, he do's make the matter, ſir,ſo daintie,
I know not what to ſay—— Dᴀᴘ. Notſo,good Captaine.

Fig. 4. STC 14751, sig. 3E6r

and distinguish between the speakers. Because typographic choice is important to early printed drama, the rend attribute can be especially useful in
encoding such visual features. Common values include italics for the italic
face and sc for small caps. The *CEWBJ* encodes the above passage in this
way:

```
<sp who="Face"><speaker rend="sc">Fac.</speaker>
 <l part="I">This is his worship.</l></sp>
<sp who="Dapper"><speaker rend="sc">Dap.</speaker>
 <l part="M">Is he a Doctor?</l></sp>
<sp who="Face"><speaker rend="sc">Fac.</speaker>
 <l part="F">Yes.</l></sp>
<sp who="Dapper"><speaker rend="sc">Dap.</speaker>
 <l part="I">And ha' you broke with him, Captain?</l></sp>
<sp who="Face"><speaker rend="sc">Fac.</speaker>
 <l part="M">I.</l></sp>
<sp who="Dapper"><speaker rend="sc">Dap.</speaker>
 <l part="F">And how?</l></sp>
<sp who="Face"><speaker rend="sc">Fac.</speaker>
 <l>Faith, he do's make the matter, sir, so dainties,</l>
 <l part="I">I know not what to say&mdash;</l></sp>
<sp who="Dapper"><speaker rend="sc">Dap.</speaker>
 <l part="F">No so, good Captaine.</l> </sp>[8]
```

In more highly structured poetry, the <lg> attribute type is used to
identify the particular verse strategy being described. Much of Jonson's plays
are in blank verse that has a fairly loose metrical structure, and grouping these
passages with the type value verse paragraph usually provides enough analytic information. But along with the basic encoding of verse forms one can
also include information about the rhyme scheme and metrical pattern using
the rhyme and met attributes (see sec. 9.4). Toward the beginning of Jonson's
masque *Hymenæi*, the character Pan speaks in quatrains in which the first

three lines contain three iambs and the fourth contains five. A sample encoded quatrain would look like this:

```
<sp who="Hymen"><speaker>HYMEN.</speaker>
  <lg type="quatrain" rhyme="abab" met="-+-+-+|-+-+-+|-+
    -+-+|-+-+-+-+-+">
  <l>'Tis so: this same is he,</l>
  <l>The king, and priest of peace!</l>
  <l>And that his Empresse, she,</l>
  <l>That sits so crowned with her owne increase!</l></lg>
</sp>
```

The immediate performance instructions that accompany the dramatic speech acts fall under the general rubric of stage directions, and the encoding strategies for this information split into two basic categories. The `<stage>` tag is used to mark the nonverbal stage directions included in a piece of dramatic text and employs the **type** attribute, while the `<move>` tag signals the actual movement of a character or characters on, off, or around the stage. This latter tag functions mainly as a supplement to the textual stage directions, filling in where actual directions are lacking or serving to help the reader keep track of the entrances and exits of all characters. The `<move>` tag is empty and usually employs three attributes: **type** (e.g., entrance or exit), **who** (identifying the character in motion), and **where** (to further specify the movement if necessary).

Toward the end of Jonson's *The Alchemist*, the two puritan characters Ananias and Tribulation are driven from the house of Lovewit by Drugger the tobacconist. The 1612 quarto edition of the play has no stage directions at all, while the 1616 folio (and subsequent editions) include the marginal note, "Drugger enters, and he beats him away." Modern editions of the play often add bracketed stage directions indicating the exit of the two puritans, but the *CEWBJ* encodes the folio version of the passage using a combination of `<stage>` and `<move>`:

```
<sp who="Ananias"><speaker rend="sc">Ana.</speaker>
  <l part="F">I will pray there,</l>
  <l>Against thy house: may dogs defile thy walls,</l>
  <l>And waspes, and hornets breed beneath thy roofe,</l>
  <l>This seat of false-hood, and this caue of cos'nage</l></sp>
```

```
<stage type="entrance" rend="italic"> Drugger enters, and he
  beats him away.
  <move who="Drugger" type="entrance"/>
  <move who="Ananias" type="exit"/>
  <move who="Tribulation" type="exit"/>
</stage>
<sp who="Lovewit"><speaker rend="sc">Lov.</speaker>
  <l part="I">Another too?</l></sp>
<sp who="Drugger"><speaker rend="sc">Drv.</speaker>
  <l part="F">Not I sir, I am no <emph rend="italic">
  Brother</emph></l></sp>
```

Speeches and stage directions make up the bulk of a play text, which is in turn typically grouped into acts and scenes. For a play presented on the popular stage, the use of numbered <div> elements along with type and n attributes provides the necessary structural framework, with the <head> element reserved for header information contained in the text (see sec. 10.2.1). The first scene in Jonson's *Poetaster* might look like this:

```
<div0 type="act" n="1">
<div1 type="scene" n="1">
  <head rend="italic"> Act I. Scene I.</head>
  <stage type="characters" rend="sc">Ovid, Lvscvs</stage>
<!-- . . . --></div1></div0>
```

While Jonson's plays employ a vertical hierarchy, his masques and entertainments are much more horizontally structured, consisting of a mixture of speeches, songs, dances, and prose commentary. In these works the use of numbered <div> elements in a flat structure may seem excessive; but mixing numbered and unnumbered <div> elements can cause processing problems, so the *CEWBJ* employs numbered <div> elements throughout the archive.

A play will often have, beyond the body of the text, one or more related components, such as a prologue and epilogue, a description of the set and lighting, information about a specific performance, and a list of characters. This last section contains a variety of fairly well structured items as well as referential links to the body of the text itself (such as the who attribute to the <sp> element discussed above), requiring a more detailed encoding strategy. *Every Man in His Humour*, the first play in the Jonson folio of 1616, has both an initial cast of characters with brief descriptions and a list at the end of the play of the "principall Comædians" in the Lord Chamberlain's Men who acted the piece in 1598. A partial list of the cast of characters for this play might be encoded using the `<castList>` element for the basic container and the `<role>` and `<roleDesc>` elements for the individual entries:

```
<castList>
    <role id="Knowell" rend="sc">Kno'well</role>
    <roleDesc rend="italic">An old Gentleman</roleDesc>
    <role id="EdKnowell" rend="sc">Ed. Kno'well</role>
    <roleDesc rend="italic">His Sonne</roleDesc>
    <role id="Brainworm" rend="sc">Brayne-worme</role>
    <roleDesc rend="italic">The Fathers man</roleDesc>
    <role id="Stephen" rend="sc">Mr. Stephen</role>
    <roleDesc rend="italic">A countrey Gull</roleDesc>
<!-- . . . --></castList>
```

Notice that the id attribute to the `<role>` element is a unique identifier to which all references to that particular character can be pointed, including the `<sp>` element. Likewise the list of actors that follows the play in the 1616 folio can be encoded using the `<castItem>` container and `<actor>` elements, with the traditional identification of William Shakespeare as the performer who first played Knowell included through the id attribute. For grouped characters the `<castGroup>` element serves to mark off a subset of performers from the larger listing of characters. For example, in the preliminary cast list for Jonson's *Epicoene*, three members of a literary salon are listed with a three-line bracket to the right that points to a single description of all three characters, a structure that might be encoded thus:

```
<castGroup rend="braced">
    <castItem><role id="Haughty" rend="sc">Mad. Havghty</role>
    </castItem>
    <castItem><role id="Centaur" rend="sc">Mad. Centavre</role>
    </castItem>
    <castItem><role id="Mavis" rend="sc">Mrs. Mavis</role>
    </castItem>
    <trailer rend="italic">Ladies Collegiates</trailer>
</castGroup>
```

Each of the above examples presents a textual unit organized in a fairly hierarchical fashion, an arrangement ideal for the structural nesting principle at the heart of XML's design. But in practice literary works rarely conform to vertical hierarchies for very long, instead evolving sophisticated linguistic patterns that overlap and overlay in complex ways. The TEI guidelines offer a number of solutions to the problem of multiple hierarchies—for example, using a lattice of pointers and targets or linking elements with location ladders—although none are completely satisfactory (see sec. 31 for a more detailed discussion of this question). When dealing with performance works in which intersecting structures are part of the fabric of the text, marking the individual pieces in an aggregate fashion and employing the `<join>` element to coordinate them all has proved especially useful (see sec. 14 for a more detailed discussion of this option). Toward the end of Jonson's historical tragedy *Sejanus*, the title character is denounced by Tiberius in a letter read before the senate. The public reading of the letter is interrupted a number of times in both stage asides and public utterances, resulting in two concurrent, overlapping structures—the speeches and the letter. The first portion of this sequence is encoded:

```
<sp who="Arruntius">
  <speaker rend="sc">Arr.</speaker>
  <l part="I">O, most tame slauerie, and fierce flatterie!</l>
</sp>
<sp who="Praecones">
  <speaker rend="sc">Prae.</speaker>
  <l part="F">Silence.</l>
</sp>
<join targets="a1 a2 a3 a4 a5 a6 a7 a8 a9 a10"
    result="letter"/>
<stage>The Epistle is read.</stage>
<sp who="Praecones">
  <p id="a1">TIBERIVS CAESAR<lb/>TO THE<lb/>
    SENATE<lb/>GREETING.</p>
  <p>If you, Conscript Father, with your children, bee in
    health, it is aboundantly well: wee with our friends here,
    are so.</p>
<!-- . . . --></sp>
<sp who="Arruntius" type="aside">
  <speaker rend="sc">Arr.</speaker>
```

```
<l>The lapwing, the lapwing.</l>
</sp>
<sp who="Praecones">
  <p id="a2">Yet, in things, which shall worthily, and more
    neere concerne the maiestie of a prince, we shall feare to
    be so cruell to our owne fame, as to neglect them.</p>
<!-- . . . --></sp>
<sp who="Arruntius" type="aside">
  <speaker rend="sc">Arr.</speaker>
  <l>This touches, the bloud turnes.</l>
</sp>
<sp who="Praecones">
  <p id="a3">But wee affie in your loues, and vnderstandings, and
    doe no way suspect the merit of our SEIANVS to make our
    fauors offensiue to any.</p>
<!-- . . . --></sp>
```

Each section of the letter is assigned a unique identifier from a1 through a10, and any program designed to process the text can reconstruct the letter as a single unit by using the information in the <join> element.

A strategy similar to <join> is used when representing simultaneous speech and action in a stage play. Each component receives a unique id and the overlapping relation is declared with the **corresp** attribute to the <stage> element (see sec. 10.2.6). For example, in the middle of Jonson's comedy *Bartholomew Fair* the ballad singer Nightingale performs a song about cutpurses while a second character is having his pocket picked and a third comments on the unfolding scene. The 1631 folio edition of this play places the commentary to the immediate right of the song with vertical braces to indicate simultaneity and the stage directions in the usual left columnar position. These visual indicators can be translated into XML thus:

```
<sp who="Nightingale" id="b1">
  <speaker rend="sc">Nig.</speaker>
  <l>But o, you vile nation of cutpurses all,</l>
  <l>Relent and repent, and amend and be found,</l>
  <l>And know that you ought not, by honest mens fall,</l>
  <l>Aduance your owne fortues, to die aboue ground,</l>
  <!-- . . . -->
</sp>
```

```
<sp who="Winwife" id="b2">
  <speaker rend="sc">Win.</speaker>
  <p>Will you see sport? looke, there's a fellow gathers vp to
    him, marke.</p>
</sp>
<stage corresp="b1 b2" type="business">Edgeworth gets vp to
  him, and tickles him in the eare with a straw twice to draw his
  hand out of his pocket.</stage>
```

The **corresp** attribute provides the processing instructions needed to reconstruct the performance circumstances in whatever format is required.

Jonson was perhaps the most typographically conscious playwright of
his time, working with London stationers to create a diverse group of quite
sophisticated publications. Scholars have shown that he contributed at every
level to the design and printing of the 1605 quarto edition of *Sejanus*, not
only arranging the complex mixture of text and commentary on the page
but also selecting the type and paper out of which the quarto was fashioned.
Likewise complex bibliographic evidence derived from a close physical study
of the justly famous folio *Workes* of 1616 shows the author participating (and
meddling) throughout the long and complicated volume. The challenges
facing the project team, then, revolve around the need to retain as much of
the expressive information embodied in the physical object as possible while
at the same time enabling scholars and students to generate new expressions.

The encoding strategies discussed above emerged out of the editors'
desire to achieve a balance between tradition and innovation, between structure and freedom. On the one hand, the *CEWBJ* will provide access to a
variety of visual representations of the source documents, including the stylized format of the modernized print edition, digital facsimiles of the source
documents, and electronic reconstructions derived from the XML-encoded
original spelling texts. On the other hand, users will be encouraged to move
beyond the received forms, employ emerging technologies to generate fresh
approaches, and imagine new ways of understanding the verbal icons that
have come down to us from the past.

NOTES

1. Among the recent overviews of editorial options a few stand out for their balance
   of theoretical acumen and practical insight. Greetham, *Textual Scholarship*; Hill;
   Shillingsburg, *Scholarly Editing*; Tanselle, "Varieties."

2. Some of the main concerns behind the project have been laid out by D. Bevington and by I. Donaldson.

3. Keyboarding was done by Remote Services, Inc., of Vancouver, Washington.

4. The second stage of proofing was carried out under the auspices of the Electronic Text Centers at the University of Virginia and University of New Brunswick.

5. Perhaps the most famous early-seventeenth-century example is the manuscript copy Jonson prepared of his *Masque of Queens* for Prince Henry. Sample facsimile pages have been published in a number of venues.

6. Such efforts did not prevent scholars from attempting to humanize their object of study. Jeffrey Masten has noted how compositor studies of the Shakespeare First Folio often include implied biographic characteristics of an anonymous printing-house worker, a "composite-compositor-sketch" (84).

7. For example, the famous first and second War of the Roses tetralogies of Shakespeare's Henry and Richard plays.

8. For a discussion of special language and character sets, see Sperberg-McQueen and Burnard, *Guidelines for Electronic Text Encoding*, ch. 4.

THE WOMEN WRITERS PROJECT: A DIGITAL ANTHOLOGY

JULIA FLANDERS

I n the transition to the digital medium, the anthology has undergone a number of significant changes—not least because the constraints that give print anthologies their distinctive character have been largely removed, while the methodological boundaries that separated the anthology from more strictly conceived editions have blurred. In describing the work of the Women Writers Project (WWP) in this case study, I discuss a collection that began in the spirit of a traditional anthology and then evolved under the influence of the past decade's debates about electronic editing and digital textuality. The result is a collection that has been described variously as an archive, an edition, and an anthology and serves, in a sense, the purposes of all three.

Despite the range of textual approaches implied by these three terms, the original spirit of the anthology still animates the creation of these new digital collections. What was essential about print anthologies was their aim of bringing together a wide range of material bound by some common factor: a period, an author, a genre, a language. The constraints of space typically require that a print anthology emphasize brief works or excerpts, and at first this may appear to be a functional constraint as well: allowing the reader to focus quickly on the qualities the anthology seeks to highlight, without having to grapple with long texts in their entirety. To manage the problem of sheer scale, the anthology, like the canon, exercises a strategic simplification. But with the digital anthology this same strategic purchase can be achieved not through exclusion and brevity but through the intelligence of the data itself, which can enable the reader to discover the thematic subcollections within a larger assembly of texts.

This emphasis on readerly discovery is part of a crucial shift that has shaped the digital collection and its editorial assumptions. The digital collection, unlike the typical print anthology, has a history of self-consciousness about editing—both in the sense of being uneasy about it and in the sense of wanting to foreground the collection's own activities. This self-consciousness has double roots in the early discourse surrounding digital texts. For one thing, the initial scholarly distrust of digital texts encouraged an emphasis on full disclosure: responsible digital projects went far beyond ordinary print practice to document their sources and methods and to provide the reader with careful linkages to the "real" textual world. At the same time, the enthusiasm for the democratizing possibilities of digital texts (typified in early works such as George Landow's *Hypertext* and Richard Lanham's *The Electronic Word*) suggested that digital texts might constitute a critique of the politics of the printed word, including those of traditional editorial practice. Digital projects in the theoretical forefront took up the challenge of giving readers access to raw, unedited textual information (hence the "electronic archive") and to whatever editorial decisions were to be made—to make the reader a potential participant in the editorial process, or at least not its unwitting and passive consumer. Early discussions of text encoding, too, foregrounded the question of whether encoding itself was, or could be, an objective process or whether it inevitably constituted an editorial intervention. Even though the climate of these debates has changed over time, they have helped establish the assumption that readers can and should be given a much more participatory and knowledgeable role in the process that brings a text finally before their eyes.

This trend has resulted in digital methods in which the source text retains a distinct existence in the electronic edition instead of being consumed and ultimately effaced by the editing process. Editors wishing to provide the reader with access to the unedited source materials and also to an edited final product can do so by using an encoding system such as SGML (or, more recently, XML), through which multiple witnesses and their complex relations may be represented simultaneously. The final editorial decisions as to which reading is preferred may be encoded as well, in such a way that the reader can explore not only a given editor's choices but also the roads not taken: other plausible hypotheses and useful representations based on the same source texts. Editions like the *Canterbury Tales* Project (see www.cta.dmu.ac .uk/projects/ctp/) or the Piers Plowman *Electronic Archive* (see www.iath .virginia.edu/piers/) offer exceptionally rich ground for such an approach— and indeed could not be conceived without it—but even in less editorially fertile collections the reader can usefully be offered choices such as whether to view modernized or unmodernized spellings, original capitalization, relevant excerpts or full texts. And although this distinction between "raw" source text and the editorial cooking it may receive needs to be tempered by an acknowledgment of how much cooking is already present in the encoding of the source, the distinction usefully reflects what is for the reader an important new set of opportunities that had not been available before.

If one result of these developments has been a tendency to view a digital collection in the spirit of an archive—as a body of source material on which may be built a superstructure of metadata, retrieval and analysis tools, and editorial decisions—the corollary has been an almost ironic interest in the materiality of the text. At its most thoroughgoing, this interest results in an approach like that of the *Rossetti Archive* (see www.rossettiarchive.org/), in which the physical details of the original text are captured and foregrounded as fundamentally constitutive of the text's significance. Few collections go to such lengths; indeed, most digital anthologies capture very little structural or physical detail from the source. But as the information transcribed diminishes, the ubiquity of page images rises, so that the information to which the reader has most direct access is in fact the physical sequence and appearance of the source. The challenge posed by projects like the *Rossetti Archive* is how to capture bibliographic codes and textual materiality in ways that represent them usefully to readers: not simply as visible cues but as data that can give one leverage on the text.

The digital anthology or collection emerges out of these debates and possibilities not so much as a particular kind of artifact but as a set of activities—activities that are actually very similar to those readers expect of other kinds of digital objects. Indeed, the distances among the digital archive, edition, and anthology are not great, because all three seek to take advantage of the same set of functions that are characteristic of the digital medium. Their differences lie rather in the reference point they choose from the print world, the emphasis they choose in cuing the reader. It might be fair to say that there is no stable category of the digital anthology, only a body of works that inherit the anthology's logic of collection. For purposes of this discussion, then, a digital anthology is a collection of texts assembled primarily (though not exclusively) for the purpose of providing convenient (or perhaps sole) access to materials that are either unavailable in other forms or that gain value from being collected together. The anthology may in fact take an archival approach, by presenting the texts in something close to a diplomatic transcription and emphasizing their materiality. It may also present a critical edition of each text (though this is rare, if only for reasons of cost).

The anthology or collection that is the subject of this case study—the Women Writers Project's online collection entitled *Women Writers Online*— is the product of the history just sketched. In what follows, I describe the decisions and processes of greatest importance in developing an anthology of this sort, including the choice of editorial approach, the methods by which the text is captured and represented to the reader, the production process and its provision for error detection and correction, the publication infrastructure, and the role of text encoding as an editorial and scholarly research tool.

THE WWP CASE STUDY: GENERAL POINTS

In presenting a specific case of a genre so broad and so likely to vary, one should emphasize not only what is distinctive but also what is exemplary: not the unfortunate quirks that have been rightly avoided by other projects but the sound decisions that are worthy of emulation. During the WWP's dozen or more years of research on the digital editing of large textbases, we have occasionally ventured down some thorny paths, but on the whole our approach has been guided by a few principles that we feel are defensible and worth generalizing.

Probably the most fundamental of these is the approach we take to the transcription of textual witnesses. As suggested above, the WWP's methodology emerged from debates about digital editing that placed emphasis on presenting readers with a set of data with which they could work rather than with an editorial fait accompli. It also seemed clear that in early women's writing, where so few texts had been republished in any form, the appropriate role for a digital collection would be to make the primary source materials available to the public and encourage their study instead of preparing scholarly editions of a few texts. It seemed premature to determine what the best text of these profoundly unfamiliar works might be, when the scholarly community was still recovering basic information about their publication, authorship, and history. As a result, the WWP's emphasis has been on representing specific documents—particular copies of particular books—at a level of detail that would support many different kinds of textual study. Although it might seem absurd to imagine such a text substituting for a visit to the physical archive, our goal was to represent all the linguistic detail that a view of the original would provide and to capture all the document's contents, even where they were almost unconnected with the main work (e.g., advertisements).

In transcribing the text, we preserve the readings of the original text, whether or not they seem correct, explicable, or intended by the author or printer. Our premise here is, first, that errors may be significant, whatever their source: they are part of the information that circulated to readers when the text was first published and are part of the evidence that literary researchers may wish to view.[1] Second, in many cases (particularly in earlier texts) it may be difficult to say with confidence that a given reading is an error. Given that our expectations about meaning and the conventions for its expression are based overwhelmingly on the textual tradition with which we are familiar, it seems theoretically important not to allow these expectations to "correct" a dissenting text into conformity.

This diplomatic transcription forms the basis for an encoded document that carries a great deal more information. The errors that we stolidly refuse to correct in the base transcription are marked and encoded, with an alternative corrected reading if one is obvious. Illegible passages are identified, with information about the number of letters or words that cannot be read, and a reading from another source is supplied if available. Unclear text, where the given reading is uncertain, is also flagged. For a subset of the collection, entitled *Renaissance Women Online* (*RWO*), we have added brief introductions and contextual materials giving historical and biographical background.[2] Finally, although the WWP does not at present encode more than one version of a given text, the possibility remains that alternate witnesses could be included and their differences encoded as variant readings. This inclusion could be made either by transcribing each witness independently and encoding all the differences between it and the others or by creating a single master document containing the data necessary to reconstruct all possible versions.

This approach owes a methodological debt to Jerome McGann, whose arguments for the importance of the historical and physical specificity of documents and their production have provided good reasons to regard the document, rather than the "work," as the central object of interest. We treat authors' specific intentions with respect to literary meaning as not only largely unknowable but also beside the point: what we wish to represent is a cultural document, a piece of historical currency whose modern readers may or may not find in it insight into the author's mind. We do not wish to minimize the difficulty—philosophical and practical—of obtaining that insight; on the contrary, we wish to emphasize the historical distance and difference that must be bridged in reading these documents.

While the editions we create do not attempt to represent the ideal text that might emerge from a realization of the author's literary intentions, they do make cautious reference to a more limited model of social intentionality that governs domains like printing conventions, orthography, and genre. Furthermore, the agency of the author and of the other participants in the document's production is clearly an operative analytic category for readers, and insofar as the document bears its traces, our encoding seeks to record that agency in a meaningful way. So for instance we distinguish between footnotes by the author and by her contemporary editors (and of course distinguish both from our own notes of whatever sort). Where a text contains sections by different authors, we can associate metadata with each section indicating its separate authorship. Most important, the header for each file includes identification of each participant—author, editor, publisher, printer, and potentially many others—together with the possibility of demographic information on each.[3]

The fact that we are dealing with a large collection of documents by different authors has some important consequences in this context as well. Although each text has a certain autonomy within the collection and can be read independently, the reader may also "read" the collection as a whole as a larger historical text representing four centuries of women's literate culture in English. The tools for this kind of reading—search and text analysis tools, concordance views, and other forms of textual manipulation—rely on our ability to identify generic commonalities and distinctions and capture these in the encoding of the texts. By using a vocabulary for describing genre and textual structure that locates the particular instance within a larger framework, we not only allow for comparisons across the collection but also potentially between this collection and others similarly prepared.

Finally, our approach is motivated by insights into what might be called information engineering. It is simpler to capture all the primary data first and then derive from it whatever second-order versions are needed than to create such a second-order version at the start and then work backward to the source. On the basis of the information we capture about documents, we can create a multitude of editions that build on specific hypotheses about intention, revision history, and the like.

TEXT REPRESENTATION

The foregoing may already have suggested some of the complexities of discussing editorial method in a medium where data can—and should—be so clearly separated from display. In describing the source data we capture, we say almost nothing about what the actual representation of the text will be like; in describing the representation, we are only discussing one of a large range of possibilities, or a set of choices offered to the reader. The distinctiveness of the approach lies in the tools and constraints that govern what readers may do with the text and what kinds of information they may expect to find there. In the WWP, our greatest investment thus far has been in the capture of the source data. Our current provision for display has been constrained by available resources, and while it responds to the needs of our most frequent users—a university classroom audience—it does not represent our final expectations for the collection.

As we currently present it, the text is displayed in a manner that preserves the most significant details of its original formatting. We preserve the more determinate features of the text more or less exactly—the original's capitalization, punctuation, and use of italics. Indentation and alignment are more difficult to reproduce with precision, because they depend on the particular size and aspect ratio of the original text block. Instead of displaying absolute positioning, we represent what might be termed the "significant position" of the textual unit—that is, the positioning that distinguishes it from its context and indicates its structural function: whether it is centered, aligned left or right, indented from one side or the other. Although we record all original line breaks, the display suppresses prose line breaks except in headings, letter closings, title pages, and similar features where they may be significant. Similarly, line-end hyphens are retained in our transcription but suppressed when the text is relineated for display. From among the readings recorded in our transcription, the display currently provides a version with typographic errors corrected and with the text's original use of *i, j, u, v,* and *w* regularized to conform to modern usage. Additionally, contractions derived from manuscript practice in very early texts (such as õ for *on*) are displayed in expanded form. These choices result in a reading text that serves a nonspecialist audience. Very shortly we will also be able to offer a display that shows the original readings and offers the ability to switch between views.

Several important kinds of textual feature are omitted both from our transcription and from our representation of the text. Most significant, we do not capture any of the graphic features of the text such as illustrations and ornaments. Our transcription includes placeholders for such features, and for figures (images with representational content) we encode a detailed description of the illustration and a transcription of any words it may contain. Nonrepresentational ornaments, ruled lines, borders, and other printers' devices are noted merely as ornament or rule without further detail. This policy may seem an impoverishment of the text, and in a sense it is; we do not regard it as an ideal approach. But the work and cost involved in negotiating rights to reproduce images of the source, and the logistics of digitizing these images, were beyond our reach at the start of the project. The result was a methodology that emphasizes the specifically textual domain: the ability to search, to manipulate the texts, to find material of interest. For graphic features, we reasoned, readers could consult microfilm or the original when necessary, whereas these options could never provide the textual power of the digital version.

Because we currently do not represent more than one copy of a given text, we do not have any apparatus representing textual variants. But in some texts we do need to represent manuscript deletions and revisions. Where a complete representation of all the marks on the page is required, we adapt marks often used in print: strikethrough to indicate deletions and square brackets to indicate additions. It is also possible in our newest interface design for the reader to choose a clear reading display that presents either the originally printed version or the revised version and so allows for easy comparison of the two. A similar approach would be used if we wished to represent textual variants from other sources: the varying text would be marked with some notation or highlighting. Clicking on the text would display the variant reading(s); the reader could also toggle between different versions. In all of these cases, our goal is to present the reader with the option to explore variation in an informed way or to choose one version as a clear reading text.

WWP IN THE CONTEXT OF OTHER PROJECTS

Large numbers of text collections now available online could be described as digital anthologies. Among those that may be considered scholarly resources—intended for a scholarly or academic audience and created with a high degree of editorial care—responsible practice has coalesced around a set of widely accepted methods, although local practice varies as to the details. There is general agreement about the importance of providing searchable text and, if possible, a page image as well. The advantages of marking up the text using an XML-based markup language are also well understood and widely accepted, although some highly regarded projects are experimenting with non-XML-based markup. The Text Encoding Initiative Guidelines for Electronic Text Encoding and Interchange (see www.tei-c.org) represent the most widely used markup language in the scholarly community (aside from HTML, whose limitations are becoming clearer as scholarly expectations of digital resources rise). While its provisions for literary editing and text representation are extensive, few projects apply this encoding in detail, largely because of cost and the lack of needed expertise. Similarly, the need for good metadata—information by which a text can be identified, located, and retrieved from a collection—is also increasingly well understood, but high-quality metadata is challenging to create and consequently rare.

The WWP is situated among a group of digital anthologies that have adopted the most rigorous practices among those sketched above. Providing page images is not practicable for us, but our full-text transcriptions and metadata are encoded in XML following the TEI guidelines with a degree of detail that is unusual (perhaps even unmatched) among projects of this sort. We are also unusual, though not unique, in providing a detailed account of our editorial and transcriptional methods to the reader as part of our site documentation. Perhaps because print anthologies typically wear their editorial practices lightly and seldom dwell on details of regularization, line-end hyphenation, and the like, digital anthologies (particularly those aimed at a student audience) are often similarly reticent.

As for the WWP's editorial practice, it too matches the range of practice accepted by the community of digital anthologies. The use of unamended or very lightly edited, diplomatic transcriptions from single sources is common and serves the goals of such projects well.[4] The WWP prefers to capture any emendation using XML encoding rather than make silent alterations; as a result our approach may lend itself more than others to offering readers alternative versions of the text (concerning the treatment of details like typographic errors or abbreviations).

PRACTICAL PROCEDURES

A number of practical procedures are worth describing here, because of their impact on the reliability of the resulting transcriptions. Our choice of source text (the edition and copy to be used for transcription) and our methods of ensuring transcriptional accuracy and encoding consistency have required careful thought and planning.

Our basic criteria for choosing a source text are in many ways unremarkable, reflecting the factors that give a text particular scholarly value. We prefer a first edition or one published in the author's lifetime; evidence that a certain edition was revised by the author will carry weight as well.[5] In a given edition, we choose a copy that is both legible and complete. From among copies that meet our criteria, we prefer one that is readily available on microfilm.

Accuracy of transcription is checked by several different kinds of proof-reading. Because some of the transcribed characters are captured in the markup itself, the first proofreading is performed with the markup visible, so that the proofreader can ensure that features such as rendition, abbreviation, typographic errors in the original, and the use of *i, j, u, v,* and *w* have been captured correctly. A subsequent proofreading is ideally performed on a formatted copy that shows only the content of the text.[6] In both cases, the proofreader does a word-by-word reading of the output against a copy of the source. In addition, we have developed tools that list the vocabulary of a given text, expressed as a unique word list, so that individual usages (those most likely to be typographic errors) can be spotted and checked; the list can also be checked against a cumulative dictionary of WWP usages to catch the most frequent errors.

Consistency of encoding is the most difficult to achieve, particularly with a complex system like the TEI guidelines. Often several encoding solutions are possible for a given textual feature, all valid SGML and many equally defensible. It is therefore important to build in checks to ensure that similar features are always tagged alike. Like most digitization projects, we rely first of all on careful and extensive documentation that our encoders use both during training and as a reference while they are transcribing. Following the initial transcription and encoding, we run a set of automated checks that scan for the most frequent kinds of encoding inconsistencies, and we check for the kinds of errors that are difficult to catch manually. Finally, each text is given a final review when the last set of proofreading corrections has been entered. Despite all these checks, differences from text to text may amount even to differing encoding aesthetics. It is not clear to what extent these affect the digital behavior of the collection. As tools for manipulating digital texts grow more powerful, we will need to develop more nuanced ways of assessing and enforcing consistency.

The WWP's example illustrates a few trade-offs that are particularly significant in the transition to digital editing. The WWP anthology emphasizes capturing editorial decisions not as finalities but as contingencies, with important effects. By capturing the text so as to represent its variability as a data structure, we are able to create a distinct editorial space that stands apart from the source transcription and from any final editorial result. This space is accessible to us as editors—it is where the editing proper can occur—but it is also accessible to readers, enabling them to inspect the decisions that have been made and choose different strategies if they wish. In our particular case, these choices operate at a broad level, on things like typographic modernization or abbreviations, but the same basic approach could apply to individual readings as well. What is crucial here is that the editorial work has not simply been displaced onto the reader, an abnegation of editorial responsibility that—though a heady possibility earlier in digital history—is no longer regarded as desirable by editors or readers. Instead, the process has the potential to be both collaborative and mutable, contingent and yet not flimsy.

This strategy, with its underlying infrastructure of XML encoding, is now increasingly the approach taken to digital editions of all sorts. And although the digital anthology is a loosely identifiable genre in the landscape of digital editions, it is also the form that landscape as a whole is taking. With the development of large-scale retrieval tools and methods of federating digital resources, not only the large digital library collections but also individual editions may be treated as part of one vast textual field. At first such a textual universe seems to have little to do with the anthology tradition: it reverses the selectivity, the annotation, the editorial uniformity, the thematic appositeness that are characteristic of the print anthology. But with care, these qualities can—and should—be relocated into the liminal space between the data and the interface, where choices about which texts, which readings, and which presentation can be made and remade. The digital anthology thus serves both as macrocosm and microcosm, a scale model of the textual world that contains everything and yet fits in the palm of your hand.

NOTES

1. Many examples of ingenious research—on the quantity of type used to set a given book, the error rates of different compositors, the possibilities of pronunciation alternatives—point to the variety of research that might be possible and illuminating if the requisite data were available.
2. See www.wwp.brown.edu/texts/rwoentry.html. These contextual materials are limited to the *RWO* collection for reasons having to do with the vagaries of funding; they were created under a generous grant from the Andrew W. Mellon Foundation, as an experiment in digital pedagogy and publication, but the experiment was not extended to the entire WWP collection.
3. Unfortunately limited resources have prevented us from developing this demographic metadata fully, but it would be a natural and extremely valuable addition to the resource and form part of the methodology we would recommend to others.
4. Digital anthology projects often wish to provide access to rare materials— women's writing, slave narratives, rare books, documentary materials—where a transcription of the original document may be of greater value to readers than an

edited version. In addition, there may be practical reasons for this emphasis; few anthology projects have the resources to create substantially edited versions on a large scale, and most prefer to put their resources into digitizing additional texts.

5. If there exist two substantially different versions of the text, we strongly consider encoding both, resources permitting.

6. Given the vagaries of XML output software, it has not always been possible to produce this latter form of proofreading output; in that case, a second round of proofreading, with encoding visible, is carried out.

AUTHORIAL TRANSLATION: SAMUEL BECKETT'S *STIRRINGS STILL / SOUBRESAUTS*

DIRK VAN HULLE

Many authors have written in two languages, usually first in their native language and from a certain moment on, often after emigration, in the language of the country to which they moved. Vladimir Nabokov first wrote in Russian, later in English; Julien Green changed from English to French. Samuel Beckett's case is more complicated. Beckett wrote in both French and English in turns and translated his own works in both directions. To complicate things further, the switch between French and English sometimes even occurred during the writing process. It did in the genesis of *Stirrings Still*, Beckett's penultimate text.

Stirrings Still was first published in English and subsequently translated into French under the title *Soubresauts* by the author himself in 1989, the year of his death. A most interesting aspect of this work is its textual genesis. It took Beckett almost six years to complete this short text of only about six pages. That this process took such a long time is to a large extent due to an extreme form of hesitation, which seems to have increased over the years. The first manuscript of *Stirrings Still* preserved at the Beckett Archives in Reading (Bryden, Garforth, and Mills) starts in French but continues in English. The second leaf of this manuscript (MS2933/1) shows the reverse scenario: Beckett started in English and continued in French. The first phase of the writing process is predominantly French, but most of the later manuscripts and typescripts are in English. This long and complex genesis with more than twenty versions makes *Stirrings Still* a particularly interesting example to discuss the scholarly genetic editing of bilingual writings.

EDITORIAL PRINCIPLES

Since bilingualism characterizes this text both before and after its publication, the aim of the genetic edition is to present the work as both a process ("stirrings") and a product ("still"). In his typology of genetic documentation, Pierre-Marc de Biasi draws a clear dividing line in a text's production process, taking the *bon à tirer* moment ("all set for printing") as the decisive "freezing point" between the fluidity of the composition and the "frozen shape of a published text" ("What Is" 37; see also Biasi, *La génétique*). According to French theoreticians of *critique génétique*, a genetic edition provides the reader with all the versions of the work's genesis in extenso. G. Thomas Tanselle also makes a clear distinction between a genetic edition and, for instance, Hans Walter Gabler's synoptic edition of James Joyce's *Ulysses* ("Historicism" 38n72).

Nonetheless, David Greetham suggests that genetic and synoptic editions do not necessarily exclude each other ("Textual and Literary Theory" 20n39). A noteworthy attempt to combine these two types is Charles Krance's editorial model for scholarly variorum editions of Beckett's bilingual works. A French and an English reading text are presented face-to-face. The synoptic apparatus is remarkable, since it marks changes between draft stages, but the sum of these draft stages does not coalesce in a continuous manuscript text. Represented as different layers, they reflect the order of the writing process. To highlight only the variants between versions, Krance avoids undue repetition in the variant synopses by using diacritical signs to indicate passages without change vis-à-vis the previous version.

One of the reasons why variorum editions do not include facsimiles and full transcriptions is the codex format. In 1996, the series editorial board was "not yet convinced of the overall desirability of electronic editions" (Krance xiii). In the meantime, electronic editing has evolved, and it is worth trying to see what the possibilities are of creating an electronic, easily searchable environment that meets the requirements and aims of a bilingual edition— that is, "to show the traces of Beckett's work in the composition of his bilingual *oeuvre*" (xiv).

While Krance readily admits that his "methods may not be as all-inclusively ambitious as that of 'hard-line' geneticists" (xiv), he rightly argues that the bilingual dimension of this work calls for a clear-text, face-to-face presentation of the French and English versions to allow careful comparison. Peter Robinson has pointed out that the number of variants can be so overwhelming that merely presenting a transcription or facsimile of all the documents may not be enough. A reading text is a useful tool, but providing the reader with this tool does not imply that the critically edited text is final. Robinson consequently pleads for a presentation of "the one text and the many texts" ("One Text"). That in *Stirrings Still / Soubresauts* one must speak of the two texts and the many texts is all the more reason to provide the reader with this tool. The double text is indeed meant as a working instrument in the variorum edition, as Krance suggests: "It will be to the user's advantage to photocopy the text(s) under scrutiny as working copy, thus obviating the need to page back and forth between text(s) and synopses" (xii). While it may seem remarkable that an edition advises its own reproduction, the idea of a working copy is essential and underlies the interface design of a digital equivalent of the face-to-face representation, to be consulted at all times.

The choice of the base text for the English reading text is complicated by the fact that there is a limited first, signed, deluxe edition (published by Blue Moon Books in New York and by John Calder in London, forty-four pages with nine illustrations by Louis le Brocquy [1988]) and a nonlimited first edition published in two newspapers (the *Guardian* and the *Irish Independent* [1989]). Starting from Biasi's typology and the prominence of the *bon à tirer* moment, one could argue that the 1988 edition should provide the base text, as it represents the text's first public appearance.

The question, however, is how public this appearance is in the case of an expensive edition limited to 226 copies. Even though the *avant-texte* and the *texte* are characterized by their respectively private and public character, the limited edition as *texte* was a rather private enterprise. It was meant as a way to support Barney Rosset, who had been Beckett's American publisher for decades and was sacked from Grove Press in the mid-1980s. The newspaper version was the first truly public edition. In the *Guardian*, Frank Kermode wrote a review of the limited edition of *Stirrings Still*, pointing out the irony that this prose, "rich only in its unmatched parsimony," was published in an edition available only to a happy few: "The purchasers can henceforth meditate the destitution of their existence and simultaneously take pleasure in their privilege. . . . It's a bit like buying a Porsche to mitigate angst."

Moreover, a leaflet in the American facsimile review copy preserved in the Beckett Archives in Reading indicates 13 April 1989 as the actual publication date of the limited edition. Its public appearance is therefore deceptive, for the so-called 1988 edition of this book was actually published on Beckett's eighty-third birthday, more than a month after the *Guardian* publication.

One of the consequences of being published in a newspaper was that the text had to make room for an advertisement. In this case, Beckett's short text, worth £1,000 or $1,500 in hardback, was draped over an advertisement of the *London Review of Books*, which said, "Read the softback before you shell out for the hard," a statement followed by an image of a softback copy of the *London Review of Books* and the slogan "The best of all possible words." If the slogan of the advertisement were to serve as an editorial guideline, the question would be whether this newspaper publication indeed contained the best of all possible words. It might have been interesting had the most democratic version allowed for the most conservative of editorial methods—that is, a best-text approach. Unfortunately the newspaper editor did not prove himself to be the best guardian of the text. Apart from introducing an unnecessary capital letter and leaving out a necessary word, he divided the text into four instead of three sections (possibly to make it comply with the newspaper house style). This last intervention makes the edition unsuitable to serve as the base text of a scholarly edition, since it is the only version that has four sections instead of three.

Still, from a sociological perspective, one might argue that this newspaper publication is a Beckettian equivalent of the 1922 edition of *Ulysses*. When Joyce's text was reprinted in the 1990s, Fritz Senn advocated this paperback edition of Ulysses: *The 1922 Text* and the decision to present the reader with "those words and phrases, misprints and all, that set the literary world astir" (461). Had any version of *Stirrings Still* set the literary world astir, it would have been the newspaper edition. But then again it must be admitted that, compared with the stirrings caused by Joyce's text, the literary world remained relatively still after the newspaper edition of Beckett's short text.

Beckett's act of self-translation has the paradoxical effect of fixing a text by reproducing it in another language. It is only thanks to the French translation (or target text) *Soubresauts* that the English version on which it is based receives the status of original (or source text). This effect might be considered as a criterion for the choice of base text of a bilingual edition. But Beckett did not always simply take the final version as his source text. In *Bing*, for example, there are instances where the English version *Ping* is based on earlier drafts (Fitch 70). Since he did not necessarily stick to one version to make his translations, the idea of an original or source text is problematized and cannot serve as a general principle to choose the base text.

An intentionalist approach is another alternative. Fredson Bowers advises the use of a fair-copy manuscript (if any survives) as copy-text in preference to the first edition set from it. The last versions of the three sections preserved in the Beckett Archives in Reading are almost identical with the limited edition, but there is one problematic instance that is symptomatic of Beckett's hesitancy. Even in the last typescript of the second section (MS 2935/4/2) the first sentence is marked by an open variant. The sentence starts as follows: "As one in his right mind when at last out again he knew not . . ." The words "he knew not" are underlined (not canceled), and Beckett added the alternative "no knowing." So, even at this late stage in the writing process, his intentions appear to be multiple. He apparently needed the act of publication (and therefore necessarily a publisher) to put an end to the endless hesitating. It is even doubtful that the octogenarian author would have published anything after *Worstward Ho* had it not been for his American publisher's unfortunate situation. This circumstance was a major impulse to finish the "Fragment" for Rosset (as *Stirrings Still* was still called in 1986). It is remarkable that neither the *Guardian* publication nor the text in the *Beckett Shorts* (vol. 11) published by John Calder mentions the dedication "For Barney Rosset." It was Beckett's concern for Rosset's situation that brought about the publication. This dedication is as crucial as the dedication "(For Mrs. Henry Mills Alden)" in the poem "Trees" by Joyce Kilmer, discussed by Jerome McGann in *Radiant Textuality* (42).

As a consequence, the choice of the limited edition "for Barney Rosset" as the base text is inspired primarily by this social circumstance: not because it is deluxe but because it was meant to help a friend. This case shows that authorial intention and social orientation are not mutually exclusive. The only misspelling in this edition ("withersoever" instead of "whithersoever" on page 4) was unintended, as S. E. Gontarski explains in his reader's edition *Samuel Beckett: The Complete Short Prose*. In a review of the limited edition in the *Irish Times* (15 Apr. 1989), Gerry Dukes pointed out the typographic error, which the actor Barry McGovern in turn brought to Beckett's attention. Beckett subsequently corrected the error in the actor's copy (Gontarski 285).

Therefore, the English base text of the electronic genetic bilingual edition is represented by a single document: McGovern's copy, in which Beckett made this one correction. This instance opens up the idea of a "continuous manuscript text" (which is Gabler's description of the left-hand pages in his synoptic edition of Joyce's *Ulysses* [1895]) to what McGann calls a "continuous production text" (*Textual Condition* 30).

This idea of a continuous production text is reinforced by the French texts, since the translations took place both before and after the dividing line of the *bon à tirer* moment (in Biasi's typology). The first French edition includes the dedication "Pour Barney Rosset." Although the Beckett Archives in Reading keep a computer printout of the translated version on which Beckett wrote, "Final," this version differs in some instances from the text published by Éditions de Minuit in 1989 (both in a limited edition of 99 + 10 copies and in a nonlimited paperback edition). The kind of changes suggests that, even though Beckett was as fluent in French as he was in English, he counted on his French publisher Jérôme Lindon to correct minor mistakes.

METHODS OF TEXT REPRESENTATION

The transcription of the documents preserved in Reading is encoded in TEI-compliant XML. The advantage of this nonproprietary format is the resulting transclusive flexibility of the textual material. Depending on the user's focus, the draft material can be rearranged in several ways: (1) in a documentary approach, based on the catalog numbers; (2) in chronological order; (3) by language; (4) with a focus on translation; (5) in retrograde direction, starting from the published texts.

1. Documents: In a menu, the list of documents is probably the most neutral starting point. The archive catalog number can serve as a unique ID of what the Text Encoding Initiative refers to as the body of the different texts. Each transcription is preferably linked to a facsimile of the relevant manuscript page, so that it can always be checked against the scanned image of the manuscript. This possibility will immediately make the user aware that a single document often contains several versions of the same paragraph. Most of the manuscripts contain units of text, but especially in the early stages of the writing process and on the left-hand pages of the so-called *Super Conquérant* notebook (MS 2934; "Super Conquérant" is printed on the front cover), Beckett wrote loose jottings. The documents approach therefore also contains a special subsection for notes (as in Krance's variorum edition).

2. Chronology: Although the catalog numbers reflect the chronology of versions, some documents, notably the *Super Conquérant* notebook, contain more than one version. The versions in this document are not successive, since Beckett made alternate use of this notebook and loose sheets of paper. The chronological order of the writing process can be indicated by means of a logical succession of ID numbers.

3. Language: In the same *Super Conquérant* notebook, Beckett had already made some translations. At a certain point he turned the copybook around and started from the back. Under the heading "Repeat in different order" he opened with a French translation of the most current English version and continued with an English translation of one of his first French

versions. Unlike Joyce in *Finnegans Wake*, Beckett did not mix languages. In *Stirrings Still*, the paragraphs can be arranged or rearranged by language using the lang attribute in the <div>, <p>, and <seg> tags. On the basis of this attribute the versions can be divided into French and English sections.

4. Translation: A simple indication of the language may not be sufficient for a thorough genetic investigation, because not all French versions are translations. To highlight the ways in which self-translation can have a generative creative power, we mark those versions that are translations with the attribute ana set to Tr. This way, they can be visualized, facing the version on which they are based.

5. Teleology: A major problem with the genetic editing of prose texts is to find a way to compare a passage in one version with the corresponding passage in another. Krance found an elegant solution for this problem by dividing the text into small units or segments, preceded by line numbers corresponding to the reading text. A practical example of an electronic edition that applies a similar division into smaller units is the critical edition of Stijn Streuvels's *De teleurgang van den Waterhoek* by Marcel De Smedt and Edward Vanhoutte. Every paragraph in the reading text can be linked to and compared with other versions of it. Vanhoutte has called this linkable unit a linkeme, "the smallest unit of linking in a given paradigm" ("Linkemic Approach").

By making the links bidirectional, this system can be expanded and applied not only to the reading text but to any version the reader happens to be reading. In Beckett criticism, the later texts are often referred to by means of paragraph numbers (Cohn 380). *Stirrings Still* consists of three sections, the first of which is subdivided into seven paragraphs. The paragraphs that made it into the published text may start with either 1, 2, or 3 (the numbers of the three sections of the text), followed by a number indicating the paragraph.

The difficulty with reference to *Stirrings Still* is that some paragraphs are too long to serve as a workable unit. Krance therefore employs a flexible criterion to divide the text: "The length of these discrete units of text varies, depending on the degree of complexity and/or extent of their variants and revisions" (xiv). If a paragraph is divided into *n* segments, each of these can be indicated by the <seg> tag. In order to indicate where a particular segment in a manuscript eventually ended up in the published version of *Stirrings Still*, the id attribute in the <seg> tag may be used. This way, all the segments indicated with, for example, the ID SS1.03.05 (i.e., all the units corresponding to the fifth segment of the third paragraph of part 1 in the published text) can be arranged in vertical juxtaposition. Apart from these segments, the texts can also be compared at <p> and <div> level, as these are also encoded with an ID (e.g., segment SS1.03.05 is part of paragraph SS1.03 and of section or <div> SS1).

The main danger of a teleological perspective is the neglect of passages (especially in the early manuscripts) that did not make it into the published text. Because there are several versions of these passages, they should be comparable too. For instance, the first paragraph of the first few versions starts with the phrase "Tout toujours à la même distance," translated as "All always at the same remove." After a few versions, Beckett abandoned this path in the writing process, so that it became a dead end. By taking the last stage in such a cul-de-sac as a reference text for the division into segments, marking them with a special initial number (distinct from section numbers 1, 2, and 3), we can map these dead ends as well, to show how Beckett's famous motto "I can't go on, I'll go on" (*Unnamable* 382) also applies to the textual process.

FORM OF TEXTUAL APPARATUS

Traditionally the notion of variants applies to variation either between copies of an ancient or medieval document by scribes or between different editions of the same work. When dealing with modern texts, a distinction must be made between transmission variants and genetic (or composition) variants. The edition of a bilingual work requires an extra category of translation variants.

1. For transmission variants—that is, variants between published versions of the text—the special section of the *Guidelines for Electronic Text Encoding and Interchange* TEI P4, devoted to the apparatus, can be applied (Sperberg-McQueen and Burnard). Chapter 19 offers three methods. Since the guidelines advise avoiding the location-referenced method, "[w]here it is intended that the apparatus be complete enough to allow the reconstruction of the witnesses," and since the double end-point attachment method is "lengthy and difficult," the so-called parallel segmentation method is the most suitable in this case.

2. For genetic variants, note that the difference between genetic and textual criticism, according to Daniel Ferrer, is connected to the focus of each, respectively, on invention and repetition. Recognizing that this division is too black-and-white, he immediately qualifies this statement and emphasizes the dialectic of repetition and invention (54) that characterizes any writing process. In this context, Brian Fitch's description of Beckett's bilingual work as a double form of "répétition" is particularly relevant: "One might

say that while the first version is no more than a *rehearsal* for what is yet to come, the second is but a *repetition* of what has gone before, the two concepts coming together in the one French word *répétition*" (157).

The advantage of a synoptic apparatus is its focus on what has changed between versions or, in Ferrer's formulation, on the invention. But in order to represent the dialectics of invention *and* repetition, it may be useful to present the whole textual context (i.e., also the repetitions). A traditional apparatus is usually designed for transmission of variants in versions that are characterized by more identity than variation. In modern manuscripts, especially in the earliest draft stages, the identity-variation proportion is often inverse. According to the French school of genetic criticism, a genetic edition in the true sense of the word presents the complete texts of all the documents in chronological order and in their entirety. But evidently an important concern of the genetic edition of prose texts is not to overburden the user with a mass of material. The edition offers users the chance to adapt the size of the textual unit they wish to compare (large, medium, small—i.e., the unit of the section `<div>`, the paragraph `<p>`, or the sentence `<seg>`), which is already a refined form of versioning. But it is possible to go further and make the edition into a critical genetic edition, where the editor indicates the genetic variants explicitly.

Except for the first extant version, a previous version can always serve as a temporary invariant against which the genetic variants can be measured, even if the writing was eventually aborted and never published. Such measuring can be called *retrospective collation*. If the work did reach the stage of publication, it is only natural that readers will also be interested in another kind of genetic variation: the difference between a version and the published text. This teleological perspective requires a *prospective collation*. In XML encoding, therefore, the genetic variants are marked in two directions, by `<rdg>` tags with a **type** attribute: `retro` for differences vis-à-vis the previous version and `pro` for differences vis-à-vis the edited reading text. The code can be visualized in different ways; for instance, on the smallest level (`<seg>`) all versions of one sentence can be displayed in vertical juxtaposition, with the retrospective variants in italics and the prospective variants in bold.

This chronological arrangement is suitable for a collation of versions in their order of composition. If users wish to compare two not necessarily consecutive versions of a particular sentence, they can select them from the chronological sequence and focus on just these two in parallel frames, which facilitates comparison.

Because this part of the edition tries to offer a teleological perspective, the absence of a word or word string that appears in the published text is indicated by a rend attribute, mentioning absence: `<rdg type="pro" rend="absence">`. The absence can for instance be visualized by means of a vertical bar. This genetic approach has the advantage that the number of diacritical signs can be reduced to a minimum. Also, variants can be indicated in their context, leaving the structure of the whole sentence intact. For bilingual works, the same system can be expanded (using for instance a type attribute `trans` to indicate variants in the authorial translation).

3. Variation in the translation further complicates the distinction between genetic and transmission variants. In theory, there is no difference between making a self-translation of a text that is already out in the open and translating a draft, since in both cases the author translates his own texts. But inevitably the act of publication has a petrifying effect. Rainier Grutman makes a distinction between "simultaneous auto-translation" and "delayed auto-translation" (20). In the case of Beckett's *Murphy*, for instance, the English version was published before the Second World War, but the French translation appeared only a decade later. Because of this delay, the English text had already led a public life, which may have limited the possibilities of further invention.

But publication or even performance (of his plays) did not prevent Beckett from introducing considerable variants in the translation. In extreme cases, such alteration may raise the question whether a self-translation should be regarded as a separate work or as a version of the same work. Klaus Gerlach argues in favor of the latter option (110), suggesting that Siegfried Scheibe's definition of *version* be enlarged to include the notion of equivalence: "Textual versions . . . are related through textual identity [and equivalence] and distinct through variation" (Scheibe 207). In translation studies, however, the notion of equivalence is central but also controversial, as Dorothy Kenny notes (77). The concept's problematic nature immediately appears in a bilingual edition. Nonequivalent instances are called mismatches by Edouard Magessa O'Reilly. Words or word strings that have no match in the facing text are underlined; a vertical bar "indicates the position that would most likely have been occupied by the matching segment, were it present." O'Reilly readily acknowledges that these are obviously not the only instances of nonequivalence. He mentions shifts of verb tense, of singular and plural, of person or register, and so on and adds that "it would be impossible to point out such an endless array of mismatchings" (xiii).

Analogous to the pro- and retrospective genetic variants, another type attribute value can be used to indicate translation variants. Such tagging has theoretical implications, for it means that the publication of an authorial translation is regarded not as the end of a genesis but rather as the continuation of the writing process after publication. In the translation approach, the English source text *Stirrings Still* and the French target text *Soubresauts* are each other's version, comparable to all the other versions at `<div>`,`<p>`, and `<seg>` levels.

What this genetic bilingual edition wants to emphasize is that the creative power of translation continues to be operative after the first publication, to the effect that the *bon à tirer* moment is less decisive than in nonbilingual works. Beckett was well aware of what McGann calls "the algorithmic character of traditional text" (*Radiant Textuality* 151): text generates text, and for Beckett translation played a crucial role in the exploitation of this self-generative power. Authorial translations give evidence of an enhanced textual awareness. As a consequence, their textual examination and scholarly editing are a crucial part of their critical interpretation.

PROSE FICTION AND MODERN MANUSCRIPTS: LIMITATIONS AND POSSIBILITIES OF TEXT ENCODING FOR ELECTRONIC EDITIONS

EDWARD VANHOUTTE

> Thinking things out involves saying things to oneself, or to one's other companions, with an instructive intent.
> —Gilbert Ryle, *The Concept of Mind*

The hypertext edition, the hypermedia edition, the multimedia edition, the computer edition, the digital edition, and the electronic edition are all synonymous labels for a concept without a definition. The use of "edition" in these labels presupposes a conventional understanding of that word and is based on the implicit assumption that there is general agreement regarding what an edition is. There is no such thing. In textual studies we certainly mean "scholarly edition," whereas in strict bibliography "the term *edition* refers quite properly to the identifiably separate type-setting of *any* book, whether it is an edition in the text-critical sense or not" (Greetham, *Textual Scholarship* 348). Any kind of available text qualifies as an edition, and any kind of electronically available text qualifies as an electronic edition, just as any printed text can be called a paper or a print edition. The words *digital* and *electronic* describe only the materiality (as opposed to *print*) by which data are presented to the reader, *computer* refers to the distribution and access medium (as opposed to *book* or *codex*), and *hypertext, hypermedia,* and *multi-*

media hint at the functionality of the electronic product (as opposed to *linear*). As John Lavagnino pointed out in a report on a lecture I gave in London in 2000, "Ten years ago, it seemed sufficient to say that you were going to create such an edition in the form of a hypertext: often with very little elaboration on just what the result would be or why it would be significant, as though the medium itself would automatically make such an edition significant."

To allow a functional debate on editing and editions in the electronic paradigm, editors should provide an explicit definition of an electronic edition as well as the kind of scholarly edition they are presenting in electronic form. They should do so not only by using qualifying adjectives or labels in the titles or subtitles of their electronic products, for which conventional terminology could be used where applicable, but also by means of, for instance, a consistent argument in a textual essay that accompanies the edition proper. To avoid confusion among different meanings and types of edition, I sketch out my definition of an electronic scholarly edition in the first section of this essay and formulate six requirements that editors could embrace to ensure that their edition is treated as such.

As the attentive reader will notice, the formulation and discussion of this definition is influenced by an interest in and concern for noncritical editing and genetic transcription of modern manuscript material, which are two of the main topics covered in this essay. My electronic critical edition of Stijn Streuvels's *De teleurgang van den Waterhoek* in the second section serves as a test case for my definition and as an introduction to some limitations and possibilities of text encoding for electronic editions of modern prose texts. The assessment of this edition is used as a starting point for elaboration on issues concerned with the production of literal (noncritical) transcriptions and genetic editions of modern manuscript material with the use of text encoding as proposed by the Text Encoding Initiative (TEI). The third section covers all these issues and introduces the French school of *critique génétique*, which has developed a decade-long theory and practice for dealing with modern manuscript texts in a specific way. I attempt to apply that school's central interest in the internal dynamics of the modern manuscript and the study of the genetic continuum in a so-called *dossier génétique* to the transcription of manuscript material by means of text encoding. The current inability to encode overlapping hierarchies and time (both absolute and relational) elegantly in (noncritical) manuscript transcriptions is the subject of most of this section.

DEFINITION AND AIMS OF
AN ELECTRONIC EDITION

My full working definition of an electronic (scholarly) edition has six parts. By electronic edition, I mean an edition (1) that is the immediate result or some kind of spin-off product from textual scholarship; (2) that is intended for a specific audience and designed according to project-specific purposes; (3) that represents at least one version of the text or the work; (4) that has been processed from a platform-independent and nonproprietary basis, that is, it can both be stored for archival purposes and also be made available for further research (Open Source Policy); (5) whose creation is documented as part of the edition; and (6) whose editorial status is explicitly articulated.

With respect to this definition, five immediate observations must be made. First, by defining an electronic edition as a result or a product that has been processed, I plead for a practice in which the construction of a digital archive that contains all data (encoded transcriptions, high-resolution image files, etc.) differs from and precedes the generation of the edition. I have called this the archive/museum model.[1] Espen Ore speaks of *Teksttilretteleggelse/arkivoppbyging* ("text constitution / archive building") and *Utgaveproduksjon* ("producing the edition") (143). Second, insofar as I define an electronic edition in productive terms, it is indeed true that, as G. Thomas Tanselle paraphrases Peter Shillingsburg, "an electronic edition is a form of presentation and, as such, does not pose a different set of theoretical issues from the one faced by editors who present their work in a different form" ("Textual Criticism at the Millennium" 33). What Tanselle and Shillingsburg here seem to overlook is that the practice of creating an edition with the use of text encoding calls for explicit ontologies and theories of the text that do generate new sets of theoretical issues.[2] Maybe they are not different sets of editorial issues, but they are certainly new sets of textual issues, such as problems of document architecture, encoding time, and so on. Third, I do not consider it a requirement for an electronic edition to display textual variation in an apparatus or in any other way, for in my view such display has a project-specific purpose. But it follows from the first requirement of my definition that the study of textual variation—where it appears—is an essential part of the research involved in creating an electronic edition. Even a reading edition cannot be made without a serious examination of the textual variants. Fourth, the requirement for the presentation of at least one version of the text or the work is not a fundamental call for a critically established editor's text. Diplomatic transcript editions (Greetham, *Textual Scholarship* 391) and facsimile editions, for instance, do not present a critically edited text, but they should not pretend to be noneditorial. The editor is always present in the organization of the material and the transcription of source documents. Point 3 in my definition specifies that a database of textual variation cannot be considered an electronic edition. If one is forced to choose between an edited text or textual variation, the edited text must always take priority. The category of electronic edition includes more than critical, diplomatic, facsimile, and reading editions. Mixed-flavor editions (which have characteristics of all of them but are none of them exclusively), archives that present editions, and editions that are organized as archives all qualify as electronic editions (e.g., McGann's *Rossetti Archive* and Robinson's *The Wife of Bath's Prologue on CD-ROM*). Fifth, the working definition does not prescribe any hypertextual features to be included in the edition, because the emphasis on hypertext in the current debate on electronic editing is still often beside the point and hypertext is about to outgrow its hype. If the use of hypertext adds no fundamental advantage to the electronic edition over the codex-based edition, it is better to stick to the book. Indeed, hypertext is just the visualization of linking that Steven DeRose and Andries van Dam define as "the ability to express relationships between places in a universe of information" (9)[3] and that should be marked explicitly or generated automatically by making use of some sort of markup and path scheme. Consequently, the syntax of this markup and of the markup language becomes essential in the design of an electronic edition with hypertext functionality. The presence of hypertext functionality in an electronic text, however, does not guarantee its scholarly integrity.

G. Thomas Tanselle defines scholarly editing as the considered act of reproducing or altering texts ("Varieties"). Whether the result of that act is published in print or as an electronic product does not matter to this general definition. Nor does it affect editing's primary aims. Above all, the scholarly edition is aimed at articulating the editors' notions, perspectives, or theories of the texts—or of what the texts should be in critical editions. By doing so, the scholarly edition can invoke literary debate by providing the materials and tools to explore new ways of understanding and studying the text. Only the format of these materials and tools will differ in the print and electronic edition, not their intentions. But the ultimate, and for technical reasons the most problematic, aim is to preserve our cultural heritage.

A CASE STUDY

My electronic edition of the classic Flemish novel *De teleurgang van den Waterhoek* (The Decline of the Waterhoek)[4] by the Flemish author Stijn Streuvels[5] (1871–1969)—the first electronic scholarly edition of any sort of a Dutch-Flemish literary work—was published as an electronic critical edition on CD-ROM by Amsterdam University Press in 2000. Unfortunately, at the time of publication, I had not defined "electronic edition" in the general introduction; neither had I spelled out the ways in which the edition was critical or provided an account of the linkemic approach toward textual variation and the eclectic approach toward conventional editorial theory the editors had taken.[6] In the absence of these explicit statements, some users and reviewers misunderstood the edition. Some criticized it as disorienting; for instance, the presentation of two critical texts, the mixed use of text transcriptions and digital facsimiles as representations of the documentary source material, and the absence of a variorum apparatus confused the user, even though these features were actually the three pivotal theoretical statements of the edition. The following short survey of the edition's main editorial procedures and problems and discussion of both the solutions suggested by the edition and the questions it raises should serve as an object lesson and case study,[7] by introducing the issue of noncritical and genetic transcription/editing of modern manuscript material.

Editorial Principles and Markup

In *Scholarly Editing in the Computer Age*, Shillingsburg defines five formal orientations of editing: documentary, aesthetic, authorial, sociological, and bibliographic (15–27). Except for the aesthetic orientation, all these were applied to editing *De teleurgang van den Waterhoek*.[8] The aim of the editorial project was to explore different ways to deal with textual instability, textual variation, the genetic reconstruction of the writing process, and the constitution of a critically restored reading text. Whereas the reading edition in book form, which was published with the electronic edition, presents one text (the edited text of the first print edition),[9] this seemingly best-text approach is countered by the electronic critical edition, where instability and versioning are the governing principles in the presentation of many texts (see Reiman, esp. ch. 10 [167–80]).

On the basis of their documentary status and appearance, the many texts in the edition could be divided into two groups:

Complex Documentary Sources	Simple Documentary Sources
the complete holograph manuscript (1927)	
	the prepublication of the novel in installments in the Dutch literary journal *De Gids* (1927)
the corrected authorial copy of the prepublication, which served as a printer's copy for typesetting the first print edition (1927)	
	the first print edition (1927)
the corrected author's copy of the first print edition, which was used as printer's copy for typesetting the second print edition (1939)	
	the revised second print edition (1939)

In the electronic edition, the documentary sources of the complex group are represented by their digital facsimiles, whereas the texts of the simple group are TEI-compliant, full-text representations. By including either a full-text version or a digital facsimile version of a documentary source, the electronic edition shows a mixed approach toward Shillingsburg's (and Tanselle's) first requirement to provide both a "full accurate transcription" and a "full digital image of each source edition" in an electronic edition ("Principles" 28). This mixed approach, however, is partly compensated by the possibility of deducing the physical form of the prepublication from the facsimiles of the corrected prepublication, and the physical form of the first print edition from the facsimiles of the corrected first print edition. Only the presentations of the holograph manuscript and the second print edition do not have a full-text and a facsimile counterpart, respectively.

For sociological reasons, the edition presents two critically edited texts: the versions of the first and second print editions. The first print edition constitutes an important moment in the genetic history of the novel: it is the first finished version of the text—we consider the prepublication as one step in the writing process leading toward the first print edition—and its reception by literary critics is the reason for the drastic revision of the text in preparation of the second print edition. This second print edition is equally important, because it is the version that generations of readers have read and that the author produced in his interaction with contemporary society.[10] In constituting these texts, we applied the principles of the German (authorial) editorial tradition, which allows only justified corrections of manifest mistakes. In these two critical texts, the emendations[11] were documented by the use of the <corr> element, containing the correction, and a sic attribute, whose value documents the original reading. The editor responsible for the correction (in this case EV for Edward Vanhoutte) was specified in a resp attribute: <corr sic="katin" resp="EV">kattin</corr>. The text of the prepublication was retained for historical reasons, and the inverse markup was used. Uncertain readings (seventy-six in all) were encoded with the aid of the <sic> element, containing a suggested correction in a corr attribute: <sic corr="kattin">katin</sic>.[12] Although both systems are equivalent for the computer, they do articulate different views on the text. In the corresponding use of the inverse markup, one can see the thin line between critical editing and noncritical or documentary editing.

A Linkemic Approach to Textual Variation

The electronic edition of *De teleurgang van den Waterhoek* contains four sections:[13] an account of the editorial principles, consisting of a genetic history of the work, an account of the constitution of the texts, and a description of the transmission and publication history; the actual edition, which presents the textual variation against the orientation text by making use of the *linkemic* approach (see below); the separate documentary sources; and the diplomatic edition of seventy-one relevant letters for the reconstruction of the textual history, selected from the correspondence of the author.[14]

The third section of the edition, documentary sources, presents the six versions of the text chronologically, allowing the user to consult each separately. It is of course true that "every form of reproduction can lie, by providing a range of possibilities for interpretation that is different from the one offered by the original" (Tanselle, "Reproductions" 33) and that the process of imaging is a process of interpretation.[15] In order for users of the edition to be able to evaluate what they see, the facsimiles are accompanied by a full account of the imaging procedure, including the documentation on the software and hardware (and settings) used in the project, which I believe is an essential requirement. No facsimile can of course substitute for the original, but it is the best approximation we can offer the interested user.

The user of the edition can also read all six versions together in the second section. This part of the electronic critical edition presents the edited text of the first print edition as the *orientation text* around which the hypertext presentation of textual variation is organized. Instead of linking the orientation text to a variorum apparatus, the editors opted for what I have called a linkemic approach to textual variation. I define a linkeme as the smallest unit of linking in a given paradigm. This unit can be structural (word, verse, sentence, stanza, etc.) or semantic. In the glossary provided with the orientation text, the linkeme is of a semantic class that can be defined as the unit of language that needs explanation. In the presentation of textual variation, it is a structural unit—for example, a paragraph. In the actual hypertext edition, one can display all the variants of each paragraph in all six of the versions on the screen. This display is made possible by a complicated architecture on the code side that allows for hypertext visualization on the browser side. This architecture was automagically generated from the digital archive by a suite of sed and awk scripts. The linkemic approach provides the user with enough contextual information to study the genetic history of the text, and it introduces new ways of reading the edition. Because a new document window, displaying a text version of the user's choice, can be opened alongside the hypertext edition, users can decide which text to read as their base text. The hypertext edition can then be used as a sort of apparatus with any of the versions included in the edition. In this way, hypertext and the linkemic approach enable the reading and study of multiple texts and corroborate such textual qualifications as variation, instability, and genetic (ontological, teleological) dynamism.

MODERN MANUSCRIPTS

Despite its strengths, this practice is problematic for a genetic edition based on modern manuscript material. In the following discussion, I start with two observations that are inherently subjective and personal but nonetheless true. I then confront the reality these observations signal with the reality of transcribing modern manuscripts out of genetic interest, which leads to a brief treatment of the goals of the mainly French school of *critique génétique*, the peculiarities of the modern manuscript, and the problems resulting from trying to achieve the work in the current TEI proposals. As an alternative I suggest that further research on a methodology and practice of noncritical editing or transcription of modern manuscript material may result in markup strategies that can be applied to the constitution, reading, and analysis of a so-called *dossier génétique*. My approach to the manuscript as a filtered materialization of an internal creative process, one that is comparable with the process of internal monologue or dialogue and that thus can be considered a form of speech, might be helpful in this respect.

Observation 1: (Non)Critical Editing

Allen Renear points out that the distribution of attention to and resources for the study of critical editing and the study of noncritical editing is in inverse proportion to their relative practical importance (25). Apart from Mary-Jo Kline's very useful *A Guide to Documentary Editing*, it is, for instance, difficult to find an extensive and coherent treatment of noncritical editing in handbooks and survey articles on scholarly editing; specialized journals mainly if not exclusively focus on the theory and practice of critical editing (Renear 24). The eight steps that Wilhelm Ott outlined for the production of a critical edition and that Susan Hockey took as the framework for her chapter on textual criticism in *Electronic Texts in the Humanities* (124–45), for instance, jump from the collection of witnesses (step 1) to the collation of the witnesses (step 2) and further to

> the evaluation of the results of the collation (step 3)
> the constitution of a copy-text (step 4)
> the compilation of apparatuses (step 5)
> the preparation of indexes (step 6)
> the preparation of the printer's copy (step 7)
> and finally the publication of the edition (step 8)

The essential, difficult, and time-consuming step of the transcription of primary textual sources is not explicitly mentioned in this outline. Instead it is silently folded into the second step—the collation of the witnesses—and thus primarily oriented toward the representations or captions of the linguistic text whose collations produce a record of the interdocumentary variation. Optimally, transcription should precede the second step, as it is the principal activity of critical editing and the epistemic foundation for all further textual criticism and textual editing. Only on the basis of transcriptions can the editor proceed to automatic collation, stemma (re)construction, the creation of (cumulative) indexes and concordances, and so on, by computer.

This neglect of noncritical editing in otherwise instructive outlines for the textual critic is the more remarkable because in the not-so-distant past— as we may recall from reading, for instance, Ben Ross Schneider's report on the *London Stage Information Bank* in his *Travels in Computerland*—up to half the time, the efforts (and the budget) of an electronic project were devoted to converting textual data into another format, in this case one machine-readable. Electronic noncritical editing is concerned with the twofold transformation from one format into another: first the transformation from the text of a physical document to the transcription of that text; second the transformation from one medium, the manuscript, to another, the machine-readable transcription.

Peter Robinson makes the important point about transcribing the *Canterbury Tales* manuscripts that there is no division between transcription and editing: "To transcribe a manuscript is to select, to amalgamate, to divide, to ignore, to highlight, to edit" ("Manuscript Politics" 10). If we consider "editing" as short for scholarly editing, then both critical and noncritical editing should always have a scholarly result. The reason for the neglect of noncritical editing in the theory and practice of textual criticism, however, is frequently the lack of a satisfactory ontology of the text on which a methodology of noncritical editing can be modeled.

In contrast with the production scheme for critical editions I have just discussed, the TEI guidelines do seem to make explicit the distinction between noncritical and critical editing by devoting two separate chapters to the transcription of primary sources (ch. 18) and the critical apparatus (ch. 19). Although it is explained that "It is expected that this tag set will also be useful in the preparation of critical editions, but the tag set defined here is distinct from that defined in chapter 19 [*Critical Apparatus*] and may be used independently of it," the DTD subset for transcription also allows the scholar "to include other editorial material within transcriptions, such as comments on the status or possible origin of particular readings, corrections, or text supplied to fill lacunae" (Sperberg-McQueen and Burnard, *Guidelines for Text Encoding* 453), which strictly speaking are not features of literal transcription. So the chapter that seemingly deals with noncritical editing in the TEI guidelines addresses issues that are central in critical editing and includes in its DTD subset tags to encode them. A provocative reading of the rhetoric of the opening paragraphs of chapter 18 could then be paraphrased as "the scholar who wants to transcribe primary source material in a noncritical way in fact uses only a small portion of the DTD subset and does not exploit its capabilities to the full." This signifier is typical of the influence of the traditional schools of textual editing on the work of the TEI. Whereas they emphasize the unimportance of noncritical editing in their theories, the French school of *critique génétique* mainly works with noncritical representations of the documents under study.

Observation 2: Methodology

According to Renear, "Non-critical editions 'transcribe,' 'reproduce,' 'present'—all these words are used—the text of a particular document, with no changes, no subtractions, no additions. It gives us the text, the whole text and nothing but the text of an actual physical document" (24). But as I have suggested, an answer to the basic question of what text is, and hence what to transcribe, is a prerequisite to the transcription of a primary source. Only when a project has a clear agreement on the ontology of the text can a methodology for text transcription be developed.

Although the TEI subset for the transcription of primary source material has "not proved entirely satisfactorily" for a number of problems (Driscoll 81), it does provide an extremely rich set of mechanisms for the encoding of older texts and documents with a fairly neat appearance, such as print editions, which are fairly static and stable. Although the TEI chapter on transcription gives examples from modern manuscript material, the result of the successful use of the TEI in critical and noncritical editing can be observed mainly in projects that deal with older material and that are interested in the record of interdocumentary variation.

The transcription of modern manuscript material using TEI proves to be more problematic because of at least two essential characteristics of such complex source material: time and overlapping hierarchies. Since SGML (and thus XML) was devised on the assumption that a document is a logical construct that contains one or more trees of elements that make up the document's content (Goldfarb 18), several scholars began to theorize that text is an ordered hierarchy of content objects (OHCO thesis) that always nest properly and never overlap;[16] they acknowledged the difficulties attached to this claim.[17] The TEI guidelines propose five possible methods to handle non-nesting information[18] but state:

> Non-nesting information poses fundamental problems for any encoding scheme, and it must be stated at the outset that no solution has yet been suggested which combines all the desirable attributes of formal simplicity, capacity to represent all occurring or imaginable kinds of structures, suitability for formal or mechanical validation, and clear identity with the notations needed for simpler cases (i.e. cases where the textual features do nest properly). The representation of non-hierarchical information is thus necessarily a matter of choices among alternatives, of trade-offs between various sets of different advantages and disadvantages. (Sperberg-McQueen and Burnard, *Guidelines for Electronic Text Encoding*, ch. 31)

The editor using an encoding scheme for the transmission of any feature of a modern manuscript text to a machine-readable format is essentially confronted with a dynamic concept of time that constitutes nonhierarchical information. Whereas the simple representation of a prose text can be thought of as a logical tree of hierarchical and structural elements (e.g., book, part, chapter, paragraph) and an alternative tree of hierarchical and physical elements (e.g., volume, page, column, line)—structures that can be applied to most printed texts and classical and medieval manuscripts—the modern manuscript shows a much more complicated web of interwoven and overlapping relations of elements and structures.

Modern manuscripts, as Almuth Grésillon defines them, are "manuscrits qui font partie d'une genèse textuelle attestée par plusieurs témoins successifs et qui manifestent le travail d'écriture d'un auteur" 'manuscripts that are considered as forming part of the genesis of a text, evidence of which is given by several successive witnesses, and that show the writing process of an author' (244). Therefore, the structural unit of a modern manuscript is not the paragraph, page, or chapter but the temporal unit of writing. These units form a complex network that often is not bound to the chronology of the page.

The current inability to encode these temporal and genetic features of the manuscript and the overlapping hierarchies with a single, elegant encoding scheme forces an editor to make choices that result in impoverished and partial representations of the complex documentary source. Further, if such an encoding scheme existed and genetic transcriptions could be produced, the current collation software would need to be redesigned to take these nonnesting structures into account. Therefore, in the electronic edition of *De teleurgang van den Waterhoek*, we opted to represent the complex documentary sources by means of digital facsimiles only, preserving in that way the genetic context of the author's dynamic writing process. By mounting these digital images in a hypertext structure that confronts them with representations of the other witnesses in the edition, the instability of the text is emphasized and the user is provided with a tool to reconstruct the writing process of the novel under study. This focus on hypertext functionality and image-based editing (which I consider a valuable and valid form of editing) could give the false impression that transcriptions become superfluous, that by astounding their audience with digital facsimiles, clickable image maps, and JavaScript-driven dynamic views of the digital images, the developers of such editions very cunningly avoid having to include a full transcription of the documentary sources—and that I have been one of them.[19]

A further example of this fear of testing systems against modern manuscript material is illustrated in an article by Eric Lecolinet, Laurent Robert, and François Role on a sophisticated tool for text-image coupling for editing literary texts. The article, which appeared in the thematic issue *Image-Based Humanities Computing* of *Computers and the Humanities*, presents

> a system devoted to the editing and browsing of complex literary hypermedia including original manuscript documents and other handwritten sources. Editing capabilities allow the user to transcribe images in an interactive way and to encode the resulting textual representation by means of a logical markup language. . . . (49)

The first figure in this article shows a complicated page of authorial interventions in Gustave Flaubert's manuscript, but the next five figures demonstrate the system at work, show a simple medieval manuscript and a simple handwritten text, neither of which contains any authorial additions, deletions, substitutions, or revisions. It almost seems that the texts used for demonstration were chosen to illustrate the limited capabilities of the demonstrated system.

This fear of testing existing transcription systems with modern manuscript material of a complicated nature in several projects may signal the fact that a coherent system or methodology for the transcription of modern material still must be developed and tested and that an ontology of the text must be agreed on.

Intermezzo

> There has never been a single standard convention for the transcription of manuscript texts, and it is not likely that there ever will be one, given the great variety of textual complications that manuscripts—from all times and places—can present. (Vander Meulen and Tanselle 201)

Genetic Criticism—*Critique Génétique*

Renear says that there are major challenges to his view of text ontology that sees literal transcription as a "literal representation of the linguistic text of a particular document" (29). Therefore, he adds, "it presents the author's linguistic achievements, not the author's linguistic intentions." One such challenge is Jerome McGann's identification and treatment of "bibliographic codes" (30). *Critique génétique* is yet another major challenge to his view of text ontology, in that it is also interested in things such as time, ductus, and topology of the page, which are strictly speaking not parts of the text.[20]

The problematic position of *critique génétique* among the other schools of textual criticism and textual editing is that its primary aim is to study the pre-text (*avant-texte*) not so much to set out editorial principles for textual representation as to understand the genesis of a literary work. Therefore, *critique génétique* does not aim to reconstitute the optimal text of a work and is interested not in the text but in the dynamic writing process, which can be reconstructed by close study of the extant drafts, notebooks, and so on. Moreover, as Tanselle points out in a dicusssion of Antoine Compagnon's introduction to a special issue of *Romanic Review* (86.3 [1995]), "French genetic critics are generally opposed to the construction of editions, on the grounds that an apparatus of variants, derived from the classical model in which variants are departures from an author's final text, is inappropriate for an authorial *avant-texte* and implies a subordination of it" ("Textual Criticism at the Millennium" 27). Rather than produce editions, the *généticiens* put together a *dossier génétique* by localizing and dating, ordering, deciphering, and transcribing all pre-text witnesses. Only then can they read and interpret the *dossier génétique*. But the publication of genetic editions is still possible. The influential French *généticien* Pierre-Marc de Biassi defines three different categories of genetic editions:

transversal edition: attempts to render works that were left unfinished because of the author's sudden death or for whatever other reason

horizontal edition: reconstructs one particular phase in the writing process—for example, the author's notebooks of a certain period

vertical edition: reconstitutes the complete textual history
(Van Hulle 375–76)

Computers have been used both to publish a genetic edition and to assemble and read a *dossier génétique*. The concept of hypertext has been used extensively to regroup a series of documents that are akin to one another on the basis of resemblance or difference in many ways, but the various endeavors to produce such hypertext editions or dossiers are too oriented toward display. In the past as well as nowadays, commercial software packages such as *Hypercard*, *Toolbook*, *Macromedia*, *Adobe Acrobat*, and even *Powerpoint* have been used for genetic purposes, with data stored in proprietary formats. Where standards for markup have been used, we see HTML as the unbeaten champion for products in which every link, color, frame, and animation has been hard-coded without a repository of SGML/XML-based transcriptions of the manuscript texts. Such transcriptions are not used, as we have seen, partly because of an absent or non-text-based ontology of the text.

Intermezzo

> The institutional and technical machinery of textual genetics should not blind us to the fact that the object that it purports to study will almost by definition escape "science." What textual genetics studies is in effect something that cannot be observed, that cannot become an object: the origin itself of the literary work. (Laurent Jenny)[21]

Putting Time Back in Manuscripts

I propose a methodology that might help us combine the study of what "cannot be observed" in very observable markup. I argue that a writing process and hence any text resulting from it (by definition) takes place in time, which immediately results in four complications for the noncritical editor and text encoder:

1. The beginning and end of the process may be hard to determine, and the internal composition of the text may be difficult to define (document structure vs. unit of writing): authors frequently interrupt writing, leave sentences unfinished, and so on.
2. Manuscripts frequently contain scriptorial pauses, which have immense importance in the analysis of the genesis of a text.
3. Even nonverbal elements, such as sketches, drawings, and doodles, may be regarded as a component of the writing process for some analytic purposes.
4. Below the level of the chronological act of writing, manuscripts may be segmented into units defined by thematic, syntactic, stylistic phenomena; no clear agreement exists about how to name such segments.

These four complexities are exactly what the TEI guidelines consider "distinctive features of speech." In chapter 11, "Transcription of Speech," we read:

> Unlike a written text, a speech event takes place in time. Its beginning and end may be hard to determine and its internal composition difficult to define. Most researchers agree that the utterances or turns of individual speakers form an important structural component in most kinds of speech, but these are rarely as well-behaved (in the structural sense) as paragraphs or other analogous units in written texts: speakers frequently interrupt each other, use gestures as well

as words, leave remarks unfinished and so on. Speech itself, though it may be represented as words, frequently contains items such as vocalized pauses which, although only semi-lexical, have immense importance in the analysis of spoken text. Even non-vocal elements such as gestures may be regarded as forming a component of spoken text for some analytic purposes. Below the level of the individual utterance, speech may be segmented into units defined by phonological, prosodic, or syntactic phenomena; no clear agreement exists, however, even as to appropriate names for such segments. (Sperberg-McQueen and Burnard, *Guidelines for Electronic Text Encoding* 258)

If we consider any holograph witness as a filtered materialization of an internal creative process (thinking) that can be roughly compared to an internal dialogue between the author and the biographical person, we may have a basis on which to build a methodology for the transcription of modern manuscript material. By combining the TEI DTD subsets for the transcription of primary sources, the encoding of the critical apparatus, and the transcription of speech, we could try to transcribe a manuscript and analyze it with tools for the manipulation of corpora of spoken language. It is interesting in this respect to observe how *critique génétique* describes authorial interventions like deletions, additions, *Sofortkorrektur* or *currente calamo*, substitutions, and displacements in terms of material or intellectual gestures, as if they were kinesic (nonverbal, nonlexical) phenomena.

This approach does not do away with the essential problem of non-nesting information, which is an inescapable fact of textual life and even results from a one-way analysis.[22]

Instead of focusing the debate on the possibilities of electronic scholarly editions and the advantages over print editions in terms of usability—as has been done too often—editorial theorists should concentrate on the possibilities of a text that can be discovered by studying manuscript material very closely. Creating a noncritical edition-transcription of such a text with the use of encoding is the closest kind of reading one can do. Those who reveal the writing out of the written work and discover the traces of the genesis of the text in its internal dynamics have something sensible to say about the text and the intentions of the author. But modern manuscripts are complex and unwilling to obey the conventional ontologies of text and systems of text encoding. Paraphrasing Louis Hay, one could say that the principal merit of manuscripts is that they demonstrate the limitations and possibilities of text encoding. From the outset there are important material limitations: it is impossible to study a nonexistent manuscript.[23] Paradoxically, existent and extant manuscripts generate, by their resistance to current systems of text encoding, new ontologies of the text and new approaches toward that encoding. Likewise, current systems of encoding lay bare new possibilities by their inability to deal with such manuscripts.

NOTES

This essay is for Alois Pichler, director of the Wittgenstein Archives, whom I'd like to thank for the many fruitful discussions on textual genetics and transcription procedures, and for Heli Jakobson, who managed to drag me from behind my desk every now and again during my stay in Norway. Research for this article has been made possible by a European Research Grant (Fifth Framework Programme Improving the Human Research Potential and the Socioeconomic Base: Access to Research Infrastructures [ARI] for research at the Wittgenstein Archives at the University of Bergen from 1 June to 7 July 2002).

1. Elsewhere I have suggested a model for electronic scholarly editing that unlinks the archival function from the museum function. "By *Archival Function* I mean the preservation of the literary artifact in its historical form and the historical-critical research of a literary work. *Museum Function* I define as the presentation by an editor of the physical appearance and/or the contents of the literary artifact in a documentary, aesthetic, sociological, authorial or bibliographical contextualization, intended for a specific public and published in a specific form and lay-out. The digital archive should be the place for the first function, showing a relative objectivity, or a documented subjectivity in its internal organization and encoding. The Museum Function should work in an edition—disregarding its external form—displaying the explicit and expressed subjectivity and the formal orientation of the editor. The relationship between these two functions is hierarchical: there is no Museum Function without an Archival Function and an edition should always be based on a digital archive" ("Where Is" 176).

2. See my and Ron Van den Branden's *Describing* for a discussion on three ways to produce a scholarly edition with the use of text encoding: digitizing an existing print edition; creating an electronic edition, for example by recording some or all of the known variations among different witnesses to the text in a critical apparatus of variants; and generating electronic editions from encoded transcriptions of the documentary source material.

3. "A *place* should be any piece of information, or at least any that exists in a stable or recoverable form" (DeRose and van Dam 9).

4. The novel tells the story about the resistance of a rural community in a hamlet

called de Waterhoek to the intrusion of industrial technology—that is, the building of a bridge—and the consequences of this new connection to the outside world. The plot is complicated by the passionate relationship between Mira, a frank village girl, and Maurice, the engineer supervising the construction. The text of the first print edition of the novel is 297 pages long and contains 117,800 words.

5. Stijn Streuvels is a pseudonym for Frank Lateur.

6. These omissions were later addressed in a series of essays. See my "Linkemic Approach" and "Display"; De Smedt and Vanhoutte. The introductory material to the edition does give an account, however, of the textual genesis and history of the text; descriptions of its physical forms and physical appearance; the rationale for editorial decisions such as emendations, the treatment of spelling, punctuation, and so on. A separate technical documentation outlines the markup strategies, the digitization process, the hardware and software used, and the creation of the electronic product.

7. For this purpose I make extensive use of the three essays mentioned in note 6.

8. The editorial project ran from 1998 to 1999 and was funded by the Royal Academy of Dutch Language and Literature in Gent, Belgium (Koninklijke Academie voor Nederlandse Taal- en Letterkunde [www.kantl.be]). The project was supervised by Marcel De Smedt, who also functioned as a coeditor. Together with the electronic critical edition on CD-ROM, a text-critical reading edition in book form was published as a spin-off product of the electronic project (1999).

9. The book contained also a glossary, an introductory article on the genesis of the novel, a description of the transmission history of the text including all the documentary sources and existing editions, an account of the principles underlying the constitution of the reading text (spelling, punctuation, corrections) with a list of corrections and end-of-line hyphenations, an account of the principles underlying the creation of the glossary, and a couple of facsimiles from the several documentary sources involved in the research.

10. After an incubation period of twenty-some years, Streuvels started writing his novel and published it in installments in *De Gids* in 1927. At the end of 1927 it was published in book form both in Flanders and the Netherlands by two different publishers using the same print. For the second print edition (1939) the text was drastically reduced (by 26.6%), because the Dutch publisher requested a shorter and hence cheaper version of the book. The author chose to cross out, among others, those passages that were of a too explicit and erotic nature and against which many Catholic critics had fulminated in their reviews of the first print edition. At the same time, Streuvels changed the end of the novel. In the first edition the protagonist couple divorce, but the author suggests that the couple may eventually reunite, and there is an allusion to an unborn child. In the drastically revised edition, the divorce is definitive and conclusive. Up to the publication of the thirteenth print edition of the novel in 1987, this version was the basis for eleven successful reprints.

11. Although the second print edition retains only 73.4% of the text of the first print edition, more emendations had to be made in it (93 and 73, resp.).

12. These examples could be paraphrased as `<corr sic="kiten" resp="EV">`; `kiten</corr>` and `<sic corr="kitten">kiten</sic>`, respectively.

13. The electronic critical edition is an autoexecutable application that launches itself when the CD-ROM is inserted in the CD drive; it comes with *MultiDoc Pro CD Browser* software. No programs need to be installed on the hard drive of the computer (PC only) on which the edition is consulted. The electronic edition is an autonomous, closed package, having no links to the Internet. This feature meets the requirements that Paul Brians voiced: "CD-ROMs at the least should be self-contained, and not require that files be installed on hard drives or permanent links be available to the Internet."

14. For the transcription and markup of the correspondence material, I developed a project-specific StreuLet DTD, which allows the encoding of letter-specific elements such as the existence of the envelope and envelope information: postmark, place of posting, sender, sender's address, recipient, recipient's address, and so on. This work has developed further into the DALF guidelines for the description and encoding of modern correspondence material and the DALF DTD. DALF, an acronym for *Digital Archive of Letters in Flanders*, focuses on correspondence by Flemish authors and composers from the nineteenth and twentieth centuries. It is envisioned as a growing text base of correspondence material that can generate different products for both academia and a wider audience and thus provide a tool for diverse research disciplines ranging from literary criticism to historical, diachronic, synchronic, and sociolinguistic research. The input of this text base will consist of the materials produced in separate electronic edition projects. See Vanhoutte and Van den Branden, *DALF Guidelines*, *Describing*, and "Presentational . . . Issues"; the DALF Web site (www.kantl.be/ctb/project/dalf/).

15. The choice of hardware and software and the parameters decided on when batch-converting a TIFF file to a lossy format such as JPEG (e.g., the application of an Unsharp Mask filter) are nonobjective moments in the digitization process and highly influence the eventual result.

16. Annex C of ISO 8879 introduces the optional CONCUR feature (not available in XML), which "supports multiple concurrent structural views in addition to the abstract view. It allows the user to associate element, entity, and notation declarations with particular document type names, via multiple document type declarations" (Goldfarb 89).

17. Suggested further reading on overlap-related problems: Barnard, Hayter, Karababa, Logan, and McFadden; Barnard, Burnard, Gaspart, Price, Sperberg-McQueen, and Varile; DeRose, Durand, Mylonas, and Renear; Durand, Mylonas, and DeRose; Huitfeldt, "Multi-dimensional Texts"; Renear, Durand, and

Mylonas; Sperberg-McQueen and Huitfeldt, "Concurrent Document Hierarchies" and GODDAG; and Sperberg-McQueen and Burnard, *Guidelines for Electronic Text Encoding*, ch. 31 ("Multiple Hierarchies").

18. The suggested methods are CONCUR, milestone elements, fragmentation of an element, virtual joints, and redundant encoding of information in multiple forms (see ch. 31 of the TEI guidelines. The *Rossetti Archive* based in Virginia, and the Wittgenstein Archives at the University of Bergen created their own encoding system—respectively, RAD (Rossetti Archive Document) and MECS (Multi Element Code System)—out of dissatisfaction with the operationality of the options suggested by TEI. See McGann, *Radiant Textuality* 88–97; *Text Encoding at the Wittgenstein Archives* (http://wab.aksis.uib.no/1990–99/textencod .htm).

19. One absurd exponent of image-based editing is the genetic edition of Flaubert's *L'éducation sentimentale* by Tony Williams and Alan Blunt (www.hull.ac.uk/hitm/). The diplomatic transcriptions were "initially prepared as Word (.doc) files, which cannot be readily converted into HTML text files, since 'raw' HTML code is unable to render the refined layout, freeform lines, and interlinear additions and other features of the transcriptions achieved through advanced use of modern word-processing software" (Williams and Blunt 198). Therefore, the editors contend, "Diplomatic transcriptions need . . . to be stored in the hypertext package as image files" (199), which they create by printing out the *Word* files and scanning them on a flatbed scanner. Hyperlinks from the transcription image file to documentary notes are then established by means of image maps. But since hypertext is usually signaled by the browser by a different text color, "the hotspots must be indicated (via words in red that do not corrupt the typographical integrity of the diplomatic rendering) in the word-processed transcription document before digitization" (200).

20. Grésillon provides a good introduction to the methodology of *critique génétique*. A good introduction in English is Falconer.

21. "L'appareillage institutionel et technique de la génétique textuelle ne saurait faire oublier que l'objet qu'elle se donne échappe presque par définition à la 'science.' Ce que scrute la génétique textuelle, c'est en effet un inobservable, un inobjectivable: l'origine même de l'œuvre littéraire" (Laurent Jenny, *Divagations généticiennes*, qtd. in Lernout 124).

22. See my "Display or Argument?" for a further discussion of nonnesting information.

23. "The principal merit of manuscripts is that they demonstrate the limitations and possibilities of genetic criticism. From the outset there are important limitations: it is impossible to study a nonexistent manuscript" (Hay 68).

PHILOSOPHY CASE STUDY

CLAUS HUITFELDT

ittgenstein's Nachlass*: The Bergen Electronic Edition* was published at Oxford University Press in 2000. This electronic edition is the first publication of the Austrian philosopher Ludwig Wittgenstein's complete philosophical *Nachlass*. It contains more than 20,000 searchable pages of transcription and a complete color facsimile. The contents and the scale of the edition as well as the editorial methods employed should make it relevant not only to Wittgenstein scholarship but also to computer-based textual criticism in general.

Wittgenstein had only one philosophical book published: *Tractatus Logico-Philosophicus*. Yet he left behind approximately 20,000 pages of unpublished manuscript. Important parts of this *Nachlass* have been edited and published posthumously (von Wright). Even so, more than two-thirds of the *Nachlass* remained unpublished until the appearance of the electronic edition (Biggs and Pichler 12).

Some of the previously published editions are selections from several different manuscripts, but the relations of the selections to the manuscripts are not recorded in any detail. The editions are results of different editorial approaches to the manuscripts, some containing a lot of intervention, others less. Most of the editions contain no critical apparatus or other detailed documentation of editorial decisions. Given this background, it is no wonder that for a long time there was a demand for a complete, text-critical edition of the entire *Nachlass*.

WITTGENSTEIN'S *NACHLASS*

Like many other modern manuscripts, Wittgenstein's writings contain deletions, overwritings, interlinear insertions, marginal remarks and annotations, substitutions, counterpositions, shorthand abbreviations, as well as orthographic errors and slips of the pen. A particular problem is posed by his habit of combining interlinear insertion, marking, and often also deletion, to form alternative expressions. In some cases he clearly decided in favor of a specific alternative; in others the decision was left open. Moreover, Wittgenstein had his own peculiar editorial conventions, such as an elaborate system of section marks, cross-outs, cross-references, marginal marks and lines, and various distinctive types of underlining.

Many of these features are results of his continuous efforts to revise and rearrange his writings. Some of the revisions consisted in copying or dictating parts of the text of one manuscript into another. The *Nachlass* therefore contains several layers or stages of basically similar pieces of text. These inter- and intratextual relations, although complicated and by no means fully known, are of interest to scholars studying the development of Wittgenstein's thought.

WHY A DOCUMENTARY EDITION?

Given both the nature of the *Nachlass* itself and its relation to the existing posthumously published editions, it was by no means obvious what a complete, scholarly edition of the *Nachlass* ought to look like. On the one hand, the repetitive nature of the material seemed to call for a synthetic, text-critical edition of some kind, where different versions of largely identical texts in different manuscripts would be represented in the form of variants on one base text. Yet editorial decisions in general, and the choice of base text in particular, would be interpretationally debatable and problematic in relation to the philosophical audience the edition was supposed to serve.

On the other hand, a documentary edition reproducing the large number of revisions and rewritings page by page, manuscript by manuscript, seemed to lead to a massive, confusing, and unnecessary duplication of basically identical material. To some extent this confusion could no doubt be remedied by cross-referencing among the different versions. But such cross-referencing might easily become so extensive that it would just add to the complexity of presentation.

The problems with a documentary edition, however, were considered acceptable if the edition was to be published in electronic form. First, the bulkiness of a documentary edition is easier to deal with in electronic form. Second, an electronic edition is more open-ended and flexible than a book edition. It was therefore decided to do an electronic, documentary edition. There was (and still is) no intention to publish this edition in book form. But clearly it could provide the basis for a synthetic edition, should that prove desirable in the future.

CONTENTS OF THE EDITION

Wittgenstein's Nachlass: *The Bergen Electronic Edition* has three main components: a facsimile, a diplomatic transcription, and a normalized transcription, each providing an interrelated but independent view of the *Nachlass*. The facsimile simply consists of digital, high-quality color images of each and every page of the *Nachlass*. The diplomatic and normalized transcriptions are differentiated not so much in terms of how much detail they convey as by their textual perspectives.

The diplomatic version records faithfully not only every letter and word but also details relating to the original appearance of the text. One might say it acknowledges that our understanding of the text derives in no small part from the visual appearance of material on the page. The diplomatic version reproduces features such as deleted words and letters, shorthand abbreviations, orthographic inconsistencies, rejected formulations, authorial instructions for the reordering of material, and marginal comments. It was assumed that one of the principal uses of the diplomatic text would be as an aid to reading the facsimile.

The normalized version, on the other hand, presents the text in its thematic and semantic aspect. Orthography is corrected to a standard form, slips of the pen and deleted materials are suppressed, shorthand abbreviations are extended, and the author's unequivocal instructions for the reordering of material are carried out. Variants have been merged to alternative readings; only one reading is always visible on-screen, while the others may be displayed on request. The result is a version that is easy to read and suitable for searching for words and phrases.

The three versions are linked, so that the reader can easily switch among them (figure 1 shows a screen with each version of the same text in a separate window). Typically, a reader will first search the normalized transcription for particular words or phrases, then consult the diplomatic transcription for further detail, and finally (e.g., if in doubt about the transcription) the facsimile. Readers can search not only for words and phrases (using wildcards, Boolean expressions, and proximity searching) but also for content elements like dates, personal names, substitutions, and formulas. Searches can be limited to particular manuscripts or groups of manuscripts, date ranges, and so on. (Figures 2 and 3 are screen shots of search templates showing some of the possible categories for searching.)

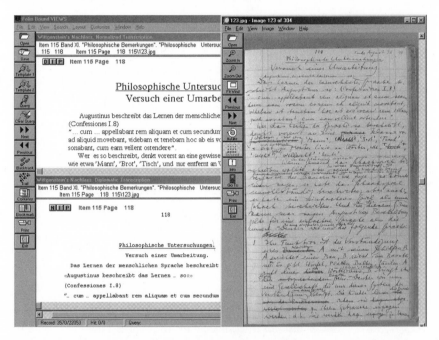

Fig. 1. Split screen showing three electronic versions of Wittgenstein's *Nachlass*: normalized transcription, diplomatic transcription, and facsimile

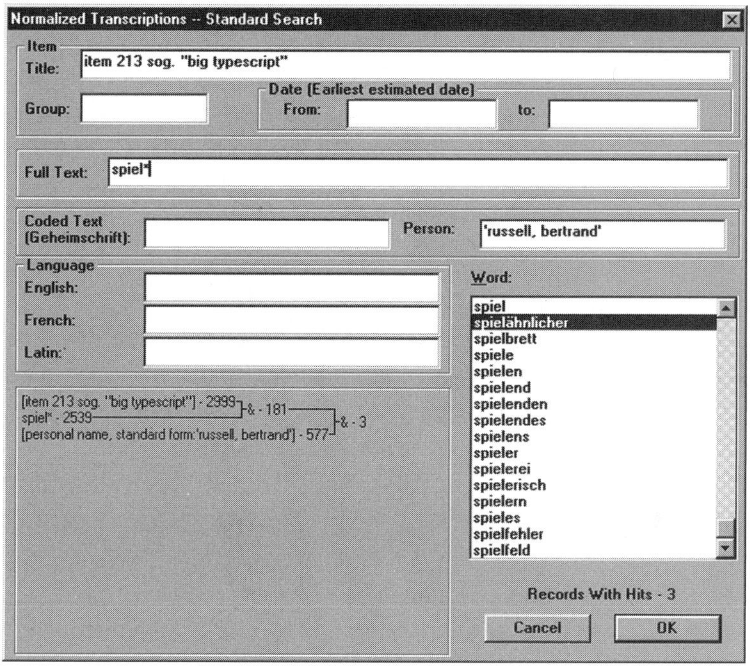

Fig. 2. Standard search template for Wittgenstein's *Nachlass*

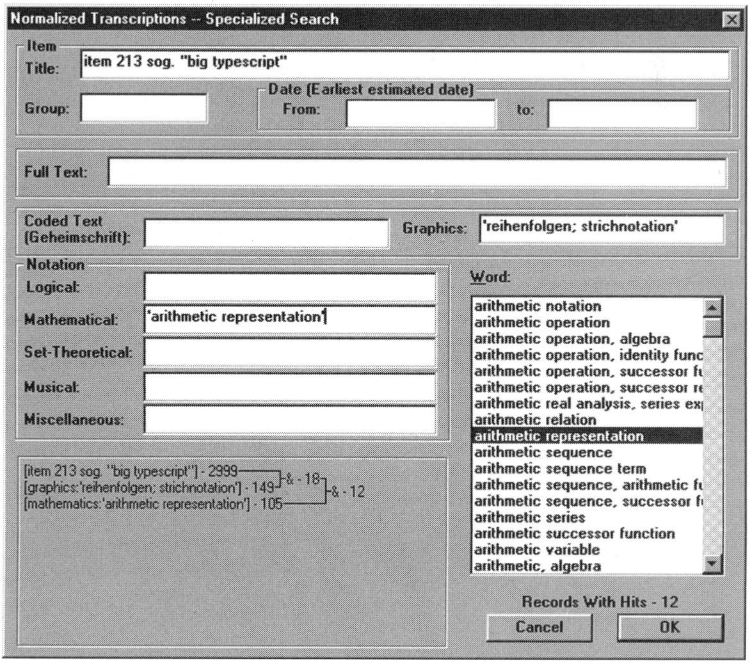

Fig. 3. Specialized search template for Wittgenstein's *Nachlass*

SOME KEY NUMBERS

The edition's 20,000 pages, all presented in these three alternative formats, comprise three million words. To interlink the three versions, approximately 200,000 links were created. In addition, a few thousand links represent Wittgenstein's own cross-references. The source transcriptions from which the edition was derived (see below) contain approximately two million coded elements (not including entity references or codes for special characters).

Even though partly based on work done earlier (Huitfeldt and Rossvær), this project took almost ten years to complete. The Wittgenstein Archives at the University of Bergen spent altogether forty man-years (including text transcription and editing, management, administration, systems development and maintenance, and all other tasks related to the project), to give an average throughput of two pages per person per day, which is high compared with other editorial projects.

AIMS OF THE EDITION

In the preparation of this edition, the following basic requirements guided the work of the Wittgenstein Archives. Transcriptions should provide a fully sufficient basis for the production of both diplomatic and normalized versions of each and every manuscript. Transcriptions should also be suited for searches for words, strings and content elements, and cross-referencing. In addition, transcriptions should include information that facilitates grammatical analysis and segmentation according to alternative criteria.

It was considered of utmost importance that the edition document manuscript details according to the highest possible standards of text-critical accuracy, that it should apply a uniform and consistent set of editorial principles throughout the entire *Nachlass*, and that it should document the exact sources for each and every piece of text.

Ideally, transcriptions should be not only (though most important) accurate and interpretationally sound, consistent and systematic, but also falsifiable. In other words, they should be guided by explicit rules, so that anyone who endeavored to repeat transcription according to these rules would, as far as possible, obtain identical results.

PRIMARY FORMAT

These requirements often implied conflicting demands. In particular, implications of the requirement for a diplomatic version easily conflicted with the other requirements. Yet for a number of reasons, most notably the concern for secure and reliable data maintenance, we decided that for any given manuscript one and only one source transcription should serve all our purposes.

To ensure the longevity of the work, we felt it imperative that the format of the source transcriptions be, as far as possible, hardware- and software-independent. It was decided to use a declarative text-encoding system—that is, to mark textual features explicitly according to a formal syntax, which would enable us to produce, with off-the-shelf or specially designed software, secondary versions that satisfied the demands set forth above.

At the time the Wittgenstein Archives were established, standard generalized markup language (SGML) was the only serious international standard to be considered. But we decided not to use SGML for this project. Instead, a special code syntax was developed for the Wittgenstein Archives, and software that allowed for flexible conversion to other formats was developed. This syntax and software were called a multielement code system (MECS) (Huitfeldt, *MECS*).

One of the reasons for not choosing SGML was that it had difficulty representing overlapping and other complex textual features. Another reason was that little relevant software for SGML existed, and there was little experience available in applying it in scholarly editorial work (the TEI guidelines did not yet exist). MECS was designed to overcome some of the problems with SGML and to provide software support for text-critical purposes beyond those provided by SGML at the time. In all other respects, MECS was kept as close to SGML as possible.

But neither the reasons to avoid SGML and instead develop a special code system for the Wittgenstein Archives nor the differences between SGML and MECS are of importance in this discussion (but see Sperberg-McQueen and Huitfeldt, "Concurrent Document Hierarchies" and *GODDAG*). Rather, I focus on examples taken from the SGML-based encoding scheme developed by the Text Encoding Initiative, since it is more widely known than our MECS-based encoding scheme.

CONSISTENCY OF ENCODING

That the TEI guidelines provide various alternative mechanisms for the encoding of many (or even most) textual phenomena is one of the strengths of the guidelines and one of the reasons why they are found applicable to a large number of widely different projects involved in text encoding. At the same time, their openness and flexibility create the danger of inconsistency.

For example, abbreviations may be encoded in basically two different ways according to the TEI guidelines. The German abbreviation *dh*, which normally stands for "das heißt" ("that is"), may be encoded in either way:

```
<abbr expan="das heißt">dh</abbr>
<expan abbr="dh">das heißt</expan>
```

A stylesheet specifying that the content of an ‹abbr› element should be replaced by its expan attribute value, while an ‹expan› element's content should be printed as is, would display both codes as "das heißt." Correspondingly, a stylesheet specifying that the content of an ‹abbr› element should be printed as is, while the content of an ‹expan› element should be replaced by its abbr attribute value, would display both codes as "dh." Any other combination of specifications would treat the two alternative representations of the same abbreviation differently.

There may indeed be a case for treating different instances of the same abbreviation differently (e.g., depending on context), but if the choice of representational form is left completely undecided by rules governing transcription and editing, the path to inconsistency is wide open. On the other hand, there may be a case for treating different abbreviations differently, independent of context. The German *dh* is a commonplace and may be regarded as a standard abbreviation, whereas "Psych," found in certain places in Wittgenstein's *Nachlass*, is by no means one. It may be an abbreviation for "Psychologie," "Psychologisch," or "Psychisch" ("psychology," "psychological," or "psychic"), depending on context and interpretation. (German capitalization rules, a further complication, are not taken into consideration here.)

In SGML, element content can be marked up but attribute values cannot. In other words, if a distinction is made between standard and nonstandard abbreviations and there is a need to mark up both, neither should be represented as attribute values. One of the great advantages of text-encoding systems like SGML is that they allow for automatic validation of document structure. What is checked, however, is the structure of the encoding, not the contents of text elements or attribute values of type text. Sometimes there is a need to check the contents of standard and nonstandard abbreviations separately. (For example, it may be desirable to check both against a list of standard abbreviations.) In such cases, both should be represented as element content, though of different element types.

The Wittgenstein Archives decided to make a distinction between standard and nonstandard abbreviations and to represent both as element content. (Had we used the TEI guidelines, we might have used the `<abbr>` element for the former and the `<expan>` element for the latter.) The point of this discussion is not to advocate a particular approach taken by the Wittgenstein Archives but to illustrate that, for virtually every textual phenomenon to be encoded, each project needs to reflect on issues like these in order to ensure the desired level of consistency.

CONSISTENCY OF EDITING AND INTERPRETATION

Consider the following, hypothetical example from a manuscript source:

To comply with the Wittgenstein Archives requirements for the diplomatic version, one must account for the facts that "weiße" is inserted above the line, that "Schloß" is overstriked, and that "große" has been misspelled "grosse."

According to the requirements of the normalized version, one must not only account for the fact that "große" is the correct spelling of "grosse" but also sort out the different possible readings of the text in question. Taken out of context, the example may seem intuitively to have at least the following possible readings:

das große weiße Haus ("the big white house")
das große weiße Schloß ("the big white castle")
das große Schloß ("the big castle")
das weiße Haus ("the white house")
das große Haus ("the big house")
das weiße Schloß ("the white castle")

In text-critical work, one will invariably rely on transcribers and editors to make their choice of possible readings using their best judgment based on a thorough knowledge of the author, the history of the text, its historical and cultural context, and other interpretationally relevant factors. Quite often, however, such considerations do not decide detailed matters like these with any degree of certainty. In such situations, leaving the choice of readings entirely to the individual transcriber without further guidance is almost certain to lead to inconsistency.

According to the editorial principles employed at the Wittgenstein Archives, the example above has exactly two readings, the first and second—these and no others, neither more nor less (unless interpretational considerations decide otherwise). I do not go into the details here of the principles leading to this decision. Which principles to employ in the choice of reading may always be discussed, and the answer will vary from project to project. In the interest of consistency, however, it is usually important to ensure that such situations are always treated the same way in the same project.

BASIC REQUIREMENTS

One might say that the aim of a diplomatic representation is to get every letter of the original right, whereas the aim of a normalized representation is to get every word and every reading right. So what we need to ensure consistency and reliability of transcription is criteria of what is to count as correct as well as procedures that will help transcribers come up with the right solution in each particular case.

The following is a brief description of the criteria and procedures developed and employed at the Wittgenstein Archives. As mentioned, the Wittgenstein Archives did not use the TEI guidelines, or indeed even SGML. However, the criteria and procedures discussed are entirely independent of such technicalities and could be adopted by any project, TEI-based or not. I start with the criteria for ensuring that a transcription is suited for diplomatic reproduction of the original text. It is not obvious what such reproduction means. According to some conventions, a diplomatic reproduction retains an almost exact positioning of every text element in two-dimensional page space, faithfully reproduces differences among allographs of the same graphemes, and represents visual markings like strikethroughs and underlinings as close as possible to the original in their visual appearance.

The Wittgenstein Archives decided to use a less strict definition: a diplomatic reproduction should reproduce the original, grapheme by grapheme; contain indication of indentation and the relative spatial positioning of text elements on the page; and include information about deletion, interlinear insertion, and a number of different kinds of underlining. It was not considered necessary to indicate every line break or allograph variation. Consequently, the markup system contained markers for phenomena of the kinds mentioned, and the procedure followed by transcribers was simply to mark up every such phenomenon with the required element. With a stylesheet, the marked-up features were reproduced according to certain conventions, and the correctness of transcriptions was checked by visually comparing the output with the original text.

The criteria for ensuring that a transcription is suited for normalized reproduction were less easy to formulate and were dealt with by means of a much more elaborate and formal approach, to be described in the next two sections.

FORMALIZATION AND OPERATIONALIZATION

Consider the following hypothetical example, which is a bit more complicated than the previous one:

Again, an obvious requirement for a normalized reproduction is that orthographic errors are corrected. In this example one will have to mark up the misspelling "Vather" so that the word can be rendered correctly as "Vater" in the normalized version. Admittedly, orthographic rules are not always clear, and texts are frequently written according to idiosyncratic or inconsistent orthographies. Further complications are that orthographic variation is quite often a literary means of expression and that orthography may in itself be an object of study. In electronic texts, spelling affects not only readability but also retrievability. Therefore, standardization is much more important in electronic than in traditional editions. While there may be a need to retain the original orthography, as in diplomatic transcription, there is also a need to standardize orthography to some set of uniform spelling rules.

But what about the variant readings? In the current example, "ein" seems to have been substituted for "eine," "großes" for "große," and "Haus" for "Hütte." At least the following readings seem to be possible:

1. Mein Vater hat eine sehr große Hütte ("My father has a very big cottage")
2. Mein Vater hat ein sehr großes Haus ("My father has a very big house")
3. Mein Vater hat ein sehr großes weißes Haus ("My father has a very big white house")

On the assumption that the inserted "weißes" is intended to apply to both the first and second readings and that the author simply forgot that the insertion of the adjective "weißes" in the first would require the inflected form "weiße," a possible reading might also be:

4. Mein Vater hat eine sehr große weiße Hütte ("My father has a very big white cottage")

As with the previous example, some kind of guidance is needed as to whether all or only some of these readings are to count as possible. But not every possible combination of *substituenda* makes sense. For example, even though "Hütte" has not been deleted, "Mein Vater hat ein sehr großes Hütte" is ungrammatical and not a possible reading. By mechanically selecting one out of every pair of *substituenda*, one can create a large number of obviously invalid readings. One needs to mark up the text in a way that does not include these.

We started out by making a basic decision: if between two transcriptions, interpretational considerations did not decide clearly in favor of one, we would decide which came closer to the ideal of what we called a well-formed text, which we defined as a unilinear sequence of orthographically acceptable and grammatically well-formed sentences that together made a coherent text unit.

Our next step was to define what we called an alpha text: a set of strings derived from a transcription according to a language-specific procedure. There was one such procedure for each language present in the transcription. The procedures consisted in assigning functions such as inclusion, exclusion, and case change to every element type.

Our final step was to define what we called beta texts. We observed that whereas a well-formed text was a unilinear sequence of sentences, a manuscript with alternative readings was multilinear. We defined a transcription's beta texts as a set of texts derived by excluding, for every substitution, all except one reading and repeating the process until all possible combinations of readings had been exhausted.

Thus, our basic requirement that transcriptions be well formed could be reformulated as the requirements that:

T1   Every alpha text derived from the transcription should be a list of orthographically acceptable graphwords in the language of that alpha text.

T2   Every beta text derivable from the transcription should be a well-formed text.

To avoid a possible misunderstanding: the set of beta texts derivable from one and the same transcription does not necessarily represent different interpretations of the manuscript in question. That a transcription derives more than one beta text may just as well be regarded as a characteristic of the interpretation in question.

TRANSCRIPTION METHOD

So far, we had formulated criteria that allowed us to identify some possible transcriptions rather than others as acceptable. What remained to be done was to prescribe a procedure that helped the transcriber satisfy these criteria. To this end, we made use of a somewhat indirect strategy: we prescribed a procedure that, given the nature of the manuscripts we were dealing with, was almost certain to produce a transcription that would not satisfy the criteria. This basic procedure we called rule A:

> Manuscripts should be transcribed page by page, from the front to the back page; each page vertically, line by line, from top to bottom; each line horizontally, letter by letter, from left to right.

The rule may seem too trivial to be of interest. It simply describes one of the most elementary features of the Western writing system. But with manuscripts like ours, this rule, if taken literally, was almost guaranteed to produce transcriptions that were neither interpretationally acceptable nor well formed.

Therefore we also defined circumstances in which transcribers were allowed to deviate from rule A. To deviate from the rule, one or more of the following criteria had to be satisfied:

> D1   It is not possible to satisfy requirements T1 and T2 unless you deviate from rule A and no interpretational considerations directly contradict the deviation in question.
>
> D2   Although a transcription according to rule A satisfies requirements T1 and T2, there is positive evidence in the manuscript in favor of a deviation from rule A and the deviation in question does not lead to violation of T1 or T2.
>
> D3   There is positive evidence for more than one reading of a specific word, one or more of these readings will not be included in the alpha text unless you deviate from rule A, and the deviation in question does not lead to violation of T1 or T2.

Finally, we decided which kinds of deviations or modifications were allowed and listed them in this order of preference: rearrangement, simple substitution, reiterative substitution, extension, and exclusion. Each of these deviations was in turn defined in terms of specific markup procedures. For example, exclusion consisted not in leaving text out but in marking it up with an element classified with a beta-exclusion or alpha-exclusion code. What is important here are not the details of these operations but that the deviations were prioritized: a lower-level deviation could be applied only if no combination of higher-level deviations sufficed to satisfy T1 and T2. For example, simple substitution should be used only if rearrangement is not enough; reiterative substitution, only if neither rearrangement nor simple substitution nor any combination of rearrangement and simple substitution suffices; and so on.

A transcription of the example from the previous section according to the rules defined by our project generates the following alpha text:

mein Vater hat eine ein sehr große großes weißes Hütte Haus

and the following beta texts:

Mein Vater hat eine sehr große Hütte
Mein Vater hat ein sehr großes weißes Haus

The alpha text satisfies T1, and the beta texts satisfy T2. It is worth noting, however, that while the procedure does produce readings 1 and 3, it does not produce readings 2 and 4, which also satisfy T2.

REPRESENTATION AND INTERPRETATION

An intriguing aspect of editing philosophical texts is that the editorial work itself exemplifies a number of classical philosophical problems, such as the relations between representation and interpretation, the subjective and the objective. Traditionally, it has been assumed that the responsibility of an editor is to provide an objectively correct representation of a text and that as far as possible editors should avoid interpretation. Because the edited text is supposed to provide the basis for interpretation of a work, the edition itself should be as free of interpretation as possible. As can be gathered from the frequent references to interpretational considerations in the discussion above, the work of the Wittgenstein Archives was not based on such a view of interpretation. Even so, the very idea of a diplomatic transcription presupposes the possibility of an objectively true and accurate representation of the original text. In particular, the whole motivation for some of the text-encoding practices employed by the project was to ensure the accuracy of the diplomatic representation.

The TEI guidelines, however, "define markup . . . as any means of making explicit an interpretation of a text." Interpretation, in turn, is described as "information which is felt to be non-obvious, contentious, or subject to disagreement" (*Guidelines* [TEI P3]). We are used to thinking of representation and interpretation as a dichotomy. If text encoding is essentially interpretational, how can it possibly help in establishing accurate and correct representations of texts? To solve this problem, we can take as our departure point what I believe to be a commonsense view on representation and interpretation. First, a text is a representation of another text if one has the same linguistic content—that is, the same wording—as the other. Second, a text is an interpretation of another text if one is not a representation of the other but expresses, explains, or discusses the meaning of the other text in other words.

On this background, I propose two steps to get us out of our problem. As a first step, let us imagine representation and interpretation as points located at opposite ends of a continuum. Our task is to find somewhere along this continuum clear demarcation lines that allow us to decide, in particular cases and classes of cases, what is interpretation and what is representation.

By stating that something is a representation, we do not exclude the possibility that it may, given some other demarcation line, legitimately be regarded as interpretive. Nor do we deny that representations and interpretations are, in some perspective, of the same kind. Nor do we claim that there are no difficult borderline cases. But we will clearly come to doubt the usefulness of a demarcation line placed at one extreme of the continuum.

At this point, we can observe that what was called representation above consists in the identification of the meaning of a text (as we read, listen, decipher). Methods for establishing such representations differ from mechanical methods of representation (such as bitmaps or OCR) in that they involve human symbol recognition and understanding and are therefore sometimes felt to be less objective and reliable. This difference is probably why the results of reading, listening, and deciphering are sometimes thought of as interpretive. In accordance with the proposed view, however, we may safely position our demarcation line so that we regard them as matters of representation.

The second step on the way out of our difficulty is that we should construe it not as a problem about the nature of text encoding but as a question about the potentials of text encoding to create certain kinds of texts—namely, representations and interpretations. This move is motivated by the commonsense view that representation and interpretation are names for relations and therefore, derivatively, for texts that represent and interpret other texts.

By extending each of these dyadic relations to a triadic one, between a pair of texts and an audience, we are able to appreciate that the demarcation line between representation and interpretation changes from case to case. This move also reflects the fact that texts are representations or interpretations of each other not in abstraction from their actual uses but only in relation to certain audiences of human beings—that is, social, historical, and cultural beings. Thus we may conclude that there is such a thing as objectivity of interpretation: the vast majority of decisions we make in this realm are decisions on which all (or most) competent readers agree or seem likely to agree.

The method described here might easily be criticized for creating the illusion that traditional text-critical scholarship, based on philological knowledge and careful interpretation, can be replaced by mechanical procedures and an artificial definition of the one and only "correct" transcription. But the requirements T1 and T2 are not intended to serve as criteria for identifying the correct interpretation of a manuscript. They direct our choice among possible interpretations in favor of some (not one) rather than others. And, as is often the case, this method as such does not in principle depend on the use of markup systems or even on computers. But it is only by marking up texts and using computer tools that the method can be implemented.

NOTE

This paper is to a large extent identical to a paper read at Informatica umanistica: Filosofia e risorse digitali, Bologna, 22–23 September 2000, and published under the title "Editorial Principles of *Wittgenstein's* Nachlass: *The Bergen Electronic Edition*," *Augmenting Comprehension: Digital Tools and the History of Ideas*, ed. Dino Buzzetti, Giuliano Pancaldi, and Harold Short, London: Office for Humanities Communication, 2004. Reprinted with permission.

ELECTRONIC RELIGIOUS TEXTS:
THE GOSPEL OF JOHN

D. C. PARKER

This survey must begin with essential questions of definition. How is one to define a religious text? It has been claimed that Marxism is a religion. If the claim was accepted, would an electronic edition of *Das Kapital* or of *The Communist Manifesto* come within the scope of this study? Again, there are texts from the Greco-Roman world that are regarded as classical or philosophical rather than religious, perhaps because they represent faiths no longer practiced. Should electronic editions of such texts be counted as editions of religious texts? The solution accepted here is a matter-of-fact one. For the purposes of this survey, those texts will be included that belong to the tradition of contemporary faith communities.

There then arises a second problem of definition. If all religious texts were to be included, the topic would be impossibly wide, covering two thousand years of Christian theological writing and yet longer traditions in the case of some other faiths. Again, the solution is pragmatic and accepts the common assumption about what constitutes a religious text. This study is restricted to those texts that a faith holds in particular esteem as revealed, inspired, or sacred. The general definition of sacred books is itself one to be handled somewhat cautiously, for several reasons. In the first place, different faiths (and the same faith at different times or in different places) have had and have very different views of what is "revealed," "inspired," or "sacred." In the second, books are used in many ways and have varying functions in different groups and places. The concept of holy books, so popular in a certain kind of study of comparative religion and popularized for a generation in teaching children, should be treated with extreme caution. To describe the Torah and Christian Bible and Qur'an as the "holy books" of Judaism and Christianity and Islam is to overlook the vastly differing functions of these texts in these three faiths and the vastly differing attitudes to their authority. It is as meaningful as comparing apples, oranges, and bananas because they are all fruit, or Australian Rules football, croquet, and rowing because they are all sports.

Having raised these points, I must refer to the particularly tender susceptibilities that may surround sacred texts. High honor is sometimes accorded, not only to the concept of a particular text, such as the Qur'an or Torah or Gospels, but to individual, physical copies. Thus, for example, a copy of the Torah in a synagogue will be one that has been copied by hand, on the ancient medium of a parchment roll, according to very strict standards of accuracy. It will be stored in a special receptacle and handled with especial care. When it is worn out, it will not be thrown away as a thing of no worth. While this process is one that applies to copies produced for the very specific purpose of use in worship, it is not unlikely to influence attitudes to scholarly editing and, indeed, to scholarly editions. Positively, it has bred the highest standards of intimate knowledge, care, and attention to details. Negatively, it may lead to hostility to alternative forms of the text, and in particular to the challenge that electronic editions offer to traditional concepts of textual authority. It may even happen that the discussion of problems of textual transmission and of text-critical issues will be completely suppressed in the interests of a claim for the unconditional authority of a particular form of text. The stakes in the introduction of electronic textual editing are, in the case of texts held in the greatest esteem by believers, extremely high, not only within particular faiths but in interfaith dialogue and in encounters between the world's cultures. Incompatibility of textual theory is not the least significant aspect of the clash of cultures in the contemporary world, and disagreement over the value of the electronic text has the potential to provide a new source of discord as well as the potential to bring about unexpected rapprochements.

The study of attitudes to electronic texts by particular groups should not focus solely on sacred texts but should include wider attitudes to electronic media. A model survey of Islam is provided by Gary Bunt in his book *Virtually Islamic*. Such a wider awareness is in fact inevitable, since on the whole one is able to glean information about electronic scholarly editions only by finding what is available more generally. In the field of world faiths, Bunt provides an invaluable print resource (*Good Web Guide*); for New Testament resources, the reader is directed to Mark Goodacre's Web site http://newtestamentgateway.com (see also http://biblegateway.com).

What swiftly becomes apparent is that while plenty of materials are available on the Web, there is a dearth of electronic scholarly editions. Plenty of scholarly editions have been digitized (or, at any rate, images of such editions), but few are *conceived as* electronic scholarly editions. The reasons for this lack are similar to the reasons why other electronically available corpora are not electronic scholarly editions conceived de novo. For some texts, there is no tradition of scholarly editing according to the terms of reference of this volume. Two possible reasons for this absence represent two extreme points of view. The one extreme is that, as has already been indicated, some groups reject the notion that the sacred text has any textual problems, so that there is in their view no scholarly editing to be done. The other extreme is that there is no anxiety about textual problems, but an acceptance of variation as either neutral or even a positive thing. If multiple text forms have happily coexisted in a particular culture, one should not expect a desire for a critical edition from within.

What emerges as a consistent theme in this essay so far is that there are no consistent themes. The title of this paper is "Case Studies: Religious Texts," but no case study, it seems, is representative: the belief systems, the scholarly traditions, and indeed the transmission histories of the sacred texts of the world are so diverse as to defy any attempt to find a representative type. It would, moreover, be the worst kind of religious imperialism to present any one set of views and experiences as a blueprint or as in any way normative. Even within the Christian tradition there is a wonderfully rich variety of attitudes to texts and of textual histories. The New Testament itself contains texts and groups of texts with quite distinct textual histories and uses. The Gospels, the Acts of the Apostles, the Pauline corpus, the Catholic epistles, and the Book of Revelation all began life separately and had differing fates along the way before they were united into "the New Testament" (for a brief survey, see D. Parker, "Text and Versions"). In terms of the original brief of this survey, then, the attempt had better be abandoned at this point. What follows is therefore not a case study, not a description of a typical foray into producing an electronic scholarly edition of a typical sacred text. It is a description of a particular set of forays, which may serve (or not) as an analogy, or a dreadful warning, of interest to editors of other kinds of text.[1] There is in fact no particular reason why the analogy need be with the editing of other religious texts. New Testament textual editing since the Renaissance has lived in close association with Western textual scholarship, shaping and being shaped, and the experiences here described may be as informative to the editor of other texts in the Western tradition as to those working with texts from quite different cultures and traditions.

The example that I take is the Gospel of John. For the reader to understand the electronic editing I describe, a brief introducion is desirable. This text is somewhat different from the other three canonical Gospels (known as the Synoptics), because while they exhibit close agreements in order and wording that point to a relationship of literary dependence, John is different both in the style of its composition and in its contents. Its presentation of the central figure is more stylized and presents his teaching in extensive discourses that are markedly different from sayings presented by the synoptists, which (even when they are combined into groups) are characteristically short and pithy. Because of its distinctive characteristics, there is far less harmonization of the text to that of the other Gospels than there is among those three, although there are still notable examples. Textual variation consists in differing interpretative forms of passages, of assimilation within the text (phrases and sentences are frequently repeated in similar but not identical ways), and in readings due to orthographical and morphological developments in the Greek language. There are also several significant additions, most notably the story of the woman (7.53–8.11) and the angel at the pool (5.3–4).

The oldest witness is a tiny fragment dated to the second quarter of the second century.[2] There are two reasonably extensive manuscripts from the period 175–225. Since the oldest complete manuscript dates at or shortly before the middle of the fourth century, there is a shortage of copies from the crucial first century of the text's existence, the period when it was at its most volatile.[3] There has thus been debate in modern scholarship as to the goal of a critical edition. Karl Lachmann, generally viewed as the editor of the first scientific edition of the New Testament, produced an edition that represented the oldest and best witnesses, of the fourth and fifth centuries, and in particular (especially for the Gospels) the Codex Vaticanus (Vatican City, Bibliotheca Apostolica Vaticana, Ms. Gr. 1209). Subsequent editions have built on his example. The evidence of the papyri is too recently known to have had a strong influence on a scholarly edition.[4]

While there are not many early copies, there are plenty of copies altogether. The database of manuscripts of the Principio Project lists 1,841 Greek manuscripts containing some or all of the Gospel of John. The vast majority of these (all but about sixty) date from the ninth century on. With some notable exceptions, they represent the various subtypes of the Byzantine text, that is, the text-type that was in use in the Byzantine Empire and that, in a somewhat bizarre form, found its way into print via Erasmus's Greek New Testament of 1516 and became the "received text" that lay behind the King

James Version. This Received Text dominated until the nineteenth century, continues as the form of text known in Greek Orthodoxy, and is still revered in some Western circles as alone representing the divinely inspired word.[5] The Byzantine manuscripts share a very similar text compared to their differences from the earliest witnesses (there are, for example, probably fewer than thirty differences between them in John 18 that define group membership). In addition, the text was copied in the Byzantine period as lectionaries, that is with passages ordered according to the lectionary rather than in continuous form. The lectionaries number approximately two thousand. Almost all are Byzantine, and their value is as witnesses to this stage of the text and not to its oldest forms. Nor is the complexity of the evidence exhausted by the number of Greek manuscripts. The Gospel was early translated into other languages, and of these two are of great importance in reconstructing the oldest recoverable forms of the text—the Old Syriac and the Old Latin. The former survives in two manuscripts, the latter in considerably more. Before they can be used in editing the text, they need to be edited themselves, and all variations likely to be the creation of a translator rather than the reading of their Greek Vorlage need to be screened out. Once this selection is done, we have evidence of forms of the text dating from the second century. Also significant for reconstructing the history of the text are four later versions of the Syriac, the Coptic (versions in a number of dialects), Georgian, Armenian, Ethiopic, Gothic (dependent on the Latin), and Old Slavonic. Finally, early Christian writers cited the Gospel, sometimes at length, in commentaries (of which the most valuable is that of Origen, written in the early third century), sometimes more briefly or loosely. Before a citation can be considered valuable as a witness to the text known to a writer, it must be carefully examined in context, since the writer may have adapted the biblical text— either by changing opening phrases in order to improve the sense or by bringing out what he believed was the most important point. In addition, the textual tradition of that writer must be examined to discover whether the text of the citation has been altered (the process of Vulgatization, adopting a citation to the form best known to a copyist, is well attested). A further problem is that there may be no critical edition of the writer: the task, for example, of editing the fifth-century writer John Chrysostom, whose extensive works are said to survive in an estimated ten thousand manuscripts, is formidable, and for the most part we remain dependent on the three-hundred-year-old edition of Bernard de Montfaucon.

The task of editing the Gospel of John involves study of an extensive Greek manuscript tradition that lasted 1,500 years, of a number of early translations, and of early Christian writers. As scholars explored libraries and collected data, the full magnitude of the task became evident. The gold standard of editions remains Constantine Tischendorf's *Editio Octava Critica Maior* of 1869–72, containing what was for its day a comprehensive apparatus criticus. Matching Tischendorf in the twentieth century was a formidable challenge. From the middle of the century on, only two groups made any attempt toward it. One was the Institut für Neutestamentliche Textforschung (INTF) in the University of Münster. The Institut's long-term goal has always been an *Editio Critica Maior*, and the first fascicles have now appeared. Both in conception and in execution, it has set new standards in critical editing, and its principles should be studied by every editor. The other was the International Greek New Testament Project (IGNTP), which completed an extensive two-volume apparatus criticus to the Gospel of Luke in 1987. Since then, the project has been at work on the Gospel of John.

The IGNTP decided to break the task of editing the Gospel of John into smaller stages of production. The first stage was the publication of transcriptions, apparatus criticus, and plates of the papyri.[6] This decision in a sense anticipated our current digital activity. We made our transcriptions and apparatus separately. But it was clear we needed a production method that brought the two together, by making it possible to generate an apparatus from transcriptions. We were trying to provide the user with the evidence (the transcriptions) on the basis of which we had constructed the apparatus as well as the evidence (the photographs of the papyri) on the basis of which we had produced the transcriptions. The goal was transparency at as many points as possible, so that the user was as little in the editor's power as possible.

Since 1995, the IGNTP has been repeating the papyrus edition for the fragmentary majuscule manuscripts. From 2000, this task was one part of the Principio Project, in which a team of researchers tackled various stages that will lead ultimately to a critical edition of the Gospel of John. But this time, using Peter Robinson's *Collate* and *Anastasia* programs, we produced a digital edition of these, containing transcriptions and apparatus.[7] Indeed, we have gone further, and produced transcriptions of all the majuscule manuscripts— approximately sixty witnesses. A series of separately funded projects will provide the final gathering of the other materials.

Collate was originally conceived and created for the editing of *The Canterbury Tales*. One interesting aspect of using it on a quite different textual tradition has been the discovery that various modifications had to be made: in the first place, the number of witnesses that it could collate had to be increased dramatically (for Chaucer, there is a maximum of sixty or so). In the second place, it turned out that Greek Gospel manuscripts show a far higher degree of correction than Chaucerian manuscripts. As a result, the way in which corrections are tagged had to be developed.

That *Collate* works by the making of transcriptions fundamentally affects how editor and user view the edition. In the first place, the user controls how materials are presented in an apparatus. In the second, the editor's attention is shifted away from textual variation as a series of short differences to textual variation as multiple copies. In the third, the manuscript as artifact comes back into its own. We adopted tagging procedures (building on what had already been done with *Collate* and working in partnership with the INTF) that allow a digital reconstruction of the layout of a manuscript. In the days of collating, one tended to focus only on the clearest way to present variations from the base. In transcribing, the textual variation is seen within the framework of re-creating the scribe's procedure of copying the manuscript.

The difficulty is to find ways to group manuscripts and select those that best represent the groups in a critical edition. Since the middle of the twentieth century, there has been a steady interest in possible methodologies. The IGNTP has used the Claremont Profile Method (CPM), which takes three sample chapters, collates a sample of manuscripts in order to determine the significant group readings, draws a profile of readings for each group, and then notes the readings of each manuscript in the selection. The resulting profile shows to which group a manuscript belongs. In two ways the CPM is now out-of-date. The first is that its creators, Frederick Wisse and Paul McReynolds, drew up their profiles using pencil and paper; we now use databases. The second follows on. The selection of group readings near the beginning of the process may have prejudged the group characteristics. We are now able, very easily, to produce complete transcriptions of the witnesses, which allows us to determine the groups on the basis of all the evidence.

Rather than profile three chapters, we are taking only one, chapter 18. We profile the earlier part of the Gospel by using the database of variants in 153 test passages in John 1–10 created in Münster. The INTF methodology is to take a sample of significant readings spread throughout a text and collect the readings of all manuscripts in those passages. The results are then analyzed, principally by comparing the oldest text form with that of the Byzantine majority, with the purpose of finding those witnesses that support the majority in less than ninety percent of the test readings. INTF will produce its analysis of the 153 test passages, and IGNTP will use the same methodology in test passages from John 18. We will thus be able to compare the results of the two methods. In a study of their comparative findings for the Gospel of

Luke, I demonstrated that the IGNTP and INTF methods are closer than has sometimes been assumed and may complement each other very satisfactorily ("Comparison"). The use of the methods for exactly the same materials in John will provide a much better basis for comparison.

In the Principio Project we used *Collate* to produce our transcriptions. In all, we have 1,147 transcriptions of John 18 in *Collate*. The IGNTP's other transcriptions are in a program called *Manuscript*, devised in the late 1980s by Bruce Morrill for the North American Committee. For profiling, the two sets have been merged into a single database.

I should here describe the level of detail in our John 18 transcriptions of minuscules. We do not record page, column, or line breaks. We do record all variations; corrections; *nomina sacra*; and spelling variations, including movable nu but excluding iota adscript.[8] Not all this detail will be of value in grouping manuscripts, but the data might be of interest to other groups. The result is a publication that we had not anticipated and that we hope will prove novel: a collection of such variants in a thousand manuscripts, with every orthographical aberration and every error that a scribe managed to make, is a resource to be put to uses that have not yet been imagined.[9]

But the main outcome of these transcriptions is a merged database of variant readings in John 18. The passage contains 800 words of the 16,000 of the Fourth Gospel and thus represents 5% of the total text. As well as profiling according to the Claremont method, we should be able to perform other tests—for example, finding manuscripts with identical texts. The database will also be studied using phylogenetic software, for whom such a large population of manuscripts will be a valuable specimen.

One of the problems with the editing of the New Testament text, as with any other text, has been that each editor or group of editors has had to go to work afresh. As standards have changed and methods developed, so collations have needed to be repeated. Even where a reliable published collation has existed, the work of placing it within an apparatus has had to be done afresh. We hope that one of the major advances of the electronic transcription will be that editorial work can become cumulative. Our transcriptions can be improved, enhanced, and made more accurate by future researchers, and the apparatus based on them can be modified rather than rebuilt from scratch. This assumes, of course, that our transcriptions will be readable by future generations. We have no way of knowing that. The most we can do is to put as many safeguards in place as we can think of.

The electronic text is affecting the editing of the Gospel of John in another important respect. It has been comparatively hard for separate projects to share results, because they are presented in such different ways, so that the benefits have scarcely outweighed the problems, and have required total agreement on almost all aspects of the undertaking. But the use of agreed computer methodologies makes it possible for separate projects to work together without losing their identity. Thus, IGNTP and INTF have been able to share certain common objectives, to their mutual benefit, without losing their individuality. This balance is important, for if everyone did things exactly the same way, textual editing would be greatly impoverished. There is no single right way of doing things, and we do not want to lose any of the good practices that we have. The partnership between INTF and IGNTP is based on the use of *Collate* and a shared set of rules for marking and tagging. There is still room for differences of opinion and presentation, since the publication package associated with *Collate*, *Anastasia*, will ignore or alter formats as it (she?) sees fit. Interesting differences in presupposition come to light in agreeing and modifying these rules and have provided a far better context for debate and advancement than would have been available in purely theoretical discussions.

Partnership has been affected in other ways as well. The Principio Project team, although spending most of their time living in different parts of the world, have been able to share views and data as though they were in the same room. On the other hand, electronic editing has caused a few problems with the team of volunteers, consisting of academics, clergy, and others, who have traditionally provided a significant portion of IGNTP's collations of manuscripts. Giving such volunteers a microfilm or a set of pictures, a copy of the collating base, and a set of rules is straightforward. It is not practicable to provide a computer and software and to train the same volunteers in the use of it. Apart from the logistics of the operation, *Collate* transcriptions need to be created fairly consistently, and the tagging of variants even in a small team needs to be monitored by continuing discussion, to maintain the necessary degree of consistency.

The project described here is a part of a major scholarly edition that will not be available for some time. By contrast, INTF is at work on an electronic edition that promises to have an instant effect. Reference has already been made to the most widely used hand edition of the Greek New Testament, the *Novum Testamentum Graece*, familiarly known from the names of its two longest-serving editors and its current edition as Nestle-Aland 27. The next edition of Nestle-Aland, announced at the International Society of Biblical Literature Congress in Berlin, July 2002, and at Studiorum Novi Testamenti Societas in Durham (UK), August 2002, will be a hybrid edition

(for more information and a sample, see http://nttranscripts.uni-muenster
.de/). The traditional blue-bound volume will not disappear, but there will
in addition be a CD-ROM containing an electronic version of the printed
text and full transcriptions of over twenty of the principal Greek manuscripts.
The provision of digital images of these witnesses is also being considered.
The text, apparatus, and transcriptions will be linked. The transcriptions will
be produced in *Collate*. Such a tool has the potential fundamentally to alter
the way in which users of the *Novum Testamentum Graece* (virtually all academics and students, as well as preachers and lay people with the skills to use
it) understand the oldest documents of Christianity. It is hard to doubt that
there will be significant implications for future use and understandings of the
text, which will shape both understandings of the tradition and its further
developments.

As has been indicated, the production of an edition that includes the
versional and patristic evidence presents an editor with a formidable set of
problems. With regard to the versions, one of the most elegant solutions
hitherto has been provided by the polyglots, such as the Complutensian
(printed 1514, published 1522), the Antwerp (also known as Plantin's,
1571–73) and Walton's (1655–57). This last edition printed the Gospels in
Greek, two Latin versions, Syriac, Ethiopic, Arabic, and Persian, with a
literal Latin translation of the four oriental versions. Walton thus provided
the user with information at several different levels. We might describe this
today as the closest thing then available to hyperlinks. The method is especially admirable, because it has this superiority over the practice of including the versional evidence in an apparatus to the Greek text, that it
provides the versions on their own terms, as evidence rather than as interpretation. The electronic text may provide ways of replicating the polyglot
without encountering the typographic challenges traditionally associated
with it. There are already publications that use the opportunities of tagging
and hyperlinks to cross-reference texts in several languages. Relevant for the
study of John is the Leiden Armenian Lexical Textbase (http://malkyn
.hum.dmu.ac.uk:8000/AnaServer?lalt4 + . + start.anv).

Electronic editing is also leading to a reevaluation of methodologies in
citing patristic evidence.[10] So far as the Gospel of John is concerned, the
problem is encountered at its most intractable in the editing of the Old Latin
evidence. The Old Latin versions are those whose creation predates the fresh
translations and revisions that (even though they are not all his doing) became
part of Jerome's Vulgate. For most of the Bible, the Old Latin versions survive
more strongly in the forms of text cited by early Christian writers than as

manuscripts. The situation is somewhat different with regard to the Gospels, where the manuscript tradition is better represented (there are approximately several dozen witnesses of John). But the patristic testimony remains of great significance and is voluminous. The editorial task consists of gathering and sifting about twenty thousand citations and grouping them to determine and recover the extant text-types. Editing the Old Latin has been the task of the Vetus Latina Institut, Beuron, Germany, for over half a century. The Johannine fascicles have been entrusted to a group working in Birmingham. The first stage, the Verbum Project, concentrating on the manuscripts, began in 2002. The use of electronic editing in this project is of interest here for two reasons. The first is that the citations will be gathered into a database and to produce one or more apparatus criticus in which (in an electronic format) different kinds of evidence may be made visible or hidden according to the requirements of the user. The second reason is that a number of databases of Latin patristic texts are available, and it would be possible to provide an interface between such a corpus and the Vetus Latina edition. The biblical citations, instead of being taken out of context and, as it were, pinned to the exhibition board, could be placed back into their context, making it possible for the user to come to an independent judgment about the editors' claim that the citations support a particular text form or reading. There are reasons why this type of evidence must be used with caution. The preferred solution is to insert a link between the Vetus Latina edition and the text of the author, providing access to the citation's context and textual variation. The result will be a tool far more critically advanced than can be attained with a print edition.

Experience has provided another important benefit from electronic textual editing: the opportunity to use the same raw data (transcriptions) in more than one way. This opportunity has led to the Byzantine Text Project, which is working to provide a critical edition of the Byzantine text of John.[11] Associated with the Principio Project yet independent, the Byzantine Project shared and augmented its transcriptions of witnesses. But the outputs of the two projects are completely different in scope and format. Using the same materials for quite different goals would not be so easily done in the production of printed editions.

Electronic editing is of course not always plain sailing. One comes up time and again against the fact that neither printed nor electronic formats can begin to represent the wealth of data provided on a manuscript page. Part of the excitement and challenge of making an electronic edition lies in looking for ways in which the inflexibility of the rules by which the computer works can be (to personify it) outwitted so that one is able to slip in additional information. At the same time, this inflexibility without a doubt improves one's skills as a textual critic, in that difficulties in deciphering manuscripts and readings have to be analyzed and described with the utmost scientific care. This new kind of discipline can only be good for textual studies.

The way we do textual editing and the way we conceive of it have changed dramatically in the past ten years. As a result, we are now able to analyze afresh the nature of past achievements, the goals ahead, and the very character of the manuscripts with which our work begins. The creation of an electronic form of a sacred text is not a merely technical or superficial matter. It will also influence the very concept of sacred text and of the text's role within the community that uses it. The way in which the witness transcription is made the main component in *Collate* moves the emphasis from a single, authoritative text to the variety of texts that have been authoritative at different points in the tradition.[12] The effect of the electronic edition on the place of sacred texts in the world's faiths, and on the relations between the faiths, will be a significant strand in future cultural developments.

NOTES

1. One thing that we have discovered in the seminars in the Centre for the Editing of Texts in Religion (now the Institute for Textual Scholarship and Electronic Editing [ITSEE]) is that the discussion of problems with colleagues working on quite different texts may provide simple solutions to problems that crop up all the time in editing one kind of text but hardly ever in editing another kind.

2. John Rylands University Library of Manchester Greek Papyrus 457. It contains the center portions of lines covering John 18.31–33, 37–38.

3. For an introduction to the issues and their wider significance, see D. Parker, *Living Text*.

4. The two major papyri (Geneva, Bibliotheca Bodmeriana, P. Bodmer II and P. Bodmer XIV–XV, numbered in the Gregory-Aland classification of Greek New Testament manuscripts as P66 and P75) were first published in 1961 and 1962. Of course, they have influenced the text of the most widely used edition, the Nestle-Aland 27 (*Novum Testamentum*). Not a full-blown scholarly edition in the sense of a roots-up reexamination, the Nestle-Aland 27 is, in its own words, "a working text . . . it is not to be considered as definitive, but as a stimulus to further efforts toward defining and verifying the text of the New Testament. For many reasons, however, the present edition has not been deemed an appropriate occasion for introducing textual changes" (45).

5. In March 2005, the INTF and IGNTP reached an agreement to produce a

critical edition of the Gospel of John in the *Editio Critica Maior*. There will be three editors from INTF (Strutwolf, Wachtel, Mink) and three from IGNTP (D. Parker, Morrill, Schmid), with Parker as executive editor. At the same time, INGTP will produce an electronic edition of the Gospel. A current challenge is to produce a set of standards for transcriptions and databases of patristic citations that will make it possible to bring together evidence from Greek, Syriac, Coptic, and Latin sources.

6. Papyrus was the most common writing material in early Christianity, until parchment began to take over in the more secure and affluent fourth century. The youngest surviving papyri are seventh-century.

7. For further information, see the ITSEE home page: www.itsee.bham.ac.uk/.

8. *Nomina sacra*: the custom of abbreviating certain important and frequent words in the Gospels, such as *Iesous*, *Christos*, *Theos*, and *Kurios*. Movable nu: in the Byzantine period, it became the rule that a final *n* was added to certain forms when the next word began with a vowel, whereas earlier the *n* often appeared when the next letter was a consonant. Iota adscript: the iota written beneath its accompanying vowel in modern Greek orthography was either absent or written after it in earlier periods.

9. I presented this data in a preliminary form at the Textual Criticism Seminar at the annual meeting of Studiorum Novi Testamenti Societas, Bonn, July 2003.

10. The problems and solutions in this area may be of interest to editors of other texts. I was able to apply it usefully to suggest an explanation for a puzzle in a sixteenth-century text, Calvin's *Commentary on Romans* (see Parker and Parker, esp. xxxii–li). For essential studies and bibliographies, see the surveys of the Greek, Latin, and Syriac patristic witnesses by G. D. Fee, J. L. North, and S. P. Brock, respectively, in Ehrman and Holmes, 191–207, 208–23, and 224–36.

11. Sponsored by the United Bible Societies and edited by Roderic L. Mullen, the project responds to a call from the Orthodox churches for modern translations based on an edition of the traditional ecclesiastical text properly reconstructed rather than on Western critical editions.

12. For discussions of the questions surrounding this plurality, including the concept of original text and of factors at work in the development of the New Testament text, see Epp; Ehrman; D. Parker, *Living Text* and "Through a Screen."

MULTIMEDIA BODY PLANS:
A SELF-ASSESSMENT

MORRIS EAVES

You've signed up for a seminar, Editing in Multiple Media. It begins
with a quiz and ends with a project, your own electronic edition. To
start, answer a few hard questions about your proposed project in the
light of the examples offered.

Why does this material need editing?

The emphasis falls on "need" and "material," because editing is a ruthlessly
utilitarian craft that trades in sensible objects. In this realm even theory has
consumable consequences.

Consider the *William Blake Archive* (www.blakearchive.org), which was
made conceivable by the coincidence of several factors, including the birth
of the Institute of Advanced Technology in the Humanities at the University
of Virginia (IATH); the advent of exciting electronic scholarship, especially
Jerome McGann's *Rossetti Archive*; but above all the prospect of putting new
media to work on an old, schizophrenic editorial legacy that emerged in
Blake's lifetime (1757–1827).

The problem originates in a fusion of difficult content with difficult
form that is unprecedented yet highly characteristic of the artist, who insisted
on both the multifariousness and unity of his artistic identity and exercised
a lifelong penchant for multimedia experimentation that was inhibited but
rarely blocked by contemporary convention. Take the medium of much of
his best-known work. He originally presented what he called "illuminated
printing"—combining the tools, techniques, and materials of writing, drawing, painting, etching, and printing—as a multimedia solution to long-
standing problems: "The Labours of the Artist, the Poet, the Musician, have

been proverbially attended by poverty and obscurity . . . owing to a neglect of means to propagate such works." Might the answer be his new "method . . . which combines the Painter and the Poet" (692–93)? As Blake discovered, some new technologies merge seamlessly into the dominant system, others replace it, while any stranded but salvageable content from less imposing technical novelties becomes eligible for conversion into the dominant forms. Instead of a solution, then, illuminated printing became a problem: Blake's ambitious innovations produced a daunting overload of information and a trail of reader resistance and resentment.[1]

Would-be supporters instinctively countered with exercises in strong editing that soon became systematic. William Michael Rossetti was among the first to articulate the vital insight that studying Blake may involve some betrayal of his original forms: "Difficult under any circumstances, it would be a good deal less difficult to read these works in an edition of that kind, with clear print, reasonable division of lines, and the like aids to business-like perusal" (see also Peattie; Eaves, "Graphicality"). The printed edition became the centerpiece of the preelectronic editorial settlement, which prepared the way for serious study and reflection on a scale previously unthinkable. Ultimately, however, dispersal, dismemberment, and translation seriously distorted the true picture of Blake's achievement. And that is primarily why we—Robert Essick, Joseph Viscomi, and I—undertook a new kind of edition.

Who needs your edition?

The first imperative of editing is to meet the needs of audiences, and the audience that has guided our imaginations is the community of scholars. Our stated goal is to create an edition aimed at "scholars doing sustained original research" (*Plan*). Blake specialists, then, are the hard core of a target demographic that softens toward the edges. Even the specialists are internally divided by discipline, usually art history or English. "Serious scholar," furthermore, includes experts who are not Blake experts. And the archive aspires to be a "public resource" (*Plan*) to all those interested in Blake's work. In this respect our edition has more in common with libraries than with scholarly books and journals. But the thin end of our wedge, specialized scholarship, explains why the archive is not primarily about reading or viewing Blake: it is about studying Blake.

Why are you multiplying media?

From one notable perspective all editions are multimedia: every medium has digested other media that are its contents. But, obviously, choosing that outer media shell is an utterly fundamental editorial decision. Choosing media of transmission and delivery dictates hard choices in hardware and software that inevitably box you into their particular corner. Editing forces such choices on us, because it puts ideas in concrete (though not necessarily inflexible) forms that are both pleasure and punishment. The *Blake Archive* attempts to break up a logjam of intractable problems by exploiting deeply—but always within painful limits created by the choices made from a range of options— the capabilities of newer media to digest several old ones that were originally produced by the traditional tools and materials of painting, writing, and the graphic arts: etched and engraved prints, watercolor and tempera paintings, manuscripts, and typographic works, among others. Digital media use entirely different systems for processing words and pictures, much as print media comprise type and halftones. And, as I have argued elsewhere ("Graphicality"), pictures have always been a problem.

What is your fundamental editorial strategy, and how are electronic media part of it?

A strategy devised in the light of the materials, the media of presentation, and the primary audience sets priorities and guides design. Editions are problem-solving mechanisms; without problems to solve, new editions would not be needed. Explicit strategy is essential, because the problems of producing hypermedia editions have not been fully faced or solved. The legacy of print offers much general but little specific guidance.

As an editorial solution, the archive takes into account the uniqueness of Blake's work and the unusual needs of its scholars. But the basic elements, texts and still images, are fundamental to cultural memory. Hence in general form our aims are easily understood.

In one sentence, then: our strategy is to employ electronic media to achieve a level of consolidation, supplementation, and extension—overlapping categories—that will overcome significant disadvantages of both Blake's originals and printed reconfigurations. Departing from traditional strategies of substitution—as when letterpress editions replace watercolored etchings— we resituate the reproduced originals at the center of a complex but coherent structure of extensions and supplements, including tools. Consolidation empowers us to adopt a documentary approach that exploits the capacity of electronic media to digest carloads of data—edited documents with their supplements and extensions—on a scale highly impractical for printed books. This is neither to deny that electronic editing must adapt to major limitations nor to claim results consistently superior to print.

Providing redundant options—the original etched script, for example, our own documentary (diplomatic) transcription, and even the transcriptions from David Erdman's standard printed edition—provides multiple perspectives instead of a blinkered view. Historically, that redundancy frees us from Blake's perspective, which left us etched script to decipher in the first place. This point is central. On the one hand, our strategy is anchored to highly controlled reproductions of Blake's original documents in order to restore his sometimes frustrating aggregations to positions of primary authority. On the other hand, we are not retrospectively surrendering authority to Blake. Editors' rhetorical deference to authors' intentions can generate disorienting questions that mislocate the real source of power. "Would Blake have approved of the *William Blake Archive*?"[2] The history of editing suggests that we care primarily about our own needs and desires (which may include our desire to honor the artist's intentions). The ultimate strategic question is not what Blake intends but what we intend for him and for ourselves.[3]

It is useful to understand this crucial principle of choice when formulating strategy, because, while some editorial features will represent the author's intentions and some supplement and extend them, others may contravene them. Did Blake want his scripts transcribed for legibility? want his works enlarged, reduced, juxtaposed, categorized? want the words of other authors who have written on his prints and drawings reproduced for their documentary significance? Our aggressive determination to make these and other scholarly actions possible is authorized not by Blake's desires but by ours, backed by the powerful electronic medium that allows us to gratify them.

Would Blake approve scholarly approaches to his work?
We may wonder, but our purpose and strategy do not address that question in practice—though, naturally, we persist in the hope that we do not murder our subject to dissect it.

How are your purpose and strategy carried through in design?
Security experts have a saying: Collecting information is one thing, analyzing it another. Your edition, like ours, will probably be a multifunctional apparatus of collection, record keeping, and analysis whose complexities (or problems) are drastically increased by multimedia commitments. Ideally, those functions will be embodied in efficient designs that optimize the advantages of the medium to achieve the interplay that sound scholarship requires.

Collection here embroils the archive in the technologies of digital reproduction, representation, and cataloging; analysis in the paraphernalia of search engines, elaborate indexes, numbering and measuring systems, comparison engines, and so on; and recording in various historical exercises (editors' notes, information about the physical object, provenance, etc.) that include recording our own editorial activity.

Consolidation bears multiple burdens. At its heart is the ecological mission of restoration. At a higher level it calls for the collection of multiple versions (two sets of Blake's illustrations to Milton's *Paradise Lost*, several versions of the *Songs*). At a still higher level it aspires to the systematic arrangement of Blake's entire corpus—now the dispersed property of individuals and institutions around the world—in one virtual place with seamless connections to all related bodies of work. This unification is of course a vision, not a reality.

The primary strategy of resynthesizing the estranged elements of Blake's editorial legacy is articulated in the treelike structure of the archive as a whole and the design of the basic "page" in particular, described and managed by the *Blake Archive* DTD (BAD).[4] The Object View Page (OVP) is the central intersection to which all roads lead. Its matrix of information, communication, and scholarly method incorporates the five fundamental constituents of the archive, which are:

    accurate images of documents
    accurate texts derived from documents
    accurate scholarly information about both texts and images
    tools for scrutinizing texts and images
    self-documentation

Editors of multimedia editions are in effect double-editing, first in discrete and then in integrated media. In a decade of intensive teamwork on the archive we have evolved a fairly elaborate division of labor that follows suit, coordinating many moments of isolated specialization in a pattern that leads ultimately to integration. Securing accurate images of objects is basic, because they reproduce the evidence from which all else derives. This undertaking keeps us heavily invested in the techniques of digital image processing: storage formats, scanning, compression algorithms, color and contrast correction, display resolution, scaling, and the like.[5] Likewise, creating accurate texts involves us in markup systems (SGML, HTML, XML) and the minutiae of textual criticism.[6] Our greatest challenge throughout is to establish appropriate benchmarks of quality with procedures to achieve and maintain them. Because these quality-assurance procedures have historical analogues in print scholarship—in the production of catalogs and facsimiles, for instance—we can compare results with those of our predecessors if we adjust them to the advantages and limitations of our media. The advantages are enormous, the limits severe. A huge pile of unsorted digital images and texts, even superb ones, could not sustain much serious scholarship. To make the images and texts meaningful and useful, we organize the information and supply contexts in three basic forms:

> ample bibliographic information (in the broad sense that includes, for example, art-historical provenances) compiled from the best current sources, including firsthand observation

> self-documentation; metadata (see *Technical Summary*; Kirschenbaum, "Documenting"); recording what is done, when, by whom (the Info button under each image reveals the technical trajectory of each object from its source in a collection to its digital destination); this exercise is motivated by the scholarly values of self-scrutiny and full disclosure— transparency for the sake of accountability

> tools that, when applied to the primary textual and pictorial materials, users employ to construct the contexts most relevant to their purposes

The tools aid and abet the fundamental scholarly goals of close scrutiny fused with broad understanding. The techniques involved are complex products of an abiding need to see less of the object of investigation—to clear the field of clutter and to magnify the object—in order to see, paradoxically, more of it. The *Blake Archive* attempts to facilitate both goals. Our tools provide ways of

> searching texts (print precedents include page and other unit numbers and the finding aids, such as tables of contents, indexes, and concordances, that use those numbers). For example, our text-searching engine can query the contents of multiple versions as well as the editorial apparatus, including bibliographies, editors' notes, and illustration descriptions. Eventually it will be able to search even the markup codes.

> searching images (print precedents include reproduction systems, such as engraving and photography, that aid record keeping and systems of managing information about pictures, such as catalogs and indexing-description schemes, most elaborately manifested perhaps in the Index of Christian Art [1917–] and Iconclass [1972–]).[7] The archive's experimental image-searching system, based on an extensive list of keywords and descriptions, mapped to visual details by means of an image grid, and viewed through *Inote* (see below), makes it possible to find most pictorial features.

inspecting by isolation and enlargement (with precedents in all manner of enlarged visual details—such as electron micrographs and maps that isolate particular aspects of a landscape—and verbal description of such details, close reading, selective quotation). Examples in the archive are our high-resolution enlargements of every image; elaborate verbal descriptions of every version of every illuminated book image; *Inote*, an image viewer-annotator that ties visual details to verbal descriptions; and *ImageSizer*, which allows users to control the scale of images. All these inspection possibilities, individually or in tandem, help users answer the fundamental question of what something is.

comparing by juxtaposition (precedents include techniques of visually juxtaposing different versions of the same image or the abnormal with the normal, which may in turn involve sequencing, and of the verbal counterparts of such images). Examples in the archive are the Compare feature, which will juxtapose any or all versions of individual works, such as the six versions of Blake's *Marriage of Heaven and Hell* currently available.

Many of these tools would apply to studying fingerprints as well as to studying art and literature. In general terms, what we face is a huge, dispersed stock of related information to be presented for study. In that light, the otherwise bizarre interface of a multimedia digital resource becomes a more understand-able, at times almost comfortable, experience or one at least as comfortable as multivolume catalogs, concordances, and variorum editions but poten-tially—and sometimes actually—far more powerful.

Launching these actions and organizing this information on a single page—our OVP—are among our greatest challenges. More than one dia-gram is required to explain it (see figs. 1 and 2), and it needs to be explained. It looks only remotely like a printed page or like Blake's original productions; it is more an instrument panel. It assuredly does not invite reading. But it invites investigative scrutiny, carried out through intensive searching, com-paring, and other high-order manifestations of "scholarly primitives." Those, according to John Unsworth's anatomy of scholarly actions, are the elemen-tary constituents of most of our labor. By combining access to documents with a set of contemporary tools, the OVP is designed to facilitate complex scholarly procedures that otherwise are difficult if not impossible.

Out of this massive organizational undertaking has evolved what strikes me as the most remarkable feature of the new editorial settlement in its first electronic incarnation: its odd relation to the editorial legacy. Despite the heavily restorative, documentary slant of our project—which is archival in that sense—we have by no means come full circle and arrived editorially

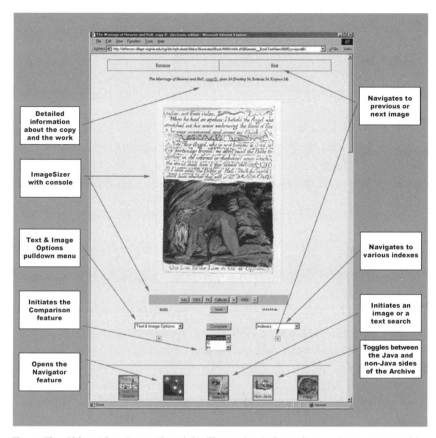

Fig. 1. The Object View Page. The Blake illustration is from the Lessing J. Rosenwald Collection, Library of Congress. © 2005 *William Blake Archive*. Used with permission

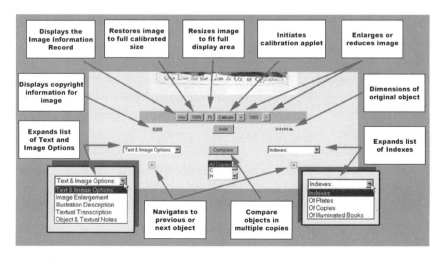

Fig. 2. The control panel

back at Blake. Instead, his old aggregations have been restored (within strict limits, imposed mostly by the present limits of the medium conspiring with other limiting factors such as time and money) but then situated among the old disaggregations: transcriptions, verbal translations of images, search engines with functions segregated conventionally into texts and images, even a (searchable) version of the standard printed edition—all digitally reprocessed and tuned to the system, that is, to new positions as servants of the originals and as concrete acknowledgments of two centuries of scholarly progress. The effect of the recuperation can be startling.

With some comparable sense, then, of what you want to do and why in this material realm, we can conclude with a glance at a few very material questions.

How will I finance my multimedia edition?

One of the attractions of electronic editing has been the ready availability of the tools of the trade. Few editors own printing presses, but many own powerful computers with Web access. Another chance to bypass the middleman and cut costs? The early fate of Blake's own illuminated inventions may be a useful cautionary tale. To date, most good electronic editions have been expensive.

Electronic editing covers a multitude of media sins and opportunities, most prominently at this point CD, DVD, and the Web. Those can in turn be packaged and distributed in various ways, restricted or unrestricted by payments and passwords. More and more often, key components of the edition can be treated as content eligible for "repurposing" and thus delivery in multiple forms. Cutting the electronic deck depends on a calculation of means, such as labor and funding, and ends, such as editorial vision and intended audience.

The *Blake Archive* has always been available on the Web as a free site, thanks to the sponsorship of the Institute for Advanced Technology in the Humanities at the University of Virginia, the goodwill of the institutions and individuals whose property we reproduce, and soft money in the form of generous foundation grants and university support.[8] It would be foolish to assume that any of these resources is permanent, and we will never be a set of volumes sitting securely on library shelves. We plow forward with no answer to the haunting question of where and how a project like this one will live out its useful life. Answers will probably begin to emerge eventually from publishers and libraries, the institutional cornerstones of print scholarship. Meanwhile, the need to persist without reassurance is one of the many unsettling conditions of life in new media. The costs and risks should not be underestimated.

Are the materials you want to edit available?

Availability is a sine qua non: if the materials can be had, strings will probably be attached in the form of permissions or payment. For printed editions this process is often made less onerous by long-established precedents that do not transfer into the digital domain.

In this sensitive area it pays to formulate tactics early and take stock of your natural advantages. We based the archive's early development on several, including the cooperation of the Library of Congress, which has no permission requirement; the Blake Trust, which had made fresh transparencies of the illuminated books for a new series of printed facsimiles; and Robert Essick, one of the archive's editors, who owns the largest collection of Blake in private hands. A modest cohort of institutions whose recent participation in the Blake Trust facsimile project had demonstrated a commitment to scholarship that we too could draw on was enough to give us a critical mass. At this writing, we have twenty contributing owner-institutions,[9] and negotiation with others has become a normal editorial duty.

How will you learn what you need to know?

You are probably an expert in the subject matter of your edition. You can learn print editing from books, editors, or the MLA's Committee on Scholarly Editions. But the history of multimedia electronic editing is short, good examples are still scarce, and nothing stays put. This book should help, but continuous reeducation is the order of the day.

Electronic editing also requires technical knowledge that must be available in some form from someone. Of course editing books requires both editorial and technical expertise, but the understanding of bookish conventions is widely shared by editors and publishers. In the electronic realm, editors usually lack the basic knowledge of the medium required to conceive or execute their projects. We have addressed the knowledge problem in two ways, first by working hand in glove with IATH, which was fortunately founded to help humanists solve that very problem; and second by working collaboratively at great distances—by e-mail discussion list (blake-proj), telephone, and the Web (Eaves, "Collaboration"). A burst of collaborative effort has been a surprising bonus of the humanists' entrée into the electronic domain. The archive's radically collaborative design is based on a model that assumes, at the editorial level, shared general expertise, highly specialized competence in different sectors of Blake studies, and specially developed competence in areas particular to the multimedia electronic edition. In the most technical sphere, we add expertise in computing (markup systems, programming, database management, etc.). We have bridged the gap between the first three and the fourth by appointing a graduate student project manager as coordinator on the scene at IATH (see Kirschenbaum, "Managing")—supplemented by assistants as required. Two previous project managers became our first technical editors: both Matthew Kirschenbaum and Andrea K. Laue are new-style PhDs in English with concentrations in humanities computing, while our current project manager, Justin Scott Van Kleeck, is more interested in Blake than in XML.

How happily do you work with other people?

Traditionally, humanists, if not quite Carmelites, are loners who find deep satisfaction in authoring, not producing, books (books, not content or product) in disorderly cells they call studies. As an editor of multimedia electronic objects, you will still have ample opportunity, perhaps more than you want, to use your study, but you will almost certainly have to share more of your time with others, taking almost nothing for granted, collaborating on decisions about everything you do. The aim is to produce precise maps of your production pipeline and everything in it. And if acronyms, technical terms, and phrases like "digital object" and "production pipeline" embarrass you with their taint of the worlds of technology and business on which you turned your back when you took the high road of humanities scholarship, you're probably in for some serious adjustments.

How much uncertainty can you bear?

"Committed to print," we say, bookishly, because print stands for a kind of commitment we understand. This understanding has shaped the modern history of editing, where the sense of prior commitment to a highly conventionalized medium has kept uncommitted editing—tentative editing—to a minimum. Digital editing is as unsettled as digital technologies. The dynamic editorial environment demands flexible theories, adaptable practices, and fast responses to unanticipated situations.

I experience it as X-editing, dominated by experimental action, Freud's label for the thoughtful hesitation before—or instead of—the leap from uncommitted thought to committed deed.[10] The opening of a new arena for scholarship on the middle ground between hypothesis and action has produced a torrent of freewheeling experimentation characterized by multilateral problem solving, trial and error, approximation, compromise, revision, and (always) unintended consequences.

In this realm, editing is speculation: by educated guesswork, we mold our practices to what seem the best bets at the time (which markup standards? which imaging algorithms?). Not that practices or consequences have ever been permanent and completely predictable in print, but the difference in editorial perspective is signaled, for instance, by the heavy traffic behind the scenes on our work-in-progress Web site, a combination editorial storeroom and testing area where we compare proposed solutions to present and future problems. The results of even the best solutions always seem to compromise our ideals.

Our protocols for diplomatic transcription are routinely insulted by our weak control over the display of texts as they travel from server to client. Every year we reconsider, revise, retest, and, if improvement seems possible, rework texts that last year seemed the best we could produce. Insider humor has generated a series of labels for our latest remodeling exercise: this year's label is "de-uglification."

On the imaging side, JPEG, a standard image-compression algorithm necessitated by present limits of memory and bandwidth, is tuned to the average picture, not to Blake's typical work. We must accept the JPEG compromise until something better comes along. So we cooperate eagerly with Vladimir Misic's experiments in combining JPEG 2000 (or JPEG2)— better but not the algorithm of our dreams—with "mixed raster content" technology.

Editing on the electronic bleeding edge is like practicing medicine— hands always tied by present limits, one eye always scanning future developments. If you listen closely to editors editing, you will hear the harsh sounds of primal conflict as visionary aspirations clash with reality. In a technocommercial world the pressures of hard necessity bear down no less on editing with electrons than on editing with ink, wood, or flesh. Evolutionary biologists think about body plans. Scholar-editors must be able to think as rigorously as they about our body plans and plans of action—including business plans—if we are going to bring adequate multimedia editions into being and keep them alive and healthy.

No question about it: "Hyperediting is what scholars will be doing for a long time" (McGann, *Radiant Textuality* 68). The future of scholarly editing is electronic. Eventually we'll develop better coping mechanisms for dealing with its slights and shortcomings. McGann proposes a sharp distinction between theory that ends in "concrete acts of imagining" (83)[11] and theory that does not, the latter being what most people in the humanities mean by theory, the former being what electronic editors are doing. We can see what he means: electronic editing, in this theoretical spirit, is a species of experiment that makes an object that then tests the idea that produced it, as buildings test architectural designs. For now, we are engaged in a great collective experiment to find the most productive editorial paths. For now, electronic editions can be cool, but they lack the respect, the "dignity," that the Victorian poet and critic Swinburne perceptively saw in "a reprint," the posthumous edition he sought for the undignified Blake of the homemade illustrated poem (114). Electronic projects are subject to a splendid array of misunderstandings—mostly to their disadvantage. Such uncertainties make multimedia editing no game for those who need insurance. In time it may become a sanctuary of formula and routine. For the time being, we wander in an editorial wilderness.

NOTES

1. I have attempted to plot these reactions to innovative artistic technology from various positions (see "To Paradise" and "National Arts").
2. The question is Miller's. Questions of authorial intention also shape the series of *Wordsworth Circle* exchanges among Cooper and Simpson ("High-Tech Luddite" and "Looks Good"), Kroeber, and the archive editors (Eaves, Essick, Viscomi, and Kirschenbaum).
3. I explore the editorial logic associated with this issue ("Why").
4. The Blake Archive Description (BAD) works in concert with the Blake Object Description (BOD). The archive also uses the Text Encoding Initiative DTD (TEI). For further information, see *Technical Summary* and the detailed descriptions of the elements on the Web site. Pitti and Unsworth explain the limitations of TEI that led, in special cases, to "locally developed DTDs."
5. For a description of the imaging protocols used in the archive, see *Editorial Principles* and *Technical Summary*; for further discussion, see "Persistence"; Viscomi. Misic explains the fundamental weaknesses of (ubiquitous) JPEG compression and proposes an alternative.
6. See *Editorial Principles*; *Technical Summary*; and Eaves, Essick, and Viscomi.
7. Both resources are gradually being converted from paper (the index in massive original files at Princeton, with four copies at widely distributed repositories in North America and Europe; Iconclass in multiple printed volumes) to electronic form.

8. For a chronicle of the archive's tenure at IATH, see *Plan*, especially part 2, "History."

9. They are listed in *Contributing Collections*, and the Blake collections are detailed in *Collection Lists*.

10. Steven Goldsmith pointed out Freud's idea to me.

11. Appendix 3 of chapter 3 of his *Radiant Textuality* is a useful complement to the present essay.

EPIGRAPHY

ANNE MAHONEY

EPIGRAPHY IN PRINT

Epigraphy is the study of texts that are inscribed onto durable materials, typically (though not always) stone. These texts include honorary and memorial inscriptions (on statue bases or gravestones), laws and decrees, and even graffiti. Although stone does not rot or burn, it can be broken or worn, and inscribed stones were often reused as building materials. As a result, many inscriptions are fragmentary texts.

Here we focus on Greek and Latin epigraphy. In the city-states of classical Greece and the Hellenistic world, from the sixth through at least the second century BC, laws and decrees were regularly inscribed on stone stelae and displayed publicly. In the Roman world, starting in about the third century BC, decree stelae were less and funerary and memorial inscriptions more common. Inscriptions of all types are an essential primary source for knowledge about the ancient world. Not only do they tell us about laws, alliances, and famous people, but they also give insight into daily life. Grave inscriptions, for example, can be mined for information about life expectancies, family sizes, and occupations. In addition, inscriptions preserve early forms of the Greek and Latin languages. Even the spelling errors give valuable information, about pronunciation.

Epigraphy has been studied systematically since the Renaissance. Inscriptions from various parts of the classical world have been collected into corpora and published in large print volumes, starting in the nineteenth century. The most important corpora are the *Corpus Inscriptionum Latinarum* and the *Inscriptiones Graecae*, both begun in the nineteenth century and still being updated today. Large university libraries will have copies of these huge, cumbersome print volumes; smaller libraries often do not. Several selections and anthologies of important inscriptions have been published, some with notes aimed at relative beginners.[1] In all these print volumes, the texts are presented in modern dress: typefaces use modern letterforms and mixed case; punctuation is added, usually according to the conventions of the editor's native language; and errors may be corrected or broken words completed, with clear indications that these are editorial changes from what appears on the stone. Photographs are included where possible, but the cost of reproducing pictures, especially when these print corpora were getting started, means that most printed inscriptions are not accompanied by photographs of the stone. As a result, it is important that the printed version of the text accurately represent what is physically present and what is an editorial addition.

Epigraphers have a standard convention for marking up texts in print, called the Leiden convention.[2] While it is common to include a diplomatic text as well (i.e., an exact transcription), nearly all epigraphic publications include an edited text, nowadays generally using the Leiden system. In this system, brackets of various shapes, underdots, and occasional other marks indicate letters added or corrected by the editor, letters on the stone that the editor judges to be wrong (e.g., misspelled words), expansions of abbreviations, blank spaces on the stone, erasures, ancient corrections, and so on. Epigraphers, thus trained to read and write semantically encoded texts, therefore often find XML markup a natural extension of what they are already doing.

A brief description of the Leiden system may be useful. In this system, angle brackets enclose letters or words that are not present in the inscription but that, in the editor's judgment, should be. Square brackets enclose letters or words that are in the inscription but are wrong. In both cases, the error could be a spelling or transcription mistake on the part of the stonecutter, or the editor could be normalizing the language or dialect. Commentary printed along with the text will generally explain which is a mistake and which a normalization.

Letters are printed with an underdot when they are not complete or not clear, as for example when the stone has been broken or worn. Suppose a particular Greek capital letter might be alpha, lambda, or delta. The editor will print the one that is most likely and place a dot under it. Sometimes context makes it clear that only one of these letters is possible. In our example, if the previous letter is nu and the following one xi, the letter in between must be a vowel, so the disputed triangular form must be an alpha. In such cases, some editors will print the alpha with an underdot, since it would not be unambiguously legible on its own, but others will print an unmarked alpha, since in the particular context there is no ambiguity.

Some ancient inscriptions include deliberate erasures, for example to remove the name of a despised Roman emperor after his death (as part of the procedure called *damnatio memoriae*). The erasure is marked with double square brackets when the letters can still be read or when it is at least clear how many letters were once there, with single square brackets otherwise.

Spacing, punctuation, and capitalization are all added or adjusted silently, as are accents and breathings for Greek. Readers are generally simply expected to know that ancient writing conventions differ from modern. The editor's commentary, however, will usually indicate the appearance of the original text. In particular, many classical Greek stones are written in *stoichedon* style (with letters arranged in a grid, as if on graph paper), and this fact is important because, if at least one line is complete, we can know how many letters are broken away from any incomplete lines.

Unfortunately, the Leiden convention is neither universal nor flawless. Since it was devised only in 1931, many published texts predate it and use similar but different conventions. Square brackets may denote additions rather than subtractions, round parentheses may denote additions rather than expansion of abbreviations, and so on. Any given book may or may not include a key to its particular markup system, so readers must become aware of different publishers' preferred styles. Moreover, because a fully marked text can be cumbersome to read, some publications omit the more complicated markings. Such omission is especially likely in texts intended for beginners and students.

A more important problem is that epigraphic markup, like most markup, encodes an editor's judgment about the text, which may be more or less certain. An editor's supplement could be almost certainly correct, as in the alpha-lambda-delta example above, or it could be pure conjecture, or anything in between. The Leiden system does not include a mechanism for indicating the editor's confidence in the proposed text. Normally this factor is discussed in the commentary, but certainty or lack of it is not encoded in the text itself. Also, editors differ in their application of markup. Some will mark any supplement or emendation, even if it is beyond any reasonable doubt; others will leave the obvious emendations unmarked—and the determination of what is obvious varies widely.

The first part of this problem, that the markup scheme in general use does not provide a way to encode certainty, can be addressed with the use of the TEI, as shown below. The second part, that editors disagree about what is obvious and what is arguable, cannot be solved by any markup scheme. We hope, though, that a scheme that provides a structured way to encode the discussion of certainty will ultimately help readers understand what editors know about a given text.

Although we focus on epigraphy here, it should be noted that the editorial and markup conventions for papyrology are similar. Textual criticism also uses similar signs in the text, and the commentary in an epigraphic or papyrological publication may include an apparatus criticus. All three fields face similar issues and have similar needs. A convention for using the TEI in epigraphy will be largely applicable to papyrology. The use of the TEI is well understood in more conventional textual criticism, which in classics involves establishing a text from several manuscripts, usually dating from the tenth to fifteenth century AD for Greek texts, sometimes rather earlier for Latin texts. The TEI tags that represent choices among variant readings are less useful in editing inscriptions and papyri, where there is generally only one copy of the text and we do not have the luxury of variants to choose from, but the tags can be used in collating prior editors' treatments of an inscription.

DIGITIZATION PROJECTS

Over the last few years, digitization projects have begun for several of the major epigraphic corpora. The epigraphic community also hopes to create a unified database of information about all known Greek and Latin inscriptions. A digitized corpus of inscriptions might contain several different representations of the inscriptions: photographs of inscriptions; photographs of squeezes of inscriptions, which are casts of the stone made in a flexible material like paper or latex; diplomatic transcriptions; edited texts; translations; and commentaries. Many projects also find it convenient to store metadata about the inscriptions in a database, to facilitate searching. The most useful metadata fields include the date of the inscription, its language, the types of letterforms in use in it, where it was found, what material it is on, and its size.

Some digitization projects complement existing print projects. Here the goal is to provide more-complicated searching than is possible with print indexes and to help produce the printed texts. The digital corpora may be made available on CD-ROM, with appropriate programs to search and display the texts and images. Some projects plan to distribute their texts on CD-ROM instead of in print. Still other projects hope to make their inscriptions available over the Web. Whatever the proposed dissemination mechanism, however, all these digitization projects face similar problems.

Digital epigraphy projects came together at the Second International Workshop on Digital Epigraphy, held at King's College, London, in July 2002. This workshop, hosted by the EpiDoc Aphrodisias Pilot Project (EPAPP), was part of a continuing discussion among epigraphers about standards and practices for semantic markup, in support of both electronic and print publication. EPAPP is a collaboration between the Aphrodisias team and the EpiDoc Group, based at the Ancient World Mapping Center, University of North Carolina. EpiDoc itself is a set of guidelines and a TEI DTD intended for use by epigraphers. It is likely to become a standard for those epigraphic projects that choose to use XML. EpiDoc was presented to the wider epigraphic community in an informal session at the XII Congressus Internationalis Epigraphiae Graecae et Latinae, the annual meeting of the Association Internationale d'Épigraphie Grecque et Latine (AIEGL), Barcelona, September 2002.

Over a dozen different epigraphic digitization projects were represented at the July 2002 workshop, covering all the classical world and including researchers from half a dozen different countries. Space does not permit detailed discussion of all the projects here; the workshop program, including links to the various projects' home pages, is available online at www.kcl.ac .uk/humanities/cch/epapp/kclwshop.html. Of the projects represented at this workshop, very few are using XML yet. The Aphrodisias Project, which hosted the workshop, is digitizing inscriptions from the Greek city of Aphrodisias in Asia Minor. Although Aphrodisias was first settled as early as the third millennium BC and the city continued to exist well into the thirteenth century AD, the project focuses on the inscriptions of late antiquity (see Rouequé and Reynolds). This project is the first major test case for the EpiDoc guidelines and DTD. The inscriptions are transcribed using this DTD, then transformed to Leiden markup in HTML for Web presentation. A database links the texts, information about the stones that contain them, photographs, and a site plan. The project began as an online reprint of *Aphrodisias in Late Antiquity* (Rouequé and Reynolds), the book in which many of these inscriptions were first published, but has expanded to include more texts and more photographs than could have been published in print. In addition, the archive contains pages from the notebooks of John Gandy Deering, who transcribed some of the Aphrodisias inscriptions in the winter of 1812–13. While such notebooks are rarely published in printed epigraphic editions, they can easily be added to an electronic edition, including both page images and transcriptions.

At Oxford, the Center for the Study of Ancient Documents (CSAD) is publishing the inscriptions from Roman Britain, which are generally on small tablets of wood or lead. Because the history of the Roman presence in Britain is part of the school curriculum there, the online publication of these texts must be accessible to children as young as eight or nine as well as to scholars. Publication therefore comprises print volumes, an online edition, and an online exhibition for nonspecialists. The texts are marked up in EpiDoc, and archaeological data and other metadata are stored in a relational database. The texts are converted to Leiden-like markup for HTML display, with some adjustment for the limited capacities of HTML: since standard HTML does not include underdots, for example, these letters will instead be shown in a lighter color. This corpus contains the well-known Vindolanda tablets, from the military base at Vindolanda near Hadrian's Wall in northern England. The tablets, small pieces of wood with text in ink, date from around the end of the first century AD; they are letters, military records, financial accounts, and other types of documents. Archaeological work continues at Vindolanda, so the corpus of texts continues to grow. As a result, the CSAD team expects to update the online edition of these inscriptions with new texts and the corresponding photographs, transcriptions, and translations, as well as with corrections or changes to earlier readings based on new materials. The print edition, naturally, will not change, so the editors must decide whether the online edition should be the printed text with a separate list of corrections or the most current text with a separate page of change history.

The oldest and largest epigraphic corpora have so much material that conversion to XML would be prohibitively difficult. Both *Inscriptiones Graecae (IG)* and the *Corpus Inscriptionum Latinarum (CIL)* began collecting inscriptions in the nineteenth century—before the codification of the Leiden markup system, let alone XML. *IG* has some 50,000 inscriptions, published in forty-nine large print volumes. The seventy volumes of *CIL* have about 180,000. Each collection also includes photographs, squeezes, and notebooks. *CIL* uses an XML-like markup internally, based on the needs of the publisher who handles the print edition, while *IG* gives its printer word-processor files. *CIL* has a large relational database storing bibliography and metadata, not the actual texts, which are transcribed and marked up in various systems, some influenced by customs from papyrology, some quite old. Converting these texts to XML would probably require a semiautomatic process, starting with a more or less accurate interpretation of the existing markup and ending with careful, manual proofreading. Given the number of texts involved and the variety of markup conventions applied over the better part of two centuries, this task is daunting. Although both projects would be happy to make at least some of their texts and photographs available online, the volume of material and the responsibility for continuing the print series do not allow it at present.

Some general considerations emerge from comparison of the various projects. Whether they are using databases, XML, or handwritten notes, all epigraphic projects have structured data, and whether they are marked up in Leiden, TEI, or an older system, all epigraphic texts are structured as well. When a new project begins or an existing one considers digitization, it faces several basic questions, some editorial and some technological.

The first question an epigraphic project must answer is whether the text or the physical object on which it is written should be considered the primary focus. That is, does the project study texts that happen to be written on stones or stones that happen to contain texts? Either approach is possible. Often projects begin from the stones, because one stone may hold several different inscriptions. If the text is primary, then information about the stone will be repeated (or referenced repeatedly) with each text it holds. It is rare, on the other hand, for a given text to appear on more than one inscription, so it is rarely necessary to repeat information about a text in the records for different stones. A project whose main concern is with language, however, might prefer to treat the texts as primary and the stones as secondary.

The next major question is the scope of the collection. A project might work on inscriptions from a particular place or time, like the city of Aphrodisias or Roman Britain, or might try to catalog all known inscriptions in a given language, as the major corpora *CIL* and *IG* do. The number of inscriptions the project expects to be working with will affect choices about how to manage them. If there are only a few dozen texts, then markup, metadata creation, and other operations can be done by hand. If the project must catalog, index, and display hundreds or thousands of texts, however, automated tools will be very useful. The project probably needs a corpus editor (see Crane and Rydberg-Cox; Rydberg-Cox, Mahoney, and Crane), who will determine what can be automated and what must be done by hand.

After these fundamental editorial questions come the technological questions, of which the most important may be how to store the metadata about the inscriptions; about the objects that contain them; and about the project's photographs, transcriptions, and editions. Although basic information about a TEI text goes into its TEI header—who transcribed it, whether it has been published before, and so on—it may also be convenient to store this information in the same place and format as the metadata about the rest of the project's collections. These issues are not specific to epigraphic projects, of course, but common to any project that deals with texts, photographs, and physical objects. Many epigraphic projects, like many more general digital libraries, use relational databases for their metadata. Some store the actual texts in the same database records, marked up in Leiden style or in XML. A sufficiently robust database system can even store photographs.

The technical question most relevant to the present chapter is how to encode and store the text.[3] There is a growing consensus that XML is the best way to encode the text, and the EpiDoc guidelines for using the TEI are emerging as a standard. XML is not the only choice, however. Projects may also use the typographic marks of the Leiden system, which has the advantage of being entirely familiar to the epigraphers who create and maintain the corpus. Unfortunately, the special brackets, underdots, and other typographic devices may not be supported by the character set of the computer system to be used. The Packard Humanities Institute inscription database, compiled and maintained by the Cornell Greek Epigraphy Project, uses *TLG* Beta Code to get around this problem.[4] In this system, every nonalphabetic character is represented by a series of characters: a marker to indicate what type of character is being represented (punctuation, bracket, metrical symbol, or the like) and a string of digits to specify the character. Thus "[4" indicates a left double square bracket, "]4" its matching right bracket, "#322" the chi-rho symbol.

If a project decides to use XML, it must then determine what DTD (or schema) to use. As in every other humanities discipline, the basic question is whether to use a general DTD, like the TEI, or to write a project-specific one. Exactly the same issues arise in the design of the database tables or other organizational schema for metadata. Some projects want databases or DTDs that are extremely specific to the types of inscriptions they are dealing with. For example, the projects that work largely or exclusively with funerary inscriptions want a standard way to record the age and sex of the person being memorialized, while projects that work with legal texts do not need this. Other projects prefer not to write and maintain their own DTD. The EpiDoc TEI guidelines are a good compromise here: the EpiDoc DTD is the TEI, with a few epigraphically oriented modifications made using the standard TEI mechanisms. There are also projects that use their own versions of the TEI, for example the project working on the Protestant Cemetery in Rome (Rahtz).

A key incentive for using XML is the ability to exchange data with other projects. Epigraphic corpora may overlap, as the time periods or geographic areas they focus on intersect. It is therefore convenient to be able to divide the labor of photographing, cataloging, and editing the inscriptions, and that means the resulting data must be in compatible forms. Using the same DTD in the same way makes this division relatively easy. While projects that store their texts as word-processor files with Leiden markup can also share data, they must agree explicitly on the details of text layout, file formats, and character encodings.

Text management must also take into account the writing systems used in the corpus. If a project is dealing only with inscriptions in Latin written in the Roman alphabet,[5] then the writing system of the inscriptions is essentially the same as that of the western European modern languages used for metadata, translations, and commentaries. Most classical epigraphy projects, however, have to deal with Greek, and projects dealing more generally with the ancient Mediterranean may have texts in Etruscan or Umbrian, which use similar alphabets; in Aramaic or Hebrew, which use very different alphabets and are of course written right to left; or even in languages that use cuneiform or hieroglyphic scripts.

The first approach to the writing-system problem is often to use different fonts, as one might with a word processor. This approach is appealing, since if the project ever wants to print its texts, it will sooner or later need fonts for the different scripts anyway. The approach is also analogous to the way texts are presented in print: we recognize that an inscription is in Greek because we see it printed in the Greek alphabet. There are long-standing conventions for the use of boldface, spaced type, and other typographic devices to represent the quasi-Roman alphabets used by the other ancient languages of Italy, like Oscan or Umbrian. Yet the font-based approach assumes that all the software that will manipulate a given text can recognize font-change markers. Some database packages do not allow change of font in a single text field, for example, and some export or interchange formats strip font information.

Unicode is a better approach when the scripts of interest are all supported, which will be the case for any script still in use by a living language (e.g., Greek or Hebrew). Hieroglyphic and cuneiform characters are not currently part of the Unicode standard, however, and even in supported scripts some old characters may not be available. In Greek inscriptions, for example, numerals are often symbols composed from the first letter of the word for the number: "fifty" would be represented as Π for *pente* (= 5) combined with Δ for *deka* (= 10): $\boxed{\Delta}$. These acrophonic numerals are generally used in print publications of inscriptions (e.g., Meiggs and Lewis, no. 72), but they are not yet part of the Unicode standard.

With XML, it is possible to define either elements or entities for unsupported characters. If the DTD contains an element called, say, `<char>`, and if the project has a controlled vocabulary for its attributes, the acrophonic numeral for 50 might be expressed as `<char type="acrophonic 50" font="numfont" pos="123"/>`, where "numfont" names a (hypothetical) font in which this character is available and "pos" is the character position of that character in that font. Alternatively, the project might define an entity like acro50 to represent this character. Either way, the XML text notes that here is the acrophonic numeral for 50, and the later rendering of the text for display or printing can substitute the appropriate character in a known font, a picture of the character, or even a numeral from a different system (the Greek alphabetic system, Arabic digits), depending on the facilities available in the target medium and on the audience for this version of the text. Approaches like these, however, assume that tools are available for these conversions; some application, transformation, or stylesheet must be told how to interpret the given element or entity.

Because so many epigraphy projects deal with large numbers of small texts, whereas literary projects in the classics more often have relatively few and larger texts (e.g., a few dozen dramas or a couple of epics), epigraphers have been quick to recognize the benefits of digitization for searching and for global manipulation of a corpus. Although many digital epigraphy projects predate XML, they are beginning to adopt it, and EpiDoc is emerging as a method.

EPIDOC: A TEI DTD FOR EPIGRAPHY

The EpiDoc initiative, under the leadership of Tom Elliott of the Ancient World Mapping Center, University of North Carolina, is working out ways to encode epigraphic data with the TEI. EpiDoc's basic assumption is that

> ancient epigraphic texts ought to be widely available in digital form for sharing and use in a variety of environments for a variety of scholarly and educational purposes. Individuals, organizations and projects require digital epigraphic texts for personal or internal use as well; if standard tools and formats were available, such needs would be more easily met. (*EpiDoc: Epigraphic Documents*)

The obvious standard for sharing and presenting texts is XML. Rather than writing a DTD for epigraphy from scratch, the EpiDoc group uses the TEI

> because TEI has already addressed many of the taxonomic and semantic challenges faced by epigraphers. The TEI-using community can provide a wide

range of best-practice examples and guiding expertise. Existing tooling built around TEI will lead to early, effective presentation and use of TEI-encoded epigraphic texts.

The EpiDoc approach has already been adopted by several epigraphic projects, and others are considering it. As noted above, Aphrodisias and the Roman Britain corpus use EpiDoc for their texts. The Dēmos project, directed by Christopher Blackwell of Furman University, is a library of materials about Athenian democracy that will include Greek inscriptions, marked up with EpiDoc, among the primary sources. The epigrapher Michael Arnush of Skidmore College is writing translations and commentaries for these inscriptions. The corpus of Macedonian and Thracian inscriptions being compiled at KERA, the Research Center for Greek and Roman Antiquity at Athens, is beginning to use the TEI and may choose to use EpiDoc.

The main product of the EpiDoc Collaborative is a set of guidelines detailing how to use the TEI for epigraphy in a standard way (Elliott, Cayless, and Hawkins). There is also an EpiDoc DTD, which is an extension of the TEI in the standard way, restricting the allowable values for certain attributes, suppressing unused elements, and adding a very small number of additional elements. The guidelines suggest what features to mark, which of a set of complementary tags to use for them (e.g., <abbr> and <expan>), and what to call the structural parts of an epigraphic publication. Projects that follow these guidelines exactly will be able to share not only their texts but also their tools. Applications written to process EpiDoc texts—transformations, stylesheets, specialized search engines, index generators, and so on—will need to handle only the cases provided for in the guidelines: they must process <abbr>, for example, but need not deal with <expan>.

The current version of the guidelines document is not complete; several sections remain to be written, and some are being revised based on experience. The basic philosophy of the guidelines, however, is clear. The simplest rule is that whatever is actually on the stone is in the content of the elements, while editorial changes and additions are in attributes. Thus EpiDoc prefers <abbr>, with the expansion in an attribute, to <expan>, with the expansion in the content and the actual abbreviation in an attribute. The next rule is that EpiDoc follows the intended semantics of the TEI guidelines: "we are not rewriting TEI," as the EpiDoc guidelines state (Elliott, Cayless, and Hawkins, sec. 6). Finally, everything that can be expressed in the Leiden system, or other similar schemes, must be expressible in EpiDoc. Moreover, there must be a one-to-one match between markup elements in the Leiden system (symbols and character formatting) and those in EpiDoc, so that the two markup schemes will be mechanically interconvertible.

An EpiDoc text is structured as a series of unnumbered ‹div›s, distinguished by their **type** attributes. Typical divisions might be the text itself, a translation, a description of the stone or other object where the text is, a commentary, or a bibliography. The EpiDoc DTD, unlike unmodified TEI, introduces a finite set of possible values for the **type** of a ‹div›, so that all users of a text can distinguish, say, the commentary from the description or the archaeological history. To ensure that this structure is used, the EpiDoc DTD does not include the numbered ‹divN› elements at all.

The EpiDoc group is also working on tools, for example XSL stylesheets, to facilitate working with EpiDoc texts; these tools can be found at the EpiDoc home page at the Ancient World Mapping Center. One tool that will be particularly important to wide acceptance of EpiDoc is a transformer that can convert between Leiden format and EpiDoc XML in either direction. This transformer, currently under development, will help projects convert their existing texts to EpiDoc format, and it will also promote the use of EpiDoc as an exchange mechanism: two projects that do not want to convert their holdings to XML can nonetheless use XML to give texts to each other. An additional desideratum is an editor with specific support for EpiDoc, as opposed to a general XML editor that can read the DTD, by analogy with the HTML editors that have the HTML DTD built in and do not claim to provide general support for other DTDs. Such an editor, tailored to the needs of epigraphers rather than general users, should help overcome the perception among some epigraphers that XML is too technical or too difficult.

Although the guidelines and DTD are primarily the work of Elliott and his colleagues at the University of North Carolina, the wider community has been involved from the beginning. Even before the first version of the DTD was prepared, EpiDoc existed in the form of a mailing list, bringing together epigraphers, historians, and humanities computing specialists to discuss how EpiDoc might work. Discussions on this list have ranged from basic philosophical questions to highly technical implementation details.

All the disputes about what to mark—like the underdot in the example above with nu, triangular broken letter, xi—don't go away as a result of encoding the texts in XML instead of in typographic form. But one advantage of structured markup is that editors can, if they choose, encode more information about how certain a particular feature is. The date of an inscription, for example, can be encoded as a range of possible dates. EpiDoc includes the TEI ‹certainty› element and the **cert** attribute to encourage editors to say whether or not they are completely confident of a given reading. After some discussion, the EpiDoc community decided that certainty should be expressed as a yes-or-no value: either the editor is certain of the reading or not. The idea of saying, "I am 95% certain of this letter, 83% certain of this letter, and only 37% certain of this letter," seemed too complicated, and it was decided that editors should be encouraged to put these details into the commentary—as they have always done. The advance of EpiDoc over the Leiden system here is simply that the editor can note certainty in a standard way in the markup, not merely in the commentary.

Other philosophical debates are how much can be assumed from applications that will work with EpiDoc texts, how best to handle characters that are not part of Unicode and will not be added, and how to handle the necessarily imprecise dates given for ancient texts. The archives of the mailing list trace the progress of the guidelines, and the guidelines themselves embody the collective wisdom of a group of practicing epigraphers and XML specialists.

The epigraphic community has a long-established practice of using semantic markup. The markup systems in use have evolved over the past four hundred years but until relatively recently have always involved special typographic symbols in the text—brackets, underdots, and so on. Some epigraphers see XML as a natural transformation of what they have always done, with all the additional benefits that come from standardization in the community.

The EpiDoc guidelines are emerging as one standard for digital epigraphy with the TEI. EpiDoc is not the only possible way to use the TEI for epigraphic texts, of course, but the tools, documentation, and examples that are growing up around it will make it a good place for new digitization projects to start.

NOTES

The work described in this essay was supported by a grant from the Digital Library Initiative Phase 2 (NSF IIS-9817484), with particular backing from the National Endowment for the Humanities and the National Science Foundation.
1. Student anthologies of Greek inscriptions include, for example, Meiggs and Lewis; Schwenk; and Tod. *Inscriptiones Latinae Selectae* (Dessau) is still used for Latin.
2. This convention was first adopted at the Eighteenth International Congress of Orientalists, Leiden, September 1932, by papyrologists and taken up by epigraphers shortly thereafter. Dow gives historical background and bibliography. Woodhead explains the system from the point of view of a student learning to

use inscriptions. Panciera summarizes more recent debates. See also Dohnicht; Finney.

3. Of course projects must also decide what format to use for digital photographs, but this question is outside the scope of this discussion.

4. Beta Code is well known as an encoding for the Greek alphabet, but it also contains representations for all the other characters that appear in the texts of the *Thesaurus Linguae Graecae (TLG)*.

5. The Greek or Etruscan alphabets were occasionally used for Latin by nonnative speakers.

PART II
PRACTICES AND PROCEDURES

EFFECTIVE METHODS OF PRODUCING MACHINE-READABLE TEXT FROM MANUSCRIPT AND PRINT SOURCES

EILEEN GIFFORD FENTON AND HOYT N. DUGGAN

The choice of a method for generating digital text from manuscript or printed sources requires careful deliberation. No single method is suitable for every project, and the very range of options can be misleading. Therefore, thoughtful consideration of the original source and analysis of project goals are essential. This essay considers two different types of source materials—manuscript and print. The discussion of manuscript sources is provided by Hoyt Duggan, based on experience in the *Piers Plowman* project, and the discussion of print sources is provided by Eileen Fenton, based on experience with *JSTOR*.

MANUSCRIPT SOURCES

Creating digital text from handwritten documents requires all the traditional editorial and bibliographic disciplines necessary for publication in print plus some mastery of SGML/XML markup. These observations are the result of the author's experiences as director of the Piers Plowman *Electronic Archive* (*PPEA*), a project designed to represent the entire textual tradition of a poem that survives in three authorial versions (conventionally known as A, B, and C) and another dozen or so scribal versions.[1] Ten manuscripts attest the A version, eleven manuscripts and three sixteenth-century printed editions the B version, and twenty manuscripts the C version. Four spliced versions of ABC texts exist as well as seven AC splices and one AB splice. Of these sixty-plus witnesses no two are identical. The complete corpus consists of well over three million word forms and ten thousand manuscript pages. The oldest manuscripts date from the last decade of the fourteenth century; most are from the first half of the fifteenth, and a handful are sixteenth-century. Most are written in professional book hands—usually varied forms of Anglicana scripts. A few of the later ones are written in a highly cursive secretary script.

Available Methods

Optical character recognition (OCR) is not a viable option for early hand-written documents with their variable letterforms and unstandardized spelling systems. Nor is OCR satisfactory for duplicating early printed texts like Robert Crowley's of 1550. The crude early fonts and the frequent instances of broken or malformed characters present even more problems than the professionally executed fifteenth-century manuscripts. Keyboard entry is the only reliable means for converting handwritten documents into machine-readable form.

Text entry from handwritten sources requires a highly motivated and well-trained staff able to comprehend a late Middle English text and to interpret a number of scripts and hands.[2] We were fortunate to have generous funding initially from the Institute for Advanced Technology in the Humanities (IATH) at the University of Virginia and, later, from three two-year grants from the National Endowment for the Humanities. Both sponsors have provided monies to employ and train a staff of highly competent young medievalists from the graduate programs in English, French, and classics at the University of Virginia. Working together, the team has transcribed forty-four manuscripts—all of the B witnesses, all but one of the A manuscripts, all of the AC splices—and has begun transcription of the C manuscripts.

What Should We Represent in a Transcription?

Naively, I had expected that editing with the computer would be a good bit faster than editing with pencil and paper, but the opposite has proved to be the case. Transcribing a manuscript electronically involves all the work that both modern print editors and medieval scribes have traditionally done. Text entry is still done one character at a time, letter by letter, space by space. Proofreading remains the same demanding activity it has always been, requiring serial rereadings to compensate for eye skip, arrhythmia, dittography, homoeoteleuton, and for the manifold other failures of concentration that have marred scribal efforts since literacy began. We have found ourselves making the same kinds of error at the keyboard that medieval scribes made when inscribing animal skins with quills. Indeed, we have introduced other forms of error facilitated by word-processing software! Moreover, if the base transcription of the manuscript readings could be miraculously rendered error-free, transcribing would still remain labor-intensive, since the electronic text with its potential for markup is capable of conveying far more information than printed editions ever attempted to convey. Such capabilities present endless possibilities for expanding the editorial project; once detailed markup has begun, it is difficult to determine where to stop.

We found, for example, that using different stylesheets and XML markup, we could represent in detail changes in hand, color of ink, script, or style. Like other late-medieval manuscripts, many manuscripts of *Piers Plowman* carry a considerable amount of textual information routinely and sometimes necessarily ignored in printed editions. Most readers of the poem will, I suspect, be surprised to learn that the B archetype (and probably B itself) was written in strophes of irregular length, marked in the best witnesses by paraphs, usually in alternating colors. The number of words and phrases given emphasis by rubrication, underlining, letters touched in red, and so forth varies from manuscript to manuscript, but it has taken electronic editions to bring their very existence to the attention of the scholars who do not have easy access to the original manuscripts. Indeed, our ability to represent on the screen the physical features of those witnesses offers a striking insight into Langland's position as a writer in late-fourteenth-century English poetic composition. As Thorlac Turville-Petre has recently written of our edition of Cambridge, Trinity College, MS B.15.17, the copy-text for the editions of Kane-Donaldson and A. V. C. Schmidt, readers who know only those printed texts "will be brought face-to-face with a fact which has far-reaching implications" (Turville-Petre and Duggan). He continues:

> Reading *Piers Plowman* as a printed text can be hugely misleading. So often students take away with them the notion of Langland as a dissident writer, operating at the margins of society, an idea encouraged by Langland himself, particularly in the C-Version, where he portrays himself as a west-country exile, perching precariously on London society, supported by a coterie of friends. For a writer of this sort, texts will surely have circulated as samizdat, clandestine writings hastily scribbled by enthusiasts, passed from hand to hand at gatherings of the disaffected? Of course nothing could be further from the truth, and no manuscript gives the lie to it more convincingly than Cambridge, Trinity College, MS B.15.17.

Such historical and bibliographic insight is enabled in electronic editions because XML markup, in addition to representing the underlying structures of the poetic text, also makes it possible to represent its formal bibliographic and codicological features in machine-readable and manipulable form.

Early in the process, the editor must determine how fine-grained the transcription is to be, because markup permits the specification in minute detail of the paleographic features of the document. The scribe of Trinity College MS B.15.17, for instance, made use of two forms of the letter *a* and three of capital *A*; two forms of *r*; and three of lowercase *s*—a long *s* appearing medially, a sigma-shaped *s* at the beginning of words, and an 8-shaped *s* at the end. Using entity references, we might well have distinguished each of these and devised fonts and stylesheets to distinguish the allographs. But because our focus in creating the archive is to edit the text, we have not attempted to represent every possible paleographic or other physical feature of the documents. We have chosen to transcribe graphemically rather than graphetically, ignoring differences insignificant for establishing the text. A student of letterforms, however, might prefer to tag features we have elided. Such tagging would be entirely feasible. Since we leave our basic ASCII transcriptions available and transparent to users, scholars with a focus on other aspects of these texts may use our transcriptions and the attached, hypertextually linked color digital images to reflect their different interests in the document. The options for markup at the time of transcription are many. We might have chosen to attach lexical and grammatical identifier tags to every word or to identify, syllable by syllable, the placement of ictus and arsis. Proper nouns might have been distinguished from common nouns, count nouns from mass nouns. Virtually any linguistic or prosodic feature of interest can be represented; consequently, editors must make fundamental choices as to what features they will mark.

Establishing Protocols

Early in the process of creating the *PPEA*, we established a set of transcriptional protocols to serve as a guide for our transcribers. They are posted on our Web site (http://jefferson.village.virginia.edu/seenet/piers/protocoltran .html) and supplied as hard copy to each of the project's editors. They have necessarily gone through several revisions since 1994, reflecting both the state of our knowledge and the stage the texts have reached.

Sources for Transcriptions

Ideally, the transcriber would work directly from the primary document. Failing direct access to the original, the transcriber should work from high-quality color digital images of each page of each manuscript. Ideal as either would be, on the *PPEA* we have had access to the original or to color images for just four of the forty-four manuscripts we have transcribed. Of necessity, we have worked from black-and-white microfilm. Initially we made photo-copy flow copies for our transcribers. But the duplications of the microfilm, itself already a copy, became a fertile source of transcriptional error, so we decided to work directly from microfilm. Microfilm, of course, does not convey elements of color; consequently additional markup must be inserted later when editors have access to color images or to the manuscript itself. When libraries become more accustomed to producing high-quality digital images as well as equipped to produce them, scholars who can find the fund-ing to purchase digital images will have a better base for scholarly editions than exists at present.

Text-Entry Software

Since 1993, we have used a variety of word-processing and text-entry soft-ware for transcribing the manuscripts. Initially we attempted to use the SGML-authoring program *Author/Editor*. Though it had the advantage of permitting us to parse the document as it was created, it was also slow and excessively complicated. At about the same time we experimented with vari-ous word-processing programs such as *Word* and *WordPerfect* on both Win-dows and Macintosh platforms and emacs on Unix. Eventually we came to use other plain-text editors. For the past five years we have used almost exclusively the shareware program *NoteTab Pro*. Using its clipboard macro feature, we have linked it to the *NSGMLS* parser.[3] Unlike *Word* and *WordPerfect*, which created problems by introducing unintended line breaks when we converted those files to plain ASCII, the ASCII editors have proved fast, cheap, and reliable.

We found it essential to create macros for the SGML tags and to persuade transcribers to use them consistently both at the time of initial file creation and later, when more information becomes available or when corrections are entered after proofreading. Individually typed tagging proliferates error.

Version and Quality Control

Both version and quality control have been steady concerns for the *PPEA*. When different people enter, proofread, and correct files, file management must be systematic. In one instance, when two different files were used for entering corrections of the same transcription, the correction of the error involved several weeks of tedious labor comparing files and an additional team proofreading (two weeks' work for two people). We have established a single copy of record kept on a single server and a standardized set of procedures for ensuring that all work is done on a single copy of record.

Quality control for the transcriptions is ensured by multiple layers of proofreading. Initially, various members of the editorial team transcribed from microfilm. We have now chosen to make a single transcriber responsible for completing the remaining C manuscripts. That transcriber proofreads each page as it is entered. Next a unique archival line number is assigned to each line using a locally produced perl script and a set of reference tags with the line numbers of the Athlone edition of the three versions. The archival line numbers will eventually be replaced with a distinctive *PPEA* reference number, but the present system, which permits users of our editions to compare our texts easily with the Athlone texts, also makes machine collation simpler than it would otherwise have been. After the line references have been inserted, a team of two proofreads the text. One sits at the computer with color digital images of each page (or at the microfilm reader when we lack digital images) and reads the text from the page, letter by letter, space by space, while the other team member checks a printout to verify the accuracy of the interpreted SGML text. To help maintain attention, these readers exchange places and roles at the page break. Each of our published texts has undergone at least three such team proofreadings. After the final team proofing, any necessary corrections are entered by two people, one responsible for text entry, the other making sure that new errors are not introduced in the process of correction.

PRINT SOURCES

Producing machine–readable text from print resources offers challenges and options somewhat different from those raised by manuscripts. Consequently an approach that works well for manuscripts may be less successful when applied to mass-produced print sources. Similarly, an approach that works well for one type of printed matter may be less successful when applied to a different type of printed matter. There is no right or wrong approach. One must find the approach that best matches the aims and mission of the project.

Once the mission to be served is clearly understood, there are a number of other factors to consider when evaluating methods for producing machine-readable text. The suggestions offered below for printed materials are derived from my experience with one particular type of print resource, the scholarly journal, at *JSTOR*. While the factors discussed here are likely to be applicable to a range of other projects and other print sources, this list is surely not exhaustive.

Background on *JSTOR*

JSTOR (www.jstor.org) is a not-for-profit organization with a mission to help the scholarly community take advantage of advances in information technologies. We pursue this mission through the creation of a trusted archive of core scholarly journals emphasizing the conversion of entire journal back files from volume 1, issue 1, and the preservation of future e-versions of these titles. To date *JSTOR* has converted over 10 million journal pages from over 240 journals representing more than 170 publishers. The archive is available to students, scholars, and researchers at more than 1,450 libraries and institutions. Each journal page digitized by *JSTOR* is processed by an optical character recognition (OCR) application (discussed below) in order to produce a corresponding text file. The resulting text files are used to support the full-text searching offered to *JSTOR* users and accomplished through a search engine that reads or indexes each word of each page and documents its location and proximity to other words. *JSTOR* does not display these full-text files to the user; their role is strictly (and literally) behind the scenes.

Fundamentals of the OCR Process

JSTOR's use of OCR is certainly not unique. Reliance on this application has become increasingly commonplace as this technology significantly improved over the last decade. Simply put, OCR converts the text of a printed page into a digital file. This process has two distinct steps: first, a digital image of the printed page is made; second, the characters of that image are read by the OCR program and saved in a text file. Sometimes these two steps are combined in one package, but technically they can be separate activities, creating different types of files that can have different uses. In *JSTOR*, we use the digital page images to present journal content to users of the archive; we also feed the images to OCR software in order to create full-text versions of the journal pages. If a digital image has not been separately produced, as may be the case with other projects, the OCR process begins by taking a digital snapshot of the page.

Next, the OCR software examines the digital image and analyzes the layout of the page by dividing it into sections referred to as zones. Zones generally correspond to paragraphs or columns of text or graphics such as grayscale or color illustrations. While this zoning task would be simple for a human reader with the ability to interpret semantic clues, it can present a variety of challenges for a machine. For example, text will sometimes be displayed in columns. If the columns are very close together, OCR software may continue to interpret from left to right across the page, interleaving the columns. Some magazines and journals will use boxes inserted into a column to explain a side issue or include an advertisement, and these may be difficult for the machine to recognize properly. When page analysis is complete, the order of the zones is determined: the software attempts to replicate the path that a typical reader seeking to understand the full text of the page will follow. The people running the software can, if they choose, review this zone order and make manual adjustments to correct it. When the appropriate zone order is established, the analysis of the characters can begin.

Most OCR applications work by looking at character groups—that is, words—and comparing them to a dictionary included with the application. Just as our eye takes in the shapes of letters and white space on the page, the software interprets black dots and white spaces and compares the patterns with the letters or even words it is trained to recognize. When a match is found, the software prints to the text file the appropriate word; when a match cannot be confidently made, the software makes a reasonable assumption and flags the word as a low-confidence output. Where a word or character cannot be read at all, the default character for illegible text is inserted as a placeholder. The focus of this process is the basic text of the page. Formatting such as bolding, italics, or underlining is not captured, nor are photos or other non-text illustrations, which cannot be read by the OCR application. If the OCR software relies on an English dictionary, non-English accents and diacritics will not be recognized. Similarly, symbols used in mathematical, chemical, or scientific notation are not recognized.

The software that completes the OCR process is sometimes referred to as an OCR engine, and OCR applications vary in the number of engines available in a particular commercial product. The software *OmniPage Pro*, for instance, contains a single OCR engine, and this application generally follows the process described above. *Prime Recognition*, by contrast, is a multiengine application, where up to six engines perform OCR and coordinate the output results in a way that aims to maximize text accuracy. The multiengine products follow the same process as the single-engine software but incorporate additional steps into the final OCR stages. After determining a best word match, each engine reports a confidence rating indicating the match's probability of error. Then, through a voting mechanism, the engines determine which match has the highest potential for accuracy, and this selection is printed to the text file. The presence of multiple engines generally improves the overall accuracy of the final text file.

Print Source Characteristics and OCR Quality

Regardless of the number of engines an OCR application includes, a variety of factors can contribute to the overall quality of the output. OCR applications perform best when the source material contains text arranged in even columns with regular margins, printed in a modern font with even, dark ink that contrasts sharply with a light paper background free of background marks or bleedthrough. Pages stained by age, water damage, or debris often lead to poor-quality OCR. Pages that contain uneven or narrow column margins, text printed over graphic elements, text that is six points or less in size, or very light or very dark printing will also generally produce poor OCR results. Printing flaws such as skewed text or echo printing, which creates an appearance similar to double vision, will also dramatically reduce OCR quality.

Key Points When Considering OCR

In deciding which approach for producing machine-readable text is right for your project, you should consider at least eight factors.

1. Select an approach for creating machine-readable text that promotes the mission of your project.
It will be important to evaluate the level of machine readability required for your project. If, for instance, you need text files that will be read by a search engine to support full-text searching, then text files produced by an OCR application may be sufficient. You may find, however, that even the best OCR output requires some manual monitoring or correction to produce satisfactory search results. To make this determination, you must carefully analyze the level of search accuracy needed and the practical implications of achieving various levels of accuracy. Is it necessary, for example, for a scholar to find every occurrence of the search term? Are some sections of the text more critical for searching than others? Similarly, you may wish to support features beyond full-text searching, which require a higher level of machine readability. In order to broaden search options, for instance, you may wish to apply SGML, XML, or other tagging to support the focused searching of key elements or sections of the text. Finally, you must decide if you will display the OCR text files to users. Should your project include display, consider how display affects the level of accuracy of OCR output. Determine what

level of tolerance the user may have—or not have—for errors in the OCR text files. An understanding of the quality expectations of the users and how the displayed files may be used will be helpful in this analysis.

2. Understand the characteristics of your source material.

The quality of the paper and the characteristics of the printed source material, including font, layout, and graphic elements, can affect the overall quality of the OCR output. Understanding the full range of features present in the source allows you to determine the most efficient way—or even whether— to employ OCR. If, for instance, your source material contains a large number of full-page graphics or a large number of special characters or scientific or mathematical symbols, develop an automated means for filtering these pages out for special OCR or other treatment. Filter those pages for which a non-English dictionary is most appropriate or for which more or fewer engines are required to achieve the desired accuracy level.

3. Develop appropriate quality-control measures.

With a clear understanding of the source material characteristics, you can establish text accuracy targets that successfully support the mission of the project. But to give these targets meaning, you must establish a quality-control program to ensure that established targets are met. Quality-control measures may vary, from a complete review of all phases of text production to a sampling approach, in which only a subset of pages is selected for review. If a complete review is prohibitively expensive, as it is for many projects, you might retain a statistical consultant to make sure that the sample drawn for quality assessment is a valid representation of the overall data population. Also have established procedures in place for any data errors that are found. Will these errors be corrected by in-house staff? Or, if the work was produced by a third party, will the rework be done by the vendor? How will quality standards be communicated to the staff involved? Whatever the approach to a quality-control program, consider carefully the staffing, budget, and space implications of the work.

4. Understand the effect of scale.

A solution appropriate for a short-term project of ten thousand pages may not be appropriate for a longer-term project of ten million. Even for short-term projects, an approach that works smoothly in the start-up phase may begin to break down as the project ramps up in scale. Be sensitive to the effect of scale and take it into account as well in project schedules and budgets.

5. Carefully assess the effect of location.

Production of OCR can be, and frequently is, contracted to a third-party vendor, but outsourcing may not be appropriate for all projects. In considering whether to outsource or to retain this process in-house, look at a variety of questions. Which approach makes the most effective use of hardware, software, and staff? Which approach provides the greatest value—as distinct from offering the lowest cost? How important is it to retain local control over all aspects of the process? How will each approach affect key production schedules? What skills can an outside vendor offer, and what benefit is lost to the project by not having these skill sets locally? Consider these and similar questions when choosing whether or not to outsource this process. Again, the best solution varies from project to project.

Addressing such questions will help you develop an understanding of the comparative advantages that each approach offers. If it is important to produce the highest quality output at the lowest possible cost, outsourcing the work may be the approach for you. But this advantage may have to be balanced with the need to build locally skills essential for other reasons—for instance, the ability to leverage knowledge across multiple projects or to help seed other initiatives at the home institution. An example from *JSTOR*'s approach to imaging illustrates this point. We decided to outsource the scanning of our journals, because scanning is a manual process with clear, measurable specifications. We can and do have various objective quality measures that we routinely apply to the vendor's work. But we chose to retain in-house the prescanning preparation work and the postscanning quality control, because through these processes we build a knowledge base about the journal content and because quality assessment is crucial to the mission of the archive.

6. More time will be required than you expect.

As a general rule and despite your best planning efforts, it will take considerable time to produce machine-readable text—in both the pre-OCR steps and the actual running of the software. The time needed to run the software can vary greatly depending on the characteristics of the source material, the specific software, the number of engines, the hardware running the process, and the quality-control measures developed for the project. Even in a single printed work, time is affected as the content varies. Running a representative test sample of the source material may help, but know that it will not fully reveal the complexities of ongoing production processes. Working with the journals in the *JSTOR* archive, whose content varies over time and discipline, we see significant variation in software processing time. A single data set of five thousand pages may require from ten to thirty hours of processing time on our particular software-hardware configuration. It is a good idea to include contingency time in production schedules, especially in the initial days of the project.

7. Consider the implications of project duration.

Given the speed of technical innovation for hardware and software, it is important to take into account the expected duration of the project. Hardware and software applications that were the best choice at the beginning of a project may become dated and require reassessment as the project moves forward. Even if the original applications continue to function, the project may save money by upgrading. A careful, periodically recurring evaluation of new developments and technologies is recommended for projects of all but the shortest duration.

8. Costs will be higher than anticipated.

While it may be relatively easy to project costs based on an initial run of sample data, it is difficult to anticipate how actual production costs will differ from such an estimate. Typically, production costs are higher than expected, especially in the early days of a project. Machines may not perform at the speed advertised or as tested; drives may fail; software upgrades may be needed. As the scale of production increases, additional purchases may be needed to reach the desired production level and to maintain server response time in an acceptable range. Similarly, as project scale increases, more staff time is required to tend to systems administration to develop a technical infrastructure suited to the operation. Anticipate the unexpected in these areas and build into project budgets, if possible, some ability to respond to unforeseen needs as they arise. The variance will be different for each project, of course. A helpful rule of thumb is that if your expectation is 1, allocate 1.5.

Considering each of these factors should help you find the best approach to producing machine-readable text for your project. But each must be examined in the context of the overall mission of the project.

NOTES

1. The received scholarly tradition, sometimes called the Langland myth, is that William Langland, a London chantry priest originally from southwest Worcestershire, wrote the three versions in the order A, B, C. Recently, scholars have

presented various arguments that would change that order, placing the B text first, with A and C representing later redactions. The chief proponents of the revisionist argument have been Anne Hudson, John Bowers, Jill Mann, and C. David Benson. For references to the relevant scholarship, see Kane, "Open Letter." David Benson's argument is to appear in a forthcoming study of the textual traditions of *Piers Plowman*.

2. A process of double keyboarding using relatively unskilled labor has been used to reproduce printed texts. This method offers nothing to the scholar who wants to create an edition from manuscript materials. Furthermore, double keyboarding depends on the questionable assumption that two typists working independently will not make the same mistake in the same place. Ubiquitous coincidental variation among the original manuscripts suggests that such errors are probable.

3. We owe grateful thanks to Daniel Pitti, project director of the Institute for Advanced Technology in the Humanities, for setting up the combined word processor and *NSGMLS* parser for us.

LEVELS OF TRANSCRIPTION

M. J. DRISCOLL

"Levels of transcription" means, essentially, how much of the infor-mation in the original document is included (or otherwise noted) by the transcriber in his or her transcription. W. W. Greg's distinction between "substantives," the actual words of the text, and the "accidentals," the surface features of the text (e.g., spelling, punctuation, word division), is well established. Few editors, however, in particular those working with manuscript or early printed materials, are content simply to record the one and ignore the other. There is, moreover, a great range of accidentals that one may or may not want to include in a transcription. At one end of the spectrum are transcriptions that may be called strictly diplomatic, in which every feature that may reasonably be reproduced in print is retained. These features include not only spelling and punctuation but also capitalization, word division, and variant letterforms. The layout of the page is also retained, in terms of line division, large initials, and so on. Any abbreviations in the text will not be expanded, and, in the strictest diplomatic transcriptions, apparent slips of the pen will remain uncorrected. Such editions are often so close to the originals as to be all but unreadable for those unfamiliar with early paleographic or typographic conventions, or in any case no easier to read than the originals (see figs. 1 and 2). At the opposite end are fully modernized transcriptions, where the substantives are retained but everything else is brought up-to-date, in some cases to such an extent as to make it questionable whether they are to be regarded as transcriptions at all. Between these two extremes a number of levels may be distinguished—semidiplo-matic, seminormalized, and so on—depending on how the accidentals of the original are dealt with. Practice varies greatly, and in some editorial traditions it may be common to normalize or regularize some features at one level while retaining others; I find it more useful therefore to identify the individual features and the ways in which they can be treated by the transcriber.

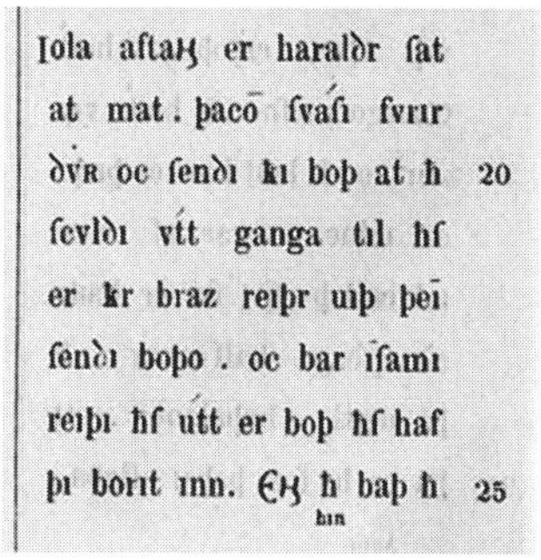

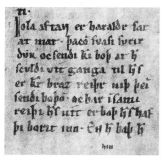

Ioia aftaɳ er haralðr fat
at mat . þaco fvañ fvrir
ðⱽʀ oc fenðı ʞı boþ at h   20
fevlðı vít ganga til hf
er ʞr braz reiþr uiþ þei
fenðı boþo . oc bar ıfamı
reiþı hf útt er boþ hf haf
þı bort mn. Eȶ h baþ h   25

Fig. 1. From Verner Dahlerup's
1880 edition of *Ágrip af Noregs
konunga sǫgum*

Fig. 2. From Copenhagen,
Arnamagnæan Institute, AM 325 II
4to, 1v, the original manuscript

Forms of Letters

Variant letterforms—high *s* and round *s*, for example—are often distinguished in transcriptions of manuscripts and early printed materials. Texts that are semidiplomatic or seminormalized will generally distinguish only between variant letterforms that are felt to have a basis in phonology distinctions, which these two forms of /s/, for example, do not. For statistical purposes, however, it may be desirable to transcribe (or register in some other way) such paleographic or typographic distinctions even where they have no apparent basis in phonology.

Punctuation

It is standard practice in diplomatic transcriptions for the punctuation of the original to be reproduced, no matter how inconsistent it may appear by modern standards. The transcriber may try to reproduce the actual signs in the original or may choose to use the nearest modern equivalent. In antiquity, for example, it was common to place points at varying heights in order to represent different degrees of pause, in ascending order of importance; the transcriber may choose to use an ordinary period instead of a mid or high dot. Similarly, an ordinary semicolon may be used for the *punctus elevatus*, the function of which was arguably the same. In many early texts, both hand-written and printed, marks of punctuation are both preceded and followed by white space; the transcriber may choose to disregard the space before the mark while faithfully reproducing the mark itself. In some editorial traditions quotation marks may be supplied to indicate direct speech, even while other features of the original punctuation are retained.

Capitalization

In a diplomatic transcription the capitalization of the original will normally be retained, although in some traditions proper names are given capital letters whether there are capitals in the original or not. In some cases it may be desirable to distinguish between large and small capitals—small capitals are letters that have the shape of majuscules but the size of minuscules. In Old Norse manuscripts, small capitals were frequently used to indicate geminate consonants; transcribing these as ordinary capitals would give a false impression of the use of capitals in the text, while replacing them with double lowercase letters would arguably involve a unacceptable degree of normalization. Some scholars would also recognize the existence of enlarged minuscules, letters that have the shape of minuscules but the size of majuscules.

Structure and Layout

By structure is meant the division of a work into its constituent parts: prose works will normally comprise a number of chapters, which contain sections or paragraphs; works in verse will be divisible into cantos or fits, these into stanzas, the stanzas into lines, and so on. Other types of texts—letters, for example—have their own structures. Layout means the arrangement of the text on the page. In medieval manuscripts and many early printed books there is rarely any connection between structure and layout. A new chapter will not necessarily begin on a new page, and poetry was frequently written out like prose, although sometimes the beginning of a new line or stanza would be indicated in some other way, through a sign or mark of punctuation. The more diplomatic a transcription, the more likely it is to favor the structure of the document—that is, the layout—over the structure of the work. In strictly diplomatic transcriptions, the line, column (if any), and page boundaries of the original are reproduced in the transcription; the structure of the work, if unmarked in the original, is left unmarked in the transcription.

In less diplomatic transcriptions the structure of the work will be given priority, while line, column, and page boundaries may be indicated by means of a vertical line (single for line boundaries, double for page boundaries, when both are indicated). In normalized and modernized texts the focus is entirely on the work itself, and there is generally no indication whatsoever of the layout of the original.

Abbreviations

The use of abbreviations, both to spare the scribe the labor of writing words that, because of their frequency generally or in a particular text, could easily be understood in an abbreviated form and to save parchment or paper and ink, is a characteristic feature of ancient and most medieval vernacular manuscript traditions and early printed books. As an aid to the reader it is common in all but the strictest diplomatic transcriptions to expand abbreviations. When a word or phrase is abbreviated, a number of letters is suppressed, and the expansion of the abbreviation thus involves supplying these letters. The letters so supplied are frequently marked in some way in the transcription—printed in italics or given in brackets, for example—but even in transcriptions that are otherwise fairly diplomatic, abbreviations may be expanded silently, especially where it can be argued that there is no doubt as to what they represent.

Corrections and Emendations

In all but the most diplomatic of transcriptions obvious errors and omissions will be corrected—the sorts of things, it could be argued, that the scribe or compositor himself would have corrected had they been brought to his attention. An editor may also want to emend the text on the basis of readings from other witnesses, common sense, or artistic inspiration, "correcting" things in the text that the scribe or compositor would presumably not have regarded as in need of correction. Such corrections and emendations can be marked in a variety of ways in printed editions; one common way is to place letters or words assumed to have been inadvertently omitted in angle brackets, while obvious misspellings are corrected and marked with an asterisk, the original form being given in a note. More extensive emendations are normally treated in the notes.

In the determination of how much information should be included, the decisions facing the producer of an electronic transcription are essentially the same as those facing the producer of any transcription. The basis for making them is much the same as well, in that the choices will depend on factors such as the amount of time available for the job and, not least, the intended use to which the transcription will be put. The great advantage of electronic texts is that many decisions need not be made: the transcriber can include a wide range of information in the transcription but then choose how much of it to make available to readers or, better still, allow readers to choose for themselves how much of it they wish to see. From a single marked-up text it should be possible, if one so desires, to produce screen or print copy at any level, from strictly diplomatic to fully normalized. Such markup must by necessity be fairly complex, and will almost certainly require several layers of input. Indeed, another great advantage of electronic transcription over traditional print transcription is that one can return again and again to one's transcription, adding further levels of markup.

How one proceeds depends to some extent on whether one is starting from scratch or working with a text already in machine-readable form. In the latter case the most logical thing to do is mark up the text feature by feature, beginning with the overall structure and layout, for example, then adding markup for abbreviations, variant letterforms, and so on. If one is starting with a blank sheet, as it were, it might make more sense to mark up these various features as one goes, or at least as many of them as one can reasonably be expected to keep track of at once. Or it might be preferable first to transcribe the text as it comes, including the abbreviations, variant letterforms, and so on, then add the structural markup.

As the text of the work and the physical object carrying that text have separate structural hierarchies, both should ideally be encoded, even in the most basic of transcriptions. To represent the structure of the text it is recommended that the ‹div› element be used for the largest structural divisions in prose texts, with a type attribute to specify the nature of the division, chapter, section, and so on. Paragraphs in these divisions can be tagged using ‹p›. Verse texts should be marked up using the tags ‹l› (for "line") and ‹lg› (for "line group," i.e., a group of lines functioning as a formal unit), again with a type attribute to identify the type of unit (e.g., stanza or couplet). Lines and line groups can also be numbered and identified using the n and id attributes. For the structure of the physical document, it is recommended that empty milestone elements be used—‹pb/›, ‹cb/›, and ‹lb/› for page, column, and line boundaries, respectively—which can also be numbered and provided with an id. (Note that ‹lb/› is an empty element used to indicate physical divisions in a printed book or manuscript, while ‹l›, which is not empty, is used for lines of verse.) A milestone tag should be placed at the beginning of the unit to which it refers. A blank space should therefore appear before rather than after the `<lb/>` tag, except where a word runs over the line break, in which case there is no space. The way these elements are handled is determined by the stylesheet. Line breaks can be made to display as such, can be marked in some other way (e.g., with a vertical bar), or can be ignored altogether. Several different stylesheets can be applied to the same text to provide different views.

Variant letterforms—indeed, any exotic (read "non-English") characters—are encoded using entity references. If one wishes to distinguish between different allographs of a single letter or other paleographic or typographic features for purposes of statistical analysis, one can define entity references for this purpose: &b1;, &b2;, and so on. The same applies to small capitals and enlarged minuscules, should one wish to retain them.

Marking up abbreviations and their expansions is one of the more problematic aspects of the transcription of primary sources. A strictly diplomatic transcription, striving to be as neutral as possible, will normally give the unexpanded abbreviation, tagged `<abbr>`; at most other levels the expanded form will be used, tagged `<expan>`. In theory it shouldn't matter which is used, since the possibility for giving the other form as an attribute value is always there. In practice, however, the situation is complicated. To begin with, what exactly is the abbreviation? Is it the mark, sign, or letter (if there is any) that indicates that something has been suppressed, or is it the entire word? Similarly, is the expansion only the letters that have been suppressed and therefore supplied by the transcriber, or is it, again, the whole word? A case could be made for distinguishing between abbreviations with a lexical reference (suspensions, contractions, and a number of brevigraphs) and those with a graphemic reference (superscript letters and signs and the remainder of the brevigraphs). It strikes one as counterintuitive to treat the former on anything other than the whole-word level, while treating the latter in the same way seems equally misconceived.

To take a simple example, MS. is a common abbreviation for "manuscript" (or, rather, "manuscriptum"). It is a suspension, actually two, where the first letter of each part of the compound word is given and the rest omitted; that it is an abbreviation is indicated by the period (frequently omitted) and by the fact that it is written uppercase (frequently it isn't). One might want to tag MS. as an abbreviation and indicate the expansion as an attribute value: `<abbr expan="manuscript">MS.</abbr>`. Alternatively, one could give the expanded form as the content of the element and the abbreviated form as the value of the attribute: `<expan abbr="MS.">manuscript</expan>`. To insist on `M<expan abbr="">anu</expan>S<expan abbr=".">cript</expan>` strikes me as patently absurd—and it produces the incorrectly expanded form "ManuScript." But even if one is prepared to overlook this problem, what should one do with the form MSS. for "manuscripts" (or "manuscripta"), where the second S is there only to indicate that the word is plural?

The superscript nasal stroke, on the other hand, has a specific graphemic reference: it stands for the letter *m* or *n*. With a word such as *fratrū*, it seems more natural to encode the expansion as `fratru<expan abbr="&bar;">m</expan>` rather than `<expan abbr="fratru&bar;">fratrum</expan>`. Doing so also makes it completely explicit which letters have been supplied and makes it possible for these letters to be displayed in italics (or round brackets), in the manner of a traditional printed edition, something that many scholars still feel to be of importance.

One solution would be to use `<abbr>` to indicate abbreviations that are left unexpanded (although the expanded form can be given as an attribute value) but `<expan>` for the letters supplied by the transcriber. Those who really do wish to have their cake and eat it—that is, derive both forms from a single markup—will probably need to find another solution, for example giving both the expanded and unexpanded forms side by side within some grouping element.

Alterations made to the text, whether by the scribe of the manuscript or in some later hand, can be encoded using `<add>` for additions and `<del>` for deletions; editorial emendations should be encoded with the `<sic>` and `<corr>` tags. It has been argued that there is in essence no difference between changes made to the text by a scribe or later reader and those made by the transcriber or editor of a scholarly edition. But there is, or should be, no more fundamental distinction in textual scholarship than between what is physically present in the source and what is not. The act of recording what actually is in the source must therefore remain entirely separate from postulating what ought to have been there but for one reason or another isn't. The simplest way to maintain this distinction is to employ separate sets of elements for the two.

The elements `<corr>` and `<sic>` function as mirror images of each other, in the same way as `<abbr>` and `<expan>` do, and the choice of which to use is made on the same grounds. In a strict diplomatic transcription, one may wish only to indicate an incorrect or suspicious reading in the manuscript without attempting to correct it; in a normalized text, one may emend an obvious error without indicating what the original reading was. The two can also be combined, with the one then acting as an attribute of the other. But `<del>` and `<add>` cannot be said to mirror each other in this way, because deletions and additions can obviously also be found in isolation.

Where a word has been supplied by the editor, the `<supplied>` tag can be used. It is customary in textual scholarship to distinguish between text now illegible or lost through damage but assumed originally to have been in the source and text assumed to have been inadvertently omitted by the scribe or compositor. This distinction can be indicated in the markup through the use of the **reason** attribute, the value being for example `illegible` in the first case and `omitted` in the second. Where the reading of another witness supports the reconstruction, it is possible to use the **source** attribute. The `<supplied>` element should be used only when the missing text can be reconstructed with a very high degree of certainty; when it cannot, `<gap>` can be used instead, with both a **reason** and an **extent** attribute.

Finally, there is the question of normalization/regularization. One can use the `<reg>` element to give regularized forms of variant or archaic spellings or the `<orig>` element to indicate that a spelling is archaic or in some other way nonstandard. The two elements mirror each other, allowing for both the regularized and unregularized forms to be given, the one as the content of the element, the other as an attribute value. If the text has only a few irregular or archaic forms, it is an easy enough matter to tag them as one proceeds, but in a text with highly irregular or archaic orthography, it is necessary to tag each word. Such tagging is probably better done afterward and could be automated to an extent.

For the most part the elements discussed here are used to tag features in the original in a way analogous to the typographic conventions of printed editions. There are, of course, elements available in the TEI for tagging many other things—dates, for example, or the names of persons, places, and institutions—all of which are useful for search purposes and indexing. And why stop there? The TEI also provides mechanisms for associating any kind of semantic or syntactic analysis and interpretation that an encoder might wish to attach to a text, including such familiar linguistic categorizations as clause, morpheme, part of speech, and so on as well as such characterizations of narrative structure as theme. Indeed, to all intents and purposes there is no limit to the information one can add to a text—apart, that is, from the limits of the imagination. One thing is clear: the more we put into a text, the more we can get out of it. If we are lucky, we wind up even finding things we didn't know were there; if we are very lucky, we find things we didn't even know it was possible to look for.

DIGITAL FACSIMILES IN EDITING

KEVIN KIERNAN

A ccording to the Guidelines for Editors of Scholarly Editions of the Committee on Scholarly Editions (CSE), the first question an editor should consider in choosing the medium of publication is, "Is the source material itself manuscript, printed, electronic, or a combination of formats?" One of the few certainties we have about authorial intentions from the Middle Ages is that neither authors nor scribes (who may sometimes be the same person) ever intended their work for print or PC. These writers nonetheless supplied their texts with meaningful text encoding, which modern editors, because of the limitations of print and the different conventions of modern literacy, have routinely ignored or unavoidably misrepresented in modern editions. Editors today can most effectively recover these significant lost features through image-based scholarly editions.

It is worth distinguishing between plain old digital facsimiles and image-based scholarly editions. The primary purpose of a facsimile in editing is to provide editors and textual scholars with a reliable version of the source document or documents. Editors of all theoretical dispensations must ultimately base their editions, whether they want to or not, on source documents, which for unique manuscripts are seldom readily available for sustained reference. High-resolution, full-color, digital images, particularly when acquired directly from the manuscripts themselves with sophisticated electronic cameras, are demonstrably more revealing, easier to access, and far more productive for further image processing than microfilm or printed facsimiles.

Like digital facsimiles, image-based scholarly editions of Old English manuscripts provide high-quality facsimiles and digital restorations for editors and textual scholars, but they also serve the broader purpose of helping modern readers negotiate a culturally strange text in its original form with all its foreign formats, including its codicology, paleography, scribal abbreviations, shifting orthography, unexpected word divisions, unknown word-hoard, missing metrical layout, and lack of any helpful punctuation or capitalization. Modern print editions of medieval texts have always approached these problems by quietly modernizing the text; replacing unfamiliar letters and ligatures with rough equivalents from the Roman alphabet; silently expanding scribal abbreviations; normalizing spellings, imposing word boundaries; emending unusual or unexpected words; laying out explicit, numbered, lines of verse; and adding Modern English punctuation.

This editorial process, excluding the major interventions of emendations and conjectural restorations, may itself easily involve thousands of changes in a long text. Although editors do not treat them as real editorial emendations, these pervasive changes from script to print should in fact be viewed as radical modernizing translations of source documents, not the usual stuff of scholarly editions. Such translating is comparable to an editor's taking a modern text and removing all punctuation from it, dividing its words into syllables, providing ancient spellings, and displaying poetry without lineation. Before the advent of digital technology, editors of medieval texts were virtually forced to make these translations of their sources, if they wanted modern readers to understand the texts. The role of the editor of medieval texts has been that of a solitary scholar, imbued with great authority by rare knowledge of primary sources, transferring a text from unique script to generic print for the less erudite masses. In the course of this work, modern editors have obscured manuscript records to an extraordinary degree. The resurgence in interest in medieval manuscripts derives from the growing recognition that modern print editions have not accurately represented them.

These editors of course included codicology and paleography of the manuscripts as part of the apparatus of their editions. But print is an extremely inefficient and inadequate means for representing manuscript texts. Codicological overviews and paleographic details in support of textual notes are all poorly portrayed without illustrations, and yet these aspects are almost always treated without them. Codicological information is usually presented in extremely austere ways. "Ff. ii, $1–3^8$, $4–6^6$, $7–10^8$, 10 wants 1," for example, means that the editor discovered by collating the leaves of a manuscript that there were ten gatherings and two prefixed leaves; the first three gatherings were made up of four sheets of eight leaves; the next two gatherings had three sheets of six leaves; and gatherings 7 through 10 again were four-sheet quires of eight leaves, but the first leaf was missing from the tenth quire.

With a complete digital facsimile of the source material there would be no reason to present the collation in shorthand so schematized as to be useless to all but experts. Print editions are increasingly providing diagrams of gatherings, but even with diagrams it is difficult to conceptualize the makeup of the book and impossible to analyze and assess the possible significance of any structural peculiarities. With access to all the images, an editor could present the collations in diagrams, indicating hair-and-flesh arrangements, sheet and quire signatures, and information on rulings, and easily link the diagrams to comprehensive image collations, from thumbnails to full-resolution views of conjugate folios.

While some people continue to think of electronic texts as exclusive of images, the fact is that digital images of manuscripts are electronic texts as well. The most compelling scholarly editions of the future will make full use of markup schemes such as XML (or its TEI manifestation), but not without extensive integration of images. The TEI has begun moving in this direction, as its guidelines indicate: "Work on areas still not satisfactorily covered in this manual will continue, and resulting recommendations will be issued as supplements to the published Guidelines. Work is expected to continue in . . . [among other areas] manuscript analysis and physical description of text" (*Guidelines* [TEI P3]). Text encoding can include coordinates in images to link text and images, so that search facilities will not only return results of text searches but also provide hypertextual links to corresponding images. It seems likely that computer science will contribute powerful additional methods for searching manuscript images, even though, with our current experience, optical character recognition (OCR) does not appear to be a fruitful approach with scribal handwriting.

The CSE guidelines assert that editors establish reliability by "accuracy with respect to texts, adequacy and appropriateness with respect to documenting editorial principles and practice, consistency and explicitness with respect to methods." Any editorial theory should be able to justify its methods in the face of its source, no matter how explicit or consistent the editorial departures from its sources might be. Textual notes should accordingly incorporate thumbnails of the documentary sources of error and expand to the full-manuscript context of the error. In addition to searchable tagging for editorial emendations; conjectural restorations by the editor; and restorations from independent manuscripts, transcripts, and collations, image-based electronic editions should provide searchable encoding and a way to link to images that correspond to such manuscript features as scribal abbreviations, accented letters, additions, alterations, letters covered or partly covered by bindings, damaged letters, deletions and erasures, readings enhanced by special lighting, faded readings, and technological restorations. For some editing projects, high-resolution digital facsimiles, acquired from a range of special lighting techniques, are indispensable for what the CSE calls the "basic task" of scholarly editing, "to present a reliable text." The reliability of editors of the future will depend not so much on historical or interpretive introductions bound to a single edition as on the editors' ability to show the relation between the edition and its documentary sources and to bring their readers to an ever-expanding digital library of supporting ancillary material.

Image-based electronic editions with thoroughly integrated text and images will thus have an advantage over traditional printed editions and facsimiles, by providing the reader with access to an edited, readable text that includes the easy, structured search of the apparatus as well as full, linked, visual representations of all the myriad uses of the source documents. Manuscripts often unabashedly highlight features that are completely ignored or deliberately submerged in print editions. One of the most exciting and interesting aspects of image-based electronic editions is that unique resources once restricted to the solitary scholar are opened to the scrutiny of all. A major advantage of image-based electronic editions over print editions is that the display of the text is transparent. The accuracy of the materials is either apparent or correctable. An image-based scholarly edition provides a very effective means of proofreading and an ever-present fail-safe for locating and correcting residual errors.

Editors of image-based electronic editions must become newly sensitive to the power of sources to reveal the different state of literacy a medieval manuscript evinces. We must presume, for example, that the communities that made and used our surviving Old English manuscripts shared a very practical, nonmagical knowledge of runes as both letters and as shorthand for words and that people then had the ability to read verse without the kind of formatting modern readers require even for accentual-syllabic rhyming verse. By making manuscript images always available, editors can help transmit insights into paleography, another aspect of medieval literacy, which the reduction to typescript strips away. Focused, comprehensive access to scribal letterforms might be mediated through the glossary, by linking all head letters to salient examples in the manuscript. However it is accomplished, examples of all letterforms should be described and illustrated, and any letter used to support an editorial emendation (for instance, typical confusion between Insular *c* and *t*) should be specifically linked to its manuscript context. XML markup is good at distinguishing different letterforms, such as Insular, Caroline, and uncial *s*, for searching of text, but for it to be of real value, the editor and the researcher should be able to link any search results to the specific instances in the manuscript images.

If the manuscript is present through images, it will both demand and enable more explicit justification than is often given for significantly different representations in the edition. The most effective way to describe the authoritative or significant texts, as well as to present the punctuation, capitalization, and spelling, is by displaying them and providing the means to understand them. For example, the strange word division of manuscripts will not be difficult to understand if the word elements are mapped together, glossed, and clearly linked as informative illustrations of the normal word divisions of the edition. In the same way the image-based scholarly edition subsumes the purpose of a diplomatic edition and removes the fruitless frustration of trying to preserve the exact layout, illumination, and physical appearance of a manuscript in print form.

The apparatus, a Help function always a click away, should be comprehensive, incorporating contents, preface, acknowledgments, introduction, footnotes and endnotes (whether explanatory or textual), glossary, appendixes, index, and bibliography. Editors of image-based scholarly editions must ask, "What kind of editorial mediation is required for a modern reader to use the manuscript images with understanding?" For editors to take full advantage of encoding strategies to inform the source with meaning, image and text must be thoroughly integrated. The most successful strategies will present image and text, manuscript and transcript or edition, in tandem. A menu bar is itself a digital image to help furnish comprehensive use of the images of the manuscript. On any given page, the menu bar containing the full apparatus should link to any topic relating to problems on that page. If there is evidence of corruption—or of reliability, such as intelligent scribal corrections and erasures—the editor should make it easy to link to it. A good principle is to link any and all tagged text to the source of information. Just as print editions move from manuscript to typescript, an image-based electronic edition must move from typescript back to manuscript.

Providing an effective, easily understood, graphic user interface (or GUI) is always an important issue in an electronic edition. Users of print editions generally know where in the edition to find introductory discussions, including descriptions of manuscripts, textual and explanatory notes, glossaries, and so on, although these important resources are not always easily or quickly accessible in print editions. In many respects, the best possible user interface is the image of the manuscript page, provided it is integrated with the encoded text. What better illustration can there be than the physical text that led to editorial intervention? By mapping links on the image, editors enable users to click on areas of interest. For example, by clicking a quire signature on an image of a folio, the user could have access to the quire it organizes, from a diagram giving the hair-and-flesh arrangement of the vellum leaves, to thumbnail gatherings, to full-resolution images of the folios in question. To investigate an emendation, the user should be able to click the editorial change and get to both the textual note, including a thumbnail image illustrating the source of the change, and a link to the full image providing the context for the presumed error. The images thus become continuing resources for deeper investigation and possibly new theories.

There is no compelling reason to place a preface or introduction at the beginning of an electronic edition, although links to them should be always available for users to examine whenever they wish. As their names indicate, prefaces, introductions, endnotes, and appendixes are all bound by the restrictive sequential order of print editions. Editors of image-based electronic editions can effectively integrate these resources into the fabric of the edition. In an electronic edition, it is much more useful to have an always available guide or Help or Apparatus that incorporates prefatory or introductory matter, matter that a reader must continually consult while using an edition. An electronic apparatus should not pointlessly mimic a print format, forcing a reader to scroll through it screen by screen. It is annoying and unnecessary to scroll through dense, scholarly discourse. Editors must intelligently employ the hypertextual environment and the supporting images they have at their disposal to guide and engage readers in efficient ways through the pertinent scholarship. There is no reason not to include bibliographic items to the links for both textual and explanatory notes, and the bibliographic items might well be linked also to online articles and image archives. An electronic edition should not simply reproduce a traditional print edition, which normally does not have free and wide access to supporting illustrations.

In the past several years it has become imperative to bring the research agendas of the humanities and computer science together to advance our abilities for representing, editing, and accessing our cultural records. What is urgently needed to take full advantage of encoding schemes of scholarly editions is the seamless integration of text and image, which will ultimately serve the interests of not only image-based scholarly editions but also the broader cultural world. The computer science research community is very interested in image search and techniques for developing efficient and accurate searching, while the humanities computing research community is absorbed in textual encoding. Neither area is likely to make real progress, however, until their complementary research agendas converge. There is an attendant need to develop interactive tools combining search strategies for images and encoded text, which would permit viewers to find an image instantly and then query any part of it to bring up informing analyses by specialists as well as technological breakthroughs: 3-D imaging; the precise understanding of size, scale, coloration, and texture; texture analysis; and other complementary insights made available by the research of computer and imaging scientists. Through cooperative cross-disciplinary research we can revolutionize the editing of texts, providing editors with robust tools to create, maintain, upgrade, and preserve image-based electronic editions and allowing readers to see with new insight and enjoyment what we read.

AUTHENTICATING
ELECTRONIC EDITIONS

===

**PHILL BERRIE, PAUL EGGERT,
CHRIS TIFFIN, AND GRAHAM BARWELL**

> The scholarly edition's basic task is to present a reliable text.
> —Guidelines for Editors of Scholarly Editions

Abook is generally seen as a trustworthy carrier of text because, once printed, text cannot be changed without leaving obvious physical evidence. This stability is accompanied by a corresponding inflexibility. Apart from handwritten marginal annotation, there is little augmentation or manipulation available to the user of a printed text. Electronic texts are far more malleable. They can be modified with great ease and speed. This modification may be careful and deliberate (e.g., editing, adding markup for a new scholarly purpose), it may be whimsical or mendacious (e.g., forgery), or it may be accidental (e.g., mistakes made while editing, or minor mistranslations by a software system). The nature of the medium makes the potential effect of these modifications greater because the different versions of the text can be quickly duplicated and distributed, beyond recall by the editor. Does the electronic future, then, hold in store something akin to medieval scribal culture? If this lack of control is the risk, will scholars be willing to put several years of their lives into the painstaking creation of electronic editions of important historical documents or works of literature and philosophy?

How can textual reliability be maintained in the electronic environment? There is a major question here of authority and integrity; if not more acute than that in the print domain, it at least has different characteristics. Especially where it is crucial that a text be stable and long-lasting—for example, in legal statutes, cumulative records, or scholarly editions—a noninvasive method of authentication is required. Following a discussion of various problems associated with the markup (encoding) of electronic texts and the danger to ongoing textual reliability that markup poses, we describe a potential model.

THE SUBJECTIVITY OF MARKUP

Verbal texts being prepared in a scholarly manner for electronic delivery and manipulation need to be marked up for structure and the meaning-bearing aspects of presentation. In the electronic domain, the features of text that in the print domain have long been naturalized by readers demand explicit categorizing and interpretation. This task is not straightforward. The most trivial things can raise tricky questions. What, for instance, is the meaning of small capitals or italics in a nineteenth-century novel? Traditionally, italics are seen either as a form of emphasis (and therefore a substantive aspect of meaning) or as presentational (as in the name of a ship or painting). Neither function can be rendered in the ASCII character set. As they cannot responsibly be ignored, a decision about their function (and therefore their presentation by the software) must be made by the human editor. Under the current paradigm, the instruction is entered into the text file.

Similarly, electronic text editors are forced to decide whether line breaks are meaningful, whether a line of white space is a section break in a chapter or only a convenience dictated by the size of the printed page and the desire to avoid widows and orphans. Editors have to decide whether a wrong-font comma, a white space before a mark of punctuation, or a half-inked character is meaningful—should it be tagged or not? The instruction (recorded in markup) will be an editorial interpretation, made, probably, in the context of what is currently known about contemporaneous print workshop practice and convention. In making explicit what in the physical text was implicit, the editor is inevitably providing a subjective interpretation of the meaning-bearing aspects of text. A later editor, or the same editor returning with new information, may disagree with the earlier interpretation.

The arduous business of entering, proofreading, amending, and consequently reproofing a transcription containing the new interpretation (the print edition paradigm) can seemingly be avoided in the electronic medium; but in fact a new state of the text will have been created. Accidental corruption of the verbal text is very possible, so collation and careful checking of the new state against the old will be necessary. The same checking is needed if interpretation of other features of text is added—for example linguistic features, historical annotations, or cross-references. Even though markup is usually separated from text by paired demarcators, as its density increases, so does the practical difficulty in proofing the text accurately.

Consider the following scenario. No one expects any two scribal copies of the same work to be textually identical: scribes will almost certainly have changed or added things, large or small. This instability is not restricted to pre-1455 or even the pre-1800 period, before the age of the steam-driven machine press. Optical collation in scholarly editing projects has proved again and again that no two copies of the same edition are precisely identical, even if printed in the industrial age. Printing involves change as well as wear and tear; inking varies, and paper has imperfections. While recent editorial theory has shown that the physical carrier can itself affect the meaning of text (e.g., McKenzie, *Bibliography*), the prospect of marking up text to record every physical variation in every known copy of a work would create a file of bewildering complexity whose reliability would be in serious doubt. No editor can foresee all the uses to which an electronic scholarly edition can be put or all the interpretative markup that will be required. The more the attempt to provide interpretative markup is pursued through increasingly heavy tagging, the more the reliability of the text is put at risk.

This situation shows the need for an automated authentication technique that separates verbal text from markup while retaining all the functionality of a computer-manipulable file. The proposal that we describe below involves such standoff markup. It also addresses another problem of markup that has often been observed. The current standard for the markup of humanities texts, that of the Text Encoding Initiative, requires an objective textual structuring to be declared on the assumption that if computers are to manipulate parts of text powerfully, then text needs to be seen as an ordered hierarchy of content objects with its various divisions and parts appropriately identified. The difficulty with this assumption is that texts are neither objective nor ideal things. They incorporate a stream of perhaps only lightly structured human decision making, of which traces have been left behind as part of the production process. Moreover, we as readers cannot help participating in the business of making meaning as we read and interpret what we see on the page. The advantage of our participation is that we, unlike computers and logic systems, can handle structural contradictions and overlaps with relative ease and safety. But if we then attempt to codify the texts for use with systems that cannot handle contradictions, the systems reveal their inadequacies. At present, only fudges—partly satisfactory work-arounds—are possible to deal with this problem.

AUTHENTICATION TECHNOLOGIES

Authentication technologies were developed by information scientists to provide a reliable basis for sending verifiable messages over networks. These technologies are based on the mathematical routines of cryptography but are designed to work with clear-text messages. (The subtle forms of meaning-bearing presentation discussed above are not normally relevant here.) The goal of such technologies is not to obscure the information contained in the message but to verify that it was sent by the person claiming to have sent it and has not been altered in the course of transmission. Meeting these requirements has allowed the development of e-commerce with such services as Internet banking.

These services require a large amount of infrastructure to support them. Changes deemed necessary to the authentication protocols and procedures must be carried out quickly because of the potential risk of criminal exploitation of a weakness. While financial institutions have the money to pay for these high maintenance costs, such resources are not available to an academic community interested in authenticating its electronic editions.[1] Authenticated financial transactions over the Internet have a lifetime of minutes if not seconds, whereas full-scale electronic editions must have a life of decades if they are to justify the investment of an editor's time and energy. The chance of an electronic edition's becoming unusable because of the obsolescence of its authentication system rules out the use of proprietary and invasive solutions.[2]

Fortunately, authentication for electronic editions is not as exacting as that for e-commerce, where it is a requirement that the creator of the message be verifiable. In electronic editions, detection of textual corruption is the primary concern. An authentication system must protect the reliability of the encoded text, by indicating if and where a file has been corrupted, thus allowing it to be replaced from a trusted master copy. The best authentication method is bit-by-bit comparison of the working copy of the file against a locked master copy. Some electronic editions at present provide their master files on nonvolatile media (e.g., CD or DVD); working files are always generated afresh from the master files. Unfortunately, this solution is very weak for long-term storage, as the master files are bound to a particular storage technology. And the system does not allow for the possibility of revised or additional interpretative markup.

Most authentication methods involve the use of hashing algorithms.[3] In its simplest form, a hashing algorithm steps through the characters of a piece of text using a mathematical formula to calculate a hash value that is dependent on their sequence. The formula is such that the resulting hash value is highly representative of the text, because small changes in the text produce large changes in the calculated value. Authentication is achieved by comparing the stored hash value of the master copy with the calculated hash value of a working file. If they are the same, it is extremely likely that the two files are identical. This technique prevents from going undetected corruptions of a file that are otherwise easy to overlook.

STANDOFF MARKUP AND AUTHENTICATION

> I want to discuss what I consider one of the worst mistakes of the current software world, embedded markup; which is, regrettably, the heart of such current standards as SGML and HTML.
> —Theodor Nelson, *Embedded Markup*

The problem of maintaining the authenticity of a text file across platforms is not a trivial one. In addition, it is desirable to prevent the proliferation of different versions of a text that would otherwise be brought about by (future) developments in or additions to markup, annotation, and cross-referencing. The use of standoff markup in an electronic text environment possessing strong authentication characteristics may allow these desiderata to be met.

To illustrate how such authentication might be achieved, let us take the case of a literary work extant in several typesettings. After the base transcription file of each typesetting was prepared, each such file would be a lexical transcription of the original but minimally marked up—since the editor's interpretative responsibilities could be fulfilled in standoff markup files. The verbal content of the base file would need to be contained in uniquely identifiable text elements. In prose, this containment could be done at the level of the paragraph; in verse, at the level of the line. The identifiers would need to be inserted in the text to act as markers, and the text proofed against the original. After proofing, the file's authenticity could be maintained by an authentication mechanism based on a simple hashing algorithm. Ideally, authentication would be done at the text-element level, so that a change to even one character would be immediately discernible when the hash value for the text element was checked. Such authentication would allow possible corruptions to be quarantined while leaving the rest of the text usable. Once the base transcription file had been prepared and proofed, markup (e.g., in SGML using a document type definition [DTD] conforming to the TEI guidelines)[4] would be inserted, its operation tested and then removed into a separate, standoff file. Standoff files would also store the hash value of the text element to which the markup could validly be applied. The result of this structuring is that the tags would carry a test of the authenticity of that portion of the text, and any attempt to reapply them to a corrupted version of the text element would result in a notified error.

A model developed along such lines would offer a number of advantages. First, by supporting the standard TEI-compliant SGML, it could be used in an SGML environment, giving access to all the available browsers and tools. But the base transcription file would not be dependent on SGML, and the separate markup files could be easily manipulated to comply with whatever markup schemes were required.[5] Second, this model would enable the text to be annotated or augmented with analytic markup, in parallel and continuously, while still retaining its integrity. Third, the levels of markup could be developed independently for different purposes and applied selectively to meet different user requirements. This independence would future-proof the edition against the obsolescence brought about by subjective markup, since any edition deemed unsuitable for a particular application is liable to spawn a competitor that will vie with the original text for maintenance resources.

To date, only one implementation of the proposed model has been developed for electronic editions: the JITM (just-in-time markup) system. It has utilities for inserting tags, subsequently removing them, and running the verification process. The embedding into the base file of the markup from the standoff files creates a virtual document—a perspective—that is inserted into a template conforming to the appropriate DTD.[6] Because any markup added to the base file is extracted into standoff markup files and the base file is authenticated "just in time" when a call is made to create the new perspective that incorporates the added markup, an automatic proofreading of the base file is in effect being continually carried out.[7] This procedure can significantly reduce the time it takes to create an electronic edition while maintaining the academic rigor required for such a project. The same authentication system continues to ensure the reliability of the edition after publication; and the same textual resources do not need to be newly transcribed or proofread afresh for each new editorial or other study.

There are further advantages. First, in the original creation of the base transcription file, proofing can, if desired, be simplified by separate checking of the markup on the one hand and the words and punctuation on the other. Second, different or conflicting structural markups can be applied to the same base file, because they are in different files and can be applied to the base file selectively. Finally, because the JITM system separates the transcriptions from the markup, the question of copyright is simplified. Since the markup is interpretative (as explained above, and more obviously with added explanatory and textual notes), a copyright in it can be clearly identified and defended. In all this, the base transcription file remains as simple as possible (thereby greatly easing its portability into future systems) and the authentication mechanism remains noninvasive. JITM is, in other words, an open rather than a proprietary system.[8]

Ensuring continuing reliability is a bigger issue for electronic editions than for print editions. The creator's responsibility to the users of an electronic edition does not end with its publication; steps must be taken to ensure that the edition is protected against corruption by the very processes and medium that gave it life. Authentication technologies can provide the required reliability, but they must be applied in such a way that they protect the long-term availability and reliability of the edition against obsolescence.

The use of standoff markup and abstracted authentication techniques potentially allows editions to have their markup revised, reinterpreted, or enhanced and their protection mechanisms easily upgraded or replaced, as future developments require it. Such maintenance will be able to be done without compromising the base transcription files or wasting the editorial labor that went into establishing them.

Notes

1. The National Archives of Canada has decided to archive only clear text in its born-digital archives (Brodie). The extra costs involved in archiving the authentication technologies necessary to authenticate the original, cryptographically secure files are considered too great a burden.

2. These authentication solutions are largely based on the idea of the digital signature, where the file to be authenticated has attached to it a cryptographic signature calculated from the contents of the file and a unique private key registered to the owner. The user of the files uses a public key provided by the message originator to authenticate the file, and the correspondence between the public key and the private key guarantees that the file was sent by the owner of the private key. The infrastructure involved in this system involves the calculation, registration, and distribution of the authentication keys. Currently these key are unique prime numbers, at least one hundred digits in length. The distribution of these keys is handled by sophisticated servers that are expensive to maintain.

3. The National Library of Australia records in its online catalog a Message Digest 5 (MD5) hash value for its digital assets in the *PictureAustralia* service so that the authenticity of the files downloaded by users can be checked.

4. The standoff markup paradigm would readily support the use of other, normally embedded markup systems in parallel, if this support were a requirement.

5. When writing for this chapter began, the P4 version of the TEI DTD had just been released. Now, the technology has progressed such that XML is the requisite language and the P5 version of the TEI DTD is almost upon us. Trusting in the stability of embedded markup for long-lived e-texts is shortsighted at best.

6. While the base transcription file does not in itself adequately represent a historical state of the work being edited, the default perspective in JITM for new users is the one that records the physical presentation of the original. More experienced users, and scholars seeking to interpret the base file or turn it to new purposes, work with the base file.

7. Each tag markup instruction incorporates a hash value for the text element into which it is to be inserted. The comparison of this stored value against the value calculated for the text element provides the automatic proofreading of the JITM system.

8. The algorithms for the JITM system and the hashing algorithm it uses are to be made public in due course. For papers about the project, go to the Australian Scholarly Editions Centre Web page at www.unsw.adfa.edu.au/ASEC/JITM and see the JITM Web site itself at www.unsw.adfa.edu.au/JITM. Just In Time Markup is copyrighted 2005 by Graham Barwell, Phillip Berrie, Paul Eggert, and Chris Tiffin.

DOCUMENT MANAGEMENT
AND FILE NAMING

GREG CRANE

This essay describes some of the things that happen to a TEI document when it enters into one particular environment, the *Perseus Digital Library* System (PDLS). The PDLS represents a middle ground between powerful and domain-specific systems and simpler, more general digital library systems. While the PDLS project is appropriate for many types of data—including plain-text, PDF, HTML, and RTF—Elli Mylonas ensured that the Perseus Project saw structured markup as a fundamental technology when work was first planned in 1986. Structured markup allows the systems that mediate between documents and human beings (and between different documents) to make more intelligent use of those documents. The PDLS itself and the code that implements it are, in my view, secondary phenomena. The PDLS is significant in that it shows concretely which functions one evolving group of humanists felt were valuable and feasible. The system reflects a cost-benefit analysis that went beyond theory. It is not an edition but a tangible interpretation of how editions can, given the limited technology and available labor power, interact with other electronic resources to serve a wide range of audiences.

I quickly describe the metadata that the PDLS automatically extracts from TEI documents; I allude to but do not describe the various services that operate on the metadata we at the project produce, setting that discussion aside both for reasons of space and because the metadata level is useful in and of itself. While the current formats and content of the metadata files are still changing rapidly, we expect that digital library systems will harvest both the TEI documents and accompanying metadata, creating their own front ends, visualizations, and metadata.

PREPARING A TEI TEXT FOR THE PDLS

Scalability is crucial to any digital library, and many of us have supported the TEI from the start, because we saw it as a mechanism that would help future generations of librarians preserve and maintain electronic documents. The TEI should allow librarian effort to grow far less quickly than the number of documents. For example, increasing the number of documents by a factor of a hundred might require twice as much labor; a thousand, three times as much; a million, six times as much, and so on. In practice, the TEI has made it quite easy for us at the project to ingest substantial collections with minimal effort. We have been able to add many third-party TEI texts to the PDLS with minimal effort. *American Memory* collections from the Library of Congress initially required a few hours of preparation; more recent setup time has been measurable in minutes. The *American Memory* collections represent a best-case scenario, since they consist of standard document types (books) and follow fairly consistent editorial practices. While we currently manage a variety of document types (dictionaries, commentaries, grammars, encyclopedias, catalogs, pamphlets), complex documents with very precise presentation schemes can require substantially more work to represent online.

The MLA's New Variorum Shakespeare (NVS) series has a very precise look and feel that go back almost to the American Civil War. Creating densely tagged TEI versions of NVS editions in a prototype for the Committee on the New Variorum Edition of Shakespeare was relatively straightforward—the TEI had adequate expressive power to represent the semantic structures that NVS editions record. We found the process of converting the TEI files into an HTML format modeled on the NVS stylesheet to be complicated and frustrating, with messy tables within tables and other formatting hacks. On the other hand, if we had simply wanted to develop an electronic representation of the information in the TEI files and had not been compelled to follow the elaborate typographic and page layout conventions of the print NVS, the task would have been much different and, we suspect, simpler.

Adding Reference Metadata to a TEI File

Many files are quite large, and users will often prefer not to see them in their entirety. The reader looking up a word in a dictionary probably does not want to download forty megabytes of data to read a single entry; the reader of Shakespeare may at different times wish to view a line, a scene, or an act as well as an entire play or an arbitrary extract. Document management systems need to know how to divide a document. Some tagging schemes (e.g., page breaks) can provide reasonably natural units, but not all documents divide so logically. Even if we impose hierarchically numbered divisions (‹div1›, ‹div›, etc.), it is not always obvious which level of the hierarchy should serve as the default unit: the highest-level division may be too large in some cases, the smallest too small.

With externally produced, TEI-compliant document collections, we have added collection-level metadata that tell the PDLS to chunk the text on page breaks. At present, we require that editors describe the units by which the system can, by default, divide a document into chunks. This information is stored in the ‹refsDecl›. The following example is typical for many simpler documents:

```
<encodingDesc><refsDecl><state unit="part"><state
  unit="chapter" n="chunk"> <state unit="page"></refsDecl>
  </encodingDesc>
```

The ‹refsDecl› above tells the PDLS that it can chunk the current document by part, chapter, and page but that chapters are the default unit. Consider the next example:

```
<div1 type="part"><head>The First Battle of Bull Run.</head>
<div type="chapter"><head>A Union View.</head>
<p> . . .
<div type="chapter"><head>A Confederate View.</head>
<p> . . .
<div1 type="chapter"><head>A Union view of the Battle of
  Fredericksburg.</head>
<p> . . .
```

The PDLS would break the document into three chunks, one for each unit with the attribute value chapter, despite the fact that two of these chunks represent a ‹div› and one represents a ‹div1›.

Displaying the Contents of the TEI File

The PDLS has a default program that displays many texts in a reasonable fashion. This program is written in the CoST (Copenhagen SGML Tool) XML conversion language. Editors can write their own specifications that build on the default specification in CoST, or they can create their own stylesheets in XSLT (extensible stylesheet language transformation), DOM (document object model), or some other specification language.

ADDING A NEW FILE TO AN EXISTING COLLECTION

It is important to assign to each actual file name a collection and identification number. At present, collections are XML files with RDF (resource description framework) metadata. This entry describes the first volume of *Battles and Leaders of the Civil War*:

```
<rdf:Description rdf:about="Perseus:text:2001.05.0007">
<dcterms:isPartOf rdf:resource="Perseus:collection:cwar"/>
<figures>/typhon/00CivilWar/5pageparsing/blcw01/figures</figures>
<pages>/typhon/00CivilWar/5pageparsing/blcw01/pages</pages>
<status>2</status>
<text>cwar/blcw01.sgml</text>
</rdf:Description>
```

The `<rdf:Description>` element provides an identification scheme for this file. Notice that the `<rdf:Description>` tag itself contains a unique identifier for the document that it describes. We therefore can, if we choose, keep this particular entry fairly succinct. A separate file can link this document to a full MARC (machine-readable cataloging) record prepared by a professional cataloger. The individual adding a document to the collection thus provides minimal data needed by the system in order to add a document.

The identification scheme describes the source of the document (*Perseus*), its basic type (e.g, text), and a unique identifier, which consists of two numbers (the Civil War collection was collection 5 for year 2001) and a serial number in the collection. The format of the identification numbers can be arbitrary—the main point is that they must uniquely describe a particular document.

The `<dcterms:isPartOf>` element assigns this document to a particular collection. The `<rdf:resource>` attribute describes the relative location of the source file. Many different machines contain versions of the PDLS, and the address is relative to a root directory in the *Perseus Digital Library* System.

The `<figures>` element describes the location of the full-resolution scans of illustrations for this book. Since illustrations take up a great deal of disk space, the source images tend to live on a central server and we thus provide an absolute path name. If we wished to include this image source data in the core digital library data distribution, we could provide a relative path.

Note that we have a separate `<pages>` element: it describes the location of page images for a book.

PROCESSING A DOCUMENT IN THE PDLS

Basic Display and Browsing

For basic display and browsing, one needs to take the following steps:

Call up an HTML version of the document by its unique identifier. Asking for `2001.05.0007` would, in the above example, call up the first volume of *Battles and Leaders of the Civil War*.

Provide a table of contents for the document.

Support the ability to page through a document by its default chunk (e.g., chapter, page).

Allow the system to override the default and chunk on some other unit (e.g., view the document as individual pages rather than as sections or chapters).

Support both interactive browsing and explicit URLs. Individuals should be able to move through a document interactively, while third parties should be able to generate links to particular sections of the document. At present, URLs can address any defined chunk (e.g., a URL can produce page- or chapter-sized chunks).

Submit a URL and return an unformatted, well-formed fragment, allowing a third-party system to format or analyze the XML source. We consider this feature to be critical, since it makes it possible for multiple systems to apply a wide range of analytic and visualization techniques to the data that we manage.

This core level of functionality does not yet provide the ability to select an arbitrary fragment of a text, so that, for example, "O, pardon me, thou bleeding piece of earth . . . groaning for burial" will resolve to Antony's full speech over Caesar's corpse in Shakespeare's play. The system should be clever enough to return this chunk in editions with different citation schemes (e.g., the Globe vs. *The Riverside Shakespeare*) and with substantive editorial differences (e.g., original vs. modern spelling). The PDLS automatically performs citation mapping, but this function needs to be developed more fully. We do not consider text retrieval at this stage, although it is clearly a core function for any document or document collection.

Processing Data Files

In processing data files, one should:

Convert SGML to XML. While we support SGML and XML, the PDLS works internally with XML, so all documents are converted to it. We maintain separate directories for each collection and separate XML files for each document. Following the example of the *Battles and Leaders of the Civil War*, this step scans war/blcw01.sgml and creates texts/2001.05/2001.05.0007.xml, a file that becomes the basis for all subsequent processing.

Extract core metadata from the XML file. Such extracting converts a variety of data into a tab-delimited field. These data include Dublin Core fields (e.g., creator, title, date, type) from the TEI header but also other categories from the body of the text. Volume 1 of the Civil War book contains hundreds of illustrations. We extract the unique identifiers and captions for these figures, generating records that indicate that document 2001.05.0007 contains (for which we use the Dublin Core relation HasPart) a particular object (e.g., 2001.05.0007.fig00017) and particular textual data associated with it (e.g., "Charles P. Stone, Brigadier-General [From a photograph]"). Data generated at this stage are stored in 2001.05.0007.met, in the same directory as the 2001.05.0007.xml file.

Aggregate the metadata for the PDL. Metadata for individual documents can live not only in the collection description file, the TEI document header, and the entire TEI document but also in other locations: full MARC records may, for example, be harvested from an OPAC (online public access catalog). All the relevant metadata are collected and stored in the ptext database. We generate a tab-delimited text file (ptext.db), which we read into whatever RDBMS (relational database management system) we happen to be using on a given *Perseus* system (at present, we alternate between PostgreSQL and MySQL).

Generate the lookup table: a list of valid citation strings for the XML file. This table contains entry points into the document. It is more involved than it may initially seem. The table allows us to divide the document into a variety of different chunks at varying levels of granularity. It must be able not only to support random access but also to identify various methods to divide the document.

Suppose we access a document by page number. We may wish to display the page or the entire chapter of which that page is a part—or we may wish to determine how to chunk the document at runtime. Chunking schemes need not follow a neat hierarchy. Speeches by the Greek historian Thucydides, for example, are very useful units of study, but they often begin and end in the middle of the conventional book–chapter–section citation scheme. We can use the lookup tables to support overlapping hierarchies, addressing a well-known drawback of BNF-style (BNF is "Backus-Naur form") grammars such as SGML/XML.

From Citations to Bidirectional Links

Web links are monodirectional: a link goes from document A to document B but not from document B back to document A. Their monodirectional nature makes the Web a directed graph and has profound implications for its topology. In digital libraries, however, having greater control over content, we can track links between documents. More important, long before computers were invented, many formal publications developed canonical schemes that gave print citations persistent value: there are various ways to abbreviate *Homer* and *Odyssey*, but Hom.Od.4.132 described the same basic chunk of text in 1880 and 1980. Not all disciplines have respected persistence of reference (Shakespearean editors, for example, regularly renumber the lines of new editions, thus making it difficult to determine the precise act–scene–line reference unless one knows the edition being used), but those that developed consistent citation schemes have a major advantage as they seek to convert print publications into electronic databases.

Persistent citation schemes cover multiple editions of the same work. Thus, when the editors of classical texts decide that the lines of a poem have been scrambled during textual tradition, they may reshuffle them into what they think to be the logical order. In a classical edition, the lines may change places, but their numbers remain the same. We find instances where line 40 precedes line 39. Such shuffled passages produce odd citations and complicate the systems that manage them, since we cannot assume that line numbers always increase. Nevertheless, this consistency of naming means that line 40 always points to the same basic unit of text, wherever the editor of a particular edition may choose to locate it.

Note, however, that if consistent reference schemes cut across editions, the text chunks pointed to by them will vary, sometimes considerably, across editions. Persistent citation schemes are fuzzy, and this fuzziness gives them flexibility. The PDLS uses the concept of an abstract bibliographic object (ABO) to capture the fact that a single work may appear in many editions. Thus we can declare two documents to be versions of the same text. The versions can be variant editions of a source text (e.g., Denys Page's edition of Aeschylus's *Agamemnon*, not that of Michael West) or a source text and its translation. In some cases, ABOs may reflect a loose affinity: citations to an original spelling edition of *Hamlet* based on the First Folio and using the through line number citation scheme (a single line count running throughout the play) are very different from those to a modern spelling edition with act–scene–line references. In other cases, text alignment may be approximate, since the word and even clause order of translations will often differ. Nevertheless, ABOs are a powerful organizational tool.

At present we use ABOs to perform two kinds of organizations. First, they allow the PDLS to aggregate versions of an overall text in a reasonably scalable fashion. Once we link a given document to a particular ABO, the digital library system can then automatically make this resource available. In practice, when the reader calls up an electronic version of the *Odyssey*, the new resource appears in the list of options. We could use ABOs to link partial versions of a text. If a translator publishes a version of a particular Pindaric ode or of the Funeral Oration of Pericles, readers would see the extra resource. The ability to mesh overlapping chunks of texts raises interface issues (e.g., how do we keep from confusing readers when they find translations by X for some poems but not others?).

ABOs are arguably most exciting when they allow us to convert individual citations into bidirectional, many-to-many links. Consider a passage from Vergil. A commentator attaches to "arma virumque cano," the opening words of the *Aeneid*, the annotation, "This is an imitation of the opening of the *Odyssey*, ἄνδρα μοι ἔννεπε 'sing to me the man.'" The system looks for Vergil *Aeneid* line 1 and then searches for the phrase "arma virumque cano." It can create a link from the source text back to the commentary. The reader who calls up the opening of the *Aeneid* sees the link back to the commentary. The link can be privileged (e.g., we are looking at a particular commentary on the commentator's own personal edition) or general (e.g., we link any comment on "arma virumque cano" in *Aen.* 1.1 to any edition of Vergil). Clearly, this service raises interesting problems of filtering and customization as annotations encrust heavily studied canonical texts, but we view such problems as necessary challenges and the clusters of annotations on existing texts as opportunities to study the problems of managing annotations.

The consequences of such linking are potentially dramatic. The Liddell Scott Jones *Greek-English Lexicon* (9th ed.) comments on about 200,000 passages in 3,000,000 words of classical Greek: individual comments directly address roughly one word in fifteen (see Liddell and Scott). Some readers will discover these comments on particular passages—though most of those reading Greek at any given time are probably intermediate students who are hard put to find a single citation buried in larger articles. In an online environment, however, the lexicon can become a commentary: that is, the readers of a text can see the words that the lexicon comments on.

The long-term consequences of converting citations in bidirectional links are intriguing: not only can an online lexicon become a continually updated database but also the individual entries—and indeed all publications about words—increase in value when their visibility increases. Nevertheless, the opportunity here raises the same challenge of information overload and need for filtering as are raised by commentary notes.

Indexing Textual Links in *Perseus*

From a practical perspective, citation linking looks for two sources. First, it scans for documents that contain explicit commentary notes on texts. These data live in the lookup table generated previously and contain the Dublin Core relation IsCommentaryOn followed by an ABO. The second source consists of citations scattered throughout documents as <bibl> or <cit> references. Note that individual documents contain both categories of links, since explicit commentary notes often contain citations to other passages as well.

INFORMATION EXTRACTION: PLACES AND DATES

Some literary works occupy spaces that are designedly amorphous, having no precise mooring in time and space. Greeks took pleasure in setting the adventures of Odysseus in various historical locations, but the poem surely assumes a never-never land of gods and monsters. But many historical documents locate themselves in very precise times and places: Dickens's novels are fictional and lack precise times, but they take place in a London with real settings. Historical documents often point to rich contextual information. The places and dates they cite often offer important clues as to their content. Time lines and maps in a set of documents can provide not only browsing aids but also information about the structure and nature of the documents. Users often explore topics that are structured by time (e.g., information about Worcester County in Massachusetts during the 1840s). We want to be able to construct geospatial queries, perhaps by selecting sections of a time line and a map.

While we can manually tag all places and dates in a document, such work is not feasible for very large collections. A fifty-year run of a nineteenth-century newspaper is far larger than the corpus of all surviving Elizabethan and Jacobean drama, but using automated methods we could create a usable edition of those fifty years of newspapers with less labor than we devote to manually editing a single Shakespearean play. Information extraction seeks to automate the process of identifying people, places, things, and the relations among them. Such automatic processes are never perfect—they seek to maximize recall (trying to find everything) and precision (trying not to collect false positives). But they can provide data that, for all their imperfections, provide a true image of a document's content and offer a starting point for those editors who wish to obtain more accurate results.

The citation extraction described above is a simpler form of information extraction, which can include many tasks. Automatic syntactic analysis, for example, is a very complex function in natural language processing that has great potential for scholarship that focuses on language. A syntactic analyzer can create a database of parse trees that identify, among other things, the subjects and objects of verbs. The output of automatic parsing is imperfect and will vary from corpus to corpus, but imperfect scalable analysis of large bodies of data can reveal significant patterns. Without syntactic analysis we could, for example, determine that *dog*, *bite*, and *man* are related, but we could not determine whether *man* or *dog* was more commonly the subject of *bite*.

Information extraction tends to be hierarchical, with more-tractable tasks serving as the foundation for further operations. Thus a morphological analyzer (which can recognize the form and dictionary entry of inflected words) is often a necessary component for a syntactic analyzer. By recognizing people and places, we can identify relations between the two: "General Grant at Vicksburg" contains references not only to a person and a place but also to a relation between them.

Information extraction tends to be domain-specific. Identifying chemical compounds encounters problems that differ from those encountered in identifying military units (e.g., recognizing "1st Mass." and "First Regiment Massachusetts Volunteers" as the same thing). Place-names are common elements of human language, but they are much easier to identify in the Greco-Roman world than in the United States. Greek and Roman place-names do not overlap as often with the names of people and things (e.g., "Christmas, Arizona," "John, Louisiana"); they are semantically less ambiguous. They also have a much better chance of being unique: there are relatively few names like Salamis (which can describe either an island near Athens or a place in Cyprus) and none so ambiguous as Springfield or Lebanon (each names dozens of places in the United States).

Members of *Perseus* have created programs to identify specific entities for particular collections (e.g., monetary quantities in dollars and pounds, Anglo-British personal names, London street names, US Civil War military units). At present, these tags are added to documents before they enter the PDLS. Ideally, the PDLS (or a similar system) would allow collections to share information extraction modules more smoothly. The generalized architecture for text engineering (GATE), developed at Sheffield, provides one model of how to integrate complementary information extraction modules and may point the way for digital library systems that incorporate these functions as a matter of course. The PDLS contains generic routines to identify references to places and dates, chosen because they can produce reasonable (if varying) results for both categories. We have not yet added a module to identify personal names (though internally we do look for clues such as "Mr." to distinguish "Mr. Washington" from places such as Washington, DC, and the state of Washington).

Extracting Places

We scan all XML files for possible place-names. The scan asks three major questions. First, has it found a word or phrase that is a proper name? Second, if it is a proper name, is it a place or something else (e.g., Washington = George Washington)? Third, if it is a place, which place is it (Washington, DC, or the state of Washington)? Each of these questions introduces its own class of errors, but results range from well over 90% accuracy for Greco-Roman place-names to roughly 80% accuracy for United States place-names. Even the relatively noisy geographic data generated from texts describing the United States allow us to identify the geographic terms for most texts.

The geographic data are stored in files with the extension `.ref`. These files associate particular instances of a place-name in a given text with various authority lists such as the *Getty Thesaurus of Geographic Names* (*TGN*). Thus, we associate references to Gettysburg with `tgn,7014060`, which describes the town of Gettysburg in Pennsylvania. The *TGN* number allows us to look up longitude-latitude data with which we can plot Gettysburg on a map. We currently combine geospatial data that *Perseus* collected for Greco-Roman sites with *TGN* data. Other data sources can be added easily to this scheme.

Extracting Dates

We scan all XML files for dates. In practice, dates have proved much easier to identify than place-names. In most documents, most four-digit numbers without commas (e.g., 1862 rather than 1,862) are dates. Furthermore, many dates have easily recognized patterns (e.g., "month," "one- or two-digit number," "four-digit number").

Problems do occur. Some texts have many isolated numbers, such as `1875`, that are not dates; in documents that use the through line number scheme to reference Shakespeare, such four-digit numbers often refer to lines in the play. Thus, general strategies must be more conservative than those aimed at a particular collection (e.g., a collection where it is more effective to assume that any number between 1600 and 2000 is a date).

Nevertheless, we found that we were quickly able to mine full text for useful date information. We were then able to generate automatic time lines that strikingly captured the chronological coverage and nature of individual documents: linear histories yield distinctive time lines, in which the dates slope downward. Likewise, we can see temporal emphasis in catalogs and more hypertextual documents that do not follow a consistent narrative (e.g., a city guide that tells the story of various buildings, constantly jumping back and forth in time). Some London guidebooks show spikes of interest in the 1660s, because many of the buildings described were damaged or destroyed in the fire then.

Because the *Perseus Digital Library* contains many documents about the Greco-Roman world, the PDLS provides reasonable support for dates styled AD, BC, CE, and BCE.

We have used the `<date>` element. All dates are converted into a standard form using the value attribute. Thus, "June 5, 1861," "the fifth of June, 1861," and "6/5/1861" are all stored as `value=1861-06-05`. We use the `<dateRange>` element to capture date ranges as well. For each XML file, we create a .dat file in which to store extracted date information in an exportable tab-delimited form.

Using Places and Dates to Identify Events

Once lists of places and dates are available, it is possible to look for associations between the two to identify significant events. David Smith reports the results of preliminary research on event identification in a heterogeneous digital library. He found that he could identify many significant events, major battles being particularly easy to find. We could (although we do not yet) generate additional metadata files listing significant place-date collocations as a part of the standard PDLS. This possibility illustrates how we can use named entity identification to elicit relations among entities (e.g., the notion that something significant occurred at a given place on a given date). Furthermore, place-date collocation detection provides an example of the kind of service that probably belongs in a general digital library system. Domain experts then have the option to refine or reconfigure such collocations—for example, one might develop a heuristics to identify such event classes as experiments or speeches.

Our experiments with the form of digital collections suggest the following general conclusions.

First, the separation of content from presentation facilitates and encourages multiple front ends to the same content. Since electronic editions can have useful life spans that extend over decades if not longer, editors need to assume that librarians or collection editors will exercise substantial control over the presentation of their work.

Second, individual editions will benefit if they can be treated not only as distinct units but also as parts of larger collections. An edition of *Macbeth* should interact with other plays by Shakespeare, with all Elizabethan and Jacobean drama, and with all online dramatic texts in any language. The more powerfully individual editions and digital libraries interact with documents that accumulate over the coming years and decades, the more useful they will be as a whole.

Third, while the sacred hand of the editor may determine every byte in the original source file, digital library systems will probably generate far more tags in associated standoff markup than are present in the original source text. This phenomenon is already visible in most texts in the *Perseus Digital Library,* where information extraction routines add <persName>, <placeName>, <date>, and other elements.

Fourth, digital library systems that mediate between edition and audience can generate new services and new audiences that the original editor did not anticipate. Informal evidence suggests that the *Perseus Digital Library* has made many Greek and Latin materials serve a diverse, geographically distributed collection. Other collections report similar jumps in the intensity and breadth of usage following open electronic publication.

The practical implications of these conclusions are immense but frustrating. We have not yet established practical conventions for electronic editions—nor are such conventions likely to assume a stable form in the near future. The structures that we add to our documents reflect elaborate (if often unconscious) cost-benefit decisions not only about the interests of our audience but also about how future systems will shape and enable those interests. Consider the simple example of place-names. We can already identify and disambiguate 80% of them in highly problematic documents about the United States. These results are good enough to generate rough maps that document the geographic coverage of a document. Nevertheless, editors can fix erroneous tags and generate a clean text that will provide much more precise geospatial data. Given the rise of geographic information systems (GIS), electronic editions where place-names are not tagged and aligned to a major gazetteer may stand at a substantial disadvantage. Similar issues arise surrounding syntactic and semantic information, where editors may find themselves including parse trees or semantic categorizations that integrate their editions into much larger frameworks.

NOTE

Since the time I wrote this, we have developed a completely new version of the Perseus Digital Library system, the first version of which was made available at www.perseus.tufts.edu in May 2005. The new system follows, however, much the same outline as the system described in this essay. Thus, while details may have changed, the essay accurately depicts the underlying system design.

WRITING SYSTEMS AND
CHARACTER REPRESENTATION

CHRISTIAN WITTERN

In a book printed on paper, the letters that make up the text are usually formed with black dots on a white surface. The specific layout selected for the page; the style, weight, size, and family of the font chosen; and the kerning and special treatment of characters running together as ligatures aesthetically and practically form a unit, the creation of which has become an art form in its own right.

The same is true for written manuscripts, which are even more idiosyncratic in their appearance and in their unit of form and appearence.

If such a text is to be brought into machine-readable electronic form—a process that as a whole has been called text encoding—the unit of form and appearance must be broken up into several layers. In one of these layers, the letters of the text will have numbers assigned to them. This process is called character encoding and does not always work as might be expected. Upper- and lowercase letterforms, for example, although representing the same letter, end up being assigned separate numbers. Another layer of this digitization process deals with the structure of the text, its division into words, sentences, paragraphs, sections, chapters, books, and so on. This layer is the domain of descriptive markup, but work on it has also been called text encoding, this time in a more specific sense. Yet another layer captures the shapes and forms that have to be used to re-create the shapes of the letters from the numbers that have been assigned in the first step: style encoding.

For all these layers there exists a competing and confusing variety of different approaches. Some word processing applications seemingly combine them all. The first and third layer are often lumped together, since the characters encoded are not directly visible, at least not in a comprehensible form—they must be represented with shapes, which can then easily be mistaken for being inherent in that layer. Levels 2 and 3 are also frequently not differentiated; in many typesetting systems, style encoding is applied directly to the appropriate sections, without the separation between the logical structure of the text and the form of presentation.

While text encoding in general has been discussed in many of this volume's essays, style encoding, which belongs largely to the realm of text processing—that is, it deals with the encoded text to produce some useful results—is largely outside of the scope of this book. This essay deals with the most basic, lowest level of the layers, character encoding.

CODED CHARACTER SETS AND THEIR ENCODING

To represent characters in digital form, we must enumerate and map them to numbers. While in the 1960s and 1970s some countries and big companies started to create encodings of their own (e.g., ASCII, EBCDIC [extended binary-coded decimal interchange code], ISO [International Organization for Standardization] 646, JIS [Japanese Industrial Standard] X 0208/), in the late 1980s it was realized that a universal character encoding was necessary to accommodate the needs of global communication and enhance interoperability.

Separately an ISO working group and an industry consortium (the Unicode Consortium) started working toward a universal character set. While their objectives were different at the outset, it was soon realized that having two competing universal character sets was not desirable, so merging these efforts was begun. Although they still operate separately, the characters encoded by ISO 10646 and by Unicode have the same name and numeric values (code points) assigned to them. They strive to encode all characters used for all written languages in current usage in the world, and in addition more and more historical writing systems are added. While the universal character set is still under development, both maintaining parties are committed to keeping them synchronized. For simplicity's sake, I discuss and mention only Unicode in this essay, but the corresponding ISO 10646 is always implied.[1]

Unicode defines and encodes abstract characters. These are identified by the names given—for example, LATIN CAPITAL LETTER J or DEVANAGARI LETTER DHA—and given corresponding numeric values (resp., U+004A or U+0927). This does not specify the visual representation of the character as it might appear on screen or paper: the exact shape of the glyph used, its size, weight, kerning, and so on. These visual aspects are completely outside the realm of character encoding.

Since Unicode had to maintain compatibility with existing national and vendor-specific character encodings, it started out as a superset of these earlier character sets. Any encoded entity that existed in these sets of characters was also incorporated into Unicode, regardless of its conformance with the Unicode design principles. To give just one example of a practical problem created by this incorporation, the Angstrom unit (Å) was assigned the Unicode value ANGSTROM SIGN (U+212B), although the LATIN CAPITAL LETTER A WITH RING ABOVE (U+00C5) would have been equally suitable for this purpose. Text encoders must be aware of such duplications in Unicode.

HOW TO FIND UNICODE CHARACTERS

Unicode characters are identified by their names; these names are in turn mapped to the numeric values used to encode them. The best strategy to find a character is therefore to search through the list of characters. As the examples of Unicode character names given so far will have shown, a name is usually derived by naming the components of a character, combining them if necessary in a systematic way. While the specific names for some of the diacritical marks may not be obvious, a look at the section where these are defined (U+0300 to U+0362) will quickly reveal how they are named in Unicode.

Not all characters have individual names. As of version 4.1, which is current at the time of this writing, Unicode defines more than 97,000 characters. More than 70,000 of these are Han characters used for Chinese, Japanese, Korean, and Old Vietnamese, and another 12,000 are precomposed Hangul forms—all these identified only by generic names, which do not allow identification of characters. There is still a large number of characters that are identified by individual names. Such characters can be looked up in the character tables of *The Unicode Standard* (*TUS* 4.0) or ISO 10646, but such searching tends to be cumbersome. Unicode provides an online version of its character database (at www.unicode.org/); there is also an online query form provided by the Institute of the Estonian Language (www.eki.ee/letter), which allows more convenient searches.

Due to the history of Unicode, many characters have more than one possible expression in Unicode. Frequently used accented letters, for example, have been given separate Unicode values (*TUS* 4.0 calls these precomposed characters), although the accents and the base letters have been also encoded, so that these could also be used to create the same character. The character

LATIN SMALL LETTER U WITH DIAERESIS (U + 00FC ü) could also be expressed as a sequence of LATIN SMALL LETTER U (U + 0075 u) and COMBINING DIAERESIS (U + 0308). We return to this problem in a moment.

To understand how Unicode is encoded and stored in computer files, we cannot avoid a short excursus into some of the technical details. This explanation is intended especially for encoders, who run into trouble with the default mechanism of their favorite software platform, which is usually designed to hide such details.

Unicode allows the encoding of about one million characters. A million is the theoretical upper limit, but at present less than 10% of this code space is actually used. The code space is arranged in 17 planes of 65,536 code points each, with plane 0, the basic multilingual plane (BMP), being the one where most characters are defined.[2]

To store the numeric values of the code points in a computer, we must serialize them. Unicode defines three encoding forms for serialization: UTF-8, UTF-16, and UTF-32 (UTF is "universal transformation format"). UTF-16 simple stores the numerical value as a sixteen-bit integer, while characters with higher numeric values are expressed using two UTF-16 values from a range of the BMP set aside for this purpose; they are called surrogate pairs. Since most computers store and retrieve numeric values in bundles of eight bits (bytes), the sixteen bits of one UTF-16 value must be stored in two bytes. Conventions of whether the byte with the higher value (big-endian) or the lower value (little-endian) comes first differ in the same way and for the same reasons as the egg openers in *Gulliver's Travels*, therefore there are two storage forms of UTF-16: UTF-16-LE and UTF-16-BE. If UTF-16 is used without further specification, it is usually UTF-16-BE (big-endian), which is the default on Microsoft Windows platforms. UTF-32 simply stores the thirty-two-bit integer directly; the same difference of LE and BE forms applies as in UTF-16.

UTF-8 avoids the whole issue of endianness by serializing the numbers in chunks of single bytes. To achieve this, it uses sequences of multiple single bytes to encode a Unicode numeric value. The length of such sequences depends on the value of the Unicode character; values less than 128 (the range of the ASCII characters) are just one byte in length, which means they are identical to ASCII. Therefore English text and the tags used for markup do not differ in UTF-8 and ASCII—one of the reasons UTF-8 is popular. It is also the default encoding for XML files in the absence of a specific encoding declaration and the recommended encoding to use. In UTF-8, most accented characters require a sequence of two bytes, East Asian characters need three, and the characters beyond the BMP need four or more.

In most cases, there is no need to worry about the specific encoding form, except to make sure that the encoding declaration, which is optionally included in the first line of an XML file in the form `<?xml version ="1.0" encoding="utf-8"?>`, does indeed faithfully reflect the actual encoding. Problems do occasionally arise with UTF-16 files read with the wrong endianness. The TEI-Emacs bundle, which is distributed on the CD-ROM accompanying this book, makes every attempt to act according to the encoding declaration. If there is a mismatch between the encoding used and the encoding declared, it is still possible to force emacs into opening a file with the desired encoding and correct the mismatch.[3]

VISUAL CONTENT AND INFORMATION CONTENT

As mentioned above, encoding of a text into digital form entails its differentiation between the visual and informational aspects of its content. This differentiation often requires analysis and an interpretative assertion to decide which of several similar-shaped characters to use. There are a number of different cases:

Multiple representations exist for the same character.
Similar but semantically different characters exist.
Visually different characters need to be encoded as identical abstract forms.
Appearance and characters must be separately encoded.

Multiple Representations of Characters

Because some Unicode characters have multiple representations, it is absolutely necessary that a text-encoding project decide which of these representations to use, that this decision be documented in the handbook of the project's encoders and in the section `<encodingDesc>` of the `<teiHeader>`, and that the decision be applied consistently in the encoding process. *Unicode Standard Annex #15 Unicode Normalization Forms* explains the problem in greater detail and gives some recommendations. In many cases, it is most convenient to use the shortest possible sequence of Unicode characters (NFC in the notation of the Unicode document [normalization form c]). This strategy uses precomposed accented characters where they exist and combining character sequences where they do not.[4]

Similar but Semantically Different Characters

Sometimes it is difficult to decide which character to encode by simply look-ing at its shape. A dash character might look identical to a hyphen character as well to a minus sign. The decision which to use must be based on the function of the character in the text and the semantics of its encoding. In Unicode, there is a HYPHEN-MINUS (U+002D), a SOFT HYPHEN (U+00AD), a NON-BREAKING HYPHEN (U+2011), and of course the HYPHEN (U+2010), not to mention the subscript and superscript var-iants (U+208B and U+207B). There are also compatibility forms at SMALL HYPHEN-MINUS (U+FE63) and FULLWIDTH HYPHEN-MINUS (U+FF0D), but these should never be considered for newly en-coded texts, since they exist only for the sake of round-trip conversion with encodings that were in use before Unicode. That the hyphen character is sometimes lumped together with a minus character is basically a legacy of ASCII, which has been carried over to Unicode. There now exists also a MINUS SIGN (U+2212) plus some compatibility forms. As for the dash character, Unicode gives four encodings in sequence up front: FIGURE DASH (U+2012), EN DASH (U+2013), EM DASH (U+2014), and HORIZONTAL BAR (U+2015). The last one might be difficult to find by just looking at the character name, but as its old name QUOTATION DASH reveals, it is also a dash character. *TUS* 4.0 has a note on this character explaining "long dash introducing quoted text," while the note for U+2014 says, "may be used in pairs to offset parenthetical text." To further complicate this specific example: if a text has the usage of a dash that fits the description of U+2015, the decision must be made whether to encode the quotation with appropriate markup (`<q>` or `<quote>` comes to mind) and encode the fact that a dash was used to set the quotation off with the rend attribute or simply retain the character in the encoded text.

While not every case is as complicated as this one, it is clear that any decision should be made by considering all possible candidates.

Visually Different Forms of Identical Abstract Characters

The issue of different forms for the same abstract character is most important in languages that do contextual shaping, like Arabic or Indian languages, but there is also one such case in Greek: the character GREEK SMALL LETTER SIGMA (U+03C3) takes different shapes depending on its occurrence within or at the end of a word. Unicode also defines GREEK SMALL LET-TER FINAL SIGMA (U+03C2), which is in violation of the principle of encoding only abstract characters, but the final sigma had to be introduced to maintain compatibility with existing encoding forms for Greek. The encoder should be careful to use the standard glyphs, not the presentation forms (even if they exist, as in Arabic, for compatibility reasons). In Greek, it must be decided by a project, and documented accordingly, how to encode the sigma character.

Separating Appearance and Encoding of Characters

In legacy encodings, visual and informational aspects of characters are sometimes lumped together and encoded as separate characters. This is the case with subscript or superscript characters, ligatures, characters in small capitals, fractions, and so on. The special formatting, if necessary, should be achieved by suitable values of the rend attribute rather than by using one of the characters that happened to make it into Unicode. Using a separate character like SUBSCRIPT TWO (U + 2082) obscures the fact that it is a digit with the value two and requires special processing; to prepare such a text for indexing and search programs, H<seg rend="sub">2</seg>0 could be used to encode this information independently but also indicate its desired rendering. Obviously, if more sophisticated formulas are required, markup vocabularies like MathML would be better candidates. A discussion of this problem can be found in the TEI guidelines, section 22.2 (Sperberg-McQueen and Burnard, *Guidelines for Electronic Text Encoding*).

REPRESENTING DIFFERENT STAGES IN A WRITING SYSTEM

In many scholarly editions, the goal is not only to produce a text as faithful to the original as possible but also to produce a derived version, using the modern conventions of the writing system for the sake of modern readers. These differences may involve mere variations in the orthography above the level of characters, but sometimes shifts occur in the characters used to represent a word. To give just one example for the writing system of English, there was a shift in the usage of *i* and *j* as well as *u* and *v* in printing after the early seventeenth century: "ivory" was once written "iuory." As well as specific markup constructs for handling such cases,[5] the TEI guidelines describe in chapter 25 a general-purpose mechanism for the definition and use of variant glyphs and characters, which is intended to make it easier and more convenient to encode both an original and a modern version of a text.[6] It should be noted, however, that this mechanism covers only variation in the usage of characters and glyphs, not orthographic variation in general.

NOTES

1. The standard reference for Unicode is *The Unicode Standard* (abbreviated as *TUS* 4.0; see Unicode Consortium); for the ISO 10646, it's *ISO/IEC 10646-1:2000* (see Intl. Organization for Standardization).
2. This architecture was finalized in Unicode 2.1. Before that, Unicode was considered to consist only of the BMP. Unicode 3.1, released in March 2001, was the first version to assign characters to code points outside the BMP.
3. The usual way to overwrite the internal detection mechanism and force a specific encoding is to press "C-x RETURN c" and type in a name of a coding system. If the problem is with UTF-16 encodings, typing "utf-16" followed by the Tab key will show the possible values.
4. Many current software applications and operating systems cannot render combining sequences as a single visual unit. To overcome this problem, some encoding projects took refuge in defining new code points in the area of the Unicode code space set aside for private usage and created fonts accordingly. This solution will make it easier for encoders to work with these characters, but care should be taken to convert such private-use characters back to the standard representation of Unicode before electronic publication of the texts.
5. The <reg> and <orig> elements and the grouping <choice> element are designed for the purpose of encoding regularizations.
6. This mechanism has been newly introduced in TEI P5.

WHY AND HOW TO DOCUMENT
YOUR MARKUP CHOICES

PATRICK DURUSAU

For one who has perused the TEI guidelines, even briefly, a chapter on documenting markup choices may seem like a chapter to read later. TEI markup is formal and complex to the point of intimidating new users with its array of choices and options for encoding. Documenting the markup choices of a particular project reduces the complexity of the TEI for encoders and potential future users of an encoded text.

Out of the welter of choices and options presented by the TEI guidelines, encoding projects should document what markup options will be used by the project. Such documentation should include features of the text(s) to be encoded, elements to be used for such features, attributes for the elements used, and the range of values for each attribute that is allowed on any element. Markup makes explicit the structures that an encoder has seen in a text. Documenting markup choices makes the decisions about what markup to use explicit as well. The process continues throughout the project, but it should be the major focus before the task of imposing markup begins.

The process varies from project to project, depending on funding and other constraints. There is no project so small that it will not derive some benefit from choosing and following a process of documenting the markup used. Benefits include cost and time savings, ease of use, longevity, and lower error rates.

I use a brief example taken from an academic journal to demonstrate the reasons for documenting markup choices by a project. It is followed by an outline of the issues suggested by the sample passage. Finally, I suggest ways that particular projects can avoid the pitfalls of not documenting markup choices.

WHY MARKUP DECISIONS SHOULD BE DOCUMENTED

Many abstract arguments can be made for documenting markup decisions—it can be used to analyze markup decisions by text type, it documents the work of the project, it facilitates reuse of markup decisions for similar texts—but the most compelling argument is made by example. Photocopy the following paragraph, distribute it among the members of an encoding project, and ask them to mark what they would encode and how they would encode it:

> In his discussion of the Eucharistic doctrine which is presented in *The Babylonian Captivity of the Church* (1520), Luther not only argues against the Catholic doctrine of the Eucharistic sacrifice but also against transubstantiation. Luther explicitly states that he was influenced on this issue by Peter D'Ailly, a Nominalist follower of William of Occam. D'Ailly and other Nominalists thought that transubstantiation was not the only possible way that Christ could be present in the Eucharist, since if God wished he could also make Christ present along with the substance of the bread and the wine. From a Nominalist perspective transubstantiation requires two actions of God, namely, the annihilation of the substance of the bread and the placement of Christ's body under the species. Therefore, consubstantiation would be a simpler account of Christ's Eucharistic presence. (Osborne 64–65)

After gathering responses, list all the features noticed; how many of the participants noticed the same features; and, most important, how many suggested the same encoding method for the feature.

Consider the rendering of "The Babylonian Captivity of the Church" in the opening sentence. A possible first reaction is simply to mimic the presentation of the printed page, which may be all that is possible in some cases. The encoder would use the `<hi>` element of TEI with an appropriate **rend** attribute to achieve that effect. Another likely reaction is that "The Babylonian Captivity of the Church" is a title of some kind and should be encoded using the `<title>` element. Another encoder realizes that it is a title but wants to construct a reference to an online English translation of the work (www.ctsfw.edu/etext/luther/babylonian/babylonian.htm) by using the `<xref>` element.

The following list contains, in order of appearance, portions of the text and possible markup options for each. It is by no means exhaustive.

Eucharistic <index>, <term> (3)
The Babylonian Captivity of the Church<hi>, <xref>, <title> (4):
    Babylonian <index>, <term><placeName><settlement> (5)
    Captivity <index>, <term> (3)
    Church <index>, <name><ref> (4)
1520 <date> (2)
Luther <index>, <name><persName> (4)
Catholic <index>, <name><ref> (4)
Eucharistic sacrifice <index>, <ref> (3)
    Eucharistic <index>, <term><ref> (4)
    sacrifice <index>, <term><ref> (4)
transubstantiation <index>, <term><ref> (4)
Luther <index>, <name><persName> (4)
Peter D'Ailly <index>, <name><persName> (4)
    Peter <index>, <name><persName><foreName> (5)
    D'Ailly <index>, <name><persName><surname> (5)
Nominalist <index>, <term><ref> (4)
William of Occam <index>, <name><persName><ref> (5)
    William <index>, <name><persName><foreName> (5)
    Occam <index>, <term><placeName><settlement> (5)
Peter D'Ailly <index>, <name><persName> (4)
    Peter <index>, <name><persName><foreName> (5)
    D'Ailly <index>, <name><persName><surname> (5)
Nominalists <index>, <ref>, <term> (4)
transubstantiation <index>, <term><ref> (4)
Christ <index>, <name><ref> (4)
Eucharist <index>, <term><ref> (4)
God <index>, <name><ref> (4)
Christ <index>, <name><ref> (4)
substance <index>, <term><ref> (4)
bread <index>, <term><ref> (4)
wine <index>, <term><ref> (4)
Nominalist <index>, <ref>, <term> (4)
God <index>, <name><ref> (4)
substance <index>, <term><ref> (4)
bread <index>, <term><ref> (4)
Christ's body <index>, <term> (3)
    Christ's <index>, <name><ref> (4)
    body <index>, <term><ref> (4)
species <index>, <term> (3)
consubstantiation <index>, <ref>, <term> (4)

Christ's `<index>`, `<name><ref>` (4)
Eucharistic presence `<index>`, `<term>` (3)
    Eucharistic `<index>`, `<term><ref>` (4)
    presence `<index>`, `<term><ref>` (4)

Markup options for grammatical or linguistic analysis as well as attribute values on the various elements have been omitted. Specialized markup that would record variant readings, overlapping hierarchies, editorial interventions in the text, elements peculiar to manuscripts, and other elements have been omitted. Despite all those omissions, the first sentence alone confronts the encoder with 4,423,680 choices using the elements listed above (3 x 4 x 5 x 3 x 4 x 2 x 4 x 4 x 3 x 4 x 4). These combinations are not unique but serve to illustrate the unlikelihood that any two encoders or even the same encoder on different days will make, without formal guidance, the same decisions. The reader should bear in mind that this level of complexity is seen in a text that is typical of a modern academic journal article. Manuscript witnesses, grammatical or linguistic analysis, critical editions, texts with overlapping hierarchies, drama, and other more complex works exhibit a greater number of markup options.

The choices offered in each case for this passage are legitimate and would result in a valid TEI document. A TEI document may be valid even when encoding choices have been made inconsistently. Validation software gauges not consistency but only formally valid markup. Inconsistent encoding will most often manifest itself during efforts to display or search the text.

Despite the emphasis on encoding texts properly, the first real test for any project is display of visual images of encoded text to department heads or funders. The stylesheet designer is responsible for creating stylesheets that will convert or display the text and will test them against samples from the project. Inconsistency means that stylesheets that work with one document may not work with another. Given the range of possible encodings, it is very difficult for a stylesheet author to compensate for inconsistent markup. Such errors are usually noticed either at the public debut of the project or while the final version is being demonstrated to the university administrators reviewing the project: portions of the text may not display properly, and some searches may not work.

Suppose "The Babylonian Captivity of the Church" does not display as a title. Thinking that the stylesheet author has failed in some regard, the user attempts to search the document for titles of works cited. Oddly enough, far fewer titles appear than are known (or assumed) to occur in the text. The next search is for personal names known to occur in the text. Like the titles of works, some are found, some are not. The encoding team knows the information is in the file, but the software is simply not finding it. Realizing that it is unlikely that both the stylesheet writer and the search engine failed on the same day, they start looking at the encoded text.

One of the problems noticed early in their review is the different encoding of the titles and personal names. Each has a legitimate argument for his or her choice, but now several hundred texts vary in ways that are not easy to find. The stylesheets can be adapted to some degree, but such adapting will not help the search for inconsistently encoded files. Time, grant money, and energy have been spent on creating texts that can be displayed only with difficulty, that cannot be accessed accurately with markup-aware software, and that will be difficult and expensive to fix. How would documenting markup choices help avoid this predicament?

DOCUMENTING MARKUP: A PROCESS OF DISCOVERY

The process of documenting markup choices is actually one of learning about a body of texts. Specialists know the text but not from the standpoint of imposing markup from a fixed set of elements such as the TEI guidelines. And it is not always obvious which TEI elements should be used for encoding, even if there is agreement about what to encode. The process of applying markup to a particular text begins with analyzing the text to be encoded.

Analyzing a text makes explicit what is understood implicitly by most readers. Few readers would not recognize "The Babylonian Captivity of the Church" as somehow different from the surrounding text. But it is possible to legitimately encode that portion of text in several ways. Since readers cannot be relied on to reach the same conclusions about a passage for markup purposes, the text must be modeled. A model might decide that all titles that appear in the article should be encoded as references to online texts whenever possible. That decision would allow for special display of the title in the running text as well as facilitate hypertext linking the title to the text it refers to.

Unfortunately for scholars (and others), the process of analyzing texts has been rarely treated outside technical markup literature. One of the more accessible attempts to address this important issue can be found in *Developing SGML DTDs: From Text to Model to Markup*, by Eve Maler and Jeanne El Andaloussi. Despite its formidable title, this book's chapter 4 ("Document

Type Needs Analysis") and chapter 5 ("Document Type Modeling and Spec-ification") can be used as guides to analyzing documents. They are written for users who are developing a DTD instead of using an existing one, but the same modeling considerations apply in either case. (Other treatments readily available are David Megginson's *Structuring XML Documents* and Rick Jelliffe's *The XML and SGML Cookbook*.) Maler and El Andaloussi present a modeling language and sample forms for analysis of any text. While the suggested process will be unfamiliar at first, scholars embarking on long-term encoding projects are well advised to adapt both the modeling language and process into their written documentation. It will not only aid in the process of analysis but also result in a record of the project's intellectual history. The alternative is ad hoc encoding decisions and practices—or undocumented ones, which are almost as pernicious.

To model texts for an encoding project, a sample should be chosen as a starting point, one that fairly represents the full range of materials to be encoded. The sample should be examined, and every feature to be encoded should be marked and the suggested encoding recorded. It is almost certain that this initial survey will not include all features. Documenting choices at the beginning of the project allows new features to be encoded consistently with choices already made. The process of analysis and modeling is not fin-ished until the last text is encoded, because it may contain new features. But consistency will be maintained throughout the project.

When proposing an encoding for texts, scholars should not assume that some features are too obvious to merit recording. Markup makes both the obvious and not so obvious structures in a text explicit, so every feature that is to be encoded in the project should be noted, even something as common as a paragraph.

Paragraphs in late-nineteenth- and early-twentieth-century grammars often appear to be numbered and followed by typographically distinct ma-terial, usually indented and set in smaller typeface. Should both the follow-ing blocks of material be encoded as paragraphs?

> 2. Among the cuneiform tablets from Tell el-Amarna, brought to light in 1887, the one which was the largest in the group happened to also be com-posed in an unknown language.[1] Only the introductory paragraph, which takes up seven out of nearly 500 lines, was written in Akkadian. From that introduction, it was learned that the document was a letter address to Amen-ophis III by Tushratta, king of Mitanni. It was logical, therefore, at the time

to assume that the rest of the letter was in the principal language of the Kingdom of Mitanni; the use of the term "Mitannian" was the natural consequence of that assumption.

> This name was employed by all the early students of the subject, including P. Jensen (cf. his articles in ZA 5 [1890] 166 ff., 6 [1891] 34ff., and 14 [1899] 173 ff.); L. Messerschmidt, Mitanni-Studien (MVGA 4 [1899] No. 4); F. Bork, Die Mitannisprache (MVAT 14 [1909] Nos. 1/2. Current usage restricts the term, as a rule, to the material in the non-Akkadian letter of Tushratta. . . .
>
> (Speiser 1)

The second block appears to offer references or remarks that explain or amplify the material in the preceding paragraph. It does not appear to be a quote of any sort. The work has footnotes, so the typographically distinct material is not any sort of mid-page note. The encoding decision is further complicated by a survey of the rest of the grammar, which reveals numbered paragraphs that appear in a similar format. (Examples in Speiser of numbered paragraphs that share this presentation are 15, 21, 26, and 78.) For some purposes, such as for a quick review, the user may wish to display only the main text, without these reference paragraphs appearing as well. A project could decide to encode the second block as a paragraph with a **type** attribute value of `reference`. The encoding team will face many such situations, but the primary rule is that if a feature is to be encoded, that encoding must be recorded and examples of the feature must be included.

Once all the sample texts have been marked with likely encodings, the participants should jointly review and decide on how the features should be encoded. It is very important that a clean version be maintained of the samples with an index of the features being encoded. This version and index will serve as documentation of the encoding decisions as well as the basis for training materials for encoders who are hired to assist in the project.

Using *The Babylonian Captivity of the Church* example above, the encoding team would record (in part):

Encode using ‹term› and insert ‹index› element. Use index list for form of name for index level and form of name. Examples: Babylonian

Encode using ‹term› and insert ‹index› element. Use index list for form of name for index level and form of name. Examples: Church

If the work is available online, encode with ‹xref› and set **target** attribute to `needsTarget`; and **type** attribute to `title`.

Note that the use of `needsTarget` for an attribute value on the `<xref>` element for the title appearing in the article reflects a multipass encoding process: a rough encoding by part-time student assistants and refinement of that encoding by more skilled users later. Since encoding is labor-intensive, it is unlikely that any scholar or group of scholars will be able to personally encode all the texts for a project. To achieve an acceptable level of quality, it will be necessary to train encoders to insert the desired markup.

DOCUMENTING MARKUP:
A PROCESS OF TRAINING

After the encoding team has reviewed sample texts and prepared a guide to what should be encoded and how, that information must be conveyed to the encoders who will be actually inserting markup into the texts. That training can be informal in smaller projects, but training of every encoder should be an explicit part of the schedule and funding. It is unfair to expect encoders to be aware of uncommunicated requirements of the project, and the errors that result from inadequate training must be corrected at a later stage.

Encoding guidelines should be conveyed to encoders in an effective manner. It might be sufficient to tell the project principals that the bound form of the noun (in Akkadian) should be noted in an attribute value, but that explanation would hardly suffice for part-time undergraduates. (Ignore for the moment that encoding at such a level would be the exclusive domain of a project specialist.) Guidelines developed with the personnel hired to perform the encoding ensure that a common understanding has been reached on what is to be encoded and how. Terminology should be used that will be understandable in answers to any question encoders may have during their work. To the extent possible, the guide should contain photocopy reproductions of several examples of each feature in the text to be encoded. The process of developing such examples will also uncover any cases of misunderstanding of encoding decisions in the project. (Misunderstandings about terminology are common even in standards committees. One goal of any project is to uncover and resolve such misunderstandings.)

An encoding guide is only as effective as the examples it contains. A guide that has no examples or ones that are incomplete or inconsistent may be worse than no guide at all. The needs of encoders will vary from project to project, but minimally any guide should cover every element that a particular encoder is expected to apply to the text. Note that it need not and probably should not cover every element that will be used by the project.

Encoders should be trained to insert the elements that are their responsibility, not attempt to correct or enter others that are not. In terms of content, a minimal encoding guide would have for every element:

> a common name for the feature in the text
> the name of the element to be used by the encoder
> examples of the features in context with no markup
> some examples of the features in context with markup

Examples of text features appearing with markup and without (without markup, photocopies from printed materials might be used) will assist encoders in recognizing situations that call for markup.

One effective training technique is to provide new encoders with the encoding guide and a nonencoded version of a text that has already been encoded and proofed for the project. The trainees can be taken through the main points of the manual and then asked to encode the sample text, which then can be compared with the proper encoding. There are a number of utilities to compare XML files for differences; whenever possible, automatic comparison should be used to test what trainees have done against texts known to represent the encoding requirements of the project.

Despite the best efforts of the team, encoders will encounter text features not anticipated by the project. They should be encouraged to bring such features to the attention of the project, even if it is ultimately decided, for consistency, that the features cannot be encoded. Except in obvious cases of misreading the encoding guide, every such question should be recorded and the answer given to the encoder who raised the question. Ad hoc decision making, just as unrecorded encoding decisions, can lead to inconsistency, which reduces the value of the project's product.

Training new encoders should be viewed as only part of the overall training process for the project. Experienced and new encoders should be brought together on a regular basis to discuss new features that have been identified and to go over one or two recent texts. The quality of the work depends on the encoders' sharing a common understanding of the markup and the texts on which it is being imposed. Periodic review of the encoding guide, of texts recently encoded, and of any new encoding issues will build and maintain that understanding, which is more important for project leaders and experienced users than for the day-to-day personnel. Paradoxically, experienced users are more likely to violate project norms and requirements, because of their deeper grasp of the goals of the project. It should always be reinforced that consistency to the encoding guide is the rule for everyone. Inconsistency, even if due to the brilliance of a particular encoder, will diminish the overall usefulness of the project result.

DOCUMENTING MARKUP: A PROCESS OF VALIDATION

Validation of markup for a project is more than simply determining that the files are formally valid; they must also comply with the encoding guide developed for the project. This compliance is a problem with vendor-based encoding services that return valid files not meeting markup requirements.

One of the advantages of having a guide with examples is that it can be used in the construction of scripts to validate encoding of particular features in a text. For example, a script can extract all the personal names that have been encoded in a certain way, and the list can be scanned to determine if anything other than personal names appears in it. More important, it can be used to search entire files for occurrences of personal names that are not so encoded. It can also make sure that indexes use the terms specified to appear as index entries. Such searching and validation would not be possible, or would be difficult, without a guide that sets requirements beyond validity for various parts of the text.

The validation of files for compliance to the encoding project's requirements should be performed on every file. Records should be kept for every problem found and corrected, and every correction should be communicated to the encoder with an explanation of the error. Such feedback ensures that any problems with the guide, training, or understanding are uncovered and corrected before the project creates hundreds of files with unknown and inconsistent encodings. Validation can be largely automated, as least as far as error detection is concerned, and it fills a much-needed quality-ensurance role for the project. Features that are likely sources of error or likely to recur across a set of texts, such as personal or geographic names, terms, and titles, should be added to the validation process as they come to light.

Any number of scripting languages, from sed and awk to Perl, can be used to validate markup in files. There are also specialized searching programs, such as sgrep, that allow the searching of markup files for particular elements and their content. Projects should develop scripts to validate markup practices before any texts are produced. Therefore, the services of a scripting language programmer should be included in the earliest planning stages of the project.

DOCUMENTING MARKUP:
A PROCESS OF REVIEW

Documenting markup is more than modeling texts, recording markup decisions, training encoders, or even reviewing encoding work. It has all those components, but treating each separately or as a static step will not meet the needs of a project. Documenting markup requires documenting those components that are part of an overall process.

The markup process itself should be made explicit. A periodic review of the encoding guide, the training materials, and the results of validation is necessary to that process. Periodic review uncovers patterns of miscoding, which, if they coincide with a shift to a new period of texts or type of material, may indicate a problem with the guide. Such shifts may also indicate training problems, lack of supervision or feedback. Such problems should be addressed as soon as they become apparent.

Like the other suggested steps in the documenting markup process, review should result in a written report of its results. Beyond satisfying the project principals that the markup guidelines are being followed, such reports also lend credence to the project's success in producing texts that meet the standard for consistent encoding.

Imposing markup on texts can create long-term resources that will benefit both students and scholars. Poorly done markup, however, consumes valuable resources, results in seldom used materials, and creates suspicion among scholars about the benefits of using markup. In other words, poorly used markup can retard study in a field of interest as surely as poor-quality publications.

Markup is a tool that ranks with the printing press, index, and lexicon as a means of advancing scholarship. It is a tool, not an end in itself. It should be judged by its effectiveness in aiding scholars in their day-to-day work. For a fair judgment to be made on the utility of markup for scholars, markup must be properly done.

Documenting markup with the techniques outlined here should result in encoded texts that serve the needs of any present-day project as well as future scholars who wish to use such texts. Documented markup offers the opportunity for scholars to contribute resources that will support future research in their field. Markup demands no less attention to detail and quality than a monograph or article that advances a particular area of study.

STORAGE, RETRIEVAL, AND RENDERING

SEBASTIAN RAHTZ

Making an electronic text is sometimes regarded as an end in itself. We spend much time making decisions on what to encode and how to formalize it, then invest huge effort in creating electronic files to represent our text. Publishing the result in some way was until recently rather hard; the amount of information encoded in a full-scale TEI text is difficult to represent in print, and we lacked easy systems to give readers access to the work. The universality of the Web changes everything; we now have a rich-featured target environment in which to present text. However, print presentation remains important, and we nearly always need to rearrange texts to publish them. In this essay, therefore, I look at transformations of encoded texts, conversion of TEI XML files for the Web, preparation of TEI XML files for print, database systems suitable for storing encoded text, and management of collections of text. In general, generic solutions using open standards are described, usually with open-source implementations.

TRANSFORMATION

Those used to preparing texts in a word processor environment usually expect to see an approximation of the final result on their screens as they write. Where they want to see an abstract, they write an abstract, and where the bibliography is to appear, they start typing it in. The fully encoded TEI XML text differs from this scenario in three important and related ways:

1. The encoder often represents two or more strands of information in a single text; it is reasonable for a TEI encoder to mark up part of speech in a text

while also representing the logical structure and the physical characteristics of a particular version.

2. The TEI offers more than one way to encode information. Notes, for instance, may be embedded in the text or placed in a section or their own and pointed to from their insertion location. The rendering sequence need not be related to the encoding sequence.

3. There is a distinct gap in many projects between the encoding and one or more representations, and the text is better regarded as a database of information than as a linear sequence. There is no one output, and the desired results may change over time.

The effect of these differences is that rendering a TEI text often means rearranging or transforming it in some way. Such transformation can involve copying, removing, moving, or generating elements. I look at examples of each of these changes in turn and then consider what tools will do the work.

Copying Elements

The most common reason for copying elements is to create useful navigation systems, like a table of contents. If the text represents an existing book that has its own list of contents, then such copying will not be needed. But in many circumstances we want to make a summary of the text and show it at the back or front. For example, in this text:[1]

```
<div>
<head><q>In Ambush</q></head>
<p>In summer all right-minded boys built huts in the furze-hill
   behind the College</p>
</div>
<div>
<head>Slaves of the Lamp Part I</head>
<p>The music-room on the top floor of Number Five was filled with
   the 'Aladdin' company at rehearsal.</p>
</div>
<div>
<head>An Unsavoury Interlude</head>
<p>It was a maiden aunt of Stalky who sent him both books, with
   the inscription, 'To dearest Artie, on his sixteenth
   birthday';</p>
</div>
```

```
<head>The Impressionists</head>
<p>They had dropped into the Chaplain's study for a Saturday
   night smoke—all four house-masters—and the three briars and
   the one cigar reeking in amity proved the Rev. John Gillett's
   good generalship.</p>
```

it would be reasonable to take each of the <head> elements and make a list at the front of the transformed text:

```
<list>
<item><q>In Ambush</q></item>
<item>Slaves of the Lamp Part I</item>
<item>An Unsavoury Interlude</item>
<item>The Impressionists</item>
</list>
```

The text nodes of each <head> element are copied to the <item> elements in the <list>. This example is trivial, but the application is widespread. Texts for reading by human beings often contain duplicate material (like many other books, every even-numbered page of Rudyard Kipling's *Stalky and Co.* repeats the title, to remind us of what we are reading). As usual in TEI work, the extent to which the encoding captures the duplication explicit in an original work very much depends on basic encoding decisions. Some TEI texts may need no transformation by copying at all.

When considering the uses of copying, it is important to remember that the <teiHeader> section may contain material that is needed for rendering and will be copied into place. For instance, the human-readable version might be annotated on each page with the date on which the text was encoded.

Removing Elements

Most TEI texts contain elements that we do not need to keep as is when rendering the material. The obvious example is the <teiHeader> containing metadata, most of which is not needed for typical rendering, but we may also choose not to show back matter or front matter, to show only a sample of the text divisions, to remove editorial notes, to suppress detailed metadata resulting from linguistic analysis, to remove stage directions from a play, or to show only those portions of text relating to a particular speaker or character.

As a simple example, we might choose to transform this:

```
<p>They had dropped into the Chaplain's study for a Saturday
   night smoke—all four<note place="end" type="editorial">King,
   Prout, White, Hartopp; but sometimes Macrea is mentioned as a
   house-master as well.  Is this reflecting the passage of
   time?</note>house-masters—and the three briars<note
   place="end" type="gloss">A briar is a type of pipe</note> and
   the one cigar reeking in amity proved the <rs key="JG11"
   reg="Gillett, John" type="person"><name>Rev. John Gillett</
   name></rs>'s good generalship.</p>
```

into this:

```
<p>They had dropped into the Chaplain's study for a Saturday
   night smoke-all four house-masters-and the three briars<note
   place="end" type="gloss">A briar is a type of pipe</note> and
   the one cigar reeking in amity proved the Rev. John Gillett's
   good generalship.</p>
```

by suppressing one type of <note> and removing the metadata about the chaplain, which might be used in other circumstances—for example, to show only those paragraphs in which he is mentioned.

Moving Elements

It may seem at first sight strange to propose reordering our carefully assembled text. But there are several occasions when we may wish to do so. For example, a text that exists in several versions may be encoded as set of separate <text> elements, but for presentation purposes we want to show each paragraph together with its variants; so the sequence of paragraphs A1, A2, A3, A4, A5, B1, B2, B3, B4, B5 will become A1, B1, A2, B2, A3, B3, A4, B4, A5, B5 as the two versions are interleaved.

Another situation in which movement of elements might be appropriate is when bibliographic citations are placed in their own section in the <back> element but are to be presented as footnotes. Thus the combination of

```
<xref type="cite" doc="BIB" from="id (TEIP4)">(TEI, 2002)
   </xref>
```

and later

```
<bibl id="TEIP4">TEI <title level="m">Guidelines for
Electronic Text Encoding and Interchange (TEI P4)</title>.
Sperberg-McQueen, C. M., Lou Burnard, Steve DeRose, and Syd
Bauman, eds. Bergen, Charlottesville, Providence, Oxford: Text
Encoding Initiative Consortium, <date>2002</date>.</bibl>
```

is turned into

```
(TEI,2002)<note><bibl id="TEIP4">TEI <title
level="m">Guidelines for Electronic Text Encoding and
Interchange (TEI P4)</title>. Sperberg-McQueen, C. M., Lou
Burnard, Steve DeRose, and Syd Bauman, eds. Bergen,
Charlottesville, Providence, Oxford: Text Encoding Initiative
Consortium, <date>2002</date>.</bibl></note>
```

by a process of interleaving.

Naturally, any sorting of elements is a process of moving, and any merging of material from a secondary file will involve its movement. An extreme form of moving (and copying) material is the rearrangement of a text into a concordance or word list.

Generating Elements

We have already seen above some generation of new elements; for instance, when we copied <head> elements to a series of list items, we had to create the surrounding <list>. There is also a TEI element <divGen> that explicitly expects a rendering application to create material. The action is determined by the type attribute, for which TEI P4 suggests possible values:

index	an index is to be generated and inserted at this point
toc	a table of contents
figlist	a list of figures
tablist	a list of tables

These actions again involve element copying of some kind; the "index" value may involve working out index entries, for instance, from all the <name> elements in a text.

A common form of generation is the addition of automated linking or the making explicit of implicit information. Thus the text used above to identify a character:

```
<rs key="JG11" reg="Gillett, John" type="person"><name>Rev.
    John Gillett</name></rs>
```

could be the key to generating a link to the section of the document where Gillett is first mentioned, or to detailed metadata about the person referred to, perhaps in a bibliography.

The Tool Kit

Unless we want to simply turn a linear sequence of TEI XML elements into exactly the same sequence of material marked up in some other way, most real-life applications involve a combination of all the techniques discussed above. It makes sense to consider all these steps *before* we worry about how precisely we want to publish the result. All the examples above apply just as much to print as to the Web, and we can operate more efficiently if we (conceptually, at least) perform all the transformations at the level of TEI XML before converting to a particular result.

A wide range of software tools can do the transformation for us. Any programming or scripting language that can handle XML has the power to do almost all the tasks, but unless you are an experienced programmer, it makes sense to stick to the recommendations defined by the World Wide Web Consortium. Three standards from the W3C are relevant here:

DOM (document object model): a specification for how programming languages should provide access to, and manipulate, the tree structure of an XML document

XPath: a specification for how to address parts of an XML document

XSLT (extensible stylesheet language transformation): high-level language for specifying transformations, using XPath

For our purposes XSLT (well described in many reference and tutorial texts, including Kay; Tennison; and the extensive pointers at www.xslt.com/) fits the bill nicely. It is available in a number of efficient implementations for most computer platforms and environments, including Web servers and clients, editors, and freestanding programs. The commonly used implementations are *MSXML*, *Saxon*, *Xalan*, *libxslt*, and *Sablotron*; they are mostly open-source or free. The language has some interesting and important characteristics:

It is expressed in XML. You can write scripts with your existing XML editor and use your existing syntax-checking tools.

It is based on a series of templates, or rules, that specify what is to happen to particular elements from the incoming text; the processor works out how to apply the rules.

Using the XPath language, any template can access any part of the document at any time. You are not constrained by a linear processing model.

XML namespaces are used to differentiate the XSLT language itself from the output.

The result is that it is simple to implement all the techniques we have discussed.

It is beyond the scope of this essay to provide a detailed introduction to XSLT, but it should be helpful to see some simple scripts. First, a script that takes each ‹div› element and puts the corresponding ‹head› element as an item in the list:

```
<xsl:stylesheet xmlns:xsl = "http://www.w3.org/1999/XSL/
  Transform" version = "1.0">
<xsl:template match = "body">
    <list>
    <xsl:for-each select = ".//div">
    <item><xsl:apply-templates select = "head"/></item>
    </xsl:for-each>
    </list>
<xsl:apply-templates/>
</xsl:template>
</xsl:stylesheet>
```

Note the xsl: prefix for statements that are part of the XSLT language; other elements, such as ‹list› and ‹item›, are placed in the output. The fragment has a single ‹xsl:template›, whose **select** attribute identifies which input element (here, ‹body›) the rule applies to. The .//div value for the **select** attribute of xsl:apply-templates is an expression in the XPath language; it means "every div element you can find below here in the document tree." The final ‹xsl:apply-templates› tells the processor to carry on and process (again, in the case of ‹div›s) all the elements inside the current element (the ‹body›).

Second, a script fragment (we omit the wrapper ‹xsl:stylesheet› element from here on) that removes some elements:

```
<xsl:template match="note[@type="editorial"]"/>
<xsl:template match="teiHeader"/>
```

By our simply supplying no body for the templates for ‹teiHeader› and no ‹note› elements with a **type** attribute of editorial, the entire element and its contents are passed by.

Third, to move some elements, we specify explicitly for an element (‹text›) what to do. Here, we say that we want the ‹back›, ‹front›, and ‹body› elements to be processed in that order:

```
<xsl:template match="text">
    <xsl:apply-templates select="back"/>
    <xsl:apply-templates select="front"/>
    <xsl:apply-templates select="body"/>
</xsl:template>
```

Note that if we omit one of the ‹xsl:apply-templates› lines, the corresponding elements would never be processed.

Last, the generation of elements. Our example of copying elements already showed how to make a crude table of contents; the following script appends a ‹note› element to each ‹name› listing the number of times that name occurs in the text:

```
<xsl:key name="NAMES" match="name" use="@key"/>
<xsl:template match="name">
    <xsl:apply-templates/>
    <note>This name occurs
    <xsl:value-of select="count(key('NAMES',@key))"/>
        times</note>
</xsl:template>
```

The ‹xsl:key› element keeps a table in memory of all the occurrences of the ‹name› element, indexed by the value of the **key** attribute; the **key** function retrieves a list from that table, and the **count** function counts them.

MAKING WEBS

If we have arrived at a transformation of a text that has the correct components in the right sequence, we can start to render it in a form suitable for
human readers. The most common way to achieve this rendering is to convert
the text to HTML; thus the TEI markup

```
<div>
<head><q>In Ambush</q></head>
<p>In summer all right-minded boys built huts in the furze-hill
  behind the College</p>
</div>
```

might become

```
<h1>'In Ambush'</h1>
<p>In summer all right-minded boys built huts in the furze-hill
  behind the College</p>
```

This transformation is, of course, no different from those discussed in the last
section; the <head> element of the <div> is used to construct the HTML
<h1> element, and the TEI <p> is turned into the similar HTML <p>. Note
also the simplification of the <q> element, which is a replaced by a matching
pair of single quotes.

This conversion to HTML involves no more or less than the transformation using copying, moving, removing, and generating described above,
if we regard the HTML language as another XML dialect. Luckily, all the
XSLT implementations have a special output mode in which they massage
their output into HTML; if the transformation turns a TEI <lb> into
(which it has to do, because the script must be well-formed XML), the XSLT
engine quietly makes that the standard HTML <br>, to satisfy older Web
browsers.

Although I describe it here as two stages, transformation from TEI to
TEI followed by transformation to HTML, most applications do both at the
same time, so

```
<xsl:template match="body">
    <list>
    <xsl:for-each select=".//div">
        <item><xsl:apply-templates select="head"/></item>
```

```
    </xsl:for-each>
    </list>
  </xsl:template>
```

would be written in XSLT as

```
<xsl:template match="body">
    <ol>
    <xsl:for-each select=".//div">
        <li><xsl:apply-templates select="head"/></li>
    </xsl:for-each>
    </ol>
  </xsl:template>
```

Writing a set of XSLT specifications for a markup scheme as large as the TEI
is not a trivial task. You will likely want to create a set of HTML files rather
than just one, in which case you need to create lots of navigational links and
take care of internal cross-references that go from one generated output file
to another. Figure 1 shows a simple rendition of a TEI text, with a table of
contents at the start and then the sections following; figure 2 shows a delivery

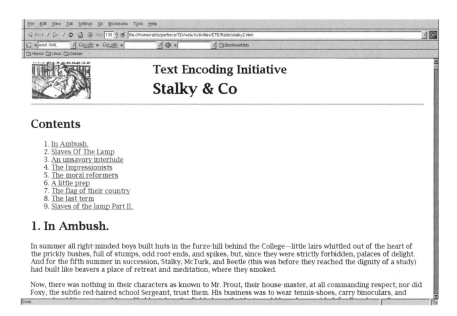

Fig. 1. Simple Web rendition of TEI document

Fig. 2. Multipart Web rendition of TEI document

in which chapters are presented in individual documents with a table of contents on the left.

Obviously an enormous number of other Web display features can be driven by TEI markup or by editorial choice. Figure 3 shows a visual rendition of the `<name>` element, from this XSLT:

```
<xsl:template match="name">
<span class="name"><xsl:apply-templates/></span>
</xsl:template>
```

Figure 4 shows the `<foreign>` elements with different colors according to the type attribute, using this XSLT fragment:

```
<xsl:template match="foreign">
<span class="foreign{@lang}"><xsl:apply-templates/></span>
</xsl:template>
```

in which a CSS (cascading stylesheets) class attribute is created using the word foreign and the value of lang. The key to these simple results, and much more complex ones, is deciding how HTML markup in the output can be created by transforming input XML.

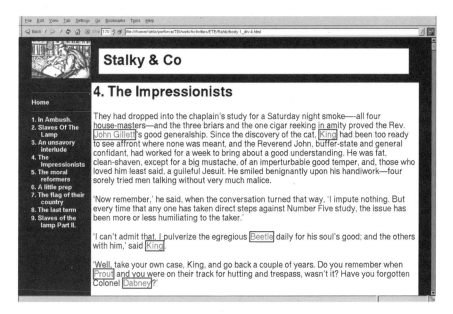

Fig. 3. Web rendition of TEI document highlighting names

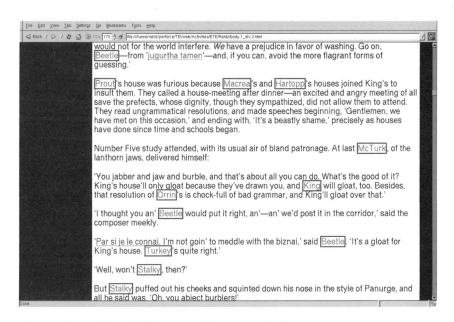

Fig. 4. Web rendition of TEI document highlighting foreign words and names

The TEI Consortium hosts a set of XSLT stylesheets by Sebastian Rahtz on its Web site (www.tei-c.org/Stylesheets) that are designed for creating Web pages. The results can be varied by providing values for over eighty parameters and by overriding individual templates.

XSLT stylesheets for TEI documents have many applications:

1. A reference to the stylesheet can be embedded in the XML file using a processing instruction. Some Web browsers, including *Internet Explorer* and the *Mozilla* family, then view the XML file directly by transforming it to HTML dynamically. This is a very easy and effective way to publish TEI XML documents, if you are sure your potential readers will use the right Web client.

2. The Web server can be set up to transform the XML to HTML on request. The *Cocoon* and *AxKit* systems, for example, trap incoming requests for XML documents, perform the transform, and return the HTML results. As the results are cached, this transformation is efficient and works with any browser. The disadvantage is that the reader does not get access to the original XML (this may also be seen as an advantage). Different renditions can be made on the server by providing appropriate instructions as part of the URL (e.g., a URL ending in .xml?style = print will process to pass the parameter **style** with the value `print` to the stylesheet engine).

3. The XML can be transformed to HTML once at source and the result uploaded to a normal Web server. This method is the most reliable and causes the least load on the server, but it is also the most cumbersome, as the text owner must remember to remake the HTML each time there is a change in the original. Any different renditions also must be precreated.

PREPARING FOR PRINT

It should be clear by now that the print version of our texts follows much the same line as the Web version. First, we define the transformations needed to present the right bits of text in the right order, then we turn the text into a print format. This format is likely to be portable document format (PDF), created by a page makeup engine. The choice here is not as clear as it is for the Web. We may prefer a dedicated publishing system with its own system of stylesheets or sophisticated interfaces for making up pages (*QuarkXPress* and *InDesign* are good examples); commercial or free systems that can create typeset pages from a semifixed page specification (XSL FO or DSSSL [document style semantics and specification language]); or conversion to a well-understood non-XML formatting language, such as LaTeX. Which you use depends on whether you want to feed material to a typesetting system where you can subsequently fine-tune and manipulate the results or whether you require automated page makeup with little need for intervention.

If you plan to use a traditional desktop publishing system, one simple way to proceed is to turn your TEI file into simple HTML and then read it into *Microsoft Word* or another similar word processor; many DTP (desktop publishing) programs can import such files. Figure 5 shows our sample text imported into *Word*. If this method is not suitable, the proprietary methods of the system will have to be used. Some programs support XSLT as part of their process (e.g., *Arbortext Epic, Advent 3B2*).

The XSL formatting objects language (XSL FO for short) and many pointers to software and tutorials at www.w3.org/Style/XSL are a W3C recommendation that provides a good basis for automated page makeup. It is a markup, expressed as XML, that describes a set of pages and the characteristics of layout objects on those pages. The core principles of the language design are conceptual compatibility with DSSSL, compatibility with CSS properties, screen properties as well as print, and no compromises on internationalization (i.e., many writing directions are supported).

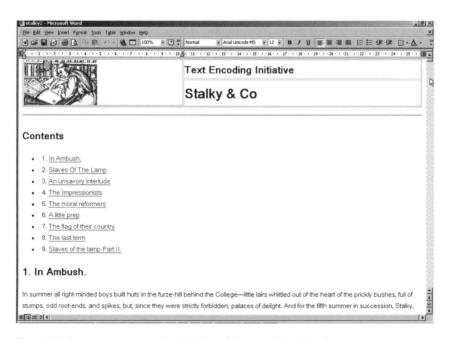

Fig. 5. TEI document converted to HTML and imported into *Word*

When one uses FO, the input XML is transformed into an output tree consisting of page masters, which define named styles of page layout, and page sequences, which reference a named page layout and contain a flow of text. In that flow, text is assigned to one of five (rectangular) regions (the page body, areas at the top, bottom, left, and right). There is also allowance for floating objects (at the top of the page), and footnotes (at the bottom), and the model covers writing in left-to-right, right-to-left, top-to-bottom, and bottom-to-top modes.

In a region of text, we find one or more blocks, tables, lists, and floats, and in a block we find inline sequences, characters, links, footnotes, and graphics.

All these objects have a large number of properties, including aural properties; borders, spacing, and padding; breaking; colors; font properties (family, size, shape, weight, etc.); hyphenation; positioning; special table properties; and special list properties—although supporting all of them is not mandatory for processors. XSL FO does not specify where line or page breaks are to occur, or precisely how to justify a paragraph, so the results from different processors can vary. A sample of XSL FO markup is:

```
<fo:block font-size="10pt"
text-indent="1em"
font-family="Times-Roman"
space-before.optimum="0pt"
space-before.maximum="12pt">&#x2018;<fo:inline
font-style="italic">Ti-ra-ra-la-i-tu</fo:inline>!
I gloat! Hear me!&#x2019; Stalky, still on his heels, whirled
   like a dancing dervish to the dining-hall.</fo:block>
```

in which a ‹block› object is described, containing an embedded ‹inline› object. The concept and some of the attribute names will be familiar to Web developers, from the CSS language.

There are several good implementations of XSL FO, both commercial and free (*XEP, Antenna House XSL Formatter, FOP*, and Arbortext's *Epic* editor), most of which take an FO document and produce PDF pages. Some can generate other formats, including PostScript, TIFF, and Windows GDI. Figure 6 shows our sample text displayed in *Acrobat* after conversion to XSL FO and then formatted to PDF using *PassiveTeX*; figure 7 shows the same FO file formatted and displayed by the *Antenna House XSL Formatter*. The differences are small but instructive. Note for instance that the line endings are not the same.

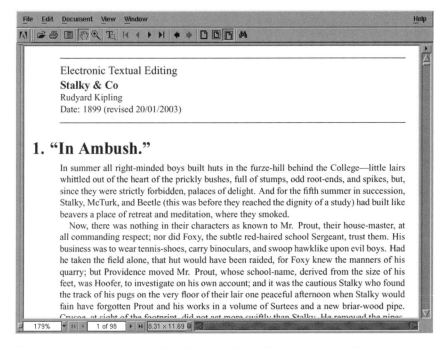

Fig. 6. TEI document converted to XSL FO and then PDF using *PassiveTeX*

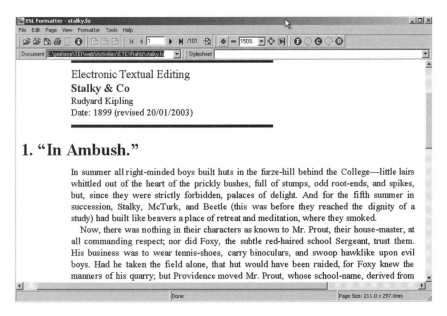

Fig. 7. TEI document converted to XSL FO and then PDF using *Antenna House XSL Formatter*

The chief disadvantage of the XSL FO approach is that it neither allows direct manipulation or specification of the page nor guarantees page fidelity. You cannot say, "I always want this figure on page 54, halfway down, with text flowing around it, regardless of how much the text changes," and you cannot be sure that your pages will have the same breaks if you use two different implementations. In practice, TEI documents tend not to be designed for the page or to require legal precision, so FO is a reasonable choice.

XSL FO is generally created by a transformation from higher-level XML; it is highly verbose and hard to write by hand. XSLT is again a good tool to perform this transformation, as the task is very similar to the creation of HTML. The TEI Consortium hosts a set of parameterized XSLT stylesheets by Rahtz on its Web site (www.tei-c.org/Stylesheets) that can be used to create XSL FO from TEI XML. These stylesheets allow for obvious layout changes, including change of page size and basic font size, choice of size and style of headings, whether or not headings are numbered, whether the text is single- or double-column, and the management of cross-references.

Orthogonal to the methodology adopted (automated or interventionist) is the method of software integration. Some systems offer closely integrated publishing solutions (e.g., *Arbortext Epic* [www.arbortext.com/html/products.html]), which cover all aspects of the document management process, including editing, stylesheets, print publication, Web publication, and database integration. The alternative is a set of loosely related solutions for each situation along the line, perhaps drawn from both commercial and open-source software. Both approaches are equally valid, and generally speaking the TEI encoder can be slightly relaxed, since the overwhelming effort is in creating the neutral XML source in the first place.

DATABASE SYSTEMS FOR TEI AND XML

Our discussion so far has been on the level of simple XML files and manipulating them individually. What if we want to present composite results from a whole collection of TEI texts? On a small scale, this presentation can be done with XSLT, since that language allows us to read multiple input files, select arbitrary subsets, and make a composite output. But all current XSLT implementations work in memory and read the documents afresh each time a script is run—a technique unsuitable for documents over a certain size or when many queries need to be run at the same time. In either situation we need to turn to a dedicated database.

Database systems have two important characteristics for our purposes; first, they do not store all the data in memory and are designed to handle arbitrarily large collections with equally efficient access to any part; second, they support multiple simultaneous queries. How do they work in the XML context? Ronald Bourret has an exhaustive discussion of the details; here I summarize four simple ways to proceed:

1. We can store entire XML documents as single-text objects in a conventional database and query them using substring operators. This method works well if we always want entire documents back, but it becomes clumsy if we want to pick out small subsets. For example, we might want all the speeches by Horatio in *Hamlet*.

2. The XML file can be decomposed into separate elements and each one stored as a separate row in a relational database. This method is rather complex but works well for some sorts of query. The problem is the overhead of reconstructing complex XML structures again (the text of *Hamlet* would be thousands of rows).

3. If the XML files are complex and static (a large linguistic corpus, perhaps), a fixed index to all the elements can be created. Such an index allows for fast querying of certain types and can be very efficient.

4. A dedicated XML database can be used. Typically, these are queried using the XPath language we saw in relation to XSLT. The big advantage is that there is no difference between retrieving the entire text of *Hamlet* and just a few lines from all Shakespeare plays, if a consistent query language is used. The problem is that XML databases are far less mature than big relational databases and present problems when it comes to updating portions of the tree.

TEI documents are likely to be fairly static but have complex, nested structures, so choices 3 and 4 are better to consider.

Xaira is an example of an XML database that works by preprocessing the input and building indexes. It provides an analytic view of a text, mainly for those interested in linguistic analysis, but it returns XML fragments that are styled under control of the user. Figure 8 shows a session with *Xaira*, selecting words that will be treated as variants of *fag*; figure 9 shows a concordance of *fag*; figure 10 shows the same concordance, but with XML markup visible.

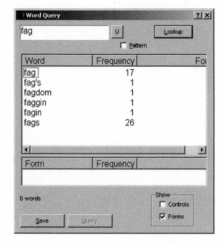

Fig. 8. *Xaira*, selecting similar words

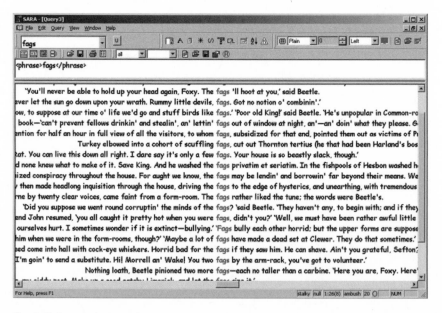

Fig. 9. *Xaira*, word concordance

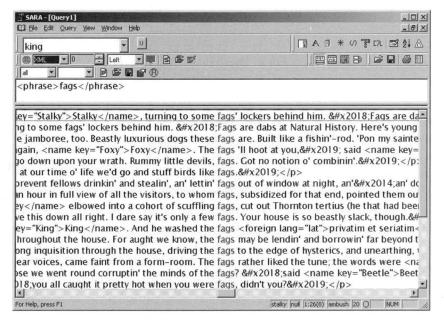

Fig. 10. *Xaira*, word concordance showing XML markup

eXist (the Apache Project's *XIndice* offers similar features) is an example of a dedicated XML database engine. It has no interface of its own but can talk to other programs or services using HTTP, XML-RPC, SOAP, and WebDAV. This feature makes it easy to deploy inside dynamic Web page systems, such Apache's *Cocoon*. The only job of the database is to return a well-formed XML tree that other applications can process. It is queried using XQuery or XPath expressions, with support for some small extensions to permit more-reasonable substring searches in element content. Examples of XPath queries follow, where the root is expressed with document and collection functions to identify a single document or named group of documents:

document('test.xml')//div   All <div> elements in document test.xml
collection('xx')//div; all <div> elements in all documents in the *demo* collection

```
collection('xx')//div[.//p[contains(.,'Hello')]]
```
All <div> elements that contain <p> elements containing the phrase "Hello"

```
collection('xx')//div[.//xref[@url='www.lexmark.co.uk']]
```
A <div> with an <xref> with a url attribute pointing to Lexmark

```
collection('xx')//list[count(item)>9]
```
Lists with more than three items

```
collection('xx')//div[starts-with(head,'Introduction')]
```
<div> elements with a title starting *Introduction*

```
collection('xx')//q[string-length(.)>100]
```
Quotations longer than a hundred characters

```
collection('xx')//person[.//surname[.='Keats' or
.='Shelley']]
```
<person> elements for Keats or Shelley

All these queries use standard syntax. *eXist* also supports some extra functions and operators that it uses to give efficient access to a full-text index, which it maintains in addition to the structural database:

```
collection('xx')//p[match(.,'[A-Z IED')]]
```
Paragraphs with words ending in *-ied*

```
collection('cem')//ab[near(.,'BOY YEARS',4) ]
```
<ab> elements with the words *boy* and *years* in a proximity of four words

```
collection('cem')//ab[.&='BORN IN ROME' ]
```
<ab> elements with the phrase "born in Rome"

```
collection('cem')//ab[.|='GOD LOVE' ]
```
<ab> elements with the words *God* or *love*

While these extensions are not necessary for most applications, they are likely to be relevant to TEI users.

We can see how *eXist* presents its results when we look at what comes back from the query against of *Stalky and Co.* of

```
//foreign[@lang='fr']
```

that is, all the words marked as <foreign> with the value fr for the lang attribute:

```
<?xml version="1.0" encoding="utf-8"?>
<exist:result
    xmlns:exist="http://exist.sourceforge.net/NS/exist"
      hitCount="19" queryTime="41">
    <foreign lang="fr"
        exist:id="12751728" exist:source="/db/kipling/
            stalky.xml"> aujourd'hui</foreign>
    <foreign lang="fr"
        exist:id="12751730" exist:source="/db/kipling/
            stalky.xml"> Parceque je</foreign>
    <foreign lang="fr"
        exist:id="12752720" exist:source="/db/kipling/
            stalky.xml"> langue de guerre</foreign>
    <foreign lang="fr"
        exist:id="12793848" exist:source="/db/kipling/
            stalky.xml"> Twiggez-vous</foreign>
    <foreign lang="fr"
        exist:id="12793938" exist:source="/db/kipling/
            stalky.xml"> Nous twiggons</foreign>
    <foreign lang="fr"
        exist:id="12799254" exist:source="/db/kipling/
            stalky.xml"> a la</foreign>
    <foreign lang="fr"
        exist:id="12804738" exist:source="/db/kipling/
            stalky.xml"> Moi</foreign>
    <foreign lang="fr"
        exist:id="12804740" exist:source="/db/kipling/
            stalky.xml"> Je</foreign>
    <foreign lang="fr"
        exist:id="12847398" exist:source="/db/kipling/
            stalky.xml"> Par si je le connai</foreign>
    <foreign lang="fr"
        exist:id="12866298" exist:source="/db/kipling/
            stalky.xml"> Je vais gloater</foreign>
</exist:result>
```

in which each result fragment is given extra attributes in the *eXist* namespace
identifying the source document and an internal identifier. These could be
easily transformed using an XSLT stylesheet to present them in any desired

way. Figure 11 shows two aspects of a Web interface to Shakespeare plays using *eXist*: the lower view shows the XML results of searching for speeches by Juliet; the upper view shows a complete retrieval of *Romeo and Juliet* formatted using XSLT.

Most XML databases suffer from the problem of the ineffective update of documents; adding in elements to a complex tree structure requires careful checking of constraints and rebuilding of indexes. The *XUpdate* proposal attempts to specify standard ways of managing updates. Another problem is making the extensions to XPath needed for fully effective database searching; the W3C *XQuery* solution is not yet fully accepted or dominant. It remains sensible to use text files as archival storage and use the XML databases for static presentation.

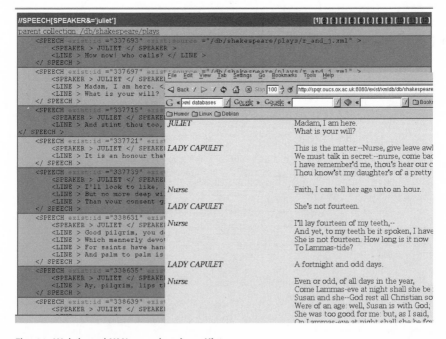

Fig. 11. Web-based XML search using *eXist*

The publisher of a TEI XML document has a wide variety of methods to access the data locked within. While any XML-aware software can do the job, we are also able to take advantage of a wide range of open standards, with commercial and open-source implementations. For transformation, typesetting, retrieval, and analysis, it is increasingly easy to use off-the-shelf packages.

NOTE

1. In this essay, example texts are mostly drawn from Rudyard Kipling's 1899 collection of stories *Stalky and Co.*

WHEN NOT TO USE TEI

JOHN LAVAGNINO

The Text Encoding Initiative guidelines describe an approach to transcribing texts for digital representation; if the principles underlying that approach seem appropriate for your scholarly project, then the next question is whether your texts are really the right kind of texts. Other essays in this volume discuss a number of common genres that are specifically covered, but this list is not exhaustive; the TEI did not intend to rule out any of the many sorts of text that interest scholars. That there are no essays in this volume or sections in the guidelines on encoding cookbooks, newspapers, guidebooks, quotation dictionaries, instruction manuals, commonplace books, or mail-order catalogs is not because they have been considered and found wanting; there just hasn't been space or occasion to discuss them specifically. For the most part these particular genres can be readily handled using the TEI's provisions for encoding prose texts, with the addition of some other elements for their distinctive features. If you are a scholarly editor of texts, then the TEI is applicable to your texts.

But scholarly editions involve the creation of new writing as well as work on existing texts: editions usually include introductions and commentary in some form and may extend to such things as analytic essays, catalogs of sources or witnesses, and bibliographies. The TEI guidelines apply just as well to creating new texts as to transcribing old ones, but other approaches may be a better choice for some highly structured collections of information. For example, the Encoded Archival Description (EAD) DTD is designed for archival finding aids, of the sort that an edition might create in the course of its work, and a finding aid in this form would be more useful to a library than a TEI-encoded description. Similarly, the Manuscript Access through Standards for Electronic Records (MASTER) DTD is specifically adapted for encoding descriptions of manuscripts; it is also based on the TEI DTD and indeed is now under consideration for incorporation into a future version of the TEI guidelines. A project that involves the creation of new software might choose to use the DocBook DTD for that software's documentation, as it is a DTD designed for that purpose and there are existing tools for using such information in ways that users of software need (Walsh and Muellner). There's good reason to adopt a practice that was developed for a specific kind of writing or scholarship and that produces encoded information that is as well documented and robust as TEI data; following such standard practices is likely to increase the utility of these specialized kinds of information.

Even if you've chosen the TEI for your project, there are further choices to make about exactly how you use it. Selecting the components you need remains important: your documents should not use every defined element. The existence of the <date> element does not imply the obligation or recommendation that every date in a text be tagged as such; some TEI elements are required in certain contexts, but a great many are optional, and it is intended that their use be left to the scholar's judgment. Extra markup is costly, so a project must decide just which features need to be marked in order to serve its scholarly ends. It is tempting to add markup that has no specific application but that might be of interest to someone in the future; but only the especially well-funded project can afford this luxury. Apart from the expense, it is worth considering how useful the encoded information will be to other scholars. Seeing the feature in question differently, they might want to develop their own encoding. Personal names, for example, may seem at first a straightforward category that requires little extra time to tag; but scholars who have worked on encoding personal names have found them to be hard to define and delimit (see Butler, Fisher, Coulombe, Clements, Grundy, Brown, Wood, and Cameron; Flanders, Bauman, Caton, Cournane; M. Neuman; McCarty; and Mikheev, Grover, and Moens; for more on the general point, see Driscoll's essay in this volume).

You will want to choose among the many ways that the TEI DTD allows you to encode features. Textual errors and corrections may be encoded using <sic>, <corr>, or <app>, for example. The work of encoding is simpler if the question doesn't need to be reconsidered every time the feature comes up. Some scholarly communities have developed their own guidelines for using the TEI guidelines, in which they specify a preferred way for handling features they often see or that are distinctive to their materials. If there is such a group in your area of work, it's a good idea to consider following its lead. (See for instance Mahoney's essay on epigraphy in this volume.)

The choice of elements needs to be based on their definitions in the TEI guidelines and not just on their names or brief descriptions: so the <l> element is for a line of verse (which might be displayed on several typographic lines) and not for a single typographic line on a page; <add> and <supplied> sound very similar but are for different things (the first for additions present in the documents you're working with, the second for additions by editors and encoders). Making such mistakes amounts to misdescribing the text. And if there isn't already a tag that can be used for what you need to describe, don't force an existing one into the role. Most projects will run into textual features that matter in their work but that aren't covered by the existing guidelines: section 1.3.2 of P4, "Future Developments," talks about some specific areas that are known to be incomplete, but generally there's plenty of territory that hasn't been covered. Extending the DTD to handle such features is the orthodox proceeding, and you should expect to have to do it. When a feature appears with some frequency, working out the details of an extension is not generally too difficult. Considering the array of examples helps reveal the general structure of the feature; the odd feature (such as a complex diagram) that appears only once or twice is harder to deal with, as generalization is harder. Depending on the needs of the project, it may be desirable to represent such unusual features with images instead of relying solely on transcription and tagging.

All these considerations have to do with the form to be taken by the ultimate products of a project, the final encoded files. But there are reasons for not using TEI at particular points during the lifetime of a project, even if a TEI product is still the result.

The most appropriate scholarly tools for the early, exploratory stages of a project may be pen and paper, or chalk and a large blackboard, or a word processor; some will find that the precision and formality required for TEI-encoded texts are not helpful at a stage when they may be entertaining many conflicting ideas about what sort of information will be in their edition and how it will be structured. Some may also find it more productive to start by thinking about ways in which the edition will be presented to its readers and not in terms of the information structures needed to achieve that presentation. Experience has shown that electronic texts closely tied to one mode of presentation tend to be short-lived. But thinking about an actual presentation to readers is still an effective way of working out what an edition will do, and in a later stage the design may be adapted for TEI encoding. The TEI guidelines certainly aren't about particular texts or the scholarly goals behind publishing them, but working out our thinking on those points is one essential stage in making an edition.

Scholars new to XML may find that devising a tagging system from scratch for their texts is instructive: you will understand a standard DTD in a different way after going through the intellectual labor of trying to create one. These explorations of an edition's form, or of its encoding system, can't go on for very long, since the resulting text is going to be hard to convert to TEI form: the explorations need to be seen as trials that can be thrown away.

During the main phase of work on a project, there may be reasons to create texts in a form somewhat different from the final one they'll take. Some projects have found that the very generic names of some TEI elements are a problem: though the existing elements are appropriate for the purpose, it may be easier to tell staff members to enter a `<stanza>` element rather than an `<lg type="stanza">` element. Such change in tagging is especially likely if the generic range of the texts is circumscribed, so that one encounters a restricted set of features. Devising a customized DTD for document creation (possibly just using the standard TEI customization mechanism) and converting the documents to a more standard markup at a later stage are reasonable measures, if the conversion can be readily automated. (At one time a version of this approach was often used: no TEI markup was used directly; instead, very specific ad hoc markup was invented—a system in which %, *, #, and other nonalphabetical characters had special meaning and were later expanded into proper markup. Circumstances have changed enough that this procedure usually isn't a good one: ad hoc systems run into problems expressing any but the simplest structures, and plenty of XML editors are now available that face no such limitation.)

The project that is well along in its lifetime and that was never TEI-based faces a difficult choice. Certainly there may be advantages to the switch, both intellectual and political, if the TEI approach is appropriate. But switching is always time-consuming and costly and will typically require some changes in thinking about the project's editorial approach. Projects that get completed are more valuable to the scholarly community than unfinished projects with better methodologies.

I have assumed so far the appropriateness of the TEI approach for your editorial project. But if the approach does not fit, it should not be used. Two of its requirements can be especially problematic: first, you need to understand your texts; second, you need to believe in the integrity and utility of selective transcriptions.

You need to understand your texts in order to translate them from stone or paper versions to digital versions. Even for the scholar with a knowledge of the language and script, there may still be difficult or ambiguous passages; unfamiliar conventions of layout raise problems as well. (See, for example, Cloud on headings in George Herbert's *Temple*; Hirst on little-known conventions of layout and markup that Mark Twain used.) There is less room in a digital edition for evading interpretive questions by printing something with an ambiguous appearance. To make an edition work as intended, it is generally necessary to interpret features and not merely reproduce their appearance.

To use the TEI approach you need to believe in transcription. It is impossible for a transcription to reproduce the original object; it is always a selection of features from that object: the words but not their size on the page or the depth of the chisel marks, major changes in type style but not variations in the ink's darkness from page to page or over time. Features that seem essential for a particular transcription can be encoded; what's impossible is notating everything. And it may be that the creation of a digital description of a feature has little value for analysis: what you really want may just be the opportunity to see an image of the original, if the limitations of digital images are less damaging in your case than the limitations of transcription. A transcription might be regarded more as an index of words in page images than as a reasonable working representation of the text in works intended as mixtures of words and images and in very complex draft manuscripts where the sequence of text or inscription is difficult to make out.

These two considerations about the appropriateness of the TEI approach apply to most systems of electronic transcription that an edition might consider. As scholarly editors we need to make specific claims about what the text is and communicate them clearly to others, and we are engaged in analyzing texts and creating new representations of them, not in creating indistinguishable replicas. But the TEI approach may not be right for a given project. Every project must take a particular view of the texts in question and choose particular scholarly goals; those decisions determine whether an edition based on transcription should be made.

MOVING A PRINT-BASED EDITORIAL PROJECT INTO ELECTRONIC FORM

HANS WALTER GABLER

L et us first recall how a print-based editorial project conceived in pre-computing times was organized, since even today, such projects, often large-scale and multivolume editions that were begun perhaps a generation or two ago, are still in operation. Project-specific editorial conventions and rules would have been developed for them. These were likely to be codified in editorial guidelines explicitly geared to traditional book production: the preparation of a comprehensive edition script as printer's copy; the reliance on publishers, editors, and professional book designers; the use of machine (or even manual) typesetting, proofreading, and conventional machine printing.

By contrast, let us imagine a print-based editorial project, begun after the introduction of the computer into the scholarly editor's study. Several of the preparatory operations for an edition are performed electronically. We can rely on the computer to assemble and store the edition script—that is, the text we are preparing—as well as the apparatus, the notes, the commentary, the introduction, and the indexes that go with it. Electronic tools have begun to modify the sequences, and perhaps even the internal logic, of the editorial task. For example, they can be used to ascertain the edition's accuracy. Verifying the data input already constitutes the principal round of proofreading; proofreading between typesetting and printing is no longer required, since that stage of the work process has become obsolete. Altogether, repeated proofreadings of the text of an edition are significantly reduced if not rendered altogether superfluous.

Similarly, the markup necessary for data input has particular consequences. On the one hand, it relates the input data to the source or sources from which they derive. On the other hand, it precodes the formatting of the book envisaged. Above all, the use of the computer alters the production process of an edition. The edition script will not be rekeyed in the printing house, as used to be done in traditional book production. In fact, the high standards of accuracy appropriate to scholarly editing demand that, once established electronically, the text not be rekeyed. But if and when the goal of a project is a printed book, its editors must now conceptualize the appearance of the edition in terms of typography and book design. As a corollary, they may find themselves in an easier position to produce the edition they imagine. Thus the dividing line between the respective domains of the scholarly editor and the professional publisher and printer as they previously existed has been fundamentally redrawn. Practically speaking, editor and publisher must agree on the format in which the edition in all its parts is to leave the editor's hands. Either the edition will be submitted as electronic data, not yet transformed into print through electronic typesetting, or the publisher will ask for camera-ready copy.

Not only the older type of precomputer project but also the more recent type, already computer-assisted in its preparation, must be defined as essentially print-based. To transfer a print-based editorial project into electronic form involves primarily consideration of how to make the project amenable to electronic processing and thus how to rework its editorial guidelines and practices in terms of computer aid. Transferring the more recent type of edition into electronic form amounts to divorcing it from the goal of the printed page and shaping, or reshaping, its electronically stored data in such a way as to enable consultation and study of the edition's several discourses—text, apparatus, notes, commentary, and introduction with its explication of the editorial rationale—via the computer screen. With the appropriate access software, the structuring and organization of the data of the edition should allow computer-based, question-and-answer interaction with the edition. In other words, the electronic medium, instead of being merely an aid in the preparation of a print edition, should become and be recognized and established as the proper site and natural environment for a scholarly edition.

It is useful to rehearse how a print-based editorial project might be transferred from a precomputer environment to a computer-based editorial practice, before focusing on what is involved in transforming a computer-assisted edition into one that is fully computerized. Before considering the electronic medium as the site most appropriate for a scholarly edition, through which it communicates and is communicated, we must account for the role of the computer as aid and tool in the making of an edition.

Designing a computer environment for an editorial project involves acquiring and coordinating computer hardware and software; inputting the data for the edition; structuring the editing work flow; and securing the stability of the results of the editing.

As regards hardware, there is a wide choice of standard, commercially available equipment. In addition to the computer unit itself with the standard peripherals of printer and CD-ROM burner, as well as a scanner of large capacity, a flat screen is an advantage, for ergonomic reasons, and to provide comfortable resolution for manuscript scans.

Software requirements are highly variable, and only a few basic considerations can be suggested here. For the input, scanning software should be able to cope with varieties of fonts and other typographic features. For data processing, the deployment of proprietary software must allow the data conversion without loss to standard ASCII, or to standard markup (such as HTML, SGML, XML).

In order to verify the input and carry out subsequent editing activities, text-processing software should have a capacity distinctly above that of a run-of-the-mill word processor. It should be particularly strong in collating, in text formatting and reformatting, and in administering and keeping a log automatically of a reference grid (e.g., reference numbering by page/[paragraph]/line/word, act/scene/speech/line/word, or chapter/paragraph/line/word). This stable reference grid should be trackable and recoverable through all editorial formatting and reformatting stages. At the final disposition of the editorial result into reference-linked blocks of text, notes, apparatus, and introduction, every reference and reference connection should be automatically generated and distributed.

For individual editing tasks, predesigned and custom-packaged software may be found useful and sufficient (e.g., the *Classical Text Editor*), but compatibilities should be carefully tested. Among systems as well as within systems, the option of interactive work on the screen should always be provided. At the same time, editors should never find themselves confined to screen and keyboard, to item-by-item surface progression through an edition (that is, they should not see, or be forced to use, the computer merely as a substitute for the typewriter). Every keystroke carries the chance of a miss, so keyboard interactivity can introduce as well as avoid error, and every correcting stroke also carries the chance of a miss. Text-processing software will prove its value by possessing powerful batch functions to automate batch-definable editorial operations and carry them out consistently.

What these operations might be is already part of the definition of the editorial work-flow structure. The editorial process, insofar as it provides an intellectual solution to given editorial demands, is independent of the computer. Yet deploying the computer as the editor's tool is likely to modify the process—for example, the proofing that is built into the verification of input by automatic collation. Collating two parallel inputs ensures a high degree of accuracy. Ideally, such a double input should be produced by separate agents or by different processes (e.g., one scanned in, the other keyed in). Where the making of an edition involves two or more versions, each input will result in the same verification effect: the differences revealed by automatic collation are due to input errors requiring correction, or else they accurately record genuine differences between the versions.

It is the collation of the verified input materials (the second collation in the work flow) that provides the textual variation that calls for editorial judgment and decision making. The crucial advantage of automatic collation is that it relieves editors of the task of wading through multiple records of text identity and allows them to concentrate on adjudicating among the variations. Furthermore, the use of the computer permits searches, to be built into the editorial work flow at will, for accuracy and consistency of text assessment and editing. These valuable auxiliary operations were either impossible or prohibitively arduous before the computer was used in editing. Automatic collation, together with coordinated formatting and referencing routines usually involving a third round of program activation, should also be capable of extracting, as well as formatting and correlating, the edition's apparatus and index sections.

The tasks of scholarly editing call for these kinds of computer assistance regardless of how the editorial results will eventually be presented—that is, whether they are made available as a book or through the electronic medium itself. Before its transfer into electronic form, a print-based editorial project must first be thoroughly cast to draw on computer assistance in the production process. The scholarly procedures for preparing an edition must be systematically designed for the computer, comprehensively applied, and rigorously carried out. This point needs emphasizing since, in terms of application and performance, the commonsense answer to particular local difficulties and special-case situations is still often, even in front of the computer screen, the intelligent shortcut. But in data processing, intelligence can be used only so long as it does not countermand the nonintelligent, as well as radically counterintuitive, procedural logic of the electronic medium. The essential prerequisite for realizing an edition in electronic form is that the computer operations that assist in the preparation of the edition, and as a consequence the electronic formatting and recording that result from them, be fully consistent in themselves, compatible with one another, and comprehensive.

Granted all this, the fundamental challenge offered by the transference of an edition into electronic form is rethinking the whole editing enterprise. The traditional emphasis of editorial endeavor has always been on production. The material nature of the printing process has encouraged us to conceive of the aim of editing in terms of that consummate artifact of cultural techniques, the book. Since we are thoroughly acculturated to the book, we perceive it as a commodity we know how to use, instead of reflecting on the modes of use implied in its sophisticated design and artful crafting. Scholarly editions in book form are assessed according to whether and how they fulfill the formal conventions of well-made editions, not for how aware they are of their inherent user potential.

Preparing editions to be realized, presented, and engaged with in the electronic medium requires that we define them from the user end and design them from the beginning with the widest possible range of uses in mind. Consider the lack of this awareness revealed by a number of enterprises from the current pioneer years of electronic text projects. These enterprises often refer to themselves (rightly) as archives or even libraries, and they tend to engage in (sometimes defensive) theorizing of the concepts of edition and editing. In so doing, they reflect a general need to reconceptualize the principles of the scholarly edition and the modes of scholarly editing. The electronic medium, then, specifically suggests that we reconsider the notions and practices of editing in relation to what purposes editions serve and how they are used. If we do not ask pragmatic questions about how users will deploy, or should be encouraged and guided to deploy, the computer in exploring a scholarly edition, we will not arrive at design solutions for the user interface, the port of entry into an edition's data and their structuring.

The user of a scholarly edition in electronic form must be clear that what is being supplied on a given CD-ROM or Web site is indeed an edition: it should announce explicitly what the edited materials are, what principles and methods have been brought to bear on them, and what the edition claims to have achieved. A discursive exposition is needed along the lines of the introductions customary in print-based editions.

The edition in electronic form will also be expected to provide an edited text. That expectation is carried over from print-based scholarly editing, and it is on the basis of this assumption that the essentials for computer assistance in the preparation of editions were outlined above. Much of the theorizing that has surrounded the archive- and library-type electronic text projects of recent years has questioned whether we need to edit for the electronic medium in the same ways that we edited in the traditional medium of print, engaging the editor's choice, critical judgment, and decision as the means of establishing the given edition's edited text. It is precisely on this issue that the various types of text projects in electronic form divide. The editor's responsible establishment and provision of an edited text in a comprehensive editorial enterprise define an electronic edition, just as they have defined every traditional edition in print. It is the incorporation of an edited text that distinguishes the electronic, or computer, edition from archives, libraries, or similar electronic text and document repositories.

At the same time, both the introduction and the edited text are parts of an edition that a user would expect, and be expected, to read as continuous material. That the electronic medium is not a particularly comfortable site for sustained sequential reading suggests the need for a double provision when an edition goes electronic. There have been a number of successful experiments with so-called hybrid editions in recent years. Such electronic editions also comprise a book component, in which their continuous texts remain presented in print form. The double provision is important: the printed sections must be included in electronic form as well, where they are incorporated not for the purpose of reading but hyperlinked for exploratory use, to correlate the whole range of discourses that the edition comprises.

In addition to edited text and introduction, there should be a textual apparatus and notes, which complement the text and report on variations in readings and versions. Commonly there is additional documentation relevant to the text and work, possibly incorporating images (facsimiles and digital scans) of the surviving witnesses to the processes of its composition and transmission. Further commentary and annotation might enlarge on content and interpretation. Lastly, to link these several discourses, editions are generally supplied with indexes and sometimes glossaries.

For the traditional print-based edition, this discursive conglomerate is structured in descending hierarchical order. The book, through which the edition's set of discourses is communicated, expects them to be organized on linear principles. We recognize that these discourses are correlated, but in the print-based edition, their correlation, except through the connections made by index and glossary, remains latent, supported at most by cross-referencing—and by the reader's and user's memory. It would surpass the capabilities of the book as medium to realize that networking of its discourses that a scholarly edition, as an intellectual construct, ideally demands.

Most opportunities provided by an electronic form to enhance a traditionally print-based edition do not arise from the electronic medium as an alternative to the book for presenting and representing continuous text: experience shows that it is generally a poor and always cumbersome alternative. Such opportunities lie, rather, in the potential that the electronic medium offers for networking the different elements of an edition—that is, for correlating and linking its entire range of tributary discourses. How such a network might be shaped and structured remains to be explored, a field of virtual resources unprospected. What it takes to transfer a print-based edition into electronic form can at present be expressed only negatively: a print-based project that aims to translate its print-oriented procedures one by one into computer-based routines clearly fails to utilize the full innovative potential of the electronic medium. From a linear and hierarchically structured product of scholarly effort, a print-based edition needs to be reconceptualized as a use- and user-oriented, relationally networked text database and electronic site for the exploration of knowledge. Only such a fundamental reconceptualization will create in its wake the required electronic techniques that we but rudimentarily possess at present.

RIGHTS AND PERMISSIONS IN AN ELECTRONIC EDITION

MARY CASE AND DAVID GREEN

I n undertaking a publishing project, whether in print or electronic format, the author-editor is immediately enmeshed in the world of copyright and contracts. From choosing the text to quoting from other authors to negotiating with a publisher, a scholar should have a basic understanding of copyright law and how contracts are used to manage the rights of creators, owners, and users of copyrighted works (see Abelman; Crews).

Most publishing contracts contain numerous clauses related to copyright, both the copyright of the author and the copyright of works used by the author. A contract often requires the author to transfer all copyrights to the publisher and to guarantee that the work does not infringe the copyright of others. The author must also agree to indemnify and reimburse the publisher for expenses incurred if a claim is made that the author has infringed a copyrighted work and the publisher is sued. The obligation to indemnify normally exists whether the claim is frivolous or not. The contract also requires the author to obtain permission for uses of works that go beyond fair use and to supply copies of each permission to the publisher. Given the responsibilities and exposure to liabilities placed on an author by a publishing contract, it is essential that authors understand copyright law even before they begin a project or negotiate a deal with a publisher. It is generally advisable for an author to engage a copyright lawyer to assist in this process.

While copyright law theoretically applies to works in all media, the details of the practical application of the law in the digital environment are hotly contested by copyright owners and users in the courts and the legislature. Copyright owners, concerned with the ease of reproduction and distribution of digital works, are seeking greater protection, while users are fighting to retain fair use rights, including those for education and scholarship. Publishing an electronic scholarly edition can provide the opportunity for a significantly enhanced research and learning experience, but it can also raise issues that place the author–editor at the center of this debate.

COPYRIGHT AND CONTRACTS

A Brief Review of Copyright Law

Copyright is a principle embedded in the Constitution of the United States. In article 1, section 8, the Constitution grants Congress the power "to promote the Progress of Science and useful Arts, by securing for limited Times to Authors and Inventors the exclusive Right to their respective Writings and Discoveries." The framers of the Constitution recognized the importance of new knowledge to the health and vitality of the nation and believed that discoveries are based on the prior research and scholarship of others. To achieve these goals, the Constitution gives Congress the authority to create incentives for authors and inventors by granting them a monopoly on their works, at the same time limiting that monopoly so that other authors and inventors will have the right to use and build on those works. Congress has implemented this limited monopoly through the granting of a set of exclusive rights and the establishment of specific limitations on those rights. These exclusive rights and limitations as applied to authors are embedded in Copyright law, which is contained in title 17 of the United States Code.

Copyright is a bundle of exclusive rights that automatically apply "in original works of authorship fixed in any tangible medium of expression . . ." (17 USC 102a, 2000). As soon as the original expression of a creator is fixed in any medium, it is protected by copyright. Covered by copyright are literary works; musical works; dramatic works; pantomimes and choreographic works; pictorial, graphic, and sculptural works; motion pictures and other audiovisual works; sound recordings; and architectural works (sec. 102a). Copyright protection does not extend to facts, ideas, concepts, procedures, and so on (sec. 102b) or to works of the government of the United States (sec. 105). Unpublished works, no matter where in the world they are created, are covered, as are published works created in the United States or in nations or states of a treaty partner (sec. 104).

The exclusive rights of authors are found in section 106 of the law. They are: to reproduce the work; to prepare a derivative work (e.g., a translation into another language, a revised edition); to distribute copies of the work to the public; to perform the work publicly; to display the work publicly; and, for sound recordings specifically, to perform the work publicly by means of digital audio transmission.

An important point to remember is that these rights belong initially to the original creator of the work. They can be transferred (or "assigned") in whole or in part to another party, usually through a contract (sec. 201). Hence the use in copyright law of the phrase "copyright owner" or "rights holder" as distinct from the author or creator. In the academic environment, some publishers require the exclusive and entire transfer of copyright as a condition of publication. But since these rights are divisible, an author can choose to retain and transfer rights in a variety of exclusive and nonexclusive arrangements. For example, an academic author could grant a publisher exclusive print reproduction and distribution rights but nonexclusive rights to reproduce, distribute, and display a digital version of the work. The management of copyrights is critical for authors to consider from the very beginning of a project. We address this issue in more detail below.

The exclusive rights granted to copyright owners are subject to limitations laid out in sections 107–21 of the Copyright Act. The most relevant to the creation of a scholarly edition is section 107, which addresses fair use. A concept critical to the scholarly enterprise, fair use permits reproduction of a copyrighted work "for purposes such as criticism, comment, news reporting, teaching (including multiple copies for classroom use), scholarship, or research." Not all uses in these categories are necessarily fair use. The statute lists four factors that must be considered in determining whether any particular use is a fair use: "the purpose and character of the use, including whether such use is of a commercial nature or is for nonprofit educational purposes; the nature of the copyrighted work; the amount and substantiality of the portion used in relation to the copyrighted work as a whole; and the effect of the use upon the potential market for or value of the copyrighted work." In quoting from the works of others or reproducing pages of a manuscript, an author must determine whether the use is a fair use or whether permission is required from the copyright owner.

Another important limitation on the exclusive rights of copyright owners is the term of copyright protection. Starting out at just fourteen years, copyright term has been extended many times by Congress, the most recent with the passage in 1998 of the Sonny Bono Copyright Term Extension Act, which added twenty years of protection.[1] In general, for works published from 1978 on, copyright protection now lasts for the life of the author plus seventy years (sec. 302a). For works made for hire and anonymous and pseudonymous works, the copyright term lasts ninety-five years from first publication or 120 years from creation, whichever comes first (sec. 302c). Works published in the United States from 1923 to 1977 with a formal notice of copyright[2] and still under copyright in 1978 have also had their terms extended as much as ninety-five years (sec. 303). Foreign works published during this time period may also still be under copyright even if they do not include a formal notice of copyright. A review of the Copyright Office information circulars[3] and a search of its registration records may be necessary to determine the copyright status of any work published between 1923 and 1977. Copyright term has expired for works published in and before 1922, which means they are now in the public domain. The publication date of a work and its copyright status are critical to knowing what uses an author can make of the work without having to seek permission.[4]

Authors working on scholarly editions may need to consult and reproduce unpublished manuscripts, diaries, and letters. These works are also protected by copyright. For unpublished works created after 1 January 1978, copyright term is the same as that for published works, the life of the author plus seventy years. Before 1978, unpublished works were granted a common-law privilege that lasted in perpetuity or until publication, at which time they became covered by federal copyright law. Congress ended this privilege with the Copyright Act of 1976, which brought the copyright term for unpublished works in line with that for published works. To help smooth the transition to this new term, Congress gave copyright owners until 31 December 2002 to publish their works, thereby extending the copyright term, or copyright would expire (sec. 303). In January 2003, the first of the unpublished works of American authors deceased for seventy years or more entered the public domain.

In October 1998, Congress updated Copyright law to take into account the digital environment (on rights in the digital environment, see Tadic). The Digital Millennium Copyright Act (DMCA) allows copyright owners to control access to their works through the use of such technological protection measures as passwords and encryption (sec. 1201). With very narrow exceptions, circumventing these measures without permission of the copyright holder is a federal offense. The law also includes a provision that makes it illegal to purposely remove, alter, or falsify any copyright management information that is associated with or contained in a work (sec. 1202). This information can include the copyright statement, title, author, terms of use, and so on. The new law also limits the liability of online service providers under certain circumstances for infringing activity by users of their systems (sec. 512).

In theory, the DMCA did not alter any of the aspects of copyright law discussed above, such as fair use and copyright term, which should apply to digital as well as printed works. But given the ease of copying and distributing digital works, copyright owners may be hesitant to grant permission for their use in a digital product. Or they may decide to charge a fee to make up for possible losses. Publishers of a digital work may be more conservative than they are in print, requiring permission for uses that would ordinarily be considered fair use. Similarly, college and university legal counsels are likely to urge authors not to use materials for which the copyright owner cannot be found and permission obtained.[5]

Implications for Scholarly Editions

One of the first things the editor of a scholarly edition must do is determine whether the work that forms the basis of the effort is still under copyright. It is generally safe to assume that anything published in the United States before 1923 is in the public domain—that is, the exclusive rights granted to the copyright owner have ceased. Anyone in the United States may now use the work without legal restrictions.

For works published between 1923 and 1978, the rules become more complex. But many more of these works are in the public domain than one might think. Unfortunately, there is not yet a convenient way to make this determination. If a work was published in the United States during this time frame and does not carry a formal copyright designation, it is likely in the public domain. For works with such designation, a search of the registration and renewal records of the Copyright Office is required. If the editor or a research assistant cannot make the trip to Washington to search the files, the Copyright Office will provide the information for a fee. The Copyright Office will not offer a legal opinion as to whether the work is in the public domain. A legal review is then necessary.

For works published outside the United States, obtaining legal advice may be a wise investment. While use of a printed work, no matter where it is published, is generally governed by the copyright laws of the country in which it is being used, the digital environment may add complications. Given the variation in copyright laws around the world, a work that is in the public domain in one country may not be in another. If your project makes publicly available on the Web a work that you believe to be in the public domain, you could be sued by the copyright owner under the laws of a country where the work was viewed or downloaded, for such infractions as copyright infringement (public display) or contributory infringement (if a user in that country makes an infringing use of the work you made available). This area of law is very unsettled in the digital age, and the advice of an attorney is essential.

If it is determined that the work is in the public domain, the editor may proceed to use the work, including digitizing it, displaying it on the Web, and publishing it, without seeking permission and without having to pay a fee. But you may find that many institutions holding public domain material will still charge a use fee (separate from any rights fee) to help defray their costs in preserving and making the material available. If the work is still under copyright, permission must be sought. In the permission process, it is important to anticipate the various uses that are to be made of the work so one does not need to go back to the copyright owner many times. As with many issues related to copyright, determining the copyright owner to begin with is not always a straightforward task; we address that process in the next section of this essay.

Compiling a scholarly edition will likely involve not only the basic literary work but also the works of other authors, previous editions of the author's work, critical essays, reviews, original manuscripts, letters, diaries, and perhaps even interviews with the author and screenplays. If any of these works are in the public domain, they may be quoted from or copied freely. If they are still under copyright, the editor must determine if the use of the material would be considered fair use. This determination requires an analysis of the four fair-use factors outlined above. Fair use applies to unpublished as well as to published works.

While fair use should apply in the digital world, there is still great uncertainty about its application (see the *Checklist for Fair Use*, compiled by the Copyright Management Center at Indiana University). Publishing a scholarly edition in an electronic format provides an opportunity for enhancing the work with features not possible in print: for example, a brief audio clip of an interview with the author or a film clip of the work as a screenplay. While limited quoting from these works for a printed scholarly edition would likely be considered fair use, a publisher may require the editor to obtain permission before incorporating such media clips into the electronic product. Because copyright owners now use technological means to search the Web to find unauthorized uses of their content, a publisher may be unwilling to expose itself to the cost of responding to potential claims, whether it believes the use is fair use or not.

With fair use a matter of judgment, reasonable people may come to different conclusions on any individual use. Most publishers and attorneys will tend to err on the side of conservatism and suggest that if there is any doubt that a use is fair use, permission should be sought. In the unsettled digital environment, they may be even more conservative and advise permission for obvious fair uses. Some in the educational community believe that if users do not invoke the fair-use limitation provided for in the copyright law, there is a good chance of losing it altogether. The author of a work has the responsibility both legally and financially to ensure that the work does not infringe the copyrights of another. If the author determines through a reasonable fair-use analysis that a particular use, such as the incorporation of a brief audio piece or a digitized copy of a few pages of a diary, is a fair use, the author should not be required to seek permission.

If a work is still under copyright and the use the author wishes to make of it is not fair use, then permission must be sought from the copyright owner. But there is no guarantee that the owner will be found. If the owner is found, there is no guarantee that permission will be granted. And, if permission is granted but a fee is charged, there is no guarantee that the author will be willing or able to pay it. In the electronic environment in particular, copyright owners may be extremely hesitant to allow their works to be digitized and incorporated into an electronic product for fear of losing control of the content. Authors must be prepared for the possibility that key works may not be usable beyond fair use.

The editor of a scholarly edition may also wish to include in the final product copies of the original manuscript, letters, diaries, or photographs of the literary author. While digitizing and publishing a single page of such material might be considered fair use, extensive reproduction, display, and distribution of it will require permission. Note that the owner of the manuscript, letters, or photographs (the owner could be a library, archive, or individual) may not have the copyright and be able to grant permission for use. Copyright law (sec. 202) provides for the distinction between ownership of a material object and ownership of its copyright. The transfer of ownership of an object does not convey ownership of the copyright unless the copyright is explicitly transferred as a part of the agreement.

Editors and Contracts

We turn now to the rights of an editor as the creator of a new work and how contracts are used to manage those rights. To begin with, if the underlying text is in the public domain, the publication of the scholarly edition will not create a new copyright in the work. If the underlying text is still under copyright, copyright remains with the copyright owner, and the copyright term is not extended. But the editor of a scholarly edition does bring much original work to the project, including the introduction, textual emendations, historical and critical essays, and—in the digital world—perhaps even programming for display and interactive tools. As soon as this editorial work or added content is "fixed in a tangible medium," it is protected by copyright. The author owns the copyright, which, as noted above, contains a bundle of rights that can be transferred or licensed in whole or in part to another party. This transfer usually takes the form of a contract, whether it is called a publishing agreement or a license of rights.

Publishers of scholarly works tend to request the exclusive and complete transfer of copyright, but there is no legal reason that an author has to accept this condition. Before signing any contract, authors should think carefully about the uses they would like to make of their own work. For example, the editor of a scholarly edition may envision multiple versions of a work—a printed volume and CD-ROM produced and distributed by a publisher and an openly available Web site hosted and managed by the editor's institution. In addition to acquiring permission for these various uses, the editor must make sure that any contract negotiated with a publisher does not inadvertently restrict the editor's rights to use the work as planned. An editor is well-advised to consult an attorney when negotiating a contract with a publisher.

Contracts are used in turn by publishers in making electronic works available to users, whether to individuals or to libraries. Generally referred to as licenses, these agreements lay out who can access a product under what conditions and what uses can be made of it. From the user and library's perspective, such licenses are often restrictive, prohibiting uses that would be allowable as fair use or by another exemption under copyright law. Since the courts are unsettled about whether licenses can preempt copyright law, libraries have actively negotiated with publishers to modify licenses to allow fair uses that would support education and research. You should think about what uses you would want to make of your product as a scholar and teacher. Then, as an editor, you should investigate a publisher's licensing practices before agreeing to publishing with it and insist that the license agreement that accompanies your electronic work allows for fair use and the uses you would expect.

THE PERMISSIONS PROCESS

Identifying the Copyright Owner

If it has been established that permission must be sought (because the material the editor wants to use is not in the public domain or its use cannot be considered fair use) or if the publisher insists that permission be obtained, the editor needs to know not simply who the copyright owner is but also, in many cases, who the owner is of the rights for the kind of use planned for the material—because rights can be assigned or transferred to others. This process can be long and involved, so it should not be left until the end of a project; otherwise it might delay publication.

Secondary Rights. Be aware from the outset that many copyrighted works themselves contain other copyrighted material for which separate permissions must be obtained for further publication or distribution.

Repositories. The repository that archives the material an editor is working on should be the first stop in the process of discovering the copyright owner. Sometimes the owner assigns copyright along with ownership of material when it is donated. But often the owner of the material and sometimes the archive may not understand that the ownership of the work and of copyright are separate. So it is important to ascertain that the archive itself knows whether copyright was assigned or not. If it was assigned, was the person who assigned it in fact authorized to do so? Did the creator of the work assign rights to a publisher, distributor, or other body? For motion pictures, songs, and some other properties, tracking down rights assigned or sold can be quite difficult.

Copyright Office. Owners of United States copyright works created before 1978 were required to register with the Copyright Office. Since 1978, registration is voluntary, although registration confers certain rights. Pre-1978 registrations can be checked in catalogs at the Library of Congress. Post-1978 registrations can be checked using either an older online system (LOCIS) or, since 2002, an experimental system (www.copyright.gov/records/). If one succeeds in finding the registrant, one must again determine whether the registrant still owns the rights or has assigned or sold them to another party. Because the Library of Congress catalogs do not include entries for assignments or other recorded documents, they cannot be used authoritatively for searches involving the ownership of rights. One can pay a search fee for library staff to conduct searches. For $75 an hour, as of 2005, Copyright Office staff members will search the indexes covering the records of assignments and other documents concerning copyright ownership. Search reports will "state the facts shown in the Office's indexes of the recorded documents but will offer no interpretation of the content of the documents or their legal effect" (*How to Investigate*). The Library of Congress has issued Circular 22, "How to Investigate the Copyright Status of a Work," to assist in this process.

Other Databases. The WATCH File (Writers, Artists, and Their Copyright Holders) is a database containing primarily the names and addresses of copyright holders or contact persons for authors and artists whose archives are housed, in whole or in part, in libraries and archives in North America and the United Kingdom. It is a joint project of the Harry Ransom Humanities Research Center at the University of Texas, Austin, and the University of Reading Library (http://tyler.hrc.utexas.edu/).

Collective Rights Societies. Collective rights societies help rationalize the permissions process by being licensed by individual copyright owners to deal with permissions. Societies tend to specialize in particular media. Especially if a work is part of a book or journal, the Copyright Clearance Center (CCC) is a good place to begin. If text material is not found at CCC, you could try the Publications Rights Clearinghouse, representing a wide variety of writers groups, from the National Writers Union to the Society of Children's Book Writers and Illustrators.

Visual Images. Although some artists handle their own permissions, many use licensing agencies such as the Artists Rights Society (www.arsny.com/) or the Visual Artists and Galleries Association (VAGA). Sometimes an organization might own publication rights but will assign digital reproductions to another agency (for example, the Ansel Adams Publishing Rights Trust owns rights to publish Adams photographs, while the commercial company Corbis has digital rights).

Audio. Should permission be required to use audio material, the editor should be aware of the possible need for several layers of permissions. In order to reproduce any music, the editor must have composition rights (for public performance), for which licensing organizations such as ASCAP (American Society of Composers, Authors and Publishers) and BMI (Broadcast Music, Inc.) act as clearinghouses; recording rights (for the recording to be used), obtained from the recording company (although rights often revert to the performer thirty-five years after release); and reproduction and distribution rights (for both the composition, handled usually by the Harry Fox Agency, and the recording, handled by the recording company). For recordings of the human voice, you must also think through the possible layers of copyright ownership. The sound archives should be the first source of information. The individual whose voice is recorded should be contacted if at all possible. Fair use also applies to sound recordings, and some would argue that streaming a sound file (rather than downloading it) would strengthen a fair-use argument.

Moving Images. There are no collectives for moving images, although RightsLine is a new entrant offering permissions software for the studios. Until recently, using movie clips was unrealistic because of limited bandwidth available to authors and editors. But as bandwidth increases, the distribution of movies will be increasingly possible. Currently, no two studios handle these issues in the same way. One author successfully dealt directly with the director of the film he wanted to use.

Foreign Collectives. The United Kingdom's Copyright Licensing Agency offers electronic and nonelectronic licenses for print works (www.cla.co.uk). The European Union is also pursuing several initiatives for solving the issues of multimedia rights clearance (see www.cordis.lu/econtent/mmrcs/verdi .htm).

Seeking Permission

Once you have verified who can give you permission, you must contact the parties and explain what you require permission for.

Your first contact should be to verify that the individual is fully authorized to give you permission for the use you require. Some publishers may require absolute assurance of authority to grant permission.

Beyond this, it is important to specify in your letter the precise use or uses for which you are seeking permission. Think through possible future uses too. In an attempt to simplify and rationalize the permissions process, some copyright-holding organizations are creating their own forms. These forms are useful to examine for the information a copyright owner is likely to need from you. See the sample Reproduction Request Form of the Art Museum Image Consortium (www.amico.org/use/reproRequest.sample .html); see also the sample letter on Georgia Harper's *Getting Permission* Web site (www.utsystem.edu/OGC/IntellectualProperty/permmm.htm).

You do not have to get permission in writing, but if you get verbal permission, make sure again that you carefully describe exactly what your use of the material will be and document your conversation with the rights holder. It would be advisable for you to send a confirming letter to the owner and ask for an initialed copy in return to ensure that the letter accurately reflects the agreement.

Seeking permission can be a lengthy and complex process, so consider copyright-related issues early in your project planning. If permission is not granted for materials that require it, you may need to seek alternatives. We encourage you to proactively exercise fair use in the republication of portions of material, but be prepared for risk-averse publishers who insist that permission be obtained. When identifying the source for permission to republish material, remember that the original copyright owner may have transferred rights to another party, so be prepared to spend time tracking down the owner of the rights you need. To expedite obtaining permission, examine sample letters and forms to make sure you give the precise information that the rights owner will need to consider. Remember also to think about future uses you may want for the material.

Be aware of your own rights under copyright law. As an author or editor of a compiled work you also have some copyright protection. Exercise your right to negotiate a contract. Publishers may have printed standard contracts, but authors should think through the uses they would like to make of their work before signing away all rights.

NOTES

1. Many in the humanities and library communities believe that copyright term has been extended beyond what the framers of the Constitution intended when they spoke of granting authors exclusive rights for "limited times." Several organizations from these communities submitted amicus briefs in support of a case (*Eldred v. Ashcroft*) challenging the constitutionality of the Sonny Bono Copyright Term Extension Act. The Supreme Court heard arguments in the case in October 2002 and ultimately upheld the act.

2. Before 1978, a formal notice of copyright was required, such as the © symbol with the year and copyright owner's name, and registration with the Copyright Office, for a work to receive copyright protection. The 1976 Copyright Act, which took effect in 1978, dropped these requirements; copyright protection now automatically applies to a work as soon as it is "fixed" in a tangible medium.

3. United States Copyright Office information circulars can be found at http://lcweb.loc.gov/copyright/circs/.

4. A chart that simplifies copyright term has been prepared by Laura N. Gasaway of the University of North Carolina Chapel Hill Law Library.

5. The United States Copyright Office is currently examining possible legislative, regulatory, or other solutions to the problem of orphan works—copyrighted works whose owners are difficult or even impossible to locate. For the latest information, consult www.copyright.gov/orphan/.

COLLECTION AND PRESERVATION OF AN ELECTRONIC EDITION

MARILYN DEEGAN

THE PRESERVATION OF EDITIONS

The world of electronic editing is a new one, and it will take time for standards and practices to settle down and become part of the established world of scholarship. The book has developed over five hundred years, the print edition has been evolving over the past 150 years, and electronic tools have been used to assist in editing for perhaps fifty years. The reconceptualization of the edition as an innovative electronic artifact has happened only over the last ten to fifteen years, so the librarians charged to acquire, deliver, and preserve this most important of scholarly tools are facing new challenges. In this essay I discuss what the different issues are in preserving electronic editions, some of which derive from the newly conceptualized modes of instantiation of electronic text, and offer some suggestions to scholars that should enable them to take the necessary steps from the beginning of an editorial project in order to ensure that what is produced is preserved to the extent possible.

Electronic editing offers a plenitude of materials that represent a work in all its different states of being. It also allows the situation of a work in a nexus of social, contextual, and historical materials, all of which contribute to the totality of its meaning. The electronic edition is itself another version of the text, one that in many cases, especially when an archive approach is taken, seeks to encompass all other versions. But it is merely another witness in the life of a text, not the final witness, and must be preserved in some form as that witness. The fluidity of the medium of creation and delivery is in a sense antithetical to that preservation, however, because preservation, being an act of fixity, may create what an editor has been trying to avoid: the text frozen at a point in time. What are editors, publishers, and librarians to do with the conundrum of preserving for scholars of tomorrow the fluid text of today? I look first at how conventional printed editions are preserved by libraries, then discuss how this preservation changes in the digital world.

Preserving Traditional Editions

Collecting and preserving conventional printed editions present few problems to librarians that they have not already been grappling with for many years. The problems that print editions present all derive from the physicality of the medium used to deliver them. They may be old and rare, in need of careful handling, controlled storage, conservation, and so on. Nineteenth-century editions may be printed on acid paper that is disintegrating into yellow crumbs or may have pages coming loose from bindings. Such editions can be repaired, or their contents can be reformatted onto another medium: microfilm, photographic facsimile, a new print volume. Reformatting raises questions about the authenticity of the material object, but the alternative might be total loss of the object and its valuable contents. Librarians are concerned mostly with the format and construction of the material object, the carrier of the content. They are not usually concerned about the content itself, other than to be able to describe it bibliographically and store it logically, so that users can access it. In the analogue world, at one level of abstraction, the physical format—the carrier—*is* the edition and all that libraries and librarians need to know in order to collect and preserve it. They are concerned, in Kathryn Sutherland's terminology, with the vehicular rather than the incarnational form of the edition (23).

In the analogue world the editor's roles and responsibilities in relation to the longevity of the work are clear. Editors are little concerned with the format or composition of a carrier, unless they are involved to some degree in font choice, cover design, and so on. Most responsibilities of editors end on the day of publication, by which time they may already be engaged in a new piece of work. The responsibility of publishers is to produce a printed volume that contains the edition, ensuring as far as possible the quality of its scholarship. This process is complex, involving many different tasks and subtasks of selecting, advising, reviewing, revising, copyediting, typesetting, proofing, designing, printing, marketing, and disseminating. Ongoing responsibilities might include reprinting or publishing a new edition, but any role in the long-term survival of the product is minimal. When an edition is out of print, it is usually unobtainable from the publisher. It is not for the editor or publisher to ensure continuing access: that task rests with libraries, especially the copyright and major research libraries. Copyright libraries receive a copy of every publication produced in a country in any one year, so a published edition that is out of print and unavailable anywhere else will almost certainly be locatable in a copyright library somewhere, even if it is more than a hundred years old. That edition should be perfectly usable and accessible, even if created according to principles different from what the user expects: it should be self-describing and contain all the explanation needed for its use.

Preserving Editions in a Digital Context

In his foreword to this volume, G. Thomas Tanselle suggests that the format in which books are delivered is irrelevant: "The use of the computer in editing does not change the questions, and the varying temperaments of editors will continue to result in editions of differing character." This irrelevance may be true for editors, and it may also be true for users of editions, but it is not true for publishers producing or libraries collecting and preserving electronic editions: for them the changes are profound, far-reaching, and the economics of how these works are produced and handled must be completely rethought. Previously, these "varying editions" would all have been treated in much the same way by both publishers and libraries. Even a uniform series of texts with a strict style guide, unchanging livery, and immutable type style can have very different kinds of editions within it. In the Early English Text series, for instance, which has existed for a century and a half, you will find very different contents underneath the brown covers: Julius Zupitza's facsimile of *Beowulf*, Hubert Jan De Vriend's edition of the Old English *Herbarium*, and D. G. Scragg's edition of the Vercelli Book are all totally different, as befits the nature of the source materials and changing editorial practices. But to the librarian such variation presents no problem: the editions can all be lined up together on the shelf, a nice neat series, as uniform as a parade of chocolate soldiers. They can be cataloged, described, borrowed, read: the early volumes from the 1860s just as easily as the most recent. For the publisher, there may be issues of different sigla to represent, alternative page layouts, different fonts, and so on, but these details normally cause few problems and entail no major rethinking of what the edition or the series is.

Tanselle goes on to say that editors working in the electronic world need to "confront the same issues that editors have struggled with for twenty-five hundred years." Again, he is right, but if their work is to survive beyond even the next five years, serious thought must be given at the start about how to create the edition in such a way that libraries can collect and preserve it alongside many other electronic and conventional editions for the benefit of scholarship in the long term as well as for users of today—a question that scholars never have had to consider before. While the traditional questions are still being asked, the plenitude of new possibilities in the electronic medium means that new questions will be asked too. In an edition of William Butler Yeats's poem "The Lake Isle of Innisfree," should the editor include the early recording of the poet reading the work? Is that recording to be considered part of the poet's output in relation to the poem? Should the song settings for "Innisfree," written later, be considered as part of the edition? How should all these materials be linked? What about including radio or film performances of plays in editions of dramatic texts? In this new world, the limits are not what will fit on the page or between the covers. The new constraints are time and money; with a sufficiency of both, the technology will allow us to go as far as our imagination leads.

For scholars contemplating embarking on an electronic textual edition, the first place to look for advice about creating a preservable edition is the CSE guidelines. If scholars can answer yes to all those questions under "Electronic Editions" in this volume's "Guiding Questions for Vetters of Scholarly Editions" that apply to their projected work, they are well on the way to producing a durable resource. The rest of this essay expands on some of the issues raised by the guidelines.

WHAT ARE THE ISSUES?

Two of the key questions the guidelines ask of potential editors are, "How important is permanence or fixity? How can these qualities be obtained?" and "Is there a possible benefit to openness and fluidity?" These points are crucial but in some ways contradictory. Openness and fluidity are significant benefits that the digital world offers to editors, and many of the contributions in this volume discuss projects that have no final point of publication of the edition or any of its parts. Some of the editions are purely networked, and it is anticipated that these will grow and change over time. Indeed, in this volume Dirk Van Hulle suggests that publication is a "freezing point," an exercise in petrification. He is talking not about edited texts but about some of the fluid published texts of Samuel Beckett's oeuvre, but this observation applies to edited as well as authored texts. Fluidity in editing can cause serious problems at the same time as it conveys many benefits. As the editors of the current volume suggest, "The scholarly edition's basic task is to present a reliable text: scholarly editions make clear what they promise and keep their promises." It is also vital to provide a stable text. Of course, there is much debate about what is meant by reliable or stable: what is meant here is that a reliable text is created according to principles that are made explicit and is based on witnesses that can be accessed by others; a stable text is fixed at some particular point in time in some known state and not changed later without those changes being explicitly recorded. This second requirement, regarding later change, is much more difficult to ensure in an electronic context, especially in a networked environment.

Fluidity can be a strength for an editor, who can adapt and change the edition as new information comes available, but a weakness for a user who may not know what changes have been made and for a librarian who needs to deliver and preserve the materials: what version of a text becomes the preservation version? Instability of citation is a critical problem; research and scholarship are based on a fundamental principle of reproducibility. If an experiment is repeated, are the results the same? If a citation is followed by a scholar, does it lead to a stable referent, the same that every other scholar following the citation is led to? If not, then we do not have scholarship, we have anarchy, and it is an anarchy that is aided and abetted by the Internet.

When planning electronic editions, one should establish standards and working practices that make them interoperable: able to exchange data at some level with other systems. These other systems might be other editions, library catalogs, databases, dictionaries and thesauri, and many other kinds of relevant information sources, those that are currently in existence and those that may appear in the future. Interoperability is difficult to achieve, and the digital library world has been grappling with it for some time. Editors should not strive to ensure the interoperability of their editions but make editorial and technical decisions that do not preclude the possibility of libraries creating the connections at a later date. We cannot expect more of editors at our current state of knowledge.[1]

It will take time for principles and practices to be established that ensure the longevity of electronic scholarly editions, and those principles and practices will need to be much more precise in many ways than those that are needed for the production of conventional editions, elaborate and precise though these already are. The underlying scholarly practices are much the same, as many of the essays in this volume make clear; it is the technical issues that need to be resolved. The resolution is difficult, because at the moment electronic editing is characterized more by innovation, experimentation, and new developments than by established practices—that is what makes it so exciting. Electronic scholarly editing is also caught up in the world of hardware, software, applications, and standards, which change with dizzying speed. An editor is caught between taking advantage of all these new developments and trying to ensure that the work survives for the long term.

Preserving Digital Data

Digital data are being preserved by libraries and other memory institutions in different ways.[2] This field is new and changing, and there are differing views on the best methods of preservation, especially in the preservation of fast-moving online data. There are Web sites, for instance, that change not every day but every minute: news sites, sport sites, and so on. We may be tempted to think that electronic editions are unlikely to change this rapidly; a glance in the pages of this volume should disabuse us of this notion. Take for instance the editions of poetry discussed by Neil Fraistat and Steven Jones, who suggest that electronic editions of poetry might offer a "potentially infinite expansion of the traditional editorial apparatus" and that users might be able to have their own customized version of an edition, based on their behavior while interacting with the materials. They also suggest that an important feature of online poetry could be the contextural relation of multiple texts on the Internet in hyperlinked clusters, where the poem interacts with many other kinds of information. In all this experimentation and innovation, it is sometimes difficult to know what at the core of a complex, ever-changing edition can be collected and preserved by a library.

The preservation of digital data has two main components: preserving the integrity of the bits and bytes and preserving the information that they represent. The first is a matter of preserving the physical media on which the digital data are recorded (CDs, DVDs, hard drives, tapes, disks, etc.) and moving them to new formats if there is suspicion that the medium is compromised in some way or if the means of accessing the material is in danger of becoming obsolete: CDs are reported to have a life span of hundreds of years, but CD drives will be obsolete long before this. The process is known as refreshing: the bit stream is not altered in any way, just moved to a different medium. As the software that created the information becomes obsolete, the information becomes more and more difficult to access unless it is stored in some future-proof format or reformatted. Reformatting means that the information must migrate to a new version of hardware and software, and it could be changed or damaged in the process, especially if moved through more than one generation of software or to completely new software. Reformatting might need to be done many times in the life of a digital object, as hardware and software change. Other methods that are being contemplated for digital preservation are: preserving the hardware and software, which could be expensive and is problematic (though some data archives still maintain old card readers, because there is still much information around on punch cards that it would be too expensive to move to another system); emulation—building hardware or software that can run obsolete programs and data; data archaeology—preserving and documenting the bits and leaving it to future scholars to work out what they mean. Every method of digital preservation has its costs, and many of the costs are unknowable. National copyright libraries are currently grappling with these problems as they collect more and more publications that now have no print equivalent.

A new approach to the preservation of complex digital data is being explored by the University of Virginia and Cornell University, together with other academic partners: the Fedora project (flexible extensible digital object repository architecture), one of a number of repository architectures that have been proposed for use in digital libraries.[3] The architecture of complex electronic editions must be planned carefully for many reasons, preservation being only one of them, and some cognizance of repository architectures could be useful for editors. Fedora is of particular interest, because it proposes new ways of reasoning about digital data, based on data objects and their behaviors rather than on the essential nature of the data. The Fedora work at Virginia was initially started as a practical response to the preservation of complex digital data being produced by research centers in the university and its library like IATH (Institute for Advanced Technology in the Humanities), much of which derives from electronic editing projects like the *Blake Archive* and the *Rossetti Archive*. The library was faced with the long-term support of objects in all media, including much born-digital data. No system existed to allow libraries to provide such mixed-media support, so the university established a digital library research and development group, which soon realized the potential of the Fedora theoretical model. Fedora was originally proposed by Carl Lagoze and Sandra Payette at Cornell University to solve some problems of the interoperability of digital objects and respositories (Payette, Blanchi, Lagoze, and Overly). Fedora is in the process of development but shows great promise in elucidating the problems of and proposing solutions to the long-term survival of complex editions.

A number of projects are looking at the problems of preserving information on Web sites. The Web is the largest and most prolific source of information that has ever been, and much of that information can be lost if not actively preserved. Initiatives at a number of national libraries that are concerned about the possible loss of considerable portions of the national heritage now being produced in online form (the Library of Congress, the British Library, the National Library of Australia, the National Library of Sweden, among others) are looking closely at the long-term preservation of Web sites. The volumes of data to be stored are enormous; it is impossible to preserve every state of a Web site as a library might preserve every edition of a book. Some projects aim to harvest Web sites every six months and preserve them for historic purposes.

Many of the experiences in the preservation of Web sites offer insights into the preservation of networked editions. For instance, if a networked edition has many links to sources of information outside the control of the editors, these links will be highly vulnerable. Link checkers can automatically report a link is broken and information missing, but rarely can anything be done except to remove the link. Another interesting Web-harvesting initiative is the *Internet Archive* (www.archive.org), which has taken a snapshot of the World Wide Web every two months since 1996 and created the *Wayback Machine* to give access to former states of Web sites, making it possible to search more than ten billion Web pages ("Bibliotheca"). Try it on your favorite Web site and see what problems this throws up.

What Are Editors to Do?

There is a real tension between the new possibilities offered by the electronic edition and the need to preserve the scholarly record. As Morris Eaves points out in discussing the *Blake Archive*, "We plow forward with no answer to the haunting question of where and how a project like this one will live out its useful life." The TEI itself was established to address many problems, but just using the TEI for preparing text will not solve them: there are many more issues than which text-encoding scheme to use. Each electronic medium has its own problems: handling, long-term storage, format, markup, the maintenance of highly prolific often unstable links.

In the past a threefold distinction was made among data, programs, and interface. It is useful to discuss that distinction here, though Fraistat and Jones warn us against the "venerable dichotomy that divides the digital world into opposing demesnes, one focused on the front end . . . and one on the back end"; for them, editors in the digital world (especially editors of poetry) need to consider the appearance of texts on particular interfaces in their decisions about editing and markup. This need is echoed by Kevin Kiernan, who opines that "providing an effective, easily understood, graphic user interface . . . is always an important issue in an electronic edition." We might expand the distinction to a fivefold one: data, metadata, links, programs, and interface. The first three contain the intellectual capital in an edition; the last two are (should be?) external. However important the programs used to create and deliver the edition and however important the interface through which it is accessed, scholars must always remember that these parts of any electronic edition are the least durable; they must plan for the design and formatting of their intellectual assets in such a way that those assets can be reused with different programs and interfaces. Easier said than done.

What do we mean here by data, metadata, and links? Data are the raw material deriving from the source itself and can be text, images, sound files, video, and so on. Metadata are added symbols that describe some features of the data. Links are strings of code that connect pieces of data to other pieces of data—either internal or external to the source. Throughout this volume, the metadata of most concern are textual markup, in particular TEI markup, but an editor may use other kinds of metadata in an electronic textual edition, some of which are discussed by John Lavagnino. It may be that the TEI is not the best metadata system to use for nontextual materials that form part of a textual edition. The TEI system is excellent for describing logical objects; there may be other metadata standards that are more useful for describing physical objects. Lavagnino suggests that encoded archival description (EAD) might be better at describing the highly structured collections of data that make up an edition, and METS (the Metadata Encoding and Transmission Standard) is being used a great deal by libraries in a digital preservation context for describing and encapsulating the structure of digital objects.[4]

Creating Preservable Assets

A number of approaches can be taken to the creation of editions that will survive for the long term. One relatively straightforward approach is to produce a fixed edition on some stable medium at regular stages in its life, as is being done for *The Cambridge Edition of the Works of Ben Jonson*, described by David Gants. The plan is to produce simultaneously a six-volume traditional edition and a networked electronic edition that will grow and change as scholarship develops and "distribute editorial power among the users." The reliable and stable text that it is so important to establish will be at the core of a conventional edition but also at the center of a highly fluid, "rhyzomatic" network of hypertext links. Fixing the text in one form and therefore being assured of its stability may permit more experimentation in the electronic medium. It will be interesting to see in what way and over what period the editions diverge and at what point the need for a new printed edition will be felt—if ever.

While this volume deals primarily with electronic textual editions, such is the power of the medium that other media can be included, which all must be created according to standards and stored in a format that is nonproprietary and well supported. Eaves observes that editors of multimedia editions should double-edit: edit first in discrete, then in integrated media. This approach makes editors think hard about what the different components of an edition are likely to be. It also helps editing in teams: different team members can prepare different parts of an edition, which can be integrated later. Indeed, such integration might point to how one should conceive of an edition's components first; work out how to capture, describe, and store them; and then determine what the links among them might be.

Applying Data Standards

The TEI has brought to the world of textual editing a standard that is durable yet flexible. Standards must change to reflect new knowledge as well as new technical possibilities, but they are useful only if they have a predictable path of change. This volume suggests how editors need to think about their work. Editing projects must create, encode, and describe their component materials according to the most robust standards available. These standards, different for different media types, must be compatible and interoperable within the project and allow for the later possibility of interoperability with other resources.

For text, the ASCII standard should always be used, with markup added that is also in ASCII. There has been great progress in the presentation of special characters through the Unicode standard, but it is preferable that characters be encoded as entity references that can be displayed in Unicode than encoded as Unicode itself: for historical reasons, some characters have multiple representations, and there are languages, ancient or Asian, that do not yet have full Unicode support. The TEI is the markup system of choice for most electronic editing projects today. One decision to make is whether markup (TEI or any other kind) should be embedded in the text or offset (sometimes called standoff markup)—that is, stored in a separate file. The advantage of embedded markup is that the text file is complete in itself: when you have the file, you have everything that is known about it—all dates of revisions, records of people who have worked on it, and so on. But TEI markup can be used to describe many different features of a textual object; such description may result in a highly complex file. Some projects are now experimenting with offset markup, arguing that the text file can be kept in a more pristine state (and therefore be a more preservable textual object) and that different kinds of markup can then be kept in separate files, all pointing to the original text file. The only markup that the text file would then hold is locational information that the offset files can use to point to the correct parts of the text. Phill Berrie, Paul Eggert, Chris Tiffin, and Graham Barwell in the volume feel that this approach maintains the authenticity of a text file across different platforms, clearly a desideratum for the preservation of text. This approach is also taken by the ARCHway Project at the University of Kentucky, which is dealing with complex manuscript traditions that need markup to describe paleographic features and physical attributes of a manuscript (collation, damage, etc.). They separate out the markup for different features into a number of DTDs, a system that is clear, concise, and easy to maintain (see Dekhtyar and Jacob).

Image data should be captured at the best quality possible to reveal all significant information about the original, then stored in a nonproprietary file format using only lossless compression (if compression is used at all). The process differs depending on the source materials: modern printed documents might yield everything they have to offer when scanned bitonally at 300 dpi (dots per inch) and stored as (for example) TIFF images with lossless compression. Such images can be stored for the long term and will yield up all the information necessary now and in the future. Complex and perhaps damaged manuscript materials need different treatment: they may be captured with the best systems currently available, at the highest possible resolution, and stored as archival masters (currently TIFFs with no compression); then lower-quality surrogates may be made available for access. That such original images, scanned with current professional digital cameras, can be up to 350 MB each in size poses huge storage problems for projects and libraries. It is vital to consider from the start what storage requirements a project has, then double or even treble this to take account of all the extra files that will be produced along the way: delivery images, thumbnails, text files, metadata, and so on. Think too about the networks that will have to move all this material around and about the backup media that will also be needed.

Audio-and-video data are even more difficult to store, being more memory-hungry than still images. Uncompressed high-quality video, for instance, has file sizes of around 28 MB per second. Audio and video standards are currently moving very rapidly because of commercial developments in the offering of streaming audio and video over the Internet. Any standards suggested here would be out-of-date immediately; projects should take the best expert advice that they can at the outset in order to establish formats and standards.

The long-term prospects of electronic editions are also affected by the naming conventions used. A complex editing project will likely produce many thousands of files that need to be kept track of. These files may be kept in different locations that change over time. File-naming conventions should be devised and documented at the early stages of project. Having names assigned automatically can reduce human error and make batch renaming simpler and more reliable later on. Bar codes, hashing functions, and databases can all be used for assigning file names. File locations are often problematic: a URL is notoriously prone to difficulties; and some other way of indicating location should be found to avoid the dreaded "Error 404: FILE NOT FOUND." Work is being done on alternatives to URLs. Uniform resource names (URNs) identify a piece of information independent of its location: if the location changes, the information can still be found. One type of identifier that has been adopted by a number of publishers is the digital object identifier (DOI). DOIs are persistent names that link to some form of redirection; a digital object will have the same DOI throughout its life, wherever it may reside. DOIs must be registered with an agency in order that the redirection process can operate, but they offer good long-term prospects for digital object naming.[5]

All these suggestions assume standards and conventions to be used when the discrete components of an electronic edition are produced, but the whole point of editing in this new format is the introduction of complexity in the interrelations among the many subparts of an edition, and it is this complexity that is the most challenging problem in preserving electronic editions. It is created mostly by the exponential growth of links; in editions of even short works there can be millions of links created. Sometimes this interlinking is managed by programs and interfaces—the most vulnerable part of an edition. But one need not rely on programs and interfaces to provide linking capability: the TEI specifies a number of mechanisms for the description and markup of links (Sperberg-McQueen and Burnard, *Guidelines for Electronic Text Encoding*, ch. 14), and the World Wide Web Consortium (W3C) has defined the XML Linking Language (XLink) and the XML Pointer Language (Xpointer) for the specification of complex links (see www.w3.org/TR/xlink). The problem with using these specifications is that there is more of a learning curve when linking is done through pointing and clicking in various kinds of authoring software. But for long-term security, links must be separated from programs.

Finally, the most important thing an editor can do to ensure the development of preservable editions is to consult widely with experts in digital preservation, metadata, digital file formats etc, and with other editors who have been grappling with the same problems. Anyone who has read this far in this volume is well-equipped to begin an editing project with most of the tools they need at their fingertips.

NOTES

1. For more information on interoperability, a useful resource is the Interoperability Focus, based in UKOLN (United Kingdom Office for Library Networking), at www.ukoln.ac.uk/interop-focus/.

2. For an introduction to the issues around digital preservation, see Deegan and Tanner; see also the National Library of Australia's PADI (Preserving Access to Digital Information) Web site at www.nla.gov.au/padi/. In the United States, the Library of Congress has a Digital Preservation Directorate at www.loc.gov/preserv/digital/dig-preserve.html, and OCLC has a Digital and Preservation Resources Cooperative with outreach services to provide training and awareness in preservation issues (www.oclc.org/preservation). In the United Kingdom, the Digital Preservation Coalition was established in 2001 to promote national awareness of the issues (www.dpconline.org).

3. For a description of Fedora and other repository architecture projects, see Staples and Wayland; Staples, Wayland, and Payette.

4. For more information about METS, see www.loc.gov/standards/mets.

5. For more information about DOIs, see Paskin. The EU-funded DIEPER project did some useful work on persistent identifiers in the context of digitized periodicals (see http://gdz.sub.uni-goettingen.de/dieper/).

NOTES ON CONTRIBUTORS

Graham Barwell has collaborated on electronic editing projects with Phill Berrie, Paul Eggert, and Chris Tiffin since 1993. He is based at the University of Wollongong, where he teaches communication and cultural studies and English studies.

Phill Berrie created the JITM (just-in-time markup) system at the University of New South Wales and has been involved with the Australian Scholarly Editions Centre, working on grants to develop further the software and projects created with it.

Lou Burnard is assistant director of Oxford University Computing Services and has been European editor of the Text Encoding Initiative since 1990. His expertise ranges from corpus linguistics to markup technologies.

Dino Buzzetti is associate professor of the history of medieval philosophy at the University of Bologna. He works on the critical edition, in digital form, of medieval texts, devoting special attention to textual fluidity in manuscript textual traditions.

Mary Case is university librarian at the University of Illinois, Chicago, and was director of the Office of Scholarly Communication of the Association of Research Libraries. She has coordinated programs and workshops on copyright and the licensing of electronic resources.

Greg Crane, professor of classics and Winnick Family Chair in Technology and Entrepreneurship at Tufts University, is editor-in-chief of the Perseus Project and author of *The Ancient Simplicity: Thucydides and the Limits of Political Realism* (1998).

Marilyn Deegan, director of research development in the Centre for Computing in the Humanities at King's College London, coauthored (with Simon Tanner) *Digital Futures: Strategies for the Information Age*. She is editor- in-chief of *Literary and Linguistic Computing*.

M. J. Driscoll, lecturer in Old Norse philology at the Arnamagnæan Institute, University of Copenhagen, has edited and translated early Icelandic works and is author of *The Unwashed Children of Eve: The Production, Dissemination, and Reception of Popular Literature in Post-Reformation Iceland* (1997).

Hoyt N. Duggan is professor of English at the University of Virginia and director of SEENET and the Piers Plowman *Electronic Archive*.

Patrick Durusau is author of *High Places in Cyberspace: A Guide to Biblical and Religious Studies, Classics, and Archaeological Resources on the Internet* (1998). He is coeditor of *Topic Maps Reference Model* (ISO 13250–5), chair of the United States Technical Advisory Group to ISO/IEC JTC1/SC34, and has been on the TEI board of directors.

Morris Eaves, professor of English at the University of Rochester, is coeditor of the *William Blake Archive* with Robert N. Essick and Joseph Viscomi. He is author of *The Counter-Arts Conspiracy: Art and Industry in the Age of Blake*. He has served in various capacities on the MLA Committee on Scholarly Editions.

Paul Eggert is director of the Australian Scholarly Editions Centre and professor of English at the University of New South Wales, Canberra. He has edited titles for the Cambridge Works of D. H. Lawrence and the Academy Editions of Australian Literature series.

Eileen Gifford Fenton is executive director of Portico, an archive that ensures the long-term preservation of and access to scholarly literature published in electronic form. She has been director of production at *JSTOR*.

Julia Flanders is director of the Women Writers Project and associate director for text-base development at the Scholarly Technology Group at Brown University. Her research focuses on digital text editing, text-encoding theory, and electronic textuality.

Neil Fraistat is professor of English at the University of Maryland and a founder and general editor of the *Romantic Circles* Web site. With Donald H. Reiman he coedited two volumes of *The Complete Poetry of Percy Bysshe Shelley* and the Norton Critical Edition of *Shelley's Poetry and Prose*.

Hans Walter Gabler recently retired as professor of English literature at the University of Munich, where, from 1996 to 2002, he directed the interdisciplinary graduate program Textual Criticism as Foundation and Method of the Historical Disciplines. He was editor-in-chief of the critical editions of James Joyce's *Ulysses* (1984, 1986), *A Portrait of the Artist as a Young Man*, and *Dubliners* (both 1993).

David Gants, Canada Research Chair in Humanities Computing, is electronic editor of the forthcoming *Cambridge Edition of the Works of Ben Jonson*, advisory board member for the *Oxford Works of Edmund Spenser*, and assistant editor of the *Humanist* discussion group.

David Green is principal of *Knowledge Culture* (www.knowledgeculture .com), which assists cultural and academic organizations in maximizing their digital resources. He was founding executive director of the National Initiative for a Networked Cultural Heritage and coorganized the Computer Science & Humanities Initiative.

Robert Hirst, who compiled the glossary for the CSE guidelines, is general editor of the *Mark Twain Project* and has served on the MLA's Committee on Scholarly Editions.

Claus Huitfeldt is associate professor in the Department of Philosophy at the University of Bergen. He was director of the Wittgenstein Archives and board member of the Text Encoding Initiative Consortium.

Steven Jones, professor of English at Loyola University, Chicago, is a founder and general editor of the *Romantic Circles* Web site. He is editor of *The Satiric Eye* (2003) and two volumes in the series The Bodleian Shelley Manuscripts. He is author of *Against Technology: From the Luddites to Neo-Luddism* (forthcoming).

Kevin Kiernan, T. Marshall Hahn Sr. Professor of Arts and Sciences at the University of Kentucky, is editor of *The Electronic* Beowulf and currently preparing an electronic edition of Alfred the Great's Old English translation of Boethius's *De consolatione Philosophiae*.

John Lavagnino is lecturer in humanities computing at the Centre for Computing in the Humanities at King's College London. He is a general editor of the forthcoming *Collected Works of Thomas Middleton* and member of the board of directors of the Text Encoding Initiative.

Anne Mahoney, lecturer in classics at Tufts University, works on Greek and Latin meter and poetics and on ancient drama. Her commentary on Plautus's *Amphitryo* was published in 2004.

Jerome McGann is John Stewart Bryan University Professor at the University of Virginia. His development group, ARP (Applied Research in Patacriticism), recently released *Ivanhoe*, a collaborative online play space for generating and analyzing acts of critical reflection.

Katherine O'Brien O'Keeffe, Notre Dame Professor of English at the University of Notre Dame, has edited the C-text of the Anglo-Saxon Chronicle (2001) and is completing a study of the textual dimensions of the Anglo-Saxon subject. She was cochair of the Committee on Scholarly Editions.

D. C. Parker, professor at the University of Birmingham, is codirector with Peter Robinson of the Institute for Textual Scholarship and Electronic Editing, coeditor of the International Greek New Testament Project, and editor of *Texts and Studies*. He is currently working on editions of the Gospel of John in Greek and Latin.

Sebastian Rahtz, information manager in IT support for Oxford University, uses TEI XML extensively for creating Web pages. He is a member of the board of directors and of the Technical Council of the Text Encoding Initiative Consortium. He is a chief architect of the revised fifth edition of the TEI's literate programming language.

Peter Robinson is professor of English and textual scholarship in the Faculty of Humanities and director of the Centre for Technology in the Arts at De Montfort University. He is developer of the textual-editing program *Collate* and director of the *Canterbury Tales* Project. In 2000, he founded Scholarly Digital Editions, a new electronic publishing house specializing in high-quality electronic publications.

Bob Rosenberg oversaw the creation of the *Thomas A. Edison Papers* Web site, which currently has more than 180,000 document images, and laid the foundation for marking up the text edition's transcriptions. He is an independent scholar in the San Francisco area.

G. Thomas Tanselle, senior vice president of the John Simon Guggenheim Memorial Foundation and adjunct professor of English at Columbia University, is author of *Textual Criticism since Greg* (2005) and a coeditor of the Northwestern-Newberry edition of Melville.

Chris Tiffin teaches at the University of Queensland in Brisbane, Australia. He is the compiler of *Mrs. Campbell Praed: A Bibliography* and editor or coeditor of *South Pacific Stories*, *South Pacific Images*, and *De-scribing Empire*.

John Unsworth is dean and professor at the Graduate School of Library and Information Science, University of Illinois, Urbana. He has been director of the Institute for Advanced Technology in the Humanities at the University of Virginia. From 1996 to 2004, he was a member of the MLA's Committee on Scholarly Editions; from 2001 to 2003, he chaired the Text Encoding Initiative Consortium.

Edward Vanhoutte is director of research at the Royal Academy of Dutch Language and Literature (Belgium). He is coeditor, with Ron Van den Branden, of the DALF Guidelines for the Description and Encoding of Modern Correspondence Material and is a member of the TEI Council.

Dirk Van Hulle, associate professor of English literature at the University of Antwerp, is author of *Textual Awareness: A Genetic Study of Late Manuscripts by Joyce, Proust, and Mann* (2004).

Christian Wittern is associate professor at the Documentation and Information Center for Chinese Studies, Institute for Research in Humanities, Kyoto University. For the TEI, he has chaired the working group on Character Encoding and now chairs the Technical Council.

WORKS CITED

Abelman, Arthur F. "Legal Issues in Scholarly Publishing." *MLA Style Manual and Guide to Scholarly Publishing.* By Joseph Gibaldi. 2nd ed. New York: MLA, 1998. 33–60.

Adams, Robert. "Editing *Piers Plowman* B: The Imperative of an Intermittently Critical Edition." *Studies in Bibliography* 45 (1992): 31–68.

Baker, Mona, and Kirsten Malmkjaer, eds. *Routledge Encyclopedia of Translation Studies.* London: Routledge, 1998.

Barbauld, Anna (Anna Laetitia Aikin). Poems *(1773): A Hypertext Edition.* Ed. Lisa Vargo and Allison Muri. *Romantic Circles.* U of Maryland. 24 Jan. 2005 < http:// www.rc.umd.edu/editions/contemps/barbauld/poems1773>.

Barnard, D. T., L. Burnard, J.-P. Gaspart, L. A. Price, C. M. Sperberg-McQueen, and G. B. Varile. "Hierarchical Encoding of Text: Technical Problems and SGML Solutions." *Computers and the Humanities* 29 (1995): 211–31.

Barnard, D. T., R. Hayter, M. Karababa, G. Logan, and J. McFadden. "SGML-Based Markup for Literary Texts: Two Problems and Some Solutions." *Computers and the Humanities* 22 (1988): 265–76.

Baum, Paull Franklin, ed. The Blessed Damozel: *The Unpublished Manuscript, Texts and Collation.* By Dante Gabriel Rossetti. Introd. Baum. Chapel Hill: U of North Carolina P, 1937.

Beckett, Samuel. Comment c'est / How It Is and / et L'image: *A Critical-Genetic Edition / Une édition critico-génétique.* Ed. Edouard Magessa O'Reilly. New York: Routledge, 2001.

————. *Samuel Beckett: The Complete Short Prose*. Ed. S. E. Gontarski. New York: Grove, 1996.

————. *Soubresauts*. Paris: Minuit, 1989.

————. *Stirrings Still*. New York: Blue Moon, 1988.

————. *Stirrings Still*. *Guardian* 3 Mar. 1989: 25.

————. Stirrings Still: *Beckett Shorts*. Vol. 11. London: Calder, 1999.

————. *Stirrings Still*. Beckett, *Samuel Beckett* 259–65.

————. *The Unnamable*. *The Beckett Trilogy*. London: Picador, 1979. 265–382.

Bédier, Joseph. "Le tradition manuscrite du *Lai de l'ombre*: Réflexions sur l'art d'éditer les anciens textes." *Romania* 54 (1928): 161–96, 321–56.

Berners-Lee, Tim. *Web Architecte from 50,000 Feet*. Sept. 1998. 24 Jan. 2005 < http:// www.w3.org/DesignIssues/Architecture.html >.

Berners-Lee, Tim, James Hendler, and Ora Lassila. "The Semantic Web." *Scientific American* May 2001. 24 Jan. 2005. < http://www.sciam.com/article.cfm ?articleID = 00048144-10D2-1C70-84A9809EC588EF21&sc = I100322 >.

Bevington, David. "Why Re-edit Herford and Simpson?" *Re-presenting Ben Jonson*. Ed. Martin Butler. Basingstoke: Macmillan, 1999. 20–38.

Biasi, Pierre-Marc de. *La génétique des textes*. Paris: Nathan, 2000.

————. "What Is a Literary Draft? Toward a Functional Typology of Genetic Documentation." *Yale French Studies* 89 (1996): 26–58.

"Bibliotheca Alexandrina." *Internet Archive*. 4 Apr. 2005 < http://www.archive.org/ about/bibalex_p_r.php >.

Biggs, Michael, and Claus Huitfeldt. "Philosophy and Electronic Publishing: Theory and Metatheory in the Development of Text Encoding." *Monist* 80.3 (1997). 25 July 1997. 4 Mar. 2005 < http://bureau.philo.at/mii/mii/node5.html >.

Biggs, Michael, and Alois Pichler. *Wittgenstein: Two Source Catalogues and a Bibliography*. Working Papers from the Wittgenstein Archives at the U of Bergen 7. Bergen: Wittgensteinarkivet ved Universitetet i Bergen, 1993.

Blake, Norman F., and Peter M. W. Robinson, eds. *The* Canterbury Tales *Project: Occasional Papers*. 2 vols. Oxford: Office for Humanities Communication, 1997.

Blake, William. *The Complete Poetry and Prose of William Blake*. Rev. ed. Ed. David V. Erdman. Berkeley: U of California P, 1988.

Bourret, Ronald. *XML and Databases*. Dec. 2004. 21 Mar. 2005 < http://www .rpbourret.com/xml/XMLAndDatabases.htm >.

Bowers, Fredson. "Some Principles for Scholarly Editions of Nineteenth-Century American Authors." *Studies in Bibliography* 17 (1964): 223–28.

Brewer, Charlotte. "Scribal vs. Authorial Writing in *Piers Plowman*." *Medieval and Renaissance Texts and Studies* 79 (1991): 59–89.

Brians, Paul. "CD-ROMs in Libraries and at Home." Online posting. 7 Feb. 2000. *Humanist Discussion Group* 13.380. 13 Jan. 2004 <http://lists.village.virginia.edu/lists_archive/Humanist/v13/0374.html>.

Brodie, Nancy. *Authenticity, Preservation, and Access in Digital Collections*. Preservation 2000: An Intl. Conf. on the Preservation and Long Term Accessibility of Digital Materials. Dec. 2000. York, Eng. 24 Jan. 2005 <http://www.rlg.org/en/page.php?Page_ID=243>.

Bryden, Mary, Julian Garforth, and Peter Mills. *Beckett at Reading: Catalogue of the Beckett Manuscript Collection at the University of Reading*. Reading: Whiteknights; Beckett Intl. Foundation, 1998.

Bunt, Gary. *The Good Web Guide to World Religions*. London: Good Web Guide, 2001.

———. *Virtually Islamic: Computer-Mediated Communication and Cyber Islamic Environments*. Cardiff: U of Wales P, 2000.

Butler, Terry, Sue Fisher, Greg Coulombe, Patricia Clements, Isobel Grundy, Susan Brown, Jeanne Wood, and Rebecca Cameron. "Can a Team Tag Consistently? Experiences on the Orlando Project." *Markup Languages* 2 (2000): 111–25.

Buzzetti, D. "Diacritical Ambiguity and Markup." *Augmenting Comprehension: Digital Tools and the History of Ideas*. Ed. Buzzetti, Giuliano Pancaldi, and Harold Short. London: Office for Humanities Communication, 2004. 175–88.

———. "Digital Representation and the Text Model." *New Literary History* 33.1 (2002): 61–88.

Byron, George. *Childe Harold's Pilgrimage*. Project Gutenberg. 1 Feb. 2004. 21 July 2005 <http://www.gutenberg.org/etext/5131>.

Calabretto, Sylvia, and Andrea Bozzi. "The Philological Workstation BAMBI (Better Access to Manuscripts and Browsing of Images)." *Journal of Digital Information* 1.3 (1998). 4 Mar. 2005 <jodi.ecs.soton.ac.uk/>. Path: Past Issues.

The Cambridge Communiqué. W3C Note. 7 Oct. 1999. 20 Jan. 2005 <http://www.w3.org/TR/1999/NOTE-schema-arch-19991007>.

Cloud, Random. "FIAT fLUX." *Crisis in Editing: Texts of the English Renaissance: Papers Given at the Twenty-Fourth Annual Conference on Editorial Problems, University of Toronto, 4–5 November 1988*. Ed. Randall McLeod. New York: AMS, 1994. 61–172.

Cohn, Ruby, *A Beckett Canon*. Ann Arbor: U of Michigan P, 2001.

Coleridge, Samuel Taylor, and William Wordsworth. Lyrical Ballads: *An Electronic Scholarly Edition*. Ed. Bruce Graver and Ronald Tetreault. *Romantic Circles*. U of Maryland. 24 Jan. 2005 <http://www.rc.umd.edu/editions/LB/index.html>.

Collection Lists. William Blake Archive. 2002. 7 Mar. 2005 <www.blakearchive.org/main.html>. Path: Resources for Further Research; Collection Lists.

Committee on Scholarly Editions. *Guidelines for Editors of Scholarly Editions*. MLA. 15 Sept. 2003. 18 Feb. 2005 <http://www.mla.org/cse_guidelines>.

———. "Guidelines for Scholarly Editions". Typescript. Oct. 1992.

Contributing Collections. William Blake Archive. 2002. 7 Mar. 2005 <www.blakearchive.org/main.html>. Path: About the Archive; Contributing Collections.

Coombs, James H., Allen H. Renear, and Steven J. DeRose. "Markup Systems and the Future of Scholarly Text Processing." *Communications of the ACM* 30.11 (1987): 933–47.

Cooper, Andrew, and Michael Simpson. "The High-Tech Luddite of Lambeth: Blake's Eternal Hacking." *Wordsworth Circle* 30.3 (1999): 125–31.

———. "Looks Good in Practice, but Does It Work in Theory? Rebooting the *Blake Archive*." *Wordsworth Circle* 31.1 (2000): 63–68.

Copyright Management Center. *Checklist for Fair Use*. Indiana U. 2002. 24 Jan. 2005 <http://www.copyright.iupui.edu/checklist.htm>.

Corpus Inscriptionum Latinarum. Berlin: Berlin-Brandenburgische Akademie der Wissenschaften, 1862– .

Crane, Gregory, and Jeffrey A. Rydberg-Cox. "New Technology and New Roles: The Need for Corpus Editors." *Proc. of the Fifth ACM Conference on Digital Libraries*. San Antonio: ACM, 2000. 252–53.

Crews, Kenneth D. *Copyright Essentials for Librarians and Educators*. Chicago: Amer. Lib. Assn., 2000.

Dahlerup, Verner. *Ágrip af Noregs konunga sögum: Diplomatarisk udgave for Samfundet til udgivelse af gammel nordisk litteratur ved Verner Dahlerup*. Samfund til udgivelse af gammel nordisk litteratur 2. København: Møllers bogtrykkeri, 1880.

Darwin, Charles. *On the Origin of Species*. 1859. *The Writings of Charles Darwin on the Web*. Ed. John van Wyhe and Sue Asscher. 2002–04. 15 Feb. 2005 <http://pages.britishlibrary.net/charles.darwin/texts/origin1859/origin_fm.html>.

Day, Colin A. *Text Processing*. Cambridge Computer Science Texts 20. Cambridge: Cambridge UP, 1984.

Deegan, Marilyn, and Simon Tanner. *Digital Futures: Strategies for the Information Age*. New York: Neal-Schuman, 2002.

Dekhtyar, Alex, and Ionut Emil Jacob. "Management of Data for Building Electronic Editions of Historic Manuscripts." *ACH/ALLC 2003 Conference Abstracts*, U of Georgia.

DeRose, Steven J., David G. Durand, Elli Mylonas, and Allen Renear. "What Is Text, Really?" *Journal of Computing in Higher Education* 1 (1990): 3–26.

DeRose, Steven J., and Andries van Dam. "Document Structure and Markup in the FRESS Hypertext System." *Markup Languages: Theory and Practice* 1.1 (1999): 7–32.

De Smedt, Marcel, and Edward Vanhoutte. "The Best of Three Worlds: Eclecticism in Editorial Theory." *The Electronic Edition of Stijn Streuvels'* De teleurgang van den Waterhoek*: Sichtungen*. Archiv-Bibliothek-Literaturwissenschaft 2001–02 (4–5): 300–11. *Sichtungen*. 13 Jan. 2004 <http://www.onb.ac.at/sichtungen/ berichte/smedt-m-1a.html>.

Dessau, Hermann, ed. *Inscriptiones Latinae Selectae*. Berlin, 1892–1916.

De Vriend, Hubert Jan. *The Old English* Herbarium *and* Medicina de Quadrupedibus. EETS 286. London: Oxford UP, 1984.

D'Iorio, Paolo. *HyperNietzsche: Modèle d'un hypertexte avant sur Internet pour la recherche en sciences humaines*. Paris: PUF, 2000.

Dohnicht, Marcus. *Zusammenstellung den diakritische Zeichen zur Wiedergabe der latein-ischen Inschrifttexte der Antike für den Unicode*. Working paper, n.d. 17 July 2000. <http://www.csad.ox.ac.uk/varia/unicode/Dohnicht.pdf>.

Donaldson, E. Talbot. "The Psychology of Editors of Middle English Texts." *Speaking of Chaucer*. New York: Athlone, 1970. 102–18.

Donaldson, Ian. "A New Edition of Ben Jonson?" *Ben Jonson Journal* 2 (1995): 223–31.

Dow, Sterling. *Conventions in Editing: A Suggested Reformulation of the Leiden System*. Greek, Roman, and Byzantine Scholarly Aids 2. Durham: Duke UP, 1969.

Driscoll, Matthew J. "Encoding Old Norse / Icelandic Primary Sources Using TEI-Conformant SGML." *Literary and Linguistic Computing* 15.1 (2000): 81–91.

———. "The Virtual Reunification of the Arnamagnaean Collection." Digital Resources for the Humanities. Saint Anne's Coll., Oxford. 14 Sept. 1997.

Duggan, Hoyt N. Rev. of *Textual Criticism and Middle English Texts*, by Tim William Machan. *Text* 10 (1997): 377–88. Mississippi State U Archives. 4 Mar. 2005 <http://www.msstate.edu/Archives/TEXT/contents10.html>.

Durand, David, Elli Mylonas, and Steve DeRose. "What Should Markup Really Be? Applying Theories of Text to the Design of Markup Systems." Joint Conf. of the Assn. for Lit. and Linguistic Computing and Assn. for Computers and the Humanities. U of Bergen, Norway. 28–29 June 1996.

Eaves, Morris. "Collaboration Takes More than E-Mail: Behind the Scenes at the *William Blake Archive*." *Journal of Electronic Publishing* 3.2 (1997). 24 Jan. 2005 <http://www.press.umich.edu/jep/03-02/blake.html>.

———. "Graphicality." Loizeaux and Fraistat 99–122.

———. "National Arts and Disruptive Technologies in Blake's Prospectus of 1793." *Blake, Nation and Empire*. Ed. Steve Clark and David Worrall. London: Palgrave, forthcoming.

———. "To Paradise the Hard Way." *The Cambridge Companion to William Blake*. Ed. Eaves. Cambridge: Cambridge UP, 2002: 1–16.

———. "'Why Don't They Leave It Alone?': Speculations on the Authority of the Audience in Editorial Theory." *Cultural Artifacts and the Production of Meaning: The Page, the Image, and the Body*. Ed. Margaret Ezell and Katherine O'Brien O'Keeffe. Ann Arbor: U of Michigan P, 1994. 85–99.

Eaves, Morris, Robert N. Essick, and Joseph Viscomi. "The William Blake Archive: The Medium When the Millennium Is the Message." *Romanticism and Millenarianism*. Ed. Tim Fulford. New York: Palgrave, 2002. 219–33.

Eaves, Morris, Robert N. Essick, Joseph Viscomi, and Matthew Kirschenbaum. "Standards, Methods, and Objectives in the *William Blake Archive*." *Wordsworth Circle* 30.3 (1999): 135–44.

Editorial Principles: Methodology and Standards in the Blake Archive. William Blake Archive. 1 Nov. 2004. 24 Jan. 2005 <http://www.blakearchive.org/main.html>. Path: About the Archive; Editorial Principles.

Ehrman, Bart D. *The Orthodox Corruption of Scripture: The Effect of Early Christological Controversies on the Text of the New Testament*. Oxford: Oxford UP, 1993.

Ehrman, Bart D., and Michael W. Holmes, eds. *The Text of the New Testament in Contemporary Research: Essays on the* Status Quaestionis*: Festschrift for B. M. Metzger*. Grand Rapids: Eerdmans, 1995.

Elliott, Tom, Hugh Cayless, and Amy Hawkins. *EpiDoc: Guidelines for Structured Markup of Epigraphic Texts in TEI*. 8 May 2002. <http://www.ibiblio.org/telliott/epidoc/downloads/EpiDocGuidelines04.pdf>.

EpiDoc: Epigraphic Documents in TEI XML. EpiDoc Collaborative. 16 Aug. 2002. 8 Mar. 2005 <http://epidoc.sourceforge.net/>.

Epp. E. J. "The Multivalence of the Term 'Original Text' in New Testament Textual Criticism." *Harvard Theological Review* 92 (1999): 254–81.

Falconer, Graham. "Genetic Criticism." *Comparative Literature* 45.1 (1993): 1–21.

Farrell, Elizabeth F., and Florence Olsen. "A New Front in the Sweatshop Wars?" *Chronicle of Higher Education* 26 Oct. 2001: A35. 24 Jan. 2005 <http://chronicle.com/weekly/v48/i09/09a03501.htm>.

Faulhaber, Charles. *Guidelines for Electronic Scholarly Editions.* MLA Committee on Scholarly Eds. 1 Dec. 1997. 24 Jan. 2005 <http://sunsite.berkeley.edu/MLA/guidelines.html>.

Ferrer, Daniel. "Production, Invention, and Reproduction: Genetic vs. Textual Criticism." Loizeaux and Fraistat 48–59.

Finney, T. J. *Converting Leiden-Style Editions to TEI Lite XML.* Working paper. 2001. 24 Jan. 2005 <http://www.tei-c.org/Sample_Manuals/leiden.html>.

Fitch, Brian T. *Beckett and Babel: An Investigation into the Status of the Bilingual Work.* Toronto: U of Toronto P, 1988.

Flanders, Julia, Syd Bauman, Paul Caton, and Mavis Cournane. "Names Proper and Improper: Applying the TEI to the Classification of Proper Names." *Computers and the Humanities* 31 (1997–98): 285–300.

Fraistat, Neil. *The Poem and the Book: Interpreting Collections of Romantic Poetry.* Chapel Hill: U of North Carolina P, 1985.

Fraistat, Neil, and Steven E. Jones. "Immersive Textuality: The Editing of Virtual Spaces." *Text* 15 (2003): 69–82.

Freud, Sigmund. "Negation." 1925. *The Standard Edition of the Complete Psychological Works of Sigmund Freud.* Ed. James Strachey et al. Vol. 19. London: Hogarth, 1961. 253–39.

Gabler, Hans Walter. Afterword. Gabler, Steppe, and Melchior 1859–907.

Gabler, Hans Walter, George Bornstein, and Gillian Borland Pierce, eds. *Contemporary German Editorial Theory.* Ann Arbor: U of Michigan P, 1995.

Gabler, Hans Walter, Wolfhard Steppe, and Claus Melchior, eds. Ulysses: *A Critical and Synoptic Edition.* By James Joyce. 3 vols. New York: Garland, 1984.

Gasaway, Laura N. *When U.S. Works Pass into the Public Domain.* 4 Nov. 2003. 30 Mar. 2005 <http://www.unc.edu/~unclng/public-d.htm>.

Gerlach, Klaus. "Zu Problemen der Edition von Bearbeitungen und Übersetzungen." *Zu Werk und Text: Beiträge zur Textologie.* Ed. Siegfried Scheibe and Christel Laufer. Berlin: Akademie, 1991. 105–10.

Getting Permission. Office of General Counsel, U of Texas. 17 Nov. 2004. 24 Jan. 2005 < http://www.utsystem.edu/OGC/IntellectualProperty/PERMISSN.htm >.

Goldfarb, Charles F. *The SGML Handbook.* Oxford: Oxford UP, 1990.

Gontarski, S. E. "Notes on the Texts." Beckett, *Samuel Beckett* 279–86.

Graver, Bruce, and Ronald Tetreault. "Editing *Lyrical Ballads* for the Electronic Environment." *Romanticism on the Net* 9 Feb. 1998. 24 Jan. 2005 < http://www .erudit.org/revue/ron/1998/v/n9/005783ar.html >.

Greetham, David C., ed. *Scholarly Editing: A Guide to Research.* New York: MLA, 1995.

———. "Textual and Literary Theory: Redrawing the Matrix." *Studies in Bibliography* 42 (1989): 1–24.

———. *Textual Scholarship: An Introduction.* New York: Garland, 1994.

———. *Theories of the Text.* Oxford: Oxford UP, 1999.

Greg, W. W. "The Rationale of Copy-Text." *Studies in Bibliography* 3 (1950–51): 19–36.

Grésillon, Almuth. *Eléments de critique génétique: Lire les manuscrits modernes.* Paris: PUF, 1994.

Griffith, John G. "A Taxonomic Study of the Manuscript Tradition of Juvenal." *Museum Helveticum* 25 (1968): 101–38.

Grutman, Rainier. "Auto-translation." Baker and Malmkjaer 17–20.

Guidelines for Electronic Text Encoding and Interchange (TEI P3). Humanities Text Initiative, U of Michigan. 2 Mar. 2005 < http://www.hti.umich.edu/t/tei/ >. Path: Other Searches; Simple Searches.

Haugeland, John. "Semantic Engines: An Introduction to Mind Design." *Mind Design: Philosophy, Psychology, Artificial Intelligence.* Ed. Haugeland. Montgomery: Bradford, 1981. 1–34.

Hay, Louis. "Does Text Exist?" *Studies in Bibliography* 41 (1988): 64–76.

Hill, W. Speed. "English Renaissance: Nondramatic Literature." Greetham, *Scholarly Editing* 204–30.

Hirst, Robert H. "Editing Mark Twain, Hand to Hand, 'Like All D———d Fool Printers.'" *Papers of the Bibliographical Society of America* 88 (1994): 157–88.

Hjelmslev, Louis. *Language: An Introduction.* Madison: U of Wisconsin P, 1970.

Hockey, Susan. *Electronic Texts in the Humanities: Principles and Practice*. Oxford: Oxford UP, 2000.

Hockey, Susan, and Nancy Ide, eds. *Research in Humanities Computing 4: Selected Papers from the 1992 ALLC/ACH Conference*. Oxford: Oxford UP, 1996.

Howard-Hill, T. "Theory and Praxis in the Social Approach to Editing." *Text* 5 (1991): 31–46.

How to Investigate the Copyright Status of a Work. United States Copyright Office. Circular 22. Rev. Dec. 2004. 24 Jan. 2005 <http://www.copyright.gov/circs/circ22.html>.

Huitfeldt, Claus. *MECS: A Multi-element Code System*. Working Papers of the Wittgenstein Archives at the U of Bergen 3. Oct. 1998. 8 Nov. 2005 <http://helmer.hit.uib.no/claus/mecs/mecs.htm>.

———. "Multi-dimensional Texts in a One-Dimensional Medium." *Computers and the Humanities* 28 (1995): 235–41.

Huitfeldt, Claus, and Viggo Rossvær. *The Norwegian Wittgenstein Project Report, 1988*. Report Ser. 44. Bergen: Norwegian Computing Centre for the Humanities, 1989.

Inscriptiones Graecae. 3rd ed. Berlin: Berlin-Brandenburgische Akademie der Wissenschaften, 1981– .

International Organization for Standardization. *ISO/IEC 10646-1:2000, Information Technology-Universal Multiple-Octet Coded Character Set (UCS)-Part 1: Architecture and Basic Multilingual Plane*. Geneva: ISO, 2000.

Jelliffe, Rick. *The XML and SGML Cookbook*. Upper Saddle River: Prentice PTF, 1998.

Jenkins, Reese, et al. *The Papers of Thomas A. Edison*. Vol. 1. Baltimore: Johns Hopkins UP, 1989.

Joloboff, V. "Document Representation: Concepts and Standards." *Structured Documents*. Ed. J. André, R. Furuta, and V. Quint. Cambridge: Cambridge UP, 1989. 75–105.

Jonson, Ben. *Hycke Scorner*. London: Wynken de Worde, 1515–16.

———. *The Workes of Beniamin Jonson*. London: Stansby, 1616.

Kane, George. "John M. Manly and Edith Rickert." Ruggiers 207–29.

———. "An Open Letter to Jill Mann about the Sequence of the Versions of *Piers Plowman*." *Yearbook of Langland Studies* 13 (1999): 7–33.

———, ed. Piers Plowman: *The A Version*. London: Athlone, 1960.

Kastan, David Scott. *Shakespeare and the Book*. Cambridge: Cambridge UP, 2001.

Kauffman, Louis H., and Francisco J. Varela. "Form Dynamics." *Journal of Social and Biological Systems* 3.2 (1980): 171–206.

Kay, Michael. *XSLT: Programmer's Reference*. Chicago: Wrox, 2000.

Kenny, Dorothy. "Equivalence." Baker and Malmkjaer 77–80.

Kermode, Frank. "A Miserable Splendour." Rev. of *Stirrings Still*, by Samuel Beckett. *Guardian* 3 Mar. 1989: 26.

Kiernan, Kevin S., ed. *The Electronic Beowulf*. CD-ROM. Ann Arbor: U of Michigan P, 2000.

———. "EPT: Edition Production Technology for Multimedia Contents in Digital Libraries." Workshop on Multimedia Contents in Digital Libs. Chania, Crete. 2–3 June 2003.

Kipling, Rudyard. *Stalky and Co.* 1899. Doubleday: Garden City, 1950.

Kirschenbaum, Matthew. "Documenting Digital Images: Textual Meta-data at the *Blake Archive*." *Electronic Library* 16.4 (1998): 239–41.

———. "Editing the Interface: Textual Studies and First Generation Electronic Objects." *Text* 14 (2002): 15–51.

———. "Editor's Introduction: Image-Based Humanities Computing." *Computers and the Humanities* 36.1 (2002): 3–6.

———. "Lucid Mapping: Information Landscaping and Three-Dimensional Writing Spaces." *Leonardo* 32.4 (1999): 261–68.

———. "Managing the *Blake Archive*." *Editors' Dispatches. Romantic Circles*. U of Maryland. Mar. 1998. 24 Jan. 2005 <http://www.rc.umd.edu/dispatches/column7/>.

Kirschenbaum, Matthew, and Kari Kraus. "Outside the Archive." Soc. for Textual Scholarship 2001 Intl. Interdisciplinary Conf. CUNY Graduate Center, New York. 18 Apr. 2001.

Kline, Mary-Jo. *A Guide to Documentary Editing*. 2nd ed. Baltimore: Johns Hopkins UP, 1998.

Knowlson, James. *Damned to Fame: The Life of Samuel Beckett*. London: Bloomsbury, 1996.

Krance, Charles, ed. Mal vu mal dit / Ill Seen Ill Said: *A Bilingual, Evolutionary, and Synoptic Variorum Edition*. By Samuel Beckett. New York: Garland, 1996.

Kroeber, Karl. "The Blake Archive and the Future of Literary Studies." *Wordsworth Circle* 30.3 (1999): 123–25.

Lachmann, Karl, ed. *Novum Testamentum Graece et Latine.* 2 vols. Berlin, 1842–50.

Landon, Letitia Elizabeth. "Verses" and *The Keepsake* for 1829: *A Hypertext Edition.* Ed. Terence Hoagwood, Kathryn Ledbetter, and Martin M. Jacobsen. *Romantic Circles.* U of Maryland. 24 Jan. 2005 < http://www.rc.umd.edu/editions/lel/ >.

Landow, George P. *Hypertext: The Convergence of Contemporary Critical Theory and Technology.* Baltimore: Johns Hopkins UP, 1992.

Lanham, Richard A. *The Electronic Word: Democracy, Technology, and the Arts.* Chicago: U of Chicago P, 1993.

Lavagnino, John. "Electronic Scholarly Editions." *Humanities Computing News.* Feb. 2001. 13 Jan. 2004 < http://www.kcl.ac.uk/humanities/cch/hcn/hcn-2001-02.html#Vanhoutte >.

Lavagnino, John, and Elli Mylonas. "The Show Must Go On: Problems of Tagging Performance Texts." *Computers and the Humanities* 29 (1995): 113–21.

Lecolinet, Eric, Laurent Robert, and François Role. "Text-Image Coupling for Editing Literary Sources." *Computers and the Humanities* 36.1 (2002): 49–73.

Lernout, Geert. "'Critique génétique' und Philologie." *Text und Edition: Positionen und Perspektiven.* Ed. Rüdiger Nutt-Kofoth, Bodo Plachta, H. T. M. van Vliet, and Hermann Zwerschina. Berlin: Schmidt, 2000. 121–42. Trans. *Text* 14 (2002): 53–75.

Liddell, Henry George, and Robert Scott. *A Greek-English Lexicon.* Rev. Henry Stuart Jones. *The Perseus Digital Library.* Ed. Gregory Crane. Tufts U. 16 Mar. 2005 < http://www.perseus.tufts >. Path: Classics; Secondary Sources; Liddell.

Loizeaux, Elizabeth B., and Neil Fraistat, eds. *Reimagining Textuality: Textual Studies in the Late Age of Print.* Madison: U of Wisconsin P, 2002.

Machan, Tim William. "Response to Hoyt Duggan's Review." *Text* 10 (1997): 388–90. Mississippi State U Archives. 4 Mar. 2005 < http://www.msstate.edu/Archives/TEXT/contents10.html >.

———. *Textual Criticism and Middle English Texts.* Charlottesville: UP of Virginia, 1994.

Maler, Eve, and Jeanne El Andaloussi. *Developing SGML DTDs: From Text to Model to Markup.* New York: Prentice, 1996.

Manly, John M., and E. Rickert, eds. *The Text of the* Canterbury Tales: *Studied on the Basis of All Known Manuscripts.* 8 Vols. Chicago: Chicago UP, 1940.

Marcus, Leah. *Unediting the Renaissance: Shakespeare, Marlowe, Milton.* London: Routledge, 1996.

Markup Guidelines for Documentary Editions. Ed. David R. Chesnutt, Susan M. Hockey, and C. M. Sperberg-McQueen. 4 July 1999. 27 May 2004 <http://adh.sc.edu/MepGuide.html#WORKFLOW>.

Masten, Jeffrey. "Ping Subjects; or, The Secret Lives of Shakespeare's Compositors." *Language Machines: Technologies of Literary and Cultural Production.* Ed. Masten, Peter Stallybrass, and Nancy Vickers. New York: Routledge, 1997. 75–107.

Maturana, Humberto R., and Francisco G. Varela. *Autopoiesis and Cognition.* Boston: Reidel, 1980.

Max, D. T. "The Electronic Book." *American Scholar* 69 (2000): 17–28.

McCarty, Willard. "Finding Implicit Patterns in Ovid's *Metamorphoses* with *TACT.*" *A TACT Exemplar.* Ed. Russon Wooldridge. Toronto: Centre for Computing in the Humanities, 1991. 37–75.

McGann, Jerome. "Editing as a Theoretical Pursuit." McGann, *Radiant Textuality* 88–97.

———. *Radiant Textuality: Literature after the World Wide Web.* New York: Palgrave, 2001.

———. "The Rationale of HyperText." *Text* 9 (1996): 11–32.

———. *The Textual Condition.* Princeton: Princeton UP, 1991.

McGillivray, Murray, ed. *Geoffrey Chaucer's Book of the Duchess: A Hypertext Edition.* CD-ROM. Alberta: U of Calgary, 1997.

McIntosh, Angus. "Scribal Profiles from Middle English Texts." *Neuphilologische Mitteilungen* 76 (1975): 218–35.

———. "Towards an Inventory of Middle English Scribes." *Neuphilologische Mitteilungen* 75 (1974): 602–24.

McKenzie, D. F. *Bibliography and the Sociology of Texts.* London: British Lib., 1986.

———. "'What's Past Is Prologue': The Bibliographical Society and the History of the Book." *Making Meaning: "Printers of the Mind" and Other Essays.* Studies in Print Culture and the History of the Book. Ed. Peter D. McDonald and Michael F. Suarez. Amherst: U of Massachusetts P, 2002. 259–75.

Medwall, Henry. *Fulgens and Lucrece.* London: Rastell, 1512–16.

Megginson, David. *Structuring XML Documents.* Upper Saddle River: Prentice PTF, 1998.

Meiggs, Russell, and David Lewis, eds. *A Selection of Greek Historical Inscriptions to the End of the Fifth Century BC.* 2nd ed. Oxford: Oxford UP, 1988.

Mikheev, Andrei, Claire Grover, and Marc Moens. "XML Tools and Architecture for Named Entity Recognition." *Markup Languages* 1 (1999): 89–113.

Miller, J. Hillis. *Digital Blake*. Digital Cultures Project Conf., 3–5 Nov. 2000, U of California, Santa Barbara. 31 Oct. 2000. 24 Jan. 2005 <http://dc-mrg.english.ucsb.edu/conference/2000/PANELS/BEssick/jhmiller.html>.

Misic, Vladimir. "Mixed Raster Content for Processing of Colored Engravings." Electrical and Computer Engineering. Diss. U of Rochester. 2003.

MOOzymandias. Romantic Circles. Ed. Neil Fraistat, Steven E. Jones, and Carl Stahmer. U of Maryland. 10 Nov. 2005 <http://www.rc.umd.edu:7000/705/>.

Nelson, Theodor Holm. *Embedded Markup Considered Harmful*. XML.com. 2 Oct. 1997. 1 Nov. 2002 <http://www.xml.com/pub/a/w3j/s3.nelson.html>.

———. *Generalized Links, Micropayment, and Transcopyright*. Almaden Research Center, IBM. 1996. 18 Feb. 2005 <http://www.almaden.ibm.com/almaden/npuc97/1996/tnelson.htm>.

Neuman, Michael. "You Can't Always Get What You Want: Deep Encoding of Manuscripts and the Limits of Retrieval." *Research in Humanities Computing* 5 (1996): 209–19.

Neuman, Yair. *Processes and Boundaries of the Mind*. New York: Kluwer Academic, 2003.

Novum Testamentum Graece. Ed. Barbara Aland and Kurt Aland. 27th ed. Stuttgart: Deutsche Bibelgesellschaft, 1993.

Ore, Espen S. "Elektronisk publisering: forskjellige utgaveformer og forholdet til grunntekst(er) of endelig(e) tekst(er)." *Vid Texternas Vägskäl: Textkritiska uppsatser*. Ed. Lars Burman and Barbro Ståhle Sjönell. Stockholm: Svenska Vitterhetssamfundet, 1999. 138–44.

O'Reilly, Edouard Magessa. "English Introduction." Beckett, Comment ix–xxxv.

Osborne, Thomas. "Faith, Philosophy, and the Nominalist Background to Luther's Defense of Real Presence." *Journal of the History of Ideas* 63 (2002): 63–82.

Ott, Wilhelm. "Computers and Textual Editing." *Computers and Written Texts*. Ed. C. S. Butler. Oxford: Blackwell, 1992. 205–26.

Panciera, Silvio. "Struttura dei supplementi e segni diacritici dieci anni dopo." *Unione Accademia Nazionale Supplementa Italica* 8 (1991): 9–21.

Parker, D. C. "A Comparison between the Text und Textwert and the Claremont Profile Method Analyses of Manuscripts in the Gospel of Luke." *New Testament Studies* 49 (2003): 108–38.

———. *The Living Text of the Gospels*. Cambridge: Cambridge UP, 1997.

———. "Text and Versions: The New Testament." *The Biblical World*. Ed. John Barton. Vol. 1. New York: Routledge, 2002. 229–49.

————. "Through a Screen Darkly: Digital Texts and the New Testament." *Journal for the Study of the New Testament* 25 (2003): 395–411.

Parker, T. H. L., and D. C. Parker, eds. *John Calvin*: Commentarius in Epistolam Pauli ad Romanos. Ioannis Calvini Opera Exegetica. Vol. 13. Geneva: Droz, 1999.

Paskin, Norman. "DOI: A 2003 Progress Report." *D-Lib Magazine* 9.6 (2003). 24 Jan. 2005 <http://www.dlib.org/dlib/june03/paskin/06paskin.html>.

Patterson, Lee. "The Logic of Textual Criticism and the Way of Genius: The Kane-Donaldson *Piers Plowman* in Historical Perspective." *Negotiating the Past: The Historical Understanding of Medieval Literature.* Madison: U of Wisconsin P, 1987. 77–113.

Payette, Sandra, Christophe Blanchi, Carl Lagoze, and Edward A. Overly. "Interoperability for Digital Objects and Repositories." *D-Lib Magazine* 5.5 (1999). 24 Jan. 2005 <http://www.dlib.org/dlib/may99/payette/05payette.html>.

Peattie, R. W. "William Michael Rossetti's Aldine Edition of Blake." *Blake: An Illustrated Quarterly* 12 (1978): 4–9.

"The Persistence of Vision: Images and Imaging at the *William Blake Archive*." *RLG DigiNews* 4.1 (2000). 24 Jan. 2005 <http://www.rlg.org/preserv/diginews/diginews4-1.html#feature1>.

Pichler, A. "Transcriptions, Texts, and Interpretations." *Culture and Value: Philosophy and the Cultural Sciences.* Ed. K. Johannessen and T. Nordenstam. Vienna: Austrian Ludwig Wittgenstein Soc., 1995. 690–95.

Pitti, Daniel, and John Unsworth. "After the Fall: Structured Data at IATH." Assn. for Computers and the Humanities and the Assn. for Literary and Linguistic Computing. Debrecen, Hungary. July 1998. 24 Jan. 2005 <http://www.iath.virginia.edu/~jmu2m/ach98.html>.

Plan of the Archive. William Blake Archive. 13 Jan. 2004. 24 Jan. 2005 <http://www.blakearchive.org/main.html>. Path: About the Archive; Plan of the Archive.

Rahtz, Sebastian. "Database Systems for Textual Data: An Experiment with Gravestones." *Literary and Linguistic Computing* 3.1 (1988): 32–35.

Rastell, John. *The Nature of the Four Elements.* London: Rastell, 1520.

Raymond, Darrell R., Frank W. Tompa, and Derick Wood. "From Data Representation to Data Model: Meta-semantic Issues in the Evolution of SGML." *Computer Standards and Interfaces* 18 (1996): 25–36.

————. *Markup Reconsidered.* First Intl. Workshop on Principles of Document Processing. Washington, DC. 22–23 Oct. 1992. 27 June 2005 <http://db.uwaterloo.ca/~fwtompa/.papers/markup.ps>.

Reiman, Donald H. *Romantic Texts and Contexts*. Columbia: U of Missouri P, 1987.

Renear, Allen. "Literal Transcription: Can the Text Ontologist Help?" *New Media and the Humanities: Research and Applications*. Ed. Domenico Fiormonte and Jonathan Usher. Oxford: Humanities Computing Unit, 2001. 23–30.

Renear, Allen, David Durand, and Elli Mylonas. "Refining Our Notion of What Text Really Is." Hockey and Ide 263–80.

Robinson, Peter M. W. "Analysis Workshop." Solopova.

———. "Manuscript Politics." *The Politics of the Electronic Text*. Ed. Warren Chernaik, Caroline Davis, and Marilyn Deegan. Oxford: Office for Humanities Communication, 1993. 9–15.

———. "The One Text and the Many Texts." *Making Texts for the Next Century*. Spec. issue of *Literary and Linguistic Computing* 15.1 (2000): 5–14.

———. "A Stemmatic Analysis of the Fifteenth-Century Witnesses to the Wife of Bath's Prologue." Blake and Robinson 2: 69–132.

———. "Stemmatic Commentary." Solopova.

———. "What Text Really Is Not, and Why Editors Have to Learn to Swim." *Computing the Edition*. Ed. Peter Shillingsburg and Fred R. Unwalla. Toronto: U of Toronto P, forthcoming.

———, ed. *The Wife of Bath's Prologue on CD-ROM*. By Geoffrey Chaucer. Cambridge: Cambridge UP, 1996.

Robinson, Peter M. W., and Robert J. O'Hara. "Cladistic Analysis of an Old Norse Manuscript Tradition." Hockey and Ide 115–37.

———. "Computer-Assisted Methods of Stemmatic Analysis." Blake and Robinson 1: 53–74.

Robinson, Peter M. W., and Elizabeth Solopova. "Guidelines for Transcription of the Manuscripts of the Wife of Bath's Prologue." Blake and Robinson 1: 19–52.

Robinson, Peter, and Lorna Stevenson, eds. *The Miller's Tale on CD-ROM*. By Geoffrey Chaucer. Scholarly Digital Eds. Rochester: Boydell, 2004.

Rosenberg, Robert. "Technological Artifacts as Historical Documents." *Text* 3 (1988): 393–407.

Rossetti, William Michael. Rev. of *Jerusalem*, by William Blake, facsim. ed. [Pearson, 1877]. *Academy* 13 (1878): 14.

Roueché, Charlotte, and Joyce M. Reynolds. *Aphrodisias in Late Antiquity*. Journal of Roman Studies Monographs 5. London: Soc. for the Promotion of Roman Studies, 1989.

Ruggiers, Paul G., ed. *Editing Chaucer: The Great Tradition.* Norman: Pilgrim, 1984.

Rydberg-Cox, Jeffrey A., Anne Mahoney, and Gregory Crane. "Document Quality Indicators and Corpus Editions." *Proceedings of the First ACM/IEEE Joint Conference on Digital Libraries.* New York: Assn. for Computing Machinery, 2001. 435–36.

Ryle, Gilbert. *The Concept of Mind.* London: Penguin, 2000.

Samuels, Lisa, and Jerome McGann. "Deformance and Interpretation." *New Literary History* 30.1 (1999): 25–56.

Scheibe, Siegfried. "On the Editorial Problem of the Text." Gabler, Bornstein, and Pierce 193–208.

Schneider, Ben Ross, Jr. *Travels in Computerland; or, Incompatibilities and Interfaces: A Full and True Account of the Implementation of the* London Stage Information Bank. Reading: Addison, 1974.

Schreibman, Susan. "Computer-Mediated Texts and Textuality: Theory and Practice." *Computers and the Humanities* 36 (2002): 283–93.

Schwenk, Cynthia J., ed. *Athens in the Age of Alexander: The Dated Laws and Decrees of the Lycourgan Era, 338–322 B.C.* Chicago: Ares, 1985.

Scragg, D. G., ed. *The Vercelli Homilies and Related Texts.* EETS OS 300. London: Oxford UP, 1992.

Segre, Cesare, and Tomaso Kememy. *Introduction to the Analysis of the Literary Text.* Trans. John Meddemmen. Bloomington, Indiana UP, 1988.

Senn, Fritz. Rev. of Ulysses: *The 1922 Text. James Joyce Quarterly* 32 (1955): 461–64.

Shaffer, Anthony. *Sleuth: A Play.* Playscript 46. London: Boyars, 1977.

Shaw, George Bernard. *Candida. Plays by George Bernard Shaw.* Signet Classic. New York: NAL, 1960. 176–235.

Shelley, Percy Bysshe. The Devil's Walk: *A Hypertext Edition.* Ed. Donald Reiman and Neil Fraistat. *Romantic Circles.* U of Maryland. 1997. 24 Jan. 2005 <http://www.rc.umd.edu/editions/shelley/devil/1dwcover.html>.

———. On the Medusa of Leonardo da Vinci in the Florentine Gallery: *A Hypertext Edition.* Ed. Neil Fraistat and Melissa Jo Sites. *Romantic Circles.* U of Maryland. 24 Jan. 2005 <http://www.rc.umd.edu/editions/shelley/medusa/medcover.html>.

Shillingsburg, Peter. *General Principles for Electronic Scholarly Editions.* Dec. 1993. 24 Jan. 2005 <http://sunsite.berkeley.edu/MLA/principles.html>.

———. "Principles for Electronic Archives, Scholarly Editions, and Tutorials." *The*

Literary Text in the Digital Age. Editorial Theory and Lit. Criticism. Ed. Richard J. Finneran. Ann Arbor: U of Michigan P, 1996. 23–35.

———. *Scholarly Editing in the Computer Age: Theory and Practice.* 3rd ed. Ann Arbor: U of Michigan P, 1996.

Smith, David A. "Detecting Events with Date and Place Information in Unstructured Text." *Proceedings of the Second ACM/IEEE Joint Conference on Digital Libraries.* New York: Assn. for Computing Machinery, 2002. 73–80.

Smith, Martha Nell. "Electronic Scholarly Editing." *Companion to Digital Humanities.* Ed. Susan Schreibman, Ray Siemens, and John Unsworth. Blackwell Companions to Lit. and Culture. Oxford: Blackwell, 2004. 306–22.

Solopova, Elizabeth, ed. *The General Prologue on CD-ROM.* By Geoffrey Chaucer. Cambridge: Cambridge UP, 2000.

Speiser, E. A. *Introduction to Hurrian.* Boston: Amer. Schools of Oriental Research, 1941.

Spencer-Brown, G. *Laws of Form.* London: Allen, 1969.

Sperberg-McQueen, C. M., and Lou Burnard, eds. *Guidelines for Electronic Text Encoding and Interchange.* XML-compatible ed. Oxford: TEI Consortium, 2001. 13 Jan. 2004 <http://www.tei-c.org/P4X/index.html>.

———. *Guidelines for Text Encoding and Interchange.* Chicago: ACH-ALLC-ACL Text Encoding Initiative, 1994.

Sperberg-McQueen, C. M., and Claus Huitfeldt. "Concurrent Document Hierarchies in MECS and SGML." *Literary and Linguistic Computing* 14.1 (1999): 29–42.

———. *GODDAG: A Data Structure for Overlapping Hierarchies.* 1999 Joint Annual Conf. of Assn. for Computers and the Humanities and Assn. for Lit. and Linguistic Computing. U of Virginia, Charlottesville. 9–13 June. 20 Jan. 2005 <http://www.iath.virginia.edu/ach-allc.99/proceedings/sperberg-mcqueen.html>.

Sperberg-McQueen, C. M., Claus Huitfeldt, and Allen Renear. "Meaning and Interpretation of Markup." *Markup Languages: Theory and Practice* 2 (2000): 215–34.

Staples, Thornton, and Ross Wayland. "Virginia Dons FEDORA." *D-Lib Magazine* 6.7–8 (2000). 24 Jan. 2005 <http://www.dlib.org/dlib/july00/staples/07staples.html>.

Staples, Thornton, Ross Wayland, and Sandra Payette. "The Fedora Project." *D-Lib Magazine* 9.4 (2003). 24 Jan. 2005 <http://www.dlib.org/dlib/april03/staples/04staples.html>.

Stevens, Michael E., and Steven B. Burg. *Editing Historical Documents: A Handbook of Practice*. Walnut Creek: AltaMira, 1997.

Stoltz, Michael. "New Philology and New Phylogeny: Aspects of a Critical Electronic Edition of Wolfram's *Parzival*." *Literary and Linguistic Computing* 18.2 (2003): 139–50.

Streuvels, Stijn. "De teleurgang van den Waterhoek." *De Gids* 91.1 (1927): 64–118; 91.2: 153–81; 91.3: 316–42; 91.4: 1–43; 91.5: 137–79; 91.6: 285–316; 91.7: 1–63.

———. *De teleurgang van den Waterhoek*. Brugge: Excelsior; Amsterdam: Veen, 1927.

———. *De teleurgang van den Waterhoek*. 2nd rev. ed. Amsterdam: Veen, 1939.

———. De teleurgang van den Waterhoek: *Tekstkritische editie*. Ed. Marcel De Smedt and Edward Vanhoutte. Antwerp: Manteau, 1999.

———. De teleurgang van den Waterhoek: *Electronic-Critical Edition*. Ed. Marcel De Smedt and Edward Vanhoutte. Gent: Koninklijke Academie voor Nederlandse Taal- en Letterkunde; Amsterdam: Amsterdam UP, 2000.

Stuart, Ian. *XML Schema: A Brief Introduction*. 17 Dec. 2003. 24 Jan. 2005 < http:// lucas.ucs.ed.ac.uk/xml-schema >.

Stubbs, Estelle, ed. *The Hengwrt Chaucer Digital Facsimile*. CD-ROM. Leicester: Scholarly Digital, 2000.

Sutherland, Kathryn. "Revised Relations? Material Text, Immaterial Text, and the Electronic Environment." *Text* 11 (1998): 17–39.

Swinburne, Algernon Charles. *William Blake: A Critical Essay*. 1868. Rpt. ed. Hugh J. Luke. Lincoln: U of Nebraska P, 1970.

Tadic, Linda. *Intellectual Property versus the Digital Environment-Rights Clearance*. Intellectual Property and Multimedia in the Digital Age: NINCH Copyright Town Meeting. New York Public Lib. 24 Sept. 2001. 1 Sept. 2002. 20 Jan. 2005 < http://www.ninch.org/copyright/2002/Tadic_rev.doc >.

Tanselle, G. Thomas. "Historicism and Critical Editing." *Studies in Bibliography* 39 (1986): 1–46.

———. *A Rationale of Textual Criticism*. Philadelphia: U of Pennsylvania P, 1989.

———. "Reproductions and Scholarship." *Studies in Bibliography* 42 (1989): 25–54.

———. "Statement on the Significance of Primary Records." *Profession 95*. New York: MLA, 1995. 27–28.

———. "Textual Criticism and Literary Sociology." *Studies in Bibliography* 44 (1991): 83–143.

———. "Textual Criticism at the Millennium." *Studies in Bibliography* 54 (2001): 1–80.

———. "The Varieties of Scholarly Editing." Greetham, *Scholarly Editing* 9–32.

Technical Summary. William Blake Archive. 30 Jan. 2003. 24 Jan. 2005 <http://www.blakearchive.org/main.html>. Path: About the Archive; Technical Summary.

Tennison, Jeni. *XSLT and XPath on the Edge.* Unlimited Ed. Hoboken: Wiley, 2002.

Tod, Marcus Niebuhr, ed. *A Selection of Greek Historical Inscriptions.* 2 vols. Oxford: Clarendon, 1951–62.

Turville-Petre, Thorlac, and Hoyt N. Duggan. *Preface.* Piers Plowman *Electronic Archive: Cambridge MS B.15.17 (W).* 27 Sept. 2000. 1 Aug. 2005 <http://www.iath.virginia.edu/seenet/piers/windows/preface.html>.

The Unicode Consortium. *The Unicode Standard.* Version 3.0. Reading: Addison, 2000.

Unicode Standard Annex #15 Unicode Normalization Forms. Unicode Technical Reports. 20 Jan. 2005 <http://www.unicode.org/unicode/reports/tr15/>.

Unsworth, John. *Scholarly Primitives: What Methods Do Humanities Researchers Have in Common, and How Might Our Tools Reflect This?* Humanities Computing: Formal Methods, Experimental Practice. King's College, London, 13 May 2000. <http://www.iath.virginia.edu/~jmu2m/Kings.5-00/primitives.html>.

Vander Meulen, David L., and G. Thomas Tanselle. "A System of Manuscript Transcription." *Studies in Bibliography* 52 (1999): 201–12.

Vanhoutte, Edward. "Display or Argument? Markup and Visualization for Electronic Scholarly Editions." *Standards und Methoden der Volltextdigitalisierung. Beiträge des Internationalen Kolloquiums an der Universität Trier, 8./9. Oktober 2001.* Ed. Thomas Burch, Johannes Fournier, Kurt Gärtner, and Andrea Rapp. Mainz: Akademie der Wissenschaften und der Literatur, 2003. 71–96.

———. "A Linkemic Approach to Textual Variation: Theory and Practice of the Electronic-Critical Edition of Stijn Streuvels' *De teleurgang van den Waterhoek*." *Human IT* 1 (2000): 103–38. 13 Jan. 2004 <http://www.hb.se/bhs/ith/1-00/ev.htm>.

——— "The Typopatamus Called 'Electronic Edition': Notes towards a Definition and Typology of Electronic Scholarly Editions." King's College London. 8 Dec. 2000.

———. "Where Is the Editor? Resistance in the Creation of an Electronic Critical Edition." *Human IT* 1 (1999): 197–214. 13 Jan. 2004 <http://www.hb.se/bhs/ith/1-99/ev.htm>. Rev. in *DRH 98. Selected Papers from Digital Resources for the Humanities 1998: University of Glasgow, September 1998.* Ed. Marilyn Deegan, Jean Anderson, and Harold Short. OHC Publication 12. London: Office for Humanities Communication, 2000. 171–83.

Vanhoutte, Edward, and Ron Van den Branden. *DALF Guidelines for the Description and Encoding of Modern Manuscript Material.* Version 1.0. Gent: Centrum voor Teksteditie en Bronnenstudie, 2002–03. 13 Jan. 2004 <http://www.kantl.be/ctb/project/dalf/>.

———. *Describing, Transcribing, Encoding, and Editing Modern Correspondence Material: A Textbase Approach.* Centrum voor Teksteditie en Bronnenstudie, Ghent. Koninklijke Academie voor Nederlandse Taal- en Letterkunde. 29 July 2005 <http://www.kantl.be/ctb/pub/2004/comedvanvanfig.pdf>.

———. "Presentational and Representational Issues in Correspondence Reconstruction and Sorting." *Literary and Linguistic Computing* 19.1 (2004): 45–54.

Van Hulle, Dirk. "Textual Awareness: A Genetic Approach to the Late Works of James Joyce, Marcel Proust, and Thomas Mann." Diss. U of Antwerp, 1999.

Varela, Francisco J. *Principles of Biological Autonomy.* North Holland Ser. in General Systems Research 2. New York: North-Holland, 1979.

Varela, Francisco J., et al. *The Embodied Mind: Cognitive Science and Human Experience.* Cambridge: MIT P, 1991.

Versioning Machine 2.1. Maryland Inst. for Technology in the Humanities. U of Maryland. 9 May 2005. 28 July 2005 <http://mith2.umd.edu/products/ver-mach/description.html>.

Viscomi, Joseph. "Digital Facsimiles: Reading the *William Blake Archive.*" *Computers and the Humanities* 36.1 (2002): 27–48.

Voloshinov, Valentin Nikolaevic. *Marxism and the Philosophy of Language.* Cambridge: Harvard UP, 1986.

von Wright, Georg Henrik. "The Wittgenstein Papers." *Wittgenstein.* Oxford: Blackwell, 1982. 45–76.

Walsh, Norman, and Leonard Muellner. *DocBook: The Definitive Guide.* Sebastopol: O'Reilly, 1999.

Wellek, René, and Austin Warren. *Theory of Literature.* 3rd ed. New York: Harcourt, 1984.

Williams, Tony, and Alan Blunt. "Hypertext and Genetic Studies: Flaubert's *L'éducation sentimentale.*" *Digital Evidence: Selected Papers from DRH 2000, Digital Resources for the Humanities Conference, University of Sheffield, September 2000.* Ed. Michael Fraser,

Nigel Williamson, and Marilyn Deegan. Office for Humanities Communication Pub. 14. London: Office for Humanities Communication, 2001. 191–203.

Williams, William Proctor, and Craig S. Abbott. *An Introduction to Bibliographical and Textual Studies*. New York: MLA, 1985.

Wittgenstein, Ludwig. *Philosophical Investigations*. London: Blackwell, 1953.

———. *Tractatus Logico-Philosophicus*. London: Kegan, 1922.

———. *Wittgenstein's* Nachlass*: The Bergen Electronic Edition*. Oxford: Oxford UP, 2000.

Woodhead, A. G. *The Study of Greek Inscriptions*. Cambridge: Cambridge UP, 1981.

Wordsworth, William. The Prelude*: 1799, 1805, 1850*. Ed. Jonathan Wordsworth, M. H. Abrams, and Stephen Gill. New York: Norton, 1979.

Zupitza, Julius, ed. Beowulf*: Reproduced in Facsimile from the Unique Manuscript British Museum MS. Cotton Vitellius A. xv*. 2nd ed. EETS OS 245. London: Oxford UP, 1959.

INTERNET RESOURCES

Apache Axkit. 29 Feb. 2002. <http://www.axkit.org/>.

The Apache Cocoon Project. 2002. 29 Feb. 2002. 24 Jan. 2005 <http://cocoon.apache.org/>.

Apache Xindice. The Apache XML Project. 29 Feb. 2002. 9 Apr. 2004 <http://xml.apache.org/xindice/>.

The Canterbury Tales *Project*. Ed. Peter Robinson. Centre for Technology and the Arts. De Montfort U. 1999. 26 May 2004 <http://www.cta.dmu.ac.uk/projects/ctp/>.

The Complete Writings and Pictures of Dante Gabriel Rossetti: A Hypermedia Research Archive. Ed. Jerome J. McGann. 1993. Inst. for Advance Technology in the Humanities. U of Virginia. 26 May 2004 <http://jefferson.village.virginia.edu/rossetti/>.

DALF: Digital Archive of Letters in Flanders. Ed. Edward Vanhoutte. Centrum voor Teksteditie en Bronnenstudie. 27 May 2004 <http://www.kantl.be/ctb/project/dalf/>.

Document Object Model (DOM). W3C Architecture Domain. 29 Feb. 2002. 19 Jan. 2005 <http://www.w3.org/DOM/>.

Epic Editor. Arbortext. 29 Feb. 2002. 24 Jan. 2005 <http://www.arbortext.com/products/epic_editor_datasheet.htm>.

EpiDoc Home Page. Ed. Tom Elliott. 2004–05. 24 Jan. 2005 <http://www.ibiblio.org/telliott/epidoc/>.

eXist: Open Source Native XML Database. 29 Feb. 2002. 24 Jan. 2005 <http://exist-db.org/>.

Extensible Stylesheet Language (XSL): Version 1.0. 2001. W3C. 29 Feb. 2002. 24 Jan. 2005 <http://www.w3.org/TR/xsl/>.

FOP: The Apache XML Graphics Project. 29 Feb. 2002. 5 Jan. 2005 <http://xml.apache.org/fop/>.

Hypertext Transfer Protocol-HTTP/1.1. Network Working Group. Jan. 1997. 29 Feb. 2002. 24 Jan. 2005 <http://www.w3.org/Protocols/rfc2068/rfc2068>.

Iconclass. KNAW (Royal Netherlands Acad. of Arts and Sciences). 9 July 2002. 24 Jan. 2005 <http://www.iconclass.nl>.

Index of Christian Art. Dir. Colum Hourihane. Princeton U. 24 Jan. 2005 <http://ica.princeton.edu/>.

Internet Archive. 24 Jan. 2005 <http://www.archive.org>.

JSTOR: Journal Storage: The Scholarly Journal Archive. Exec. Dir. Michael Spinella. New York: 2000–04. 17 May 2004 <http://www.jstor.org>.

Namespaces in XML: World Wide Web Consortium, 14 January 1999. W3C. 29 Feb. 2002. 24 Jan. 2005 <http://www.w3.org/TR/REC-xml-names/>.

PassiveTeX (XSL FO processor, implemented in *TeX* by Sebastian Rahtz). Text Encoding Initiative. Mar. 2003. 24 Jan. 2005 <http://www.tei-c.org/Software/passivetex/>.

The Piers Plowman *Electronic Archive*. Ed. Hoyt N. Duggan. 1994. Inst. for Advanced Technology in the Humanities. U of Virginia. 26 May 2004. 24 Jan. 2005 <http://www.iath.virginia.edu/piers/>.

Renaissance Women Online. Women Writers Online. Dir. Julia Flanders. Brown U. 26 May 2004 <http://www.wwp.brown.edu/texts/rwoentry.html>.

Romantic Circles. Ed. Neil Fraistat, Steven E. Jones, and Carl Stahmer. U of Maryland. 24 Jan. 2005 <http://www.rc.umd.edu>.

Sablotron: XSLT, DOM and XPath Processor. Ginger Alliance. 29 Feb. 2002. 11 Jan. 2005 <http://www.gingerall.com/charlie/ga/xml/p_sab.xml>.

Saxon: The XSLT and XQuery Processor. Michael Kay. 29 Feb. 2002. 8 Oct. 2004 <http://saxon.sourceforge.net/>.

Latest SOAP Versions (Simple Object Access Protocol). W3C. 29 Feb. 2002. 24 Jan. 2005 <http://www.w3.org/TR/SOAP/>.

WebDAV (World Wide Web Distributed Authoring and Versioning). 26 Nov. 2004 <http://ftp.ics.uci.edu/pub/ietf/webdav/>.

The William Blake Archive. Ed. Morris Eaves, Robert N. Essick, and Joseph Viscomi. 8 July 2004. 24 Jan. 2005 <http://www.blakearchive.org/main.html>.

Xaira Page. Oxford U Computing Services. 26 Nov. 2004 <http://www.oucs.ox.ac.uk/rts/xaira/>.

Xalan-Java Version 2.6.0 (XSLT Processor). The Apache XML Project. 29 Feb. 2002. 24 Jan. 2005 <http://xml.apache.org/xalan-j/>.

XEP Engine: XSL FO and SVG Processor. RenderX. 29 Feb. 2002. 24 Jan. 2005 <http://www.renderx.net/Content/tools/xep.html>.

The XLST C Library for Gnome (libxslt). 29 Feb. 2002. 24 Jan. 2005 <http://xmlsoft.org/XSLT/>.

XML and XSL-FO to PDF with High Quality SVG, MathML and Multilingual Support for over Fifty Languages. Antenna House XSL Formatter. 29 Feb. 2002. 21 Jan. 2005 <http://www.antennahouse.com/>.

XML General Downloads. MSDN Lib. 24 Jan. 2005 <http://msdn.microsoft.com/library/default.asp?url=/downloads/list/xmlgeneral.asp>.

XML-RPC Home Page. Userland Software. 29 Feb. 2002. 3 July 2003. 24 Jan. 2005 <http://www.xmlrpc.com/>.

XSL Transformations (XSLT): Version 1.0. 1999. W3C. 29 Feb. 2002. 24 Jan. 2005 <http://www.w3.org/TR/xslt>.

XUpdate: XML Update Language. The XML:DB Initiative. 26 Nov. 2004. 24 Jan. 2005 <http://xmldb-org.sourceforge.net/xupdate/>.

INDEX

A page number in boldface indicates a glossary definition (pp. 34–39). An italicized *f* refers to a figure or illustration.